THE FOUR NOTES TO CALL FIRE....

Almost immediately, kigh danced on a half-dozen wicks, barely defined features flickering and changing, tiny eyes of brilliant white the only constant. A little surprised at both their size and number, she Sang calming and safety until the dance grew less frantic.

Although fire was the most self-absorbed of all the kigh, Karlene could feel them reaching out to her. She couldn't sense why. Apprehension a subtle harmony within the Song, she asked if they were afraid. When it became obvious they were, she asked if they were afraid of being trapped.

Every candle on the altar burst into flame. A blazing tower of kigh surged toward the vaulted ceiling, individuals swallowed up in the terrifying column of white and red and gold. Gulping great lungfuls of heated air, Karlene fought to Sing over the fire's roar.

She could smell her hair begin to singe....

FIFTH QUARTER

Tanya Huff

DAW BOOKS, INC.

DONALD A. WOLLHEIM, FOUNDER

375 Hudson Street, New York, NY 10014

ELIZABETH R. WOLLHEIM

SHEILA E. GILBERT

PUBLISHERS

First Printing, August 1995

7   8   9

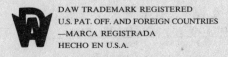

For Fe,
once again,
because she wanted it so badly.

Chapter One

There were guards on duty at the entrance to the marshal's tent but they'd expected that and were accustomed to using less obvious entrances. Problem was, there were guards on duty at the sides and rear of the tent as well.

"Looks like they're expecting us," Bannon whispered, his mouth lightly touching his sister's ear, the esses softened to prevent the sound from carrying.

Vree nodded, right hand rising to brush at the lingering caress of warm breath, eyes locked on the flickering circle of torches that left no paths of darkness.

The guards were spaced in such a way that removing one would alert the others.

She gestured at a sputtering flame; the thick knob of oil-soaked hemp had nearly burned away. Soon, it would have to be replaced. Bannon signed his agreement.

They were in position, ready, when the marshal's personal body servant appeared with a new torch. As the nearest guard half-turned to watch the exchange, they rose from a sheltering hollow and raced into the skirts of shadow around the base of the tent. His gaze sweeping a heartbeat behind their movement, the guard resumed scanning his assigned area.

Contorted to fit into the triangle of darkness, they

could hear only one voice from inside, but as it rose and fell in a conversational cadence, they assumed the marshal had company.

Pressed flat against the ground, Vree slid under the weighted edge of canvas and continued to slide under the red-and-gold patterned carpet laid to define the floor. When she felt Bannon's touch on her ankle, she dug fingers and toes into the dirt and began to creep on her belly around the perimeter. The marshal's voice grew louder, and for the first time she heard the rough whisper that answered. Commander Neegan. She grinned. They'd expected as much and made allowances for his presence.

The crushed and dying grass beneath the carpet made breathing difficult, but Vree sucked air past her teeth and kept moving through the thick growth. A parade of heavy-footed officers had mashed the floor flat in the center of the tent, but out where the billowing walls touched the earth, it rose and fell like the dunes of Hedyve. Between the patterns in the carpet and the flickering shadows—the marshal was well known for conserving lamp oil—an extra pair of lumps in the floor would not likely be noticed. When Vree finally paused, she could feel Bannon's movement in the vibrations of the fabric against her shoulder blades. But only Bannon's movement. She froze, listening. Wood and leather creaked above and to her left. Both marshal and commander were seated, discussing possible routes for a massed attack.

"They know we're coming; what makes you think they haven't moved the furniture around?" Bannon asked, rubbing his palms together as he peered down at the diagram sketched in the dirt.

"Two reasons." Vree sat back on her heels. *"First, the marshal always sits facing the entrance. Always.*

That doesn't leave a lot of options with a map table that size. Second . . ." She looked up at her brother and drew a circle around the sketch with one seemingly delicate, long-fingered hand. ". . . they don't think we can make it that far."

Bannon grinned in anticipation. A shadow-bladed knife flickered against his palm, then disappeared back into a hidden sheath, the motion almost too fast to follow. "More fools they."

"Well, Neegan . . ." The marshal leaned back in the folding camp chair and set the empty flagon on the table with a sharp crack. ". . . second watch is nearly over and still no sign of them."

"Too early to relax, Marshal." Commander Neegan's whisper had been given him many years before by an enemy archer. The commander had not only survived the battle but seen to it that the archer did not.

Marshal Chela smiled, the expression bracketing the rounded curves of her face with deep creases. "I never relax," she said cheerfully. "It's why I've lived to a ripe old age." She reached for the flagon, remembered it was empty, and sighed. "There's another bottle in that case behind you, Neegan. Get it, would you."

"Allow me, Marshal." In one lithe motion, Bannon rose to his feet, set the clay bottle on the table, and lightly touched his blade to the commander's neck, just by the white pucker of the old scar.

Chela leaned forward slightly, eyes narrowed. "Aren't you removing the wrong target?" she murmured.

Vree tapped the older woman gently on the shoulder and laid a line of steel across her throat. "Don't move," she warned. "It's very sharp."

Apparently oblivious to the knife tip dimpling his

skin, Neegan held out his hand. "You owe me forty crescents, Marshal. I told you they could do it."

"I don't want this becoming a siege; they're on springs and we aren't." Marshal Chela laced her fingers over her ample belly, the silver and ruby ring that proclaimed her a priestess of Jiir, Goddess of Battles, gleaming on her shield hand. "Any suggestions?"

Commander Leesh stepped forward, her voice a bare shade off eager. "Why don't we just charge the city? They wouldn't survive an all-out attack."

"Neither would most of us," Chela pointed out dryly. Leesh was the youngest of her four commanders and anxious to prove a political promotion deserved in spite of evidence to the contrary. "And try to remember that the people of Ghoti are as much citizens of the Havakeen Empire as you are. It is our duty to attempt to find a solution that doesn't end in slaughter."

"Governor Aralt commands a great deal of personal loyalty." Neegan's harsh whisper quieted the rising mutter of speculation. "His people follow him, not a series of . . . misguided ideals." The dead and dying of another, earlier rebellion made themselves heard in the pause. "He promises them glory, a return to days of petty kingdoms and hollow crowns." With a graceful gesture, the commander sketched that past in the air. "What chance does the Empire's promise of peace, order, and good government have against that?" Then he spread his hands, offering the answer. "Aralt is the key. Everything revolves around him. Remove him, and this rebellion falls apart."

"And how do we remove him?" Chela asked, although she strongly suspected she knew what his answer would be. Although his most recent promotion responsibilities kept him from exercising his skills,

Neegan was quite possibly the best military assassin in the seven armies. "Aralt's locked himself up tight in the governor's stronghold."

"I have two who could do the job."

Leesh snorted in disbelief.

The marshal ignored the interruption. "Aralt's no fool for all his posturing. He'll be expecting the attempt."

"Yes," Neegan agreed.

"These the two who removed Pahbad?"

"Yes."

"You're assuming that two will succeed where a single assassin might fail." *He'd fought to have them trained together using that very argument and had been proven right time after time but, this time, Chela shook her head.* "No. They'd never get to him."

Neegan smiled. "Would the marshal care to place a small wager. . . ."

As she slid her dagger back in its sheath, Vree felt the familiar bleakness that came with the end of a mission. One moment, she and Bannon were a single unit with the use of not one pair of eyes or ears or hands, but two; the next, she stood alone. This time, the dislocation was almost painfully abrupt. This time, they had no retreat, blood singing, back to safety. This time the separation occurred just as senses climaxed at the "kill."

And there's nothing worse then melodrama in the middle of the night, she told herself scornfully as she made her way around the table to Bannon's side, ignoring with long practice the sexual undertones in the original, melodramatic thought.

The marshal fought the urge to touch her throat where she could still feel the cold pressure of the blade. "I'm inclined to believe Commander Neegan's assurances that you two can target the governor. When can you go in?"

"We've been mapping the stronghold since the army arrived, Marshal." Bannon spoke for them both. "If the weather holds, we could make an attempt as early as tomorrow night."

Chela nodded. At this time of the year in the southern part of the Empire, there would not be rain. "Make it then."

As they left the tent, Bannon reached out and smacked one of the guards at the entrance on the butt. "Nice work," he said, loudly enough to turn heads.

"How'd you get in there, you little shit!" the soldier demanded, flushing a ruddy scarlet in the torchlight.

Bannon laughed, dancing back out of his way. "I can't believe you didn't see us march right by."

Well aware that this failure would mean nights spent at other, less prestigious duty posts, the guard weighed the odds of nailing the brother before the sister reacted and decided discretion was the better part of not having his throat slit. "Sod off," he snarled.

Bannon laughed again and draped his arm across Vree's shoulders as they moved out into the camp. "How about wasting a quarter-crescent in the baths."

She glanced over at him, fighting the tremors that started under his touch, telling herself they were caused by the tension of the last few hours, nothing more. His dark eyes glittered in the charcoal mask and she could feel the brittle energy coming off him in waves. "Wasting?" she asked, pointedly wrinkling her nose.

Ivory flashed in the shadow of his face as he lifted his hand to grin at the smudge of lighter skin showing through the camouflage. "Well, there's always a bit of cold water in a borrowed helmet. . . ."

The baths, one of the many businesses that followed the seven armies with the intent of separating soldiers from their pay, shut down at the end of the second watch. It took an extra half-crescent to convince the proprietors to keep the fires going a little while longer.

Vree lay back in the warm water and tried not to listen to the appreciative murmurs of the bath attendants as they scrubbed her brother. It made no difference that they'd murmur the same nonsense over her had she not made it very clear that she preferred to wash herself. Fingers puckering, she sighed and dragged herself out of the tub.

"You're too skinny, sister-mine. You should eat more."

Vree snorted and straightened, reaching for one of the soft cloths hanging on the line beside her. "I'll remind you of that at the next wall we have to go over."

"And I'll deny every word." He lifted an arm and tried to snake it around the slender waist of the departing attendant. She twisted lithely away, damp braid flicking a practiced dismissal as she left. Bannon turned to her companion who backed up a step.

"Forget it, Bannon," the young man declared, tossing a cloth at the tub and covering a yawn. "You're finished, and we're closing."

A few moments later, as the lamps went out behind them, Bannon rubbed a dribble of water off the back of his sister's neck and asked, "Coming with me?"

Vree shook her head. "No." He always asked. The answer never changed. After a kill, he needed distraction, but she needed quiet. "You going to Teemo's?"

The whores at Teemo's were regularly inspected by the army healers. An empire had not been won by ei-

ther ignoring the needs of its soldiers or the conse-
quences of disease.

"I thought I might."

"Remember we're working tomorrow night. Don't
stay too late."

His sigh lifted the damp hair off her forehead as he
leaned forward and smacked a kiss down on the crease
between her brows. "Don't fuss, sister-mine. I'm old
enough to take care of myself."

Old enough. As she watched him stride away, Vree
heard the echo of a piping voice demanding to know
why *she* always had to be older and when would it be
his turn. Sometimes that one year difference stretched
impossibly far. The one year between six and seven;
the corporal had brought the news of their mother's
battlefield death to her, she'd had to tell Bannon. The
one year between fourteen and fifteen; Neegan had
wanted them both in his command, had been able to
pull enough strings to get them there, so she'd been
held back for further training until army regulations
said Bannon was old enough to be posted. The one
year between twenty and twenty-one ... Old enough.

Except he'd always be her little brother.

And that's the problem, isn't it? she asked herself as
he disappeared into the night. Spitting the taste of self-
pity out of her mouth, Vree started back to camp.
Mooning about it wouldn't change anything. There
wasn't anything she could change....

The baths, the brothels, all the extras, were officially
outside the patrolled perimeter—although the marshal
had been heard to remark on more than one occasion
that she knew what the Sixth Army would rush to defend if it came to an attack. Vree slipped unseen past
a sentry grown bored near the end of an uneventful
watch and picked her way carefully around snoring

bodies until she came to the place where the Fourth Squad, Second Unit, First Company, First Division, Sixth Army had been ordered to sleep. The weather had been hot and dry, so hardly anyone had bothered unfolding the tiny, oiled-canvas tents the army issued as shelter to the common soldiers, and she found her gear right where she'd left it, piled next to Bannon's. Others might lose possessions to petty pilfering, but no one messed with an assassin's kit.

She nodded to Corporal Emo hunched over his wineskin, then glanced up at the sky. The Road to Glory arced overhead and The Archer continued to aim away from the heart of the Empire. A priest of Assot, God of Music and Prophecy, had long ago declared that the Empire would endure until The Archer turned his bow. Vree, inclined to believe that the priest had been sucking back too much sacramental wine, checked anyway—just to be certain.

Head pillowed on her arms, she closed her eyes and listened to the sound of the army. It was like being in the belly of a great benevolent beast, wrapped in protection, secure in the knowledge that if death came in the night, it would have to come a long way and through many lives to get to her.

Tensions the bath had been unable to touch leached out of her muscles. Slowly, her breathing slid into the cadence of those breathing all around her, and it was as a part of the greater whole that she finally slept.

One moment she was asleep, the next she knelt on the shoulders of a young recruit, her dagger point hovering over the wildly rolling surface of his left eye. As her brain caught up with the responses trained into her body, Vree could hear Corporal Emo and several others howling with laughter, could see the terror on the boy's face, and could smell the result of his fear.

She flipped the knife in the air, caught it, sheathed it, and stood. "You joined us just before we left the garrison, didn't you?"

The boy stuttered out an affirmative as he scrambled to his feet.

"What's your name?"

"Avotic." He noticed the moisture spreading over the front of his kilt, realized suddenly what it meant, and flushed a deep red. Although he had to be at least fifteen to have been posted, embarrassment dropped his age a good four years. "Th–they call me Tic."

Vree shook her head. "Let me give you some advice, Tic. When a corporal orders you to shake someone awake who wears a black sunburst . . ."

Tic swiveled his head to stare down at her pack. Scuffed and faded from years of use, the six sunbursts stamped into the worn leather still showed they had once been dyed black. His eyes widened and he swallowed, hard.

". . . you tell that corporal to stick his head up his ass and salute it." She had to raise her voice to be heard over the laughter. "Do you understand what I'm telling you, Tic?"

"Y–yes." It didn't seem to matter that he was at least a foot taller than the woman he faced.

"What?"

"If I wake you up again, you'll kill me."

Watching from his bedroll, Bannon snickered and Vree tried not to smile in response. "Close enough. Go clean up, you stink." As the kid ran off, she turned on Emo. "One of these day, I *will* kill one."

"Not a chance." Wiping streaming eyes, the corporal heaved a satisfied sigh. "You're too good. And now the little shit knows he can die. Thanks to me, he's a better soldier."

"Thanks to *you?*" Vree snorted, bending and dragging her kilt out of her pack. "Which brings up another question," she continued, buckling the limp, blue pleats around her waist. "Why am *I* always chosen to give these little lessons of yours?"

"Because you look so sweet when you're asleep," Emo told her, secure in his rank. Those of the Fourth Squad standing closest to him made exaggerated movements away. "That pointy little face of yours goes all soft and you have the cutest habit of cupping your cheek with one hand." His voice lost its false, syrupy tone, and he snorted. "Your brother, on the other hand, looks dangerous only while he sleeps."

"That's because I'm dreaming of you, Emo." Bannon stood and scratched at the triangle of brown hair in the center of his chest. His nose wrinkled at the smell of unwashed bodies, latrine trenches, and great vats of boiling mush. "Life in the army," he murmured. "Gotta love it."

" 'Cause you can't do shit about it," several voices answered in unison.

"Vree? You going out tonight?"

Vree turned her head and stared incredulously at the woman standing just beyond weapons' reach. "No, Shonna. I was feeling bloated and I thought I'd check if my black breeches, my black tunic, and my black ankle boots still fit."

Shonna shrugged and rubbed the back of her neck with one hand while the other traced circles in the night air. "Yeah, well, I mean . . ." She sighed deeply and started again. "Look, do you think that maybe, on your way back you could pick up a chicken or something?"

"I'm on target, Shonna."

The other woman looked uncomfortable but dragged up half a grin. "So kill a chicken, too."

The food provided by the seven armies was nourishing but monotonous. A number of establishments outside the perimeter took advantage of that and for a price no one had to live on mush, black bread, and sausages.

"You lost at dice again." Vree knew her too well for it to be a question.

"Yeah, but I'll come around. It's just . . ."

"It's just more of the same. And the answer's no."

"Then lend me a crescent." Shonna took a step forward, hand outstretched. "Until payday."

"No."

Shonna's hand dropped under the weight of Vree's response and she wiped her palm against her kilt. "I thought I meant something to you."

A few hours of pleasure, an attempt to raise a barricade around other desires . . . "Not after you tried losing *my* money at dice."

"I should've known better," Shonna muttered sullenly. "Your kind doesn't *have* feelings." Her voice straddled the line between challenge and insult.

Vree merely stared, expressionless, until the other woman nervously began to back away.

As she turned and stomped toward the center of camp, sandals slapping against the packed dirt, Bannon separated from the shadows to stand at Vree's shoulder. "She wasn't good enough for you, sister-mine," he said softly. "But then, who is?"

Her gaze pulled around by his tone, Vree caught a

glimpse of an expression she couldn't identify and wondered, not for the first time, how much he knew.

The Sixth Army had camped close enough to Ghoti to intimidate and far enough away to maneuver, leaving a large expanse of scrubby ground to be crossed under the eyes of enemy sentries perched on top of hastily erected earthen defenses. Fortunately, shadows were plentiful and the sentries were distracted—not only by the might of the Empire arrayed against them but by the growing fear that they just might have made a fatal mistake.

Access to the town was limited but far from impossible.

Did they honestly think that would stop us or do they just not think? Vree wondered as she followed her brother into the wedge of darkness between two buildings. She sifted the night, searched the sights and sounds and smells for threat, and signed, "All clear." The town could be empty of life for all the notice it took of them. When Bannon nodded, she led the way down a garbage-strewn alley toward the governor's stronghold.

In this, the southernmost part of the Empire, walls were made of formed mud, broader at the bottom out of necessity and angled gently upward toward a red-clay tiled roof. By sunlight, the city was an attractive patchwork of orange-brown. By starlight, the vibrant colors had muted to shades of gray. The smell of chilies fried in oil lingered in the shadows and through the shutters that closed off one deeply recessed window, Vree could hear a low voice singing to a fretful baby.

"... I will feed you bits of rainbow/red for laughter, blue for sorrow ..."

... yellow kisses, green tomorrows. Their garrison-

mother had been fond of the song, and Vree wondered
if she'd been from Ghoti or if the lullaby had traveled
across the Empire. She glanced at Bannon to see if
he'd heard and found him waiting for her to confirm
that no danger lay concealed in the open market they
had to cross. Calling herself several kinds of fool, she
slapped her mind back to the job at hand. The danger
in an easy target came from falling off the edge.

The governor's stronghold—an octagon-shaped wall
enclosing a tall central tower and a number of squat
outbuildings—was both the oldest structure in Ghoti
and the only one made of stone. The wall showed signs
of recent reinforcing and the massive gates were shut,
barred, and guarded.

Vree gestured to her left and Bannon nodded, slipping past her to take point. She could feel herself responding to the new level of danger, could see the
same response in the way her brother moved.

Over the last few months of rebellion, Governor
Aralt had swept clear the area around the stronghold,
destroying anything that might provide shelter for the
enemy should they force him back to a final stand. The
darkness, combined with one of the eight angles, provided all the shelter that Vree and Bannon needed. Fingers and toes found purchase in cracks a lizard would
have ignored. Head to head, pressed flat against the
wall's rough capstones, they scanned the enclosure,
hidden by the uneven ridge of an unfinished and unus-
able sentry box. They'd come this far once before, but
from now on, every move would be the first move.

*"Aralt's no fool for all his posturing. He'll be ex-
pecting the attempt."*

Vree touched her brother lightly on the shoulder. He
winced as he saw the three heavily armed and wary
rebels march across the court and disappear behind one

of the outbuildings. Up in the tower a trio of shadows bristling with weapons carried a flickering lamp past a narrow window.

Patrols, he mouthed.

She nodded. It looked like Aralt was, indeed, expecting them.

The stone grew warm beneath them as they watched. *No pattern,* Bannon signed at last.

They both knew that a pattern would eventually emerge; that people were incapable of sustaining truly random action. A pattern would make their job easier, safer, but could take several nights to determine. A delay would please no one except, perhaps, the governor.

As yet another three-rebel patrol paused directly below them, Bannon nudged her and flicked his thumb up. *No surprise,* Vree mused. In five years, he'd voted they turn from the target exactly twice. The first time, they'd returned the next night equipped to deal with the unexpected, four-legged guards. The second, they'd gone in farther than they should have, started back too late, and ended up trapped together for a full day in a hidey-hole barely big enough for one of them. Unable to move, barely able to breathe, it was the only time Vree had ever had more than enough of her brother and had found herself, after hours of his chin digging painfully into her shoulder, wishing that she worked alone. *And why am I dwelling on old failures now?*

She spat on her palm to chase away bad luck.

Staring down at the skinny, dark on dark silhouette of a teenage boy, his spear held tightly across his body, trembling angles announcing that he'd rather be anywhere and doing anything else, she finally nodded.

The interior of the tower was vastly more complicated than it appeared from the top of the wall. Over the years, countless divisions had created a jumble of small rooms and crooked corridors that followed no logical course. Cloaked in darkness, the assassins avoided two patrols and then were very nearly discovered by a grumbling servant stomping around complaining about all the noise.

"... up at dawn and 'spects me ta sleep wi' all this racket ..."

Bannon mimed slitting her throat. Vree rolled her eyes and motioned for him to get moving. The old woman hadn't seen them; there was no need to kill her.

Their information—and they knew better than to ask how Commander Neegan had gotten it—put the governor's quarters on the top floor of the tower. Hugging the inner wall of a wide curved hall, they found a flight of stairs, climbed seven steps, and emerged onto a carpet so plush they could have marched the entire Sixth Army across it without making a sound. The room contained only a trunk beneath a high arched window and across from it, a pile of cushions broken into squares of shadow by the night. Opposite the door they came in was another, the beaded curtain hung across it so thick that it appeared from a distance to be a solid barrier.

"Sandalwood," Bannon murmured, his breath brushing the word against her ear.

It took her a moment to understand what he meant and then another to separate the scent of the beads from the scent of him.

There were no sounds coming from the other side of the curtain; no sounds, no light, no patrol. As Vree used the back of her wrist to lift the strands nearest the door frame away from the polished stone, Bannon slid through the narrow opening. Vree counted three heartbeats, moved to follow, then froze. From the other side of the curtain came the flicker of an open lamp and the sound of marching feet.

A patrol. They'd have to go back. She turned and suddenly realized it wasn't one patrol she heard but two. They couldn't go back. The leading edge of approaching lamplight already threw three grotesquely elongated shadows against the stone just outside the room. The short flight of curved stairs had hidden the second patrol until it was almost too late.

Heart pounding, Vree dove for the tiny angle between the bottom cushions and the wall. Face pressed against the tile floor at the edge of the carpet, she squirmed into the only shelter the room had to offer. The patrol was on the threshold when she realized Bannon wasn't going to join her.

Too late to join him.

He's hidden on the other side. There was no question about it, but she didn't like discovering that they'd separated. *Not alone. Just apart.* Barely breathing, she listened to the footsteps grow louder, then suddenly stop as the carpet caught the sound and held it.

Then she heard the rattle of sandalwood beads closely followed by a muffled curse.

"Blow it, Eline, I could've killed you."

"Had to hit me first," a second voice growled. "Whacha so jumpy about anyway?"

"Place looks different in the dark." This new voice was young, not quite settled into adult depths, and Vree found herself thinking of the boy with the spear.

Eline snorted. "Gotta lamp, doncha? Hardly dark."

"Where have you just come from?" This was the first voice again. She still sounded irritated.

"Storerooms, if you must know."

"Did you see anything?"

Eline, Vree realized, had come through the curtain. *You didn't see anything . . .*

"Lotta dark. Nothin' else." He yawned, noisily. "Don't expect to neither. Fool's hunt this."

"At least they've put a fool on it."

"Up yours, too," Eline told her genially. "Come on," he snarled at his silent companions. After a moment, Vree heard the stone pick up the scuff of their footsteps.

"What is it?" The boy's patrol was still in the room.

"Something's not right . . ."

"That'd be Eline," muttered a second woman.

The first snickered and agreed.

Vree waited until the beads stopped whispering warnings against each other, then rose swiftly to her feet, cushions tumbling forward. Although training and instinct both told her she was alone, exposing herself a little at a time would do no good if someone *had* been left behind.

No one waited in the gray wash of starlight that spilled though the arced window.

No one.

She crossed the faint trail dragged through the air behind a heavily sweating body and stood by the curtain.

No sound.

Bannon . . . ?

There was nothing on the other side except corridor. Stairs curved down the outside wall to her right, gray shading quickly to black, and a narrow hall disappeared in darkness to her left.

Bannon! She'd have heard it if he were captured or killed, but knowing that didn't stop the sudden erratic beating of her heart. *Patrols coming at him from two directions. He can't go back because the curtain keeps him from seeing how close the danger is. The only thing he can do is go on.* Her back pressed against the wall, eyes useless in the total lack of light, Vree followed. They'd planned for separation the way soldiers planned for the loss of an arm or a leg in battle.

A change in air currents drew her to the other side of the corridor where questing fingers found an arched and open doorway. With a patrol on his heels, Bannon would've gone through it. She slid one foot forward and the toe of her soft boot nudged up against a step. The governor's quarters were on the top floor of the tower. Bannon would've gone up these stairs. Fully aware she'd be trailing him, and as much able to put himself in her place as she could put herself in his, he'd wait for her the moment he found a hole secure from passing patrols.

The stairs, barely wide enough for two to walk abreast, rose straight from darkness to the gray outline of another door and offered no security.

Halfway to the top, Vree grunted as the stone dipped first to the right then the left and the height of the risers abruptly changed. Any intruder who ran up these stairs would be in for a rude shock and a painful stumble if not an out-and-out fall. It was a simple precaution but—on other occasions with other intruders—an effective one.

The stairs ended at a balcony set into the side of the tower. A pair of narrow windows looked out onto it and a low stone balustrade separated it from the night. Nowhere to hide, no choice but to keep moving. As Vree crawled rapidly toward the far end, the large, complicated set of chimes hanging between the two windows caught her attention. *Shrine to the winds. South wind,* she amended, glancing over her shoulder at the position of the stars.

Flat on her belly against the cool tiles, she slid sideways and carefully snagged the lowest of the pale blue ceramic disks. Although she wore Jiir's medallion around her neck, the Goddess of Battles had never insisted on exclusive worship and Vree firmly believed in taking every possible precaution. Overhead, bits of paper and fabric hung limp in the still air. With nothing to tie to the shrine with her prayer, Vree smudged a bit of charcoal across the center of the disk. Then she smiled. The bottom curve had already been marked.

Bannon.

Another long flight of stairs, identical to those she'd just climbed, finally brought her to the top floor of the tower. Flames danced in the copper bowls of open lamps set into the wall all down the short corridor and more light spilled out through an open door halfway down one side.

The governor's apartments. If there'd been a guard, Bannon would have waited in the darkness at the top of the stairs. He'd know she was close behind him and that it was vital the guard not give the alarm. But he wasn't waiting. So there hadn't been a guard. With no cover in the corridor, he'd be waiting just inside the first room.

Why hadn't there been a guard?

Squinting, senses straining, Vree moved toward the light. The banded wooden door had not only been left open but secured back. She frowned. An open door was an invitation to enter. A trap? Possibly.

Where was Bannon?

The room was empty. No furniture, no brother, no governor. Only green and white tiles, a large hanging lamp, and yet another open door.

Something was wrong.

The hair on the back of her neck lifted and she was

halfway across the room before she realized she'd moved. Fists clenched against her thighs, she forced herself to be still, to listen . . .

Nothing in the next room.

But in the room after . . .

Something large fell; too large for even the plushest carpet to absorb the impact.

Vree had heard bodies fall on every surface, in every state of dying.

The taste of iron in her throat, she ran.

The second room passed in a blur of shelves and scrolls and books and a low table she went over not around.

In the third room was a carved wooden bed, the embroidered coverlet a tumbled heap of jeweled brilliance in the lamplight. Crumpled at the foot of the bed, was a body.

Not Bannon.

Her heart started beating again and training surged past the remnants of her panic.

The old man collapsed at the foot of the bed fought to hold onto life. His lungs struggled to lift the weight of his ribs high enough to breathe. His hands spasmed against the rich folds of his robe. His fingertips, lips, and eyelids were already tinged with blue.

On the carpet beside him was a metal goblet and on the carpet beside the goblet, a spreading stain.

Vree dropped to one knee and bent over the spilled wine, then straightened and spat the scent of poison off her tongue. A certain death but far too slow. Still on one knee, she studied the old man.

Governor Aralt.

Why he'd chosen to kill himself when he knew the Empire would save him the bother was a question best left between him and his gods.

Where was Bannon?

She'd seen his mark at the wind shrine; he *had* to have come this way. An irrational fear began to drag icy fingers down her spine and she desperately searched for another answer. The room was crowded with heavy pieces of furniture piled with cushions and draped with silk—an unattractive mix of north and south that could provide a hundred hiding places for her brother. Was he here? Had he come in, found the governor, heard her coming, and hid? It was the sort of stupid joke he might find amusing.

So would she if it meant the end of being without him.

She couldn't have gone past him and he wouldn't have gone on, so he *had* to be here.

"Haul your ass out of cover, Bannon, and let's get going. This isn't funny."

Her whisper pierced the shadowed corners, pierced the shroud that dying had wrapped around the governor.

He opened his eyes. Unfamiliar features twisted into a familiar expression. "Vree . . ."

She stared, not believing.

"Vree . . ." Cold fingers clutched at her wrist and pressed out a pattern only her brother knew.

The world became a dark and unfamiliar place. "Bannon?"

Chapter Two

". . . saw no guard, knew I should've waited, but . . ."
His face twisted and even the shadow resemblance to
Bannon disappeared. He was an old man, in agony.
And as unbelievable as it seemed, he was her brother.
"Hurts, Vree."

"I know." Knew exactly what the poison was doing
to the body he now wore. Knew there wasn't anything
she could do about it but watch him die.

"Have to tell you . . ."

His fingers were freezing. She fought a futile urge to
try and rub warmth back into them. "I'm here,
Bannon."

"He was in the room. Don't know how he saw me.
He smiled. Drank. Motioned me forward. Knew you
were behind me, so I . . . went." He'd been sucking in
air between each short burst of words but had to stop
and breathe a moment just to live.

Vree felt as though iron bands had been wrapped
tight around her ribs. Obviously, whatever had happened, she hadn't been close enough behind him.
Hadn't been close enough to save him. She wanted to
close her eyes but was afraid he'd die while they were
closed—half believed that only her attention kept him
alive.

A soldier who died off the battlefield became one of

Jiir's ravens, doomed to feed off the fallen, off the discarded bodies of those who were granted a place in Her host. But surely assassins were allowed a wider battlefield? Vree thought of the great clouds of winged scavengers that settled down to feast on the bloody flesh scattered over the ground when the fighting ended and nearly shuddered. *Goddess, please* . . . But Jiir listened to pleas only when they were accompanied by a sword thrust.

She remembered Emo grunting into his wineskin, "You live, you die, you rot," and found less comfort in that.

"Something about him . . ." Bannon had gathered enough strength to continue. ". . . drew me."

The governor had not been a physically attractive man; not judging from the wreck he'd left behind. "What drew you?"

"Don't know." He frowned, the expression pure Bannon although the features were not. "Calm," he answered at last. "Strength. Don't *know!*"

"Shhh, it's . . ." She couldn't say that it was *all right* because it would never be all right again.

"No. Got to . . . tell you." A purpling tongue scraped against his lips. "Looked at me. I was him . . . and he was . . . me and then he jumped."

"Jumped where?"

"To me. Then . . . pushed me into him." A shudder ran down the length of the old man's body and his teeth clattered together like dice. "Dying."

"He pushed you into his old body and he took yours?" Not all the training in the Empire could have kept the shrill note of disbelief out of her voice. She stiffened, head cocked, but no one appeared to have heard. Apparently, the orders the governor had given to keep everyone away still held. With a fingernail grip on her self-control, she turned back to her brother. "That's impossible!"

The expression on the face of the man lying in front of her said everything necessary. She'd seen that expression a hundred, a thousand times. Obviously, it *wasn't* impossible. "He can't have gone far. I'll go after him. Bring him here. Make him give you your body."

Bannon shook his head. "No time. Be dead . . . when you got back. Vree . . ."

He wanted something from her. She recognized a tone she'd heard all her life.

"Oh, come on, Vree, just this once . . ."

But he had only one thing left to want; only thing that she could give him. *Nothing should hurt this much and not kill you.* Teeth clenched around a howl of pain, she began the movement that would drop a dagger out of a forearm sheath into her hand. *When this is over, I'm going to find Aralt and I'm going to make him* beg *me for death.*

"Vree, let me share . . . your body."

The dagger snapped back into the sheath. "What?"

"I know what . . . he did. How he did it. Moment we shared . . . took it. Let me jump . . . into your body."

Vree opened her mouth and closed it again. Bannon was all she had, all she'd ever had besides the army. But to die for him? To allow herself to be pushed into a dying shell?

He read her thoughts off her face and shook his head. "No. Two separate actions. I jump. I don't push. You stay."

"We share?"

"Yes."

"My body?"

"Yes . . . Till we get . . . my body . . . back."

To have Bannon in her body. *And isn't that what you've been wanting?* she asked herself, desperately clamping her will around a hysterical desire to snicker. To have Bannon be a part of her. Know everything she was. Everything. No. But weighed against the only alternative, against going on alone . . .

"Vree?"

No time left to decide. Her heart slammed against her ribs and sweat trickled down her spine. She could smell her terror and his death. "Do it."

Invasion! A kaleidoscope of images tried to force an entry into her mind.

Vree fought to pull the barricades down. *This is Bannon! Let him in or he dies!* A crack appeared and then another and then he was in, and she nearly lost herself in a maelstrom of shared memories subtly skewed and alien emotions; of being just for an instant, someone else and knowing what they knew, feeling what they felt. She struggled to hold on, to accept, to not fight it although every instinct demanded she defend herself.

I trust him with my life. He trusts me with his life. I trust him with . . .

Vree? Vree! Wake up! We haven't got time for this!

She could feel the dry, dusty fibers of the carpet pressing into her cheek. Smell the poison mixed with wine spilled out onto the floor. Hear . . .

Slaughter it, Vree! Wake up!

"Bannon?" Eyes opened, all she could see was a pale hand curled up like a great, bloated, dead spider. When she tried to lift her head, her body felt as though it no longer quite fit. "Bannon?"

I'm here.

"It worked?"

Don't be an idiot, of course it worked. Now get up. Aralt, that carrion eater, is getting away.

The muscles in her thighs began to spasm. Her legs jerked and kicked and her feet scrabbled for purchase against the floor. "Bannon, stop it!"

Vree, no! Bannon's voice rose to a near incoherent shriek that slammed against the inside of her skull. *Don't.*

Panting, she forced herself to relax, to not expel the invader. Her brother. Gradually, she gathered all the bits of her body back under her control and, slowly, got her hands under her and pushed herself up onto her knees. "Just let *me* do the moving. Understand?"

Yeah. He sounded subdued, but she knew it wouldn't last. *I understand.*

Ignoring the corpse sprawled beside her, Vree stood. Every movement was surer than the one before as, with every movement, she reclaimed more of her scattered self. Although constantly aware of Bannon's presence, as long as he remained a passive passenger, she felt she could ignore him enough to manage. He had, after all, always been a constant presence in her life. *Kind of like ignoring a nagging toothache . . .*

I heard that.

Not now, Bannon. We haven't time for . . . Which was when she realized that she wasn't speaking aloud. *Shit on a stick! Do you know *everything* I think?*

No. You have to put it into words, then I hear it the way you hear me.

Because the alternative would be unbearable, she believed him. *But you can hear me when I speak?*

I can hear what you can hear. And I see through your eyes. And I feel what you touch.

It's like the opposite of what we always had while we worked—two sets of senses, one directing will.

I guess.

She felt her shoulders rise and fall in a gesture she had no control over. "Bannon!"

Look, I'm sorry, but it's hard.

I know . . .

No. You don't.

Yes, she did, because she felt *his* bitterness and *his* pain and *his* fear of dying. Like a wave she barely managed to keep her footing under, his emotions rolled over her and retreated. Fists clenched, she ground her teeth in anger. Aralt had a great deal to answer for, and she'd enjoy making him pay. "We'll get your body back," she murmured as though Bannon still stood beside her. "And we'll cut Aralt loose to shriek in the darkness."

Tentatively, for the floor was not always exactly where she thought it should be, she walked to the window, careful to remain out of the line of sight from below. Time had not stopped just because the impossible had occurred and she—they—were still in the heart of an enemy stronghold. Her hand held the heavy swag curtains motionless and she looked out at the sky. The stars had danced most of the night away.

"We've got to get out of here."

Agreed.

But instead she stood staring at her hand as though she'd never seen it before. It was too slender, a strong hand but a woman's hand. The nails were too even, they should have been ragged, chewed to the quick. The white line of scar from the second knuckle to the base of the thumb—where had it come from?

"Bannon."

The sound of his name barely carried past her lips but he heard it.

Not mine . . .

"No. Mine." And suddenly, it was her familiar hand again. She felt his presence draw in on itself, wrapped around equal parts of torment and terror. She wanted to reach out and touch him . . .

. . . with her hand . . .

. . . hers . . .

. . . but she couldn't, so she settled for getting them safely out of the stronghold instead.

By the time they were over the wall and back into the city, her body was responding with the fluid grace and economy of movement they had always shared. If Bannon occasionally added his control to hers, Vree couldn't tell, and she supposed that was all that mattered.

Head for the South Road.

She paused, one foot half raised. *What?*

Aralt is going north, toward the Capital. If the city had another name, no one remembered it. No one had used it in generations.

And we'll go north right after we tell Commander Neegan what's going on.

No.

Vree slid into the shadow cast by the damp, above-ground wall of a cistern. *What do you mean, no?*

Commander Neegan won't believe you.

Her protest died, unformed. In the commander's place would she believe that an old man had stolen her brother's body and pushed his life out into a dying shell? Would she believe such an impossible story without the presence of Bannon's thoughts beside her own?

He'll think I died in there and you've gone crazy,

Bannon insisted. *The army thinks assassins are half crazy anyway. You'll be shackled so you don't hurt anyone. Probably drugged. We'll *die* like that, Vree.*

The commander has known us all our lives.

So what. His hostility surprised her.

We could convince him. But in the face of Bannon's certainty, she was no longer convincing even herself.

We've got to go north now or we'll lose all chance of catching Aralt and my body.

If we leave the army like this—if we desert—they'll hunt us down. Assassins who deserted were under an immediate death sentence; an Imperial edict designed to reassure the citizens that the army's more subtle killers remained under control.

Slaughter it, Vree! Why would they think we deserted? They'll think the odds finally caught up to us and we died in Ghoti. And if you'd stop arguing, we could have him by dawn and be back in camp before they even miss us.

Don't be an idiot, Bannon ...

*He's in *my* body; I should know how far he can get! He's only a couple of hours ahead of us.*

And it's less than a couple of hours till dawn. Very pointedly, Vree turned to face the east. Whether the frustration she felt was his or hers, she had no idea. *If Aralt was ready for you, he was ready to travel. He might even be on horseback.*

No, no horse.

How do you know?

*I just know, okay? I just *know.**

She ground her teeth and struggled to find order in the emotional maelstrom inside her head; fought to separate her reactions from his. *So we skirt the army for the South Road, and then what?*

And then we find Aralt and reclaim my body.

You really think it's going to be that easy?

His anger started her heart racing. *I don't care a crow's ass about how easy it is or isn't going to be! I want my body!*

We'll never be able to go back. The silence in her head was the loudest sound she'd ever heard. *Bannon?*

It's me or the army, Vree. Your choice.

An assassin has no family but the army. But it wasn't a choice and he knew it.

They crossed the South Road, east to west, on the Ghoti side of the embankment—the sentries patrolling along the top unaware of the enemy slipping through the darkness behind them—and getting out of town was as easy as getting in. Driven by Bannon's uncompromising need, Vree stayed as close to the road as she dared, stealing from one bit of shadow to the next, using the night as cover. How, she wondered, had Aralt managed? While he had Bannon's body, he wouldn't have the skill to manipulate it. *At least we didn't find him pinned to the road by arrow fire from the top of the embankment.*

Shut up, Vree.

Just for a moment, she'd forgotten what *he* meant and had, for the same moment, forgotten that her thoughts were no longer her own. *Sorry.*

The terrain began to climb and the road with it.

There'll be a squad where the road crests the ridge.

I know. She kept moving toward the dim glow of the banked watchfire.

What are you doing, Vree?

Aralt is going to have to swing wide around; if we cut close, we'll gain on him.

And if you cut in too close, you'll be seen. His tone bordered on the edge of accusation.

Vree stopped, crouched in the shadow of a thorn tree. Her teeth were clenched so tightly together that a muscle jumped in her jaw. *And just what's that supposed to mean?*

You don't want to leave . . .

So I'll allow myself to be seen? She spat the thought at him. *So I'll have to go back to camp or be shot as I cross the perimeter? Do you think for an instant that I want you in my head for the rest of my life?*

Do you think I want to be here? Bannon snapped back.

Panting slightly, Vree stared at a thorn, four inches long and silver-gray in the starlight. When they were children, armed with thorn daggers, they'd saved the Empire from a thousand rebels, winning honor and glory and the notice of the Emperor himself. Together. Always together. She forced her fingers to uncurl. Who was she going to hit? *We'll get your body back. I promise.*

Bannon remained silent as she moved closer to the watchfire, but she could feel him holding back, in no way adding his skill to hers, allowing her to prove her commitment. Black shapes stood around the fire that had been lit in the middle of the road; kilts and sandals and tunics, round helms and shields and pikes imposing uniformity on the silhouettes. Vree could hear the quiet murmur of voices, then a loud laugh, then . . .

"Slaughtering bugs!"

"Not lice *again*."

"Bugger you. Something just bit me."

"Good," muttered someone else. "Now it'll die and not bite us."

She knew those voices. All of them. The Fourth Squad, Second Unit, First Company, First Division, Sixth Army had provided the soldiers who were watching the road. Knowing what to look for, she began to pick out individual shapes. Nub had a way of wearing his helm that made his head look as though it sloped straight from crown to nose. Wora slapped the shaft of her pike constantly from palm to palm. They said she'd be corporal when Emo finally took his wineskin into one battle too many. The slim figure pacing nervously around the perimeter of the light could only be Tic, his youth radiating off him.

Her squad. Their squad. Hers and Bannon's.

Vree?

No.

But I . . .

*Just *no*, okay? Be quiet.*

They'd be easier to pass than strangers because she knew their habits. Harder because she knew them and there was no way to even say good-bye. She had no idea why that should matter, but it did.

As she drew even with the fire, a burly shadow shambled off the road and straight toward her. Corporal Emo. She froze, trusting the night to keep her hidden, eyes narrowed to slits so that the whites would not betray her. He continued to come directly at her. They'd served together five, nearly six years. Did he know something?

Then, less than a body-length away, he stopped. And there was a dagger in Vree's hand.

Kill him!

I know what I have to do. But as she hesitated, Emo hiked up his kilt, reached into his sling, and directed a stream of urine practically at her feet. *He doesn't see me, Bannon.*

He's probably too soaked to see anything. Vree could feel relief under the derision. *What if he'd aimed six inches higher?*

Then I'd have killed him on principle. She felt almost giddy. *How can he piss for so long?*

How can he drink so much? Bannon asked in turn, a shrug implied.

Emo finally tucked himself away, belched, and turned to go. Then he stopped, frowned, and stared into the shadows. Vree felt his eyes meet hers, saw recognition dawn, and she slowly stood. His gaze dropped to the dagger in her hand, then went back to her face.

He knew her speed, he knew her skill, and he wasn't so drunk that he didn't know, at that moment, how close he stood to death.

No one in the squad would be surprised if Emo died in the bushes, too drunk to have seen the enemy. Vree could feel the weight of the dagger she held, feel the familiar grip under her fingers. This close, she *couldn't* miss; could close her eyes and with a flick of her wrist still bury it in Emo's throat.

You don't see me, she mouthed. *I wasn't here.*

Vree! What are you doing?

Emo stared at her, startled. She wondered what he saw. Who he saw. Finally, after several lifetimes, he nodded. *I don't see you.*

You've brought the hunt down on us, Bannon snarled when the watchfire had faded to a glow in the distance.

Vree remembered a younger man with large callused hands and a ready laugh; Emo before the wineskin became his constant companion. *He won't say anything.*

How do you know?

He was a friend.

He was my friend, too, but I'd have killed him.

That was not an argument she wanted to get into. Bannon hadn't been the one with the dagger in his hand and those kinds of choices were easier to criticize than to make. *There was no need to kill him.*

Bannon gave a mental snort. *You think he'll keep his mouth shut just because you used to fuck him? Think again. They'll know you didn't die in the city. They'll come hunting for you, Vree, and when you die, I die, too.*

All at once she was very, very tired. *So we'll try to get your body back before that happens.*

They hadn't caught up to Aralt when dawn began to elongate the shadows and brush the cloaking night away. But neither had there been any indication that they themselves were being followed.

Keep going! He can't have gone that much farther!

As Bannon's thoughts bounced around her head, brittle and beginning to shatter, Vree realized how tightly his sanity had been tied to finding Aralt quickly. What if he lost it? Would he drag her down with him, or would madness dissolve their unnatural union and send him screaming off as a disembodied spirit?

Vree! Her name echoed in her skull as she moved farther away from the road. *What are you doing?*

Locking her fear away, she chose her words carefully because her calm appeared to be the only thing holding her brother together. "I'm taking advantage of this water hole," she murmured, as her approach sent a trio of wild goats bounding away. "I'm going to take a long drink, and then I'm going to make myself a little less obvious for day travel."

But we have to catch Aralt! His protest was shrill enough to be almost painful.

"We will." Her tone suggested she spoke to a small and frightened child, not a young man only a year her junior. "But it's going to be hot, and I don't know when we'll find more water."

Slaughter it, Vree, don't patronize me! I hate it when you do that. I've always hated it!

Always hated it?

Pursing her lips, she pressed her face against the water and carefully sucked from just below the surface. It was still night-cool but with a faint, flat taste of the heat it had held the day before. Fortunately, the goats hadn't had the chance to stir up much of the gritty silt. Vree drank past desire, until she sloshed when she moved, then took a dagger to her tunic and breeches.

First the long sleeves, then the high collar, then a double hands span ripped ragged from the bottom of each leg—the fine, closely woven cotton, dyed and redyed to match the darkness, tore easily. She knotted the narrow ends of the sleeves and filled them with the weapons she could no longer hide as well as the supple ankle boots that were a better indication of her profession than any number of concealed daggers. A fistful of damp sand scrubbed the charcoal from hands and face.

After a thorough roll in the pale dirt, Vree bent and forced herself to take one last drink. As she lifted her head, she frowned at a shadowy indentation, newly delineated by the rising sun. *Bannon, look there.*

I look where you look, he muttered. Then she felt his mood change as he saw what she saw. On the other side of the watering hole, an earlier visitor had braced his weight, leaned forward to drink and left a clear impression of the heel and thumb of his right hand. *Mine. That's my handprint. He came this way, Vree! I told you so! We're almost on him. Get up! Get going!*

She'd trusted her brother's judgment in a thousand situations where a mistake would mean both their deaths. She trusted it now although she could see nothing familiar in the curves pressed into the damp earth. Securing her narrow pack with the silken length of her garrote, she slung it across her body and hurried north.

It was mid-morning when Vree heard the sound of a horse approaching from behind. She turned, shaded her eyes against the glare from above and the stone dust glare from below, and squinted back down the South Road. "Courier." The word was flat, inflectionless, but her heart began to pound a little faster. They should have expected this; in this part of the Empire the South Road was the only road the army bothered to keep way stations on. In this part of the Empire, it was the only road that went anywhere. "The marshal's probably sending news of the governor's death to the garrison."

The governor isn't dead.

"He is as far as the Sixth Army is concerned. There's a body and there's no one to lead the rebellion. What more do they need?"

Us?

"If Emo squealed, we'd have had to kill someone long before now."

Yeah, but Emo's a drunk, Vree. We can't count on him not to spill his guts the next time he crawls into a wineskin. Or the next time. Or the time after that.

"You're right." She started back the way they'd come. "Let's go back and kill him."

What are you doing? We have to find Aralt!

Then you shut up about Emo! Maybe I should've killed him, okay? But he's alive and he knows and there's not a slaughtering thing we can do about it!

As the courier rode closer, she dropped her head and continued slogging north, shoulders hunched, bare feet splayed out against the heated stone, nothing in her bearing suggesting she'd ever marched behind the Empire's banner.

She needn't have bothered. The courier trotted past, the sunburst pennant on his lance tip snapping, eyes under the crested helm locked ahead on the distance still to be covered. One skinny, filthy traveler meant nothing to him. After all, the Empire had built the roads to be traveled on.

As horse and rider and road disappeared behind an outcrop of faded pink stone, Vree scrubbed at a dribble of sweat between her breasts and shook her head. "Bannon, this is impossible. We need more to go on than *Aralt went north.* Didn't you get anything else?"

I don't know.

Very slowly, she set her right foot back down on the road beside her left. "You don't know?"

Come on, Vree, there were a lot of memories and stuff thrown at me . . .

This emotion, she recognized. In the past, jobs had always been weighted toward her planning and his instincts. He always wanted the overview and hated dealing with the details.

. . . and I haven't exactly had a chance to sort them out.

"Do it now." Vree lowered herself into a slice of shade.

But Aralt . . .

"Could be anywhere. I'm not moving until you've sorted things out.*

But ...

"No."

*Look, he's in *my* body!*

"And this is *mine,* and it's not moving until you give it a direction." He believed weariness where he would have argued with anger. She listened to the high-pitched whine of a buzzbug protesting the heat, scratched the top of one foot with the heel of the other, and waited.

Did we pass something that looks like this?

An image of a jagged ridge, half the face sheared off and huddled at the base, was shoved in front of her mind's eye. Vree jerked her head back and slammed it against the rock behind her.

Ow!

"You felt that?" She raised a hand and gingerly touched the lump coming up on her skull.

Of course I did. Well?

The ridge. Vree frowned, remembering. "It was off on the left side of the road about an hour ago, just past the last milestone."

There's a valley behind it, with a spring. Aralt has a villa there. That's where he's gone.

"But he isn't ..."

He instructed the servants to follow the orders of anyone showing up with his signet.

Vree nodded and stood. "Smart."

Not smart enough. He didn't plan on me surviving.

Nice place. Vree wiped sticky fingers on her thighs. The oranges had been bitter, but she'd been too hungry to care. At the head of the valley stood a sprawling, single-story house, its thick mud walls bleached a pale cream color by the constant sun. There were stables, and gardens, and the less attractive buildings that housed Aralt's servants. One slope of the valley held olive groves while the other grew oranges.

How do you think we should go in? Bannon asked.

If she didn't turn, she could believe he was crouched beside her. *We'll follow the line of trees to those currant bushes, behind them to that building, up onto the roof, a short jump up onto the house, and down into the central courtyard.* There had to be a central courtyard—there were almost no windows in the outside walls.

They'll be able to see us from the kitchens.

Vree squinted down at the open-sided building. *It's noon,* she said. *And hotter than a garrison whore. Everyone's asleep.*

Everyone except us.

Mad dogs and officers . . . In spite of everything, she grinned at the quote and felt Bannon's grin as he responded.

What does that make us?

The grin faded. *Desperate.*

They listened to the heartbeat they shared for a moment. Finally, when it became obvious that Bannon wasn't going to break the silence, Vree started toward the villa.

Vree, there's a dog.

I see it. Half rolled on its back, one paw in the air, the huge animal snoozed in the shade of the stables.

Are we upwind?

*I don't think there *is* a wind.* The air hung down from the searing heights of a yellow-blue sky like the beaded curtain in the governor's stronghold—not quite solid but a physical barrier nevertheless. Vree could almost feel the heated beads brush against her skin.

One foot on top of the low stone wall; both hands flat against the tiles; bare toes dug in for purchase; and she was on the first roof. The dog twitched but had no intention of abandoning its dream.

It would take a running leap to reach the roof of the main house, and during that one exposed moment disaster would be a single person glancing upward.

The windows in the servants' quarters stared like eyes. Vree could feel them watching her as she gathered herself for the jump. *They can't all be asleep* . . .

*They *have* to be.*

The run.

The jump.

The landing, nearly silent against the earth packed onto thick supporting logs.

A pigeon burst out of its shadowed corner, wings beating noisily at the air. Below, the dog jerked awake.

Slaughter it! It'll wake the dead, let alone the servants. We should have killed it.

Shut up, Bannon. Pressed flat, trying to push herself into the roof, Vree tried to hear past the dog's frenzied barking. It wasn't easy. Either the animal really hated pigeons or it had seen them. Her.

"Shaddup, ya stupid mutt!"

The dog yelped in pain.

"Hey, shithead! Don't throw things at my dog!"

"No problem." Something metal and hollow—a brass pitcher from the sound—clanged off a wall.

"Hey! Ya coulda killed me with that!"

"Not likely, I was aimin' at yer head."

"Yeah?"

"Yeah."

"Feis, leave the dog along and come back to bed."

"Ya gonna protect her when I rip her apart, Sova?"

"Touch my Feis and I'll rip you apart, you dickless wonder."

The three voices began to weave an intricate cacophony of name-calling and it no longer mattered just what the dog had been barking at.

Time to go.

Vines hung from the trellises that edged the deserted courtyard and in the center, a shallow pool reflected the sky. Quickly, her weight spread over as much area as possible, Vree moved to one of the carved pillars supporting the trellis and climbed down it. Training and experience turned her toward the rooms unmistakably occupied by the master of the house.

What if he's not in there?

Then we search the rest of the place. She kept her mental voice matter-of-fact as she padded across the cool tile to the louvered doors.

What if he's left already.

He was up all night. He has to sleep. No point in adding she'd also been up all night because she *couldn't* sleep, not yet, so why think about it.

Through the angled slats of faintly scented wood, she could see a northern style desk and chair and the low, cushion-piled rectangle of the bed. On the bed lay a body. Bannon's body? There wasn't light enough in the room to be sure. Fighting the tremors that racketed through her in the wake of her brother's nearly chaotic emotional response, she slid a long, narrow dagger from its sheath on her thigh.

What are you doing! That's my body! Mine!

Her hands began to spasm. *Bannon, stop it! No one tries to run with a knife at his throat. I'll hold him, you get back in.*

Slowly, he calmed. Vree could almost hear him panting. *My body,* he repeated. *Mine.*

Slowly, more out of concern that Bannon would try to take control again than any fear of discovery, Vree pushed open one side of the louvered doors just far enough to slide through. With the scorching heat of midday unable to penetrate the narrow windows and thick walls, the room had a cavelike feel about it. No longer instantly evaporating, sweat plastered her filthy clothes to her skin as she crossed silently to the bed. Just before her toes hit the edge of the cotton pad, she stopped and stared at the naked man stretched out amidst the cushions.

It *was* Bannon's body. Aralt had bathed at some point, for the short brown curls sprang crisply back from his temples and the taut sheath of dark olive skin stretched over lean muscles seemed almost oiled. There the scar where the barbed Ohkan spear tip had been dug out; there where a dying rebel had managed to open a line across his ribs; there the puckered rosette on the crown of his knee where at nine he'd knelt on an ember. Her gaze lingered on the long muscles of his thighs, moved upward, swept past the soft protrusion of his sex—in spite of a sudden urge to linger she knew came from the brother within—and locked on his face. His chin came to less delicate a point than hers and his cheekbones angled higher and sharper. Combined with the arc of his brows, the length of his lashes, and the wide bow of his mouth, they gave him a feral beauty that would look at home in any shrine of the Wild God. It wasn't difficult to imagine a rack of horns sweeping up off his brow.

Bannon remained quiet, almost withdrawn, while she stared down at his body. Although his curiosity was unmistakable, he was wrapped too tightly for her to separate out any other emotions. She supposed that

was for the best as her own emotional fabric had begun
to fray. *This is my brother. This is not my brother.*

Mine . . .

Hush, Bannon, I know.

There was something wrong, but she couldn't put
her finger on it. She'd seen Bannon asleep a thousand,
a hundred thousand times, but . . .

But Bannon never slept on his back.

Shifting her grip on the dagger, she reached down
with her free hand to lightly touch the broad chest that
rose and fell to another man's rhythm.

He opened his eyes.

They were still so dark a brown that they seemed to
be all pupil. They looked like they always had and
were, at the same time, completely different.

Now, Vree! Now! The knife!

Her instant of hesitation was all he needed. Vree
suddenly found herself caught up in an iron grip and
flung to the floor. She twisted to avoid his knees slamming at her gut, shoved a foot into his armpit, and
kicked out hard. She'd sparred with her brother many
times in the past, but this time he had all the advantages. He was obviously trying to kill her. She couldn't
hurt him. He was rested. She was exhausted. He had a
single life driving him. She had two, for Bannon kept
flinging bits of her about.

With the pressure of his chest grinding her against
the floor, his hand closed around her wrist; the other
reached for her throat. To her surprise, she broke his
grip with a desperate move that Bannon should have
been able to counter easily.

Not all the advantages.

This wasn't Bannon. Aralt might have Bannon's
body, but he'd only been in it for hours. He didn't
know it. Didn't know what it was capable of. Didn't

have the training that made physical responses instinctive.

And a man fighting naked had areas he *had* to protect—whether he did it consciously or not. She crammed her hip into his groin. When he turned to shield it, she threw her weight against his shoulders and this time, hitting the floor, she rode him.

His skin was cool, smooth. The nest of hair between his legs brushed against her ankle as they struggled. They were so close she could smell the peppers on his breath.

Then the blade kissed his throat and he froze, a pulse throbbing just above the steel.

"Now, Bannon! Do it now!"

She felt him surge forward and for an instant, he was both in her and looking up at her.

Then he was gone. The place he'd been echoed, empty. He stared up at her for another instant, triumphant; then his eyes widened in fear. Then they were a stranger's eyes again.

NO! Somehow, she reached out and clutched at the life being hurled into oblivion. For a heartbeat she was Bannon, she was Vree, then, as terror—hers; not hers—scraped jagged edges of panic against the inside of her skull, she slid into darkness.

Chapter Three

The rough hemp rope abraded skin as the corporal secured wrist to iron bolt. Her mouth set in a grim line, she muttered, "You both should've known better." as she tied off the last knot.

Head up. Don't let them see you're afraid. At the last flogging, the recruit had blubbered like a baby even before the first welt rose on his back.

A tug against the binding nearly brought panic. It was one thing to know that movement would be impossible and another thing entirely to be held immobile. *No. Don't struggle. Don't give them the satisfaction.*

So maybe it had been a stupid bet. But they'd been cooped up inside the garrison for far too long; it was time to fly. After all, wasn't this what they were being trained to do? What difference was there between sneaking out of the garrison after lockup and sneaking into an enemy camp?

What difference? Lips twisted into a trembling parody of a smile. *Nine lashes.*

Wood pressed against shoulders, belly, and thighs. the breezes felt cooler than they should against bare, exposed skin.

Getting out had been easy. They'd danced through the shadows of the town, picked up the proof the bet

required, and danced back. The feeling of freedom had
been exhilarating; even the night air had seemed
sweeter. They'd almost made it.

We should *have made it.*

From behind, the lash snapped out, striking a practice blow at nothing.

Swallow with a throat gone suddenly dry.

Shake off the comforting clasp of fingers. The corporal had bound them together before lashing their
inner wrists to the punishment beam.

We would've made it if I'd seen that rotten board.
Impossible not to tense, anticipating the pain. *I
should've . . .*

. . . seen that rotten board. Vree struggled to pull
herself out of the memory before the lash could fall.
She'd gone through it once when she was fourteen and
had no intention of going through it again. And then
she realized. That hadn't been *her* memory. *Bannon?*

No . . .

Bannon!

Vree? She could almost feel him pulling himself
together, drawing all the scattered bits into a confused and fearful whole. *What . . .?*

They realized they were bound at the same instant
and for a moment their combined memories of pain
and humiliation threatened to overwhelm them. Only
exhaustion kept their struggle against the binding from
tipping over into panic.

A frenzied throbbing that threatened to smash the
bones of her skull dragged Vree out of the gestalt.
Fighting the instinctive urge to push Bannon away, she
clung to herself and finally forced her body to still.

"That's better. You haven't a chance of breaking
free."

The tone was urbane, amused. The voice was almost familiar.

Gritting her teeth, Vree heaved her eyelids up.

Bannon—not Bannon—stood watching her from a double-body length away. He'd put on a pale green robe that didn't quite fit and his expression contained more curiosity than threat. Beside him, piled on the end of the bed, were not only the weapons she'd been forced to carry in her makeshift pack, but also every weapon that had remained on her body.

Shit.

Not that it really mattered because she was obviously going to be given no chance to use them. She'd been tied, with what appeared to be silk scarves, to the heavy, northern-style chair she'd seen from the doorway. Although bruised from the fight, the greatest amount of damage seemed to have been caused by the sudden desperate grab for her brother's life. Her head still rang as though all seven armies were marching through it.

"You must be the sister."

It was so weird hearing the timbre of Bannon's voice changed by a stranger's inflections. Vree flinched as long, cool fingers took firm hold of her jaw and raised her head.

"You look very much alike. Do you know that?" Bannon's lips smiled. "Of course you do. I have to admit, I never thought to meet you—although you were close to the surface of your brother's thoughts, he believed himself to be alone and I certainly didn't expect you to be following so close behind. Had I known, I'd have lingered long enough to take care of things." He released her and wiped his fingers fastidiously on the billowing folds of his robe as he straightened. "Mind you, I couldn't possibly have expected you to gather the poor boy to your bosom, metaphorically speaking, and come trotting after me determined to shove him back into his fleshy shell. If asked, I'd have declared it an impossible situation. Obviously, I would have been wrong." His eyes narrowed. "That doesn't often happen. I don't like to be wrong."

Say something, Vree.

Say what? He doesn't seem to need any encouragement from me.

The man who had been Governor Aralt walked over to the pile of weapons and prodded it gently, then he turned to face her again. "Vree. A diminutive of Vireyda. But no one calls you that, do they? Tell me, Vree, after this morning's little adventure, are you still sane?"

"Yes." The question surprised an answer out of her. "Is he?"

I'll soon show you how sane I am, you thieving son of a diseased pig!

"I know you're still holding him. I felt you drag him back from the brink of oblivion."

"He's sane." Vree spit the words from between tight lips.

"This is fascinating." Bannon's body folded itself gracefully into a cross-legged position on the end of the bed. "Absolutely fascinating."

He'll find it fascinating all right, with a dagger shoved up between his ribs!

Try to remember that they're your ribs. She clamped her will down on her left arm, stopping its futile struggle against the russet scarf that bound her to the wooden arm of the chair. *And stop doing that.*

"You're talking to him, aren't you?" Bannon/Aralt leaned forward, elbows braced against his knees. "Your eyes develop an inward cast and . . ."

"Can I ask you something?" Vree broke in before he could begin another monologue.

He spread his hands. "Ask."

"Why haven't you killed me? Us."

"A good question. You intrigue me. And there isn't a lot capable of that anymore." He grinned, and the familiar expression plunged her into confusion. "My turn. Did you have any idea of the risks you took, or did you act in total ignorance of the danger?"

"What danger?"

"Insanity. Loss of self. Death. When you allowed him to jump into your mind—and I assume you allowed it, he didn't just force himself in?" He read the answer off her face. "Yes, well, when you allowed him in, you should have been pushed out. Destroyed. Your life sacrificed for his."

"I trusted him."

"Very commendable." His voice picked up a sardonic edge. "I trusted someone once. But what made you think that you could hold two lives in one frail shell? No, wait." He raised his hand as a thought occurred to him. "You didn't think, did you? It was the only thing to do, so you did it. Blind faith succeeds where reason would have failed. That's so touching it makes me ill."

Vree leaned back in the chair, subtly testing the knots that held her. "So now what?"

"Another good question." Aralt/Bannon stared down at his foot as though fascinated by the strength and flexibility of his toes. "You could still go insane."

"I don't think so."

"How would you know?"

"I'd know." She ground the words out through clenched teeth, and he smiled.

"Yes, I believe you would." He leaned forward suddenly, and for the first time, his eyes met hers. "If I let you live, you'll continue trying to push me out of your brother's body, won't you?"

Yes!

Bannon, no!

But he wasn't listening. She felt him throw himself forward over the fragile bridge of her gaze, felt him slam into an impenetrable barrier, once again had to grab him and drag him back.

This time, at least, she remained conscious. When her vision cleared, Bannon/Aralt was standing over her. "You can't," he said simply. "I've done this too often. I'm far too strong."

Her head felt like it was being ground between two large rocks. "Then you'll have to kill me. Us." At the moment, death didn't look so bad.

"No. I have a better idea. I have something you want. Something you need." He spread his hands. "This body. Which, I might add, is a fine physical specimen—young, strong, handsome. I'm sure we can come to some sort of an agreement."

Vree glared at him. "And what do I have that you want?"

"Skill. Training. Experience. How old are you? Your brother is twenty, so you'd be twenty-two? Twenty-three?" He sighed and shook his head. "You're not going to tell me, are you? No matter. You're a military assassin and a very good one if you've been doing it since you were fifteen."

"Twenty-one."

Why are you telling him?

She winced as Bannon's protest drove yet another spike of pain into her head. *What difference does it make? We need him to deal.*

*We don't *need* anything from him.*

*Except *your* body.*

*Which I'll *take* back!*

How?

"Children . . ."

Nobody spoke to her like that. Not if they wanted to live to see morning. After everything else that had happened; after discovering Bannon in a dying body not his own; after finding the precarious balancing point that let them both exist in her head; after tracking Aralt; after confrontation and capture—that smug patronizing tone was just too much. Vree's eyes narrowed and she began working her strength against the scarves securing her; if the silk wouldn't give, perhaps the chair would. All at once, it became very easy not to see her brother in the man sitting on the bed.

Vree, stop it. You'll hurt yourself.

She could see his mouth moving, white teeth flashing between curved lips, but she couldn't hear what he said over the roaring in her ears.

Vree, let it go. It isn't worth it. Listen to him.

You said we didn't need anything from him. Rage clipped each word to its bare essentials.

I was wrong. She felt him sigh. *He has my body. We have to deal.*

How come you're so slaughtering composed all of a sudden?

Because you aren't? Bannon's laugh still held a hint of hysteria, but his thoughts felt clearer than they had. *We're a team, remember. I see the dangers you don't. You spot the dangers I miss. I want my body back, Vree, as much or more than you want me out of your head. I, I can't force my way in . . .* He hated to make the admission—Vree could feel him struggle with it. *. . . so we have to listen to him. We don't have a choice.*

She drew in a long breath and managed to unclench her teeth before she slowly let it out. *Maybe I should've fallen apart hours ago.*

Maybe.

"You haven't been listening to me, have you?"

"No." With the fury gone, Vree sagged against the scarves.

Bannon/Aralt shook his head and sighed. "Family matters? No, never mind." He raised a cautioning hand, a gold signet gleaming on his second finger. "I don't really want to know. I shall present the case once more. This time, I suggest you pay attention." Steepling his fingers, he leaned forward slightly, the action at odds with the flesh he wore. "As admirable as this body is, it comes with none of the little extras that make life worthwhile, and I have no wish to remain in it for very long. So, did you stop to tell any of your comrades about what happened in Ghoti or did you rush blindly after me?" He read the answer on her face and smiled. "Good. You will use your skills to help me get another body."

"One with *extras?*"

"Precisely."

"What kind of extras?"

"Wealth. Power. Position."

"Why do you need me? Us? You seem to have managed fine so far."

"Yes, well, the body I have in mind—if you'll pardon the expression—will be heavily guarded and I'll need you to help me get close enough to make the transfer. When that happens, your brother will have his body back."

"What happens to the life from this new body?"

"Why should you care?"

Why should she? As long as Bannon got his body

back, what difference did the death of one stranger make? "Who is it?"

"Prince Otavas."

The youngest of the Emperor's four children, Prince Otavas, at seventeen, had just begun to take his place in public life. His coming of age had been celebrated across the Empire and the Sixth Army had happily drunk a river of beer in his honor. Pounding heads made for a silent parade the next morning, but the swearing of allegiance had rung out with enough volume to echo off the garrison walls lest word get back to the Emperor that the Sixth Army was less than sincere in their support of his son. Vree, her own head eggshell fragile, had shouted as loudly as the rest although she'd aimed her voice directly at Bannon, who'd turned a pale green at the noise.

"No."

Bannon/Aralt smiled. "Aren't you being just a bit hasty? Don't you think you should talk it over with your brother first? I mean, you do realize what your alternative is . . ." Picking up one of her daggers, he tested the point against the ball of his thumb and frowned at the crimson bead of blood. "Very sharp."

Vree . . .

No. We swore an oath to serve the Imperial House. We've been serving the Imperial House all our lives. Don't ask me to break those oaths, Bannon. She tried to swallow around the sudden obstruction in her throat that seemed to have edges sharper than her dagger. If he asked her, she'd have to do it and then there wouldn't be anything left of her at all. She'd already given him the army, surely he couldn't want her honor, too.

Do you think I could break those oaths so easily?

I . . .

His mental voice held equal amounts of hurt and anger. *I've served the Imperial House just as you have. I've killed for them. I've bled for them. What makes you think your oaths mean more to you than mine do to me?*

Vree closed her eyes, shutting out the distraction of Bannon/Aralt. *He has your body.* It was the only answer she could give him.

*And that's all he's getting."

I'm sorry. I should've known.

Yeah. You should have. He sounded as though he'd been betrayed.

She was too tired to react, too tired for that underlying accusation to cut as deeply as it would have under other circumstances. Given the way she felt—physically drained and emotionally flayed—a quick death looked almost inviting. She only wished they could have died in battle. *I wonder if we'll get stuffed into the same crow.*

What?

Because we'll die in one body, she explained, wondering why he hadn't understood. It'd seemed obvious to her.

We're not going to die.

Bannon, I'm tied like a festival goose. What am I supposed to defend myself with? Spit and a prayer?

Lies.

What?

His grin lit up the inside of her head. *We're going to lie to him. It's a long way to the Capital and the prince, and we'll be chewing at his defenses the whole time.*

And if we can't get through?

*Vree, there're two of us to one of him. And we're

the best. There's never been a defense we couldn't get through. Has there?*

No . . .

So we agree to give him the prince, but we get my body back before we have to.

He'll think he's safe because I won't hurt the body he's in, and he doesn't think you're strong enough to push him out.

That's the only reason he would have made the slaughtering offer. His tone held an approving nod. *The arrogant carrion eater.*

"I'm waiting for a decision."

Vree opened her eyes. "We'll help, on one condition."

Vree!

Shut up, I'm trying to make this believable.

"I hardly think that you—either of you—are in a state to be imposing conditions, but what is it?"

"After you're in the prince and Bannon has his body back, we're to be given time to get away. No yelling for the guards."

"And what makes you think you can trust me?"

She lifted both brows and layered silent sarcasm onto her response. "The same thing that makes you think you can trust us. We have something you need."

"You won't after I'm in the prince."

"I won't be tied then." Vree dropped her gaze pointedly to her weapons. "After all the trouble you're going through to become the prince, I'd think you'd like to live a while longer."

"If you kill the prince . . ."

"*You'll* have already killed the prince!" she snarled.

"Very well. If you kill the prince's body, the palace guards will kill you. Both of you."

She shrugged. "We're not afraid to die."

He stared at her strangely and murmured, "But I notice you're choosing life, regardless."

"I said we weren't afraid, not that we wanted to. Besides, if we die after you've taken the prince, at least we'll have the satisfaction . . ."

The pleasure!

". . . of taking you with us."

He studied her as if weighing her sincerity, then he smiled. "I think I can meet that condition."

"Then you have a deal." Except that he'd be dead and out of Bannon's body long before they reached the prince. Bannon was right. There'd never been a defense they couldn't breach together. "Now, if I'm, we're, going to help you, you can start your part of the bargain by cutting me free."

"Of course. Pardon me." The dagger he chose was the long, slender blade she'd carried into the room. He slid it between silk and skin, and she shivered at the caress of the chilled steel. The silk parted like water around stone, flowing away from the edge.

"Very sharp," he repeated approvingly, turning the knife and offering it to her, hilt first.

His fingers laid warm pressure against hers during the exchange.

"Is something the matter?"

Vree shook her head. "No." Safest to stick to single syllables. Or maybe not. "Just so you know . . ." The dagger whispered promises as she slid it back into the thigh sheath. ". . . I know twenty-seven ways to kill you with no weapons at all."

The theatrical recoil was so Bannon it was difficult to remember that it involved Bannon's body alone. He clutched a handful of the robe over his heart. "You're scaring me to death."

She cocked her head thoughtfully. "Twenty-eight." Two could play at that game.

Impossible not to laugh with him. With Bannon's body. *I'm so tired.*

"You need to sleep. Come, there's a guest room just next door you can use. I'm afraid you'll have to share . . ."

Vree, that's not funny.

Sorry. She swallowed a chuckle, recognizing how close she was to losing control—a very bad idea when trapped in enemy territory—and scooped up the rest of her weapons. "What will you tell the servants?"

"That my traveling companion has joined me and we'll both be leaving in the morning." He waved the signet ring under her nose as he pushed open one of the louvered doors and led the way out into the courtyard. "Governor Aralt prepared the servants for my arrival."

"How will you explain me just appearing? I didn't come in through the front door, you know."

"I'm sure you didn't, but you'll agree there's no need to tell them that." The next room was identical to the one they'd just left except there was no desk, no chair, and no pile of knotted scarf fragments. "If you insist on journeying in the heat of midday, you have to expect a lack of a welcoming committee when you arrive. Fortunately, I'm a light sleeper. I heard and I brought you in."

"And they'll believe you?"

"As long as I'm wearing this ring. There's a pot in that small chest if you need it."

She paused just inside the room, toes curling against the raised pattern in the braided straw mat. "What do I call you? Obviously you're not Aralt anymore. At least not here."

He stared at her for a long moment and she had the oddest feeling that he was actually seeing her for the first time. "You may call me Gyhard," he said at last. "Gyhard i'Stevana."

"Gyhard i'Stevana? That's a strange name."

"Perhaps. But it's the one I was born with." He sketched her a courtly bow. "I haven't used it for some time."

The glass mirror had cost him a great deal, but from the moment he'd seen the clarity of the reflection they cast he'd wanted one. The artisans who knew the secret of joining liquid mercury, tin, and glass lived in one small, but very wealthy city on the shore of the Fienian Sea. He'd gone there himself in the time before he became Governor Aralt, risking the dangerous overland route and paying nearly everything he had for an oval mirror no larger than a man's hand.

It was very important he be able to see clearly who he was.

"Gyhard i'Stevana." His reflection looked young and confused. "Why did I give her that name?" He hadn't used that name in . . . A quick frown knitted in the high arc of the brows as he counted back. He hadn't used that name in over ninety years.

He'd just jumped into his third body, had just used his *ability* deliberately for the first time. He'd been haunted and lonely when high in the Cemandian Mountains he'd met someone in infinitely worse shape.

The hand holding the mirror began to tremble and memory laid the reflection of a dark-haired, dark-eyed young man over Bannon's brown on brown features. It wasn't a handsome face, it could even be called plain—except for the dark beauty of the eyes.

"No." He'd worn that face for only five short years and had no desire to remember any of them. Forcing the memories aside, he stared down once more at the image of the boy he'd become, and then slid the mirror carefully back into its padded case. The dark eyes had rotted with the rest of the discarded body, and the man who had found them beautiful was no doubt long dead.

It had, after all, been over ninety years.

He should've pulled a name from the air. One that didn't drag the past along with it.

Jaw set, he lightly touched his throat where the assassin's blade had caressed the skin. He couldn't take the name back. He couldn't let even the suspicion of weakness disturb the tenuous balance of power necessary to achieve his goal.

Still, it was only a name.

"And none of this," he muttered, his voice self-mocking, "explains why I gave it to her in the first place."

Vree folded her arms behind her head and stared up at the shadowed ceiling. The edges had all been rounded and the whole gentle arc, extending about two hand spans down the wall to a dark tile border, had been painted a pale blue. She supposed it was intended to mimic the outdoors and give the room a feeling of openness, but it made her feel as though the sky were closing in on her.

You think we can trust him?

Bannon's presence shifted, as though he were pacing in the confines of a cage. *Who? That carrion eater in my body? Probably as much as he can trust us—and the first chance we get, he's out of there.*

Great. Her jaw creaked with the force of her yawn. *Can you keep watch while I sleep?*

Depends. Can you sleep with your eyes open?

Sighing, she pulled a dagger with each hand and arranged herself into a more defensive position. *This doesn't seem to come with any advantages.*

Yeah well, I'm alive . . . Vree?

Her eyes closed, pretty much of their own volition. *What?*

Thanks. I mean, thanks for taking the chance, for not . . . you know.

For not wanting to go on alone. Vree bit her lower lip to keep it from trembling.

*Are you *crying,* sister-mine?*

Sister-mine. It had always been as much a possessive as an endearment, and this was the first time he'd used it since he'd landed in her head. She ignored the moisture trickling out from under the corners of her lids. *No. Of course not.*

Of course not, he repeated.

She didn't want to guess what he meant.

Vree?

What?

*Remember if you have to defend yourself, don't strike to kill. I mean, it *is* . . .*

. . . your body. Don't worry, Bannon. The dagger hilts lay loose within the circles of her fingers. *I'll remember.*

Almost asleep, she barely heard him call her name again.

Vree?

What? In spite of everything, she smiled. This was beginning to remind her of too many nights in the children's barracks when Bannon had kept her awake with question after question.

I always thought I was taller. . . .

* * *

Hunger woke her. She lay, frozen in place, fingers tight around her dagger hilts, senses straining the silence for threat. She couldn't hear anything. At all. For a moment she was afraid that she might have somehow, inexplicably, gone deaf while she slept.

Vree?

Shhhh.

The whisper of her hair against the cotton blanket as she turned her head sounded unnaturally loud. Very slowly, muscles tensed, she sat. Used to working in darkness, she found the dim, late evening light slanting through the narrow windows and the double louvered door leading to the courtyard more than sufficient.

What is it? Bannon demanded.

Can't you hear it?

I can't hear anything.

That's what I mean. A life spent in barracks and army camps hadn't prepared her for the quiet. She'd learned—everyone learned—to sleep through almost anything but she'd never woken up to such a total lack of noise.

It's like we dozed off on target, murmured Bannon, wonder touching his mental voice. *Maybe everyone's cleared out.*

Vree's nose twitched and her stomach growled loudly in response. A small stone crock, a dipper, a cup, and a covered bowl had been set on the low table beside the bed. Lips pressed tightly together in disgust, she sheathed her daggers and crossed her legs beneath her. *They could've just pushed a pillow over my face and saved themselves the bother. I can't *believe* I didn't hear them bring this in.*

Good servants walk on shadow feet. Commander Neegan always says that more assassins are screwed by personal body servants than by guards. What's in the bowl? I'm starved.*

I'm starved, Vree corrected absently, leaning forward and lifting the lid. *Cold millet and cooked slaughtering veg. Just like home.*

*Sniff again, sister-mine. When the army cooks this, it smells like onions. This smells like . . ."

. . . hot peppers and . . . With her nose nearly resting on the edge of the bowl, it didn't even look like the grayish-brown, sticky mass she was used to. *. . . and orange. And there's more than just a couple of half-cooked chunks of zucchini in there, too.* Her right hand jerked to a stop, the scoop of food on the first two fingers nearly at her mouth. *Bannon!*

What if he's trying to poison us?

Vree swallowed a curt, *What if he is?* along with a mouthful of saliva and considered the question. *No. He's grown used to having power and he needs us . . . me to get more. He won't give up the chance.*

How can you be so sure?

Ever hear of an officer turning down a promotion?

The food tasted better than it smelled. The crock held cold water with slices of lime floating on the surface—Vree ignored the cup and drank straight from the dipper. It was a beautifully crafted piece of metalwork, shaped into the likeness of a broad-petaled flower on a gently curving stem, and if she'd had her pack . . . The army officially frowned on looting but pragmatically ignored most of the less blatant occurrences.

The pot was almost too pretty to use.

Thumbs tucked under the drawstring, she shucked her breeches down and squatted. Things got complicated for a few moments.

Bannon, what is it with you!

Nothing.

Something's wrong. You'd think you never saw me piss before.

*I've never *been* you pissing before.*

*So what? It's still *my* body.*

Yeah, but I'm in here, too, and ...

And what?

Nothing!

Nothing? She looked down. Realized the problem. And couldn't stop the snicker—instantly regretted. Male obsessions that called for a wisecrack under other circumstances were no longer funny. *I'm sorry, Bannon.*

You're not a man. You don't understand. You can't understand. The next thought was so soft she hardly heard it. *I'm not a man.*

Frowning, Vree straightened and shoved the pot back into its cabinet with the side of her foot. He was partially right—she wasn't a man and she didn't understand—but she could feel his distress and wanted to ease it. *Look, being a man is more than just ... I mean, you're still you, and. ... Well, slaughter it, Bannon, you're *not* a woman.*

I'm in a woman.

Yeah? Not for the first time.

It's not the same thing. But this protest carried the feel of a reluctant grin and his next words proved that she'd managed to distract him. *Mind you, I've always wondered. Vree, if I'm stuck in here for a while, do you think you could ...*

Her face grew hot. *No.*

Just once?

Bannon!

"Am I interrupting something?"

Embarrassment gave her only one response.

Gyhard stared at the throwing dagger buried to the hilt in the door frame by his head, then he turned to stare at the young woman scowling at him. Although his heart raced and the highly conditioned body he now wore trembled with the need to react, he kept his tone mild. "I suppose I should have knocked?"

Vree fought to bring her blushing under control, which only made it worse. "What do you want?" she snarled.

"I thought, now that you've rested, that you might like to visit the bathhouse." He held out one of the flowing house robes he, as Aralt, had provided for guests. "I didn't want to mention this earlier, but you're filthy."

Soaped, scrubbed, rinsed, and feeling almost relaxed, Vree leaned back in the soaking pool until the warm water lapped at the point of her chin. *I could get used to this.*

They feel strange.

What do?

Breasts. They sort of float. Or they would float if they were bigger.

Up yours. The water level rose as Gyhard lowered himself into the pool and she shifted position. "Aralt did all right by himself."

"There were certain perks involved in being district governor," he admitted, stretching his arms out along the submerged tile ledge. "Probably why I stayed with it for so long."

Vree circled a finger above the water, indicating not only the soaking pool but more-or-less the entire bathhouse; the lush curtains of hanging plants, the mosaics, the clusters of scented candles. "I'm amazed you wanted to give this up."

He shrugged, the motion sending ripples out from his shoulders. "I was old. While I'd allowed it to happen, I found I didn't care for it much. The older you are, the closer you are to a death that can't be avoided."

He's about three feet from his death right now.

As soon as we get a chance, Bannon. I promise.

From under half-lowered lids, Gyhard watched the minute changes in his companion's expression and wondered how she managed to so closely coexist with another life. *Still, I suppose all those years in barracks and field camps are as good a training for lack of individuality as you can get.* He'd barely touched young Bannon's memories during the transfer as, at the time, he'd had no desire to know the man he was displacing. Now, he wished he'd been just a little more thorough, if only to have gained more information on the sister. Considering her trade, there was a sense of vulnerability about her that he found astounding.

"So . . ." She jerked as he broke the silence. "How is your brother?"

How am I? I'll show that carrion eater how I am the moment he drops his guard, the slaughtering son-of-a-sow, the . . .

"He's angry." Vree interrupted the internal tirade. "And he wants his body back."

Gyhard flexed his ankle and gloried in the response of young muscle. "Well, tell him from me that it's a superb body and I'm not surprised he wants it back."

"Tell him yourself. He can hear you."

"He's using your senses?" The concept intrigued Gyhard. "Is he able to exert any physical control?"

Below the surface of the water, Vree unclenched the fist Bannon had made. "No," she lied, sneering slightly. "He's a passenger. That's all."

I am not!

For Jiir's sake, Bannon, remember who we're talking to. The less he knows the better.

Yeah. I guess you're right.

But she could tell he didn't like it, that he hated the thought of being considered a passive observer. She'd have hated it also had their positions been reversed. Levering herself out of the pool, she reached for a drying cloth. "What now?"

"Now we eat a late but excellent supper and then we get some sleep. We'll be leaving for the Capital in the morning. I assembled most of what we'll need while you were sleeping. Can you ride?"

"No." The cloths were both incredibly soft and absorbant. Vree wondered if they'd miss a couple. "And neither can you."

Standing in the pool, Gyhard stared up at her. "What are you talking about? I've ridden all my life."

Vree smiled unpleasantly. "Your head has, but that body's never been on a horse. Even if you know what to do, you'll have to teach the body how to do it."

"I am *not* walking all the way to the Capital."

"Then I guess all three of us will have to learn to ride."

Teeth clenched, Gyhard muttered profanity under his breath.

You enjoyed that, didn't you?

She tugged the house robe down over her head. *Uh-huh.*

Saddle sores won't be so funny.

I'm used to the body I'm wearing. I know what it's capable of. He isn't and he doesn't.

Great. My butt suffers alone.

You won't be in it.

On it.

Whatever.

The robe settled down on her shoulders in time to see Gyhard stepping up out of the pool. He might be in Bannon's body, but he didn't move like her brother and the effect was strangely disconcerting. All at once, she found she couldn't look away. *Bannon?*

I want to see.

No need to make an excuse this time. Heart pounding, she let him stare.

Gyhard paused, spine arced as he dried his back. "What's the matter?"

Tell him that I'm just making sure he hasn't lost anything.

When she repeated it, Gyhard smiled but his gaze remained locked on her face and she could see a question in his eyes.

Bannon's eyes.

Not Bannon's eyes.

"Tell your brother," he said softly, "that he's unbelievably vain."

"Tell him yourself," Vree snapped, but her mouth was dry.

It was too quiet. Vree lay stiffly under the weight of the cotton blanket and stared into the darkness. The sights, the sounds, the smells of the army were missing. No comforting barricade of life surrounded her. She could smell the lingering perfume of the bath; could hear the pounding of her own heart; could see nothing. Couldn't sleep.

What is it?

Nothing. She forced her eyes closed and stared instead at the patterns flaring across the lids.

Sure is quiet.

Everyone's asleep.

You're not.

Moisture spread from her palms to the leather-wrapped hilts lying against them.

You thinking about him?

She rubbed her hands dry on the blanket. *No. There's nothing we can do about him now.*

Yeah, I guess.

The room that had seemed so confining before, now seemed infinitely large. She couldn't get any sense of the other lives in the villa and felt as though she were floating alone in the night with no reference points to ground her.

Vree? You're not alone. His voice laid an arm across her shoulders and pulled her into a loose embrace. *I'm here.*

A night bird screamed. The silence swallowed the cry.

What were they doing, Emo and the others? Had they fought? Had they died? Was her pack still sitting where she'd left it? When would they divide her kit? When would they be sure she wasn't coming back?

Her palms were damp again.

Hey, do you remember how Ugy used to snore? How crazy it used to drive you? You'd get up and slip across the barracks to pinch his nose closed, oh, two or three times before you finally got so pissed off you'd throw something heavy and hard at him. It'd crash and he'd swear and half the squad'd wake up ready to pound him. . . .

As Bannon built a wall of memories around her, Vree began to relax. The night filled with the familiar, with the known, and his voice became one of many voices. When she finally surrendered to sleep, she took the last words she heard with her.

It's all right, sister-mine. We'll go together. . . .

Chapter Four

His last companion had gone to pieces days before. He wasn't sure how many days, sunrise and sunset had grown so much alike of late, but he remembered holding her tenderly as the last of her flesh rotted beyond the point where it would contain her. When it was all over and her kigh had fled shrieking into the darkness, he'd taken one of her few remaining finger bones, threaded it on a silver wire, and added it to the multitude hanging from the silk cord he wore around his neck.

He kept a bit from all of them. They were his family, his friends, and he owed it to them not to forget.

If he lifted his head, he could see the Capital growing like a carbuncle on the horizon. Although old muscles ached, he was too near his destination to rest.

As he walked, he scanned the faces of the other travelers on the road. A glance, no more, and then his gaze moved on. He'd been searching for so long, he no longer remembered what it was he searched for—he only knew it was important and that he couldn't be complete until he'd found it again.

His heart began to pound uncomfortably quickly as he finally distinguished the first of the stone tombs that lined the road. Trembling fingers tightened around the carved, bone knob of his walking stick. Once it had been part of a shoulder joint which had, in turn, been part of a young shepherd he had loved. They'd stayed with him longer back then, back before age had weakened his Song.

The sun had risen past the center of the sky when he reached the first tomb, and he shuffled gratefully into the small bit of shade it offered.

"When I was alive," he muttered, tracing the stone letters as he read, *"I was a candle-maker. I was the first to add the scent of oranges or lemons to the wax. My candles burned in the Imperial Palace. I gave one tenth of all I made to the temple of Leetis. . . .* Who in the Circle is Leetis?" He'd never been able to keep track of the Empire's gods—not that it made any difference in the end. Once it had enraged him that the Circle had a place for gods created from nothing more than a bit of misremembered history but no place for him. He'd grown too old for rage, but he still felt the old pain, the old betrayal. *"Every festival, I gave two dozen beeswax candles to the healers. I employed three craftsmen and twelve laborers. My name was Elkan. My mother was Yolandis."*

He tapped a ridged and discolored nail against the crudely cut bias relief of a man dipping candles. "Elkan Yolandis. A good name. My name is . . . is . . ." He frowned. No one had called him by name for so long, he had trouble remembering. "Well," he sighed after a moment, "it doesn't matter." Clearing his throat and hacking a mouthful of phlegm into the dust at the side of the road, he began to hum.

A number of those jostling past on their way along the East Road to the Capital grew suddenly uneasy and began to hurry. No one paid any attention to the old man in the travel-stained brown robes as he padded about the tomb.

His circuit complete, he sagged against the barred and bolted door. Although three of the eight panels prepared for epitaphs had been filled, no one had answered his call.

"Too old. Too old." A long drink of brackish water from his leather flask did nothing to wash away his disappointment. Shoulders slumped, he continued on his way, less certain now that he'd find the companionship he so desperately desired.

He almost didn't recognize the funeral when he saw it approaching. It took up fully half the road, and the noise rising from the crowd seemed more likely to wake the dead than lay them to rest. As most of the traffic grumbled its way over to the remaining side of the road, he hovered near the edge of a small cluster of the curious.

"Would you look at that." A beefy arm waved at the four blue-veiled figures carrying a small but working fountain between them. "What's the point in paying for a blessing of the goddess at a tomb?"

"I heard the family'd paid for a sickbed blessing. I heard they'd paid and the priestesses were getting ready to leave and the healers said not to bother."

"What? The goddess was late?"

"That's what I heard. And just *try* getting your coin back from the temple."

He sidled a very little closer to the pair of middle-aged women who'd set down their baskets and seemed ready to enjoy the opportunity for gossip the procession created.

"Look at all the mourners. That must have cost a crescent or three."

"You'd think as they were so close they wouldn't have minded sharing."

They? More than one? He strained to see past the

white-robed men and women who appeared to be performing a stylized, scripted grief. Between the simu-
lated mourning and honest sorrow—a dozen or so
friends and family, many with tears washing channels
through the thick white makeup that covered every
face—came a pair of biers.

Two young men.

He somehow managed to stop himself from darting
forward. Two. Young men. And dead less than a day.

"They were cousins, you know."

"I heard they were lovers."

"Everything has to be sex with you, doesn't it? It's
not enough they were cousins?"

The second woman shifted uncomfortably. "I heard
it was bad fish."

"*What* was bad fish?"

"Bad fish killed them."

"Who said?"

"*My* cousin."

"The fishmonger?" Her voice rose in disbelief.

"No, my *other* cousin, the butcher."

Food poisoning. The bodies would be whole.

He made his camp in the rough ground behind the
tombs, dug a small fire pit, and coaxed a flame from
bits of broken brush. Carefully, he measured honey and
herbs into a sooty cup and filled it with the last of his
water. When the tisane had warmed so that he could no
longer feel it against the inside of his wrist, he drank
it slowly, and as the moon rose, he sang the exercises
that would tone an aged voice. To lose this opportunity
would be heartbreaking.

He had no need to call when he finally approached
the tomb. He could feel the kigh, could feel their confusion, could feel them trying to cling to the life they'd

lost. It was often that way with those who died young and healthy.

"Hush," he murmured, struggling with the heavy bar securing the door. "I've come to help."

Had the tomb not been opened that afternoon, he knew he wouldn't have been strong enough to force the rust-pitted metal up out of equally worn brackets. As it was, his arms trembled and he gasped for breath as he finally leaned the bar against the stone.

Fortunately, the hinges still glistened with oil and the door swung easily, silently open. He pushed it back until it would go no farther, then jammed it in place with a fist-sized rock. The spill of moonlight would provide all the illumination he needed.

The smell as he entered the tomb was familiar, comforting, and he breathed deeply of it as he shuffled into the narrow central aisle. Designed to hold eight bodies—the carrying poles of the biers slipping into iron cradles on the end walls—five places had already been filled before this double death. The lower three of the four resting to the left of the door had been stripped by time and rats to bare bone. The fourth wore enough bits of dried flesh for him to recognize a beautiful woman—although no one else could probably have seen her in the desiccated ruin that remained. To the right of the door, the lowest place held a body and a large brown rat.

They stared at each other for a moment, then the rat picked up the finger it had been gnawing and disappeared into the shadows.

Heart pounding, he leaned forward to check the fingers and toes of the two young men lying stacked above and sighed in relief when he found them whole. Although their faces and hands were marked with white smears of makeup from the farewell kisses of friends and family, the scavengers had not yet begun to feed.

"So young." His voice held more anticipation than sorrow as he touched each gently in turn. They'd been broad-shouldered, stocky young men who'd worn their brown hair cut short in identical round caps and had shared a slight family resemblance about the jaw. One had been a little taller, the other a little more heavily muscled. He didn't know their names or what they'd done in life—for their epitaphs had not yet been carved—but it didn't matter. They'd be able to tell him themselves soon enough.

He cleared his throat, took a deep breath, and Sang.

The kigh responded joyfully until they touched the bodies. First the lower jerked and then the upper, an arm flung out to dangle down beside the bier.

He felt the pair of kigh begin to struggle and he threw more into the Song. When they tried to twist away, he caught them. When they balked, he shoved. It always happened thus, no matter how much they'd wanted to return before it began. Over the long years, he'd become well practiced in overcoming the fear of the kigh.

His voice cracked and wavered. The Song slipped into mere sound for a heartbeat before his desperate need for companionship lent him strength and he wrapped it around the kigh once again.

The bodies of both young men were now shaking so violently their teeth clattered in spite of the cords securing their jaws.

Hands clasped together around his staff, praying that he'd been strong enough, he finished the Song.

The silence rang with it for a moment.

Two pairs of brown eyes snapped open.

He had to help them to stand, Singing gentle Songs

of comfort to them as their bodies spasmed and they moaned in terror. Lost and confused, they turned to him. He stroked them and calmed them and reassured them that the stiffness would pass. They were like children, his children, and he felt the familiar rush of love spill out over into his Song.

"All right, I know yer in there. Drop what yer holdin' and step outside where I can see ya."

A guard. He should've known there'd be a guard. These tombs were an open invitation to looters. He murmured a brief prayer of thanks to whatever gods were listening—had the guard shown up before he'd finished the Song. . . . Leaning heavily on his staff, he led the way out into the night.

The guard snorted when she saw him, brows nearly disappearing under the padded edge of her round helm. "Well, yer old enough to know better, Gramps." A wave of her loaded crossbow directed him to one side. She glared into the tomb. "The rest of ya can get out here, too. Yer not gonna make me believe this old geezer was workin' a . . . Goddess protect us, yer alive."

"Nooo." The taller of the two young men fought to pull air in and then push it out in the shape of words. It wasn't easy as he no longer needed to breathe. "We . . . are dead."

She swallowed and backed away a step, obviously wanting to run, forcing herself to stay. "But yer, yer standin'. Yer movin'. Ya gotta be alive if yer movin'."

The second young man lurched forward to stand shoulder to shoulder with his cousin. His mouth worked, but no sound came out.

The guard had seen death in many forms before. She'd picked it up in pieces after the food riots of eighty-seven. She'd dragged it frozen out of the gutter every winter. She'd held it when her son had been taken, the healer standing helpless to one side.

These men were dead.

Her finger tightened on the trigger. The crossbow quarrel slammed quivering into the dirt at the cousins' feet. She stared at it, then slowly lifted her gaze to their faces.

These men were most certainly dead.

And they knew it.

Another step back. Then another. Then, biting off a scream, she turned and ran.

Halfway through the first verse, Karlene realized she should never have agreed to sing a love song. His Imperial Highness, Prince Otavas had pulled his cushion close, drawn one knee up to his chest—not an easy thing to do with any modesty considering the short style of kilt currently favored around the Imperial Court—and was staring at her with his heart in his eyes. Although at seventeen, he was a strikingly handsome young man, with his father's dark coloring and the heavy bones of his mother's northern heritage, those dark, intense eyes were his most devastating feature and he knew how to use them to their best advantage. He was also charming. Intelligent. *And very, very young.*

If anyone had told me when I left Shkoder that the hardest part of serving in the Empire would be keeping a love-struck princeling at arm's length, I'd have laughed in their face.

It wasn't that he was rude, or pushy, or even particularly imperious about his infatuation—he was just persistent. Without appearing to be following her about, he always seemed to be where she was. Had he not been an Imperial prince, a gentle Bardic Command could have cleared up the problem in short order, but as it was, she could only dance around his feelings and try to convince him that certain gifts were inappropriate.

The worst of it was, the prince's attentions had caused a fascinatingly beautiful lady of the court to politely—or perhaps politically—surrender the field. Nor did it help that the only other bard in the Havakeen Empire thought the whole situation incredibly amusing and had already written a not-very-funny song about it. *Could be worse, I suppose. At least with the prince's involvement so obvious, he can't sing it anywhere.*

She sang the final verse with less emphasis than usual on the "Love conquers all," but as the prince's expression remained besotted, she suspected she needn't have bothered.

A babble of voices rose as the last note faded. Karlene smiled and inclined her head. Pushing her heavy, blonde braid back over her shoulder, she set her quitara to one side and stood.

"You must be thirsty." Prince Otavas stepped forward to claim her before any of the others could. "Would you care to join me for a drink? They've chilled lime juice tonight, I think. I remember you saying once how much you like it."

Those beautiful eyes looked so hopeful, she couldn't deny him. Besides, she was thirsty. A pity he'd read a deeper meaning than intended into the ritual response. "It would be my pleasure, Highness."

"I wish you'd call me Tavas." Beaming, he fell into step beside her.

"That's what your family calls you, Highness. I couldn't presume."

"They wouldn't mind. They like you."

Smothering a sigh, Karlene fell back on the standard Imperial response. "I'm honored, Highness."

"Tavas."

"Highness . . ." She turned to face him. "While I am . . ." *Well, there really isn't another word for it, is there?* ". . . honored by your attention, I feel it only fair to tell you again that I have no interest in men in that way."

He shrugged and grinned. "I'm not men. I'm me."

"*And* that I'm eleven years older than you are."

"You don't look a day over . . ."

She could see him rapidly examining ages, discarding them, and finally settling on:

". . . twenty-one." He bowed deeply, one hand keeping the back of his kilt from riding up. "Maybe twenty-two."

Impossible not to laugh.

Flashing a triumphant grin, the prince straightened and extended his arm. Shaking her head, Karlene laid her hand on his wrist and allowed herself to be led to the refreshment table.

In warm weather, the Imperial Court spent its informal evenings in a second-floor room with more window than wall. This evening, the three wide pairs of louvered shutters to both the east and west had been folded back to allow the passage of cooling breezes delicately scented by the night-blooming flowers in the gardens below. As always, refreshment tables had been set up at the narrower, south end of the room to either side of the arched entranceway. Karlene often wondered how the guards could stand so close to such mouthwatering bounty and be able to resist throwing themselves on the food.

She bowed slightly as Prince Otavas handed her a goblet of juice, ignored the not-entirely-hidden, indulgent smile of the servant who'd poured it, and nabbed a skewer of spiced chicken before any more of it disappeared. At the far end of the room, a low dais made it possible for her to see the Emperor and the Princess Verika involved in a spirited discussion. *Probably about hawking,* Karlene decided, studying the hand motions. It wasn't that difficult a guess as they were both crazy about the sport and could argue for hours over the relative merits of one bird over another.

The prince sighed as he followed her gaze. "They were talking about water rights at the last council meeting and ended up in a shouting match about marsh hawks."

"It's nice that the Emperor has someone to share his interests, Highness."

"It does take the pressure off the rest of us," Otavas admitted with a smile. He turned to face her, smile broadening. "And while I don't mind accompanying them occasionally, I personally have a deeper interest in mu ..." A gust of wind tore the rest of the words from his mouth and nearly knocked him over. Fighting for balance, he stared at the bard being buffeted back and forth by a swirling column of air. He tried to reach her, was flung away, and could only watch helplessly as she staggered and almost fell.

Somehow, Karlene managed to get both feet firmly beneath her in spite of the surrounding kigh. Long, pale fingers clutched at her clothing and hair. Above the wind-sketched outlines of elongated bodies, thin and sharply pointed faces wore nearly identical expressions as each of the kigh tried desperately to get her attention. By the time she found her voice, there were ten, maybe twelve pairs of stormy gray eyes trying to peer into hers.

"Gently, gently," she Sang although only the kigh

could find words in the pure tones. *"It's all right. I'll take care of it. Gently, it'll be all right."*

She continued Singing reassurance as the whole cluster slowed, made one final circuit around her, then sped out through the same window they'd entered, their passage throwing an elderly courtier hard against the tiles and extinguishing the torches that lined the balcony.

A babble of voices rose into the silence that followed. The prince, taking advantage of both rank and proximity clutched at the bard's arm. "Was it the air spirits?"

Brow furrowed, Karlene nodded.

"What were they so angry about?"

Tugging her tunic back into place, she turned to face him. "The kigh weren't angry, Highness. They were terrified."

"What could trap the kigh, Gabris? That's the question." Karlene walked to the window and stared out at a distinct absence of kigh. Three or four kigh—different kigh, the same kigh; no one could tell—usually hung about the windows of the bardic suite. Today the skies were clear. The kigh she'd called had fled the moment she'd released them. "I mean, even the most powerful of bards can't compel the kigh to do something they don't want to."

"Can't or don't?" asked the middle-aged man yawning up at her from behind the scribe's table that dominated the room.

Frowning, the younger bard moved back to the table. "What do you mean?"

"Bards take vows," Gabris reminded her. "The kigh are our allies, not our servants. Except in cases of great emergency, they are not to be compelled. However, if they *can* be compelled, perhaps they can also be trapped."

"Are you saying that it's a bard they're terrified of?" Karlene demanded incredulously. "Because if it is, you're wrong. First of all, I know the Songs they use to name every living bard, and so do you. Secondly, I've heard the kigh identify new talent. Remember when we started testing for Imperial fledglings?" Before Gabris could answer, she continued. "Remember when Ullious showed up? It seemed that with every step he took toward the Capital, a new kigh appeared to tell us he was coming. This *wasn't* the same thing. Trust me." The strides that returned her to the window were jerky and uneven. "This was darker. Older. At the risk of sounding melodramatic, it was unclean."

"I wasn't accusing anyone," Gabris told her gently. "I just want you to keep your mind open to all possiblities."

Karlene shrugged without turning. "All right. It's open." There were still no kigh outside the window. "If it's been around for as long as they say it has, why haven't we run into it before? I can't recall the kigh being afraid of anything." Pivoting on one heel, she returned to the table. "Can you?"

"No. I can't. I didn't." Both bards had spent most of a sleepless night in a light trance, sifting Bardic Memory for precedents. Gabris waved the quill he held toward a chair. "Karlene, please, sit down."

"Sorry." She sank down, shoulders slumped, one hand covering her eyes.

"Better. It's difficult to think with you bouncing all over the room like that." Staring up at the arc of the ceiling, he flicked at his chin with the end of his pen.

At the first *shunk, shunk, shunk,* Karlene straightened, lowered her hand, and glared across the table at him.

Shunk, shunk, shunk. Whether deep in thought or half asleep, he didn't notice.

He'd been doing it all morning, off and on, and the sound of the goose feather against the short, gray bristles of his beard was driving her crazy. She couldn't take it anymore. Teeth clenched, she snaked a long arm across the table, grabbed the older bard's wrist, and forced his arm down flat against the wood. "Please," she ground out through clenched teeth, "don't do that."

Gabris stared at her, confused, and, as she released him, the feather rose. "Don't do what?" *Shunk.*

"THAT! With the feather! Don't do it anymore." She leaned forward, fingers curled into fists. "Or I'm not going to be responsible for my actions."

"I think you're getting a little too worked up about this, Karlene." His voice rough with fatigue, Gabris very carefully set the pen to one side while he spoke.

"You weren't there. You didn't feel their terror. I am *not* getting too worked up about this!" She surged to her feet. "The Emperor is demanding to know what the kigh are frightened of, but all we've managed to get out of them is that they're afraid of being trapped, they don't want to talk about it, and could we *please* get rid of it for them."

"The Emperor is a lot more reasonable than he appears," Gabris pointed out, smothering another yawn. "When you've been here a little longer, you'll realize that his bark is much worse than his bite."

"It's not the Emperor I'm worried about." Arms folded, she paced back to the window and stared out at the city beyond the walls of the Imperial Palace. It was probably only her imagination, but the shadows seemed darker, defying the light. Something was very wrong.

"May I come in?"

Imperial princes didn't *have* to knock. Karlene swung around and leaned against the sill as Gabris welcomed the Emperor's youngest son and invited him to be seated.

"Thank you, no." Prince Otavas politely acknowledged the older bard, then directed all of his attention at Karlene. "I just stopped by to see if you've discovered what caused the air spirits to act so strangely last night."

In spite of a miserable morning, she had to admire the way he made it sound as though that was his only concern. His expression rather ruined the effect, but for a young man not yet eighteen with no bardic training it was an excellent effort. "I'm very sorry, Highness, but the kigh aren't cooperating."

"Is there anything I can do to help?"

Behind the prince, Gabris wagged both brows suggestively.

Karlene fought off the urge to grind her teeth. "I'm sorry, Highness," she said again, "but no."

He spread his hands, the dozen or more narrow gold bands he wore adding drama to the gesture. "I wish I was one of the nine, then I'd be of some use to you."

It had taken years to convince the Emperor to allow his citizens to be tested for the ability to Sing the kigh, but nine Imperial fledglings now studied at the Bardic Hall in Elbasan—the first five would return to the Empire some time before Third Quarter festival, ready to Walk their own land. Eventually, there'd be a Bardic Hall built in the Capital.

All at once, Karlene wondered if the prince's infatuation with her masked a hidden pain. It had to be difficult for him; the youngest in a family dynastically secure three Imperial children before he was born. Perhaps he was desperately searching for a purpose, a purpose represented by the individual freedom and power of the bards. Had it hurt him to see others given that chance?

"Tell me, Highness . . ." She used a gentler tone than she usually dared use given how little encouragement the prince needed, and ignored the startled look Gabris shot her because of it. ". . . do you really wish you were one of the nine? Do you want to be a bard?"

"I'd rather be a prince." He shrugged, not at all embarrassed by the admission. If he was hiding pain, it was obvious that he didn't realize it. "Besides, I was tested. No talent. Couldn't carry a tune if I got the servants to do it for me. I *would* like your ability to Command others to tell me the truth, though."

"You're a member of the Imperial House, Highness," Gabris interjected. "You *can* command others to tell you the truth."

"Not really." Otavas flashed a slightly rueful smile over his shoulder at the older bard. "Everyone tells me what they assume I want to hear." Then he ducked his head and shot a smoldering look at Karlene from under the fringe of thick, black lashes. "Well, almost everyone."

Karlene sighed. *Twenty-eight shouldn't feel this old.* "We haven't really got time for that this morning, Highness."

"You're right, of course. I am sorry." Settling down beside her on the broad windowsill, he smiled expectantly from one bard to the other. "What do we do now?"

"We, Highness?"

"Yes. His Majesty has suggested I give you every assistance."

Gabris barely got his fist to his mouth in time to cover a sudden spasm of not very believable coughing.

Shooting him a look that singed rather than smoldered, Karlene indulged in a number of treasonous thoughts about His Imperial Majesty, who'd probably been maneuvered into shouting the suggestion at his youngest son in order to get some peace. "We were discussing what we were going to do next before you came in, Highness," she said at last. "We've spoken to the kigh, but as I mentioned, they're not cooperating."

"Have you spoken to the others?"

"Others?" The two bards repeated the word in unison.

"The other kigh," Otavas offered, a little confused at their reaction. "I mean, I know you both Sing three out of the four quarters because soon you'll have to walk around the Empire with our new bards and His Majesty, King Theron never allows bards who Sing earth to leave Shkoder and . . . What's wrong?"

"Nothing's wrong, Highness." Karlene resisted the urge to beat her head against the window frame. "Gabris and I, however, are idiots."

"You hadn't thought of it?"

"No, Highness, we hadn't."

"That's all right." He looked pleased with himself. "You're tired. I'm just glad I could help."

When Otavas' mother, the Princess Irenka of Shkoder, came to the Havakeen Empire to join with their crown prince, she brought with her an enduring political alliance, a much younger Gabris, and a religion that enclosed all beliefs, all philosophies within the Circle. As the years passed and more people began to appreciate a system that accepted all gods and vastly simplified a complicated calendar of feast days and obligations, the princess had a Center built in the Capital—endearing herself to the taxpayers by paying for it herself.

The round, stone building dominated the upper half of Temple Street, style and material both looking remarkably out of place beside the local architecture.

As Karlene followed Gabris through the eastern doors and into the cool interior of the Center, she breathed a sigh of relief. Summers in the Empire were much hotter than summers back in Shkoder. She allowed a brief moment of pity for the prince's guards, now flanking each of the Center's four doors and undoubtedly baking in their armor, then hurried to catch up to the two men.

They'd been unable to convince Prince Otavas to stay behind.

"I was standing right beside you last night when the air spirits arrived," he'd pointed out. *"Nothing happened to me."*

A startled priest emerged from behind the central altar, eyes wide as she recognized the three approaching.

"If it isn't an inconvenience, Your Grace," Gabris began, bowing gracefully in spite of age and bulk. "My companion and I should like to use the Center for a few moments so that we might Sing fire and water in a protected setting."

"An inconvenience?" The priest returned the bow. "You have only to ask, honored Bard." She bowed to Karlene. "Honored Bards." Then she remembered the prince and, slightly flustered, added a deeper bow, the wide, quartered sleeves of her robe sweeping against the stone floor. "Your Highness."

Karlene nodded in turn, her opinion of Prince

Otavas rising as he ignored the priest's unfortunate
lapse. With only two bards in the Empire—even if
there'd been two bards in the Empire off and on for the
last twenty-two years—they were still a novelty, and
for those who'd accepted the enclosure of the Circle, a
bard actually Singing the kigh became a religious experience. "Unfortunately, Your Grace, we must also
ask that you leave us." The priest looked so disappointed Karlene nearly relented but, remembering the
buffeting she'd taken in the assembly room, stood
firm. Bad enough that they'd be responsible for the
prince's safety.

With a final, reluctant bow, the priest sketched the
sign of the Circle over her heart and left the building.

Gabris indicated that the prince should be seated on
one of the curved benches that filled the area between
the walls and the altar, settled down beside him, and
gestured for Karlene to go ahead.

"Why aren't you Singing as well?" Otavas asked
him in some surprise.

"Two reasons, Highness. One of us needs to witness
and Karlene's voice is considerably younger than
mine."

"She has a beautiful voice, doesn't she?"

"Yes, Highness, she does."

"Oh, great, encourage him," Karlene muttered under
her breath as she stepped out into the open space surrounding the three-tiered altar. She drew in a deep
breath of air heavy with the familiar scents of beeswax, water, and earth and found herself unexpectedly
homesick. Shkoder and the Bardic Hall suddenly
seemed a very long way away. *And suppose we find
out what's frightening the kigh. What then? There's
only the two of us.*

Wiping damp palms on the front of her robe, she

pushed the mood aside with a simple, two-octave scale, then focused on the nearest of the huge candles that crowded the highest tier of the altar and Sang the four notes to call fire.

Almost immediately, kigh danced on a half-dozen wicks, barely defined features flickering and changing, tiny eyes of brilliant white the only constant. Still Singing, Karlene heard an admiring murmur from the prince and the rustle of fabric as Gabris leaned forward. A little surprised at both their size and number, she Sang calming and safety until the dance grew less frantic.

"If fire and water have been frightened as well," Gabris had said, *"perhaps calling them into the Center will make them feel secure enough to tell us what's wrong."*

Although fire was the most self-absorbed of all the kigh, Karlene could feel them reaching out to her. She couldn't sense why. Apprehensions a subtle harmony within the Song, she asked if they were afraid. When it became obvious that they were, she asked if they were afraid of being trapped.

Every candle on the altar burst into flame. A blazing tower of kigh surged toward the vaulted ceiling, individuals swallowed up in the terrifying column of white and red and gold. Gulping great lungfuls of heated air, Karlene fought to Sing over the fire's roar.

She could smell her hair begin to singe.

Hands raised to protect her eyes, she stumbled back a step.

Then another voice joined hers, wrapping a tenor line around her Song, pouring in enough additional power to reach the heart of the holocaust. After a moment, the kigh began to listen. When together the two voices Sang a gratitude, the kigh whirled in one final, flaming vortex over the center of the altar and disappeared.

Karlene coughed and waved away the streams of smoke and the stink of burned beeswax. The candles as big around as her arm had been completely consumed. Puddles of black grease dribbled down over the edge of the altar and into the circular fountain sucked dry by the heat.

"Are you all right?" Gabris panted, dragging her around to face him.

Was she? The skin over her cheeks and forehead felt tight and hot and questing fingers pulled off curled and brittle bits of hair. A quick check found brows and lashes still present. "I got a little scorched," she muttered, licking cracked lips and tasting blood. "But I'm okay."

A gentle touch against her arm turned her toward the prince. A weight she hadn't realized she carried lifted when she saw him, pale and scared but unhurt. "What happened?"

"What happened?" Karlene repeated, glancing down at the blisters rising on the backs of her hands. "I asked the kigh if they were afraid of being trapped."

"What did they say?"

"Yes."

"That's all?" The two bards followed his gaze as he stared up at the arcing vault of the ceiling. Soot streaked the stone ribs in a circle the exact diameter of the altar forty feet below.

Her heart pounding, fully aware of how close she'd come to losing control of the kigh entirely, Karlene could only give thanks that Her Majesty had insisted on both traditional dimensions and materials.

"All they said was *yes?*" The prince's voice threatened to crack.

"Well, they said it pretty loudly." All at once, she was shaking so hard her teeth slammed together like some kind of macabre percussion instrument. She grabbed blindly for support as two pairs of hands settled her gently down on a bench. "I'm okay," she insisted.

"What we need to find out now is what specifically they're afraid of. What is it they think can trap them?" Gabris murmured. Although the skin of his face looked stretched, he'd taken a lot less heat and a lot less damage.

In unison, the prince and the two bards turned to look at the dry fountain.

"If you don't mind," Otavas said with a shaky laugh, "I'm heading for higher ground before you Sing water."

Chapter Five

Vree'd never worn silk and she wasn't certain she cared for it. The soft caress of both long-sleeved tunic and wide-legged trousers against her skin made her feel as though she were wearing the wind and not much else.

What's wrong with clothes that feel like clothes?

Bannon lifted her shoulders, just to feel the fabric move. *I like it.*

Can't say as I'm surprised. She curled her toes against the heavy sandals, also provided from Aralt's storeroom, and wished she dared to wear her boots. In a motion half comfort, half preparation, she lightly touched each concealed weapon and the medallion around her neck.

With a last word to Aralt's stablemaster, Gyhard nodded a dismissal and started across the yard toward her. With no daggers to hide, he wore a sleeveless vest, the brown silk embroidered with deep green leaves. The graceful folds of green silk trousers flowed around his legs like water as he walked. While he also wore heavy leather sandals, his were dyed the exact shade of his vest. A thick gold bracelet encircled his left wrist and the tiny gold hoops her brother had always worn in his ears had doubled in size.

When we get rid of the carrion eater, Bannon preened, *we're keeping the clothes. I look terrific!*

As far as Vree was concerned, he looked rented and all he needed was a little rouge and some scented oil to take his place under Teemo's canopy. She buried the thought. And the one that came after it.

When we get down off of this thing, I'm going to slit its throat.

Vree's fingers twitched around the reins. *We'd manage a lot better if you'd stop trying to take over!*

Maybe I'd be better at it!

Not in my body!

Fine! You can slaughtering well learn to do it yourself.

He pulled back so quickly a muscle spasmed in her leg.

Her horse danced to one side, shouldering up against its companion, away from the unexpected pressure of her heel.

"Trouble?" Gyhard asked through clenched teeth as the sudden contact of their mounts slammed their inside knees together.

Vree glared and fought the urge to yank the gelding's head around. Years of training had emphasized that a quiet touch could accomplish more than brute force—from blades to horses, the lesson remained valid. "I can handle it."

"Good. I'm pleased to see that you're catching on so quickly."

Her lip curled at the gentle sarcasm in his voice.

"Your brother's body has a finely developed sense of balance and superb reflexes." As the horses moved apart, he added, "You'd do better if you'd relax."

"Up here?" She regretted the words the moment they left her mouth.

Gyhard stared at her in exaggerated astonishment. "It can't be the height. I'm sure you could walk naked along a ridgepole in a high wind on a moonless night with a dagger in your teeth and a garrote in each hand if you wanted to." She ignored him so completely, he couldn't help but smile. "So what are you afraid of?"

A crossbow bolt in the back.

The skin between her shoulder blades crawled. Bannon's reaction or hers? *If I tell him that, he'll kill me—us—and leave the body for the hunt to find. You heard him; he's intrigued by us, but he doesn't really need us, and the last thing he does need is the hunt on his trail.*

Maybe you can convince him that Emo won't talk.

Sod off, Bannon, she suggested wearily.

"Vree?"

The patronizing, son-of-a-sow was waiting for an answer. Let him. "How long will it take us to get to the Capital?"

"At this rate?" Gyhard reached down to stroke the dapple-gray shoulder of his horse as it rose and fell in a gentle walk. He'd intended to ride a young stallion that he—as Aralt—had purchased specifically for the trip, not one of a pair of well-schooled geldings. "Thirteen days."

Thirteen days? You'll be out of my body in three, carrion eater!

A subtle tension in her hands and face made it, if not easy, possible for him to tell when Bannon spoke; "What did your brother say?"

Vree tossed her head, eyes narrowed. "He just pointed out that it's going to be a long trip."

* * *

"What do mean, that's where we're staying?"

The inn looked like a smaller, dirtier version of Aralt's villa—without the surrounding orange groves. Tucked in a hollow just off the east side of the road, it stood in the center of either a very small village or a large cluster of outbuildings.

Gyhard turned his horse off the road with the exaggerated care of a man close to the end of his resources. "Surely you didn't think we'd just toss a bedroll on the ground for the night?"

"Why not?" Vree imitated his movement, although she strongly suspected the horse would follow its companion regardless.

"Two reasons. The first, because the horses have to be fed. In case you hadn't noticed, we're not carrying fodder. The second reason is that we can afford better and what's more," he gestured broadly at the inn, "we deserve better." As a grubby adolescent shambled out through the latticed doors of the main building and started toward them, he shook his head and added grimly, "Much better. But, unfortunately, this is all there is." He heaved himself out of the saddle, a day spent relearning to ride having robbed him of grace. When his weight came down on his legs, his knees buckled and only a death grip on the tooled leather cantle kept him from pitching face first into the churned dirt of the yard.

Vree! What's he done to my body?

I don't know. She kicked both feet out of the stirrups, swung her left leg up and over the horse's head and slid to the ground. All the way to the ground. Growling profanity, she levered herself up on her arms, then, leg muscles screaming a protest, managed to stand.

"You got off the wrong side of the horse," Gyhard

gasped. "I told you, always mount and dismount from the left."

Vree stared at him in disbelief, wiping grit off her chin. "What slaughtering difference does it make?" she snarled. "Both sides look the same."

"A valid point." He struggled to free his saddlebags, then staggered toward the door, shoving the reins at the waiting teenager. "Come on. I'll do the talking if you don't mind."

Dragging her own bag over her shoulder, she pushed one leg in front of the other by strength of will alone.

Vree?

What?

I wonder if my body hurts as bad as yours does.

Odds are good. Old Gyhard's walking like a wounded duck.

Vree?

What?

I'd welcome a crossbow bolt in the back right about now.

She couldn't help it, the look on his face was more than she could bear. Snickers turned to howls of laughter and soon she was holding her stomach, gasping for breath.

"What is so funny?" Gyhard demanded.

"Y–you. W–when you realized this . . ." Sagging against the wall, Vree waved a hand, unable to go on.

He'd asked for the best room in the house. They'd been shown to a corner of a common loft with narrow shuttered windows opening in two directions and thick straw pads rolled up at the base of the wall. For an extra crescent, the innkeeper threw in a pair of reasonably clean blankets each. Except for the patina of old grime, the place could've passed for one of the barracks back at the garrison.

Gyhard's scowl set her off again. Finally, the nervous energy died and she took a deep, steadying breath. "We've got to work the stiffness out, or we won't be able to walk tomorrow let alone ride."

"I assume they have a bathhouse. . . ."

"Yeah, but would you care to sink your bare butt into it?" An eloquent wave took in the surrounding filth. Pushing herself away from the wall, she started to stretch the abused muscles in her legs.

After a moment, Gyhard began awkwardly imitating her, breath hissing through his teeth at the sudden intensifying of what had become a constant background pain.

Vree snickered and twisted him into the proper position. "What's the matter with you? You've done this a hundred times."

No, he hasn't, Vree.

All at once it wasn't funny any more.

She woke from dreams not her own and found herself crouched in the center of the straw mat, the blankets thrown aside, a dagger in her hand, waiting for an enemy.

Bannon?

He shared her pounding heart, her sudden surge up out of sleep. *What's wrong?*

Both windows were open to catch the night breezes. Moonlight painted sharp-edged shadows down the length of the loft. The empty loft. She cocked her head and sifted the sounds of the night. No threat.

Nothing. Nothing's wrong.

Then why are we awake? he muttered, settling

back into her mind and trying to pull oblivion up over
consciousness.

Why indeed? She sheathed the dagger and turned to
look at the man lying beside her. Sleep smoothed away
the small differences of expression and gesture, leaving only her brother's face and her brother's body. Her
fingertips caressed the air above an angled cheekbone,
traced the arc of an imperious brow, hovered over the
sensuous curve of a full upper lip. Impossible not to react sometimes as though this were still her brother instead of, or maybe as well as, the presence in her head.
How could she treat her brother's body as though it
was *not* her brother's body?

Dangerous.

So, what are you afraid of?

Of being alone.

Pillowing her chin on folded arms, she stared out the
window at the stars and tried to see them as a thousand
campfires, Jiir's army bedded down across the sky. A
rustle of leaves from the scraggly garden below lifted
the hair on the back of her neck. She held her breath
and closed her fingers around a familiar hilt.

It's a cat. Go back to sleep, Vree, I'm tired.

And if it isn't?

*Then they'll have to come to us. We'll deal with it
then.*

No point in reminding the goddess to allow them to
die together if the battle went against them—they were
no longer able to die apart.

No, Bannon. Forget it. I'm not going to do it.

So you'll help him kill the prince?

No!

*Then we have to get the son-of-a-sow out of my

body and me back in and the only way we're going to do that is if something distracts him.*

*I am *not* going to sleep with you . . . him.*

"Doesn't that hurt?"

Vree carefully turned to glare at her companion. Horses, she'd discovered during the last eight days, were not as smart as they looked and responded to any number of obscure physical cues. "Doesn't what hurt?"

"That expression." Gyhard smiled pleasantly at her. "You've got your jaw so tightly clenched I can see the muscles jumping."

"No."

"No?"

"No, it doesn't hurt," Vree snarled and went back to staring at the road through the definition of her horse's ears. *Why is sex your solution to everything?*

He ignored the question. *We're more than halfway to the Capital. Only five more days . . .*

*I *know* that.*

Gyhard watched her profile and wished, not for the first time, that he could be privy to the private conversations that caused such a visible increase in tension. "Are you terribly disappointed that your attempt to dislodge me last night came to nothing?" he asked suddenly.

When the hand resting on her thigh folded itself into a white-knuckled fist, he assumed he'd made an accurate guess. Shifting his weight in the saddle, he shrugged apologetically. "I did warn you that I was too strong for you to shift—even when rudely awakened." He scratched at the day's stubble. "I'd like to point out that even should you decide to risk knocking me and young Bannon's body out cold, I have to be conscious to be moved. Or perhaps I should say, removed."

Vree swiveled her head to face him again, upper lip

curled off her teeth. "Or perhaps you should say nothing at all."

"My apologies." He inclined his head graciously. "We'll be arriving in Kiaz shortly. I'll leave you to your . . ." The pause lingered long enough to be unmistakably deliberate. ". . . own thoughts until then."

Biting back her response, she forced herself to relax and tried to be less aware of the man riding at her side. How quickly the strange became the norm when only the strange remained. Over the last eight days, she'd almost grown used to her brother's thoughts mixed in with her own. She'd guarded against instinctively reacting to Gyhard as though he were Bannon, found herself reacting to Gyhard as Gyhard instead, and couldn't decide which was worse.

The feeling of exposure hadn't changed. Used to marching surrounded by thousands or slipping quietly over distance shrouded by night, to ride under the sun on the South Road as one of only two kept her in a constant state of semidread that had barely lessened as day followed day and it became obvious Emo had kept his teeth closed on what he knew.

You can't shut me out, Vree, so unless you want to help him slaughter the prince, a member of the Imperial Family you swore to serve, you come up with a better way to get him out of my body.

Better than going to his bed. Better than . . . She clamped down on the image. *No.*

She heard him sigh, which was strange as she breathed for them both. *Don't tell me you don't want to, Vree.*

I'm telling you I won't do it. How much did he know, sharing her mind? How much did he only guess after sharing her life for so long? She couldn't ask.

Look, sister-mine . . . His voice had gentled, and

she didn't want to know why. *. . . it won't mean anything. You won't be sleeping with your brother. I'm
here.*

Although he wore her brother's body, the man who
rode beside her was not her brother. *Although he wore
her brother's body.* Her fingers grew sweaty on the
reins. She had to do something or the prince would die.
This was all they had left to try. She stared at a low
line of distant hills rolling dusty brown along the bottom edge of a pale blue sky, listened to the hollow
sound of hooves against stone and the roar of her
blood in her ears. The wind lifted a strand of mane
back over her hand and she stroked the coarse length
over the ridge of callus on her palm. *What if he
doesn't want to sleep with me?* she asked at last.

Bannon almost laughed. *I know that body. He'll
want to sleep with someone by now.*

*Maybe he won't let your body rule him the way
you did.*

What's that supposed to mean?

Nothing. He'd always been able to find willing
partners. A quick tumble here. A heated moment there.
A trip to Teemo's when he had the cash. There'd been
a simplicity to his couplings she'd always envied.
What do I do?

What do you usually do?

He sounded like he thought she was kidding. Vree
allowed herself the luxury of a smile. *I sleep with
women, there's no chance of little soldiers then.*

You sleep with men. But it was almost a question;
he'd seen less of her life than she had of his.

Now and then. When it's safe.

Safe? She could almost hear him as he silently
counted the days. *Vree, you're going to . . .*

*Soon. Don't sweat it, Bannon. I'll deal with it. I've

been dealing with it once a moon for years.* Another time, his near panic at the possibility of sharing her flows would've been funny.

So it's safe now?

She thought of her body moving under his and safe was the one word that didn't come to mind. *Yeah.*

Okay, here's what you do. Make him think you're interested in him. Get him talking about himself. That always works.

And then?

Slaughter it, Vree. You're a woman, he's a man. Just let nature take its course.

And then kill him.

We both know there're worse ways to go.

Kiaz, a prosperous trade town at the junction of the Pymba River and the South Road, boasted half a dozen inns, from three waterfront dives to a well-guarded facility that catered to the Empire's nobility. As the town had gained its prominence well within the security of Imperial borders, there were no walls and the streets were laid out in a planned grid to the west of the road, behind the inns and markets.

Traffic had increased as they'd approached Kiaz, and Vree had been forced to concentrate on controlling her horse, leaving no time to worry about drawing Gyhard into conversation. "Why aren't we stopping?" she demanded as the gelding took offense at a cart of fish and danced a couple of steps to one side. "We've passed two perfectly good inns."

"Perhaps by your standards," Gyhard told her, the memory of other inns evident in his voice. "We'll be spending the night at Evion's, across the bridge."

"Who's Evion?"

Gyhard smiled at her suspicious tone. "I assume he

was the original owner of the inn and it kept his name."

"Oh. You've been there before?"

"No, but it comes very highly recommended by a number of Governor Aralt's acquaintances."

She snorted, her opinion of the late governor's acquaintances clear. "Are you sure they'll let us stay?"

"Why shouldn't they?" Gyhard asked absently, his attention momentarily distracted as one of the brothels lining the road folded back the shutters around the second-floor balcony, indicating it had opened for business. Dragging his gaze off the taut, silk-covered curves of the robust and very flexible young man securing the tall, louvered panels against the far wall, he cleared his throat and repeated, "Why shouldn't they?"

Told you. Bannon's mental voice was matter-of-fact. *Another day or two and he won't be able to keep his kilt down.*

Vree ignored him. "If this inn caters to rich travelers, why would it accept two butt-sore riders?"

"Because we have a great deal of money." He patted his bulging belt pouch. "And what's more we're very well-dressed, riding expensive animals, and I intend to behave as though I have every right to be there. An attitude I'm sure you've had intensive training in assuming given that you usually work where you have no right to be. What are we missing?"

The road ahead had momentarily cleared. As her horse seemed inclined to continue toward the bridge, Vree glanced over at her companion. "We have no servants," she said.

"Died."

"What?"

"They died." Gyhard smiled, his expression suddenly so like one her brother had molded those same

features into that Vree started and had to hurriedly relax her grip on the reins. "Died of one of those flux
diseases while we were in the south."

"Both of them? How? No rich sot would go to a
place without healers."

"Oh, there were healers, but our servants were
Olaki."

"Why would anyone hire one Olaki let alone two?"
The Olaki were a small sect who believed their god
would heal them with no direct intervention up to and
including, in extreme cases, bandaging. They were a
standing joke in the army where the burial squads were
often called Olaki healers.

"Because besides being stupidly mortal, the Olaki
also believe that a life of service will strengthen the
bond with their god. This makes them excellent, albeit
frequently replaced, servants."

"What about their horses? Or did our loyal but stupid servants run alongside?"

"We sold their horses for a tidy profit as we had no
wish to lead the now useless beasts all the way back to
the Capital."

Distracted by the necessity of guiding her horse
through traffic and up over the arc of the wide stone
bridge that lifted the South Road above the Pymba
River, Vree wondered when this riding nonsense became instinct as Gyhard kept assuring her it would.
"It's an asinine story," she muttered through clenched
teeth. "*You* can tell it."

"I had every intention of doing so."

A wide marble portico separated Evion's from the
North Road. As Gyhard led the way up to one of the
columns, a well-scrubbed girl of about ten ran out to
take their reins.

"Will you be staying the night, sirs?" she asked as Gyhard dismounted.

"We will." He flipped her a quarter-crescent.

She snatched the coin out of the air with practiced dexterity, and it disappeared into a fold of her blue tunic. ".Very good, sirs."

After eight days in the saddle, Vree no longer returned to earth feeling as though she'd gladly cut off her own legs. Muscles hurt more from hours of use than abuse. "What about the saddlebags?" she asked when Gyhard started for the inn's double doors.

"Leave them. The page will bring them to the rooms."

Vree stared down at the girl who stared fearlessly up at her. "If anything's missing, I'll cut your living heart out and feed it to you. With onions."

The page made a face as she vowed not to touch a thing.

"I never imagined that you'd have such a way with children," Gyhard murmured as they went inside.

Not bad.

Vree felt her lips purse to whistle and forced them flat.

It's not like we haven't seen places like this before, she reflected.

Yeah, but we saw those after dark with knives in our hands and garrotes in our pockets.

"I hope you don't mind that I turned down the services of a bath attendant," Gyhard said, coming out of the larger of the two bedrooms wearing a loose robe, "but you're not exactly schooled in the behavior this establishment expects, and I didn't want to put unnecessary pressure on you."

Vree shrugged. "If they swallowed that stupid story

you told about the servants without choking, they'll
believe anything."

*You know, Vree, insults aren't usually considered
foreplay.*

I said the story was stupid. I didn't say he was.

Watching her eyes narrow, Gyhard smiled. "I'll
leave you two to discuss whatever it was you were discussing while I bathe. Don't worry about going second.
Our private chamber taps into the boilers that supply
the common baths, so there'll be plenty of hot water."

As he brushed past her, Vree stepped aside, very
aware of his body under the light cover of the robe, not
wanting them to touch.

You should follow him. Offer to wash his back.

She turned and headed for the smaller bedroom.

Vree?

*If I do anything at all, Bannon, I'll do it when I'm
good and ready.*

Gyhard settled into the steaming water and allowed
himself to relax for what seemed like the first time in
eight days. The journey thus far had been less stressful
than he'd feared it might be and much too stressful to
have been comfortable. He shuddered to think what it
might have been like without the riding lessons forcing
his brooding companion to cooperate.

His six-day gallop to the Capital had been drastically amended by the army's insistence on using infantry above all else. It had never occurred to him that the
inevitable assassin whose body he intended to steal
would not be able to ride. And it had certainly never
occurred to him that said assassin would be part of a
team.

Stretching the kinks out of his back, he reached for
a loofah and froze. Suppose the sister had arrived in

Aralt's tower first? Could he have made the jump into a woman's body? Would he?

"I am luckier than I have any right to be," he murmured. "And far stupider than I would have thought." He'd had an equal chance of the assassin being a woman right from the beginning and he'd never even considered the possibility. *Perhaps I'm getting old.*

He frowned, pushing the thought aside. In the beginning, one hundred and thirty-two years ago, he'd wondered if, in spite of an infinite supply of new bodies, his life force would someday weaken and he'd die, sharing the fate of everyone and everything else. It had been some time since he'd allowed that speculation to surface.

He would live forever.

He would never die.

And soon, I'll once again have a life worth living. He'd been rich and he'd been poor. Rich was better. Rich and powerful, better still.

There was nothing wrong with the body he now wore. On the contrary, there was a great deal right with it. He worked the muscles in his arms, watching them roll beneath the slick surface of the skin. He could understand why young Bannon wanted it back.

Only five days left, my children. When are you going to make your next move? Scooping a handful of soft soap from the glass jar on the edge of the bath, he began lathering his hair. They had to be planning something, that was a given. But what? Young Bannon didn't seem the type able to beat his own body to the point where the life in it barely held to consciousness. For that matter, Gyhard doubted that his loving sister could strike the blows.

He rinsed, surfaced, and remember the feel of her gaze. She had amazing eyes. Darker than her brother's,

almost too large for her face; every now and then over
the last eight days they'd burned with emotions too intense for her to contain. Hatred. Rage. Frustration.
Fury. Her lithe assassin's body like a sculpted vessel
made to hold dark passions. . . .

Unable to stop himself, Gyhard burst out laughing.
*Gods keep me from thinking like a bad poet or an ap-
prentice bard.* Glancing down the length of his body,
he shook a chiding finger at his groin. Governor Aralt
had been an old man. It had been a long time since
he'd had such a spontaneous reaction. "And you, you
should be ashamed of yourself. Your own sister."

Except that she wasn't *his* sister.

And she was a beautiful woman.

And not only does she intend to kill you, he reminded himself. *But you intend to ensure that neither
sister nor brother remain as a threat once they've
helped you achieve your new life.*

If anything, that intensified the physical response.

I'd forgotten the immediacies of being twenty, he
sighed and surrendered to the moment.

Strenuous exercise and a scalding hot bath had
helped Vree regain both her composure and her distance. Dinner threatened to undo it all.

A parade of servants in blue tunics carried dish after
dish to the low table in the center of the suite's main
room. Sitting cross-legged on a pile of cushions—
while the inn's dining room provided benches and
chairs, Gyhard had requested the suite with southern
furnishings—Vree stared at the food and wondered
what half of it was.

"I'm going to enjoy this," Gyhard declared, scooping what she thought might be rice onto his plate.

"Aralt lost his sense of taste years ago and nothing we've had so far can equal the cooking at Evion's."

"Or so you've heard," Vree muttered, trying to identify a platter of heavily sauced meat.

"You can't spoil this for me." Grinning broadly, he passed her a bowl of glazed vegetables. "So you needn't bother trying."

He seems awfully relaxed, Bannon observed.

Why shouldn't he be? He knows what he's eating. What do you think this is?

Vree, I'm tasting exactly the same thing you are.

So what is it? She popped another small piece into her mouth.

I think it's pork.

Pork? Army pork swam in a puddle of grease. *What did they do with all the fat?*

Beats me.

Suddenly aware of being watched, she glanced across the table. "What are you staring at?"

"You."

"Well, don't."

"I was just wondering, actually, what you see when you look at me."

Vree closed both hands around the table edge and stared at him.

He paused to chew and swallow, then continued. "I mean, I was wondering if you see your brother or if you see me?"

"That's the most ridic . . ."

It's a good question, Vree. I've wondered, too.

She sighed, closed her eyes, and opened them again. The very last thing she needed was for the two of them to start agreeing on things. "I see my brother's body," she said. "But you wear it differently."

What do you mean differently?

I don't know. Differently. He doesn't move as much as you did. And when he does, he's not so . . . well, extreme about it.

What did I do? Jerk around all over the place?

No. He's older, Bannon. He's going to move less.

Grumbling inaudibly, Bannon subsided.

"I'm sorry." To her surprise, Gyhard actually looked as if he meant it. "I hadn't intended to cause a fight between you."

She raised a hand to both accept his apology and cut off any further discussion. As silence could too easily be broken by dangerous subjects, she asked questions about the meal until they'd emptied every dish on the table. Gyhard was amusing, articulate, and not only knew what they were eating but also how it had been prepared and how it could've been prepared differently. Vree actually found herself laughing at a story of sheep's eyes and Aralt's old chamberlain. When she noticed she was enjoying his company, she almost choked on the guilt.

"I'm afraid I've been monopolizing the conversation," he said as they stood. "So I'll apologize up front. It's been a long time since there's been someone I could be myself with." And then he paused as though he'd just realized what he'd said. He looked almost startled.

Vree rose as well, wishing she hadn't eaten quite so much. An overfull stomach brought with it a dangerous loss of control. "Don't try and convince me you've been living in a tragedy, 'cause I'm not buying."

"I wouldn't dream of it." He inclined his head, as he would to an equal. "We'll be leaving early in the morning. Sleep well."

She watched him pick up a lamp and disappear into

his bedroom, strangely unwilling to move until he was out of sight.

A spill of brilliant moonlight lay diagonally across the bed. Beyond it, the room was dark and so quiet she could hear the rustle of the blanket against her body as she breathed. What had awakened her? Slowly, silently, she closed her fingers around the hilt of the dagger lying on the mattress beside her.

Instinct, training—both told her she was no longer alone.

Closer now, almost at the bed. Moving with an assassin's stealth.

Muscles tensed, she waited. Whoever it was, in order to strike a killing blow, would have to bend into the moonlight. When they did, they'd die.

A heartbeat. Another. A shadow at the edge of the illumination.

"Bannon?"

The sudden realization delayed her long enough for him to shove the pillow he carried down over her face. She twisted and fought while her lungs screamed for air and finally got both hands against his chest and pushed with all her remaining strength.

VREE!

Bannon?

VREE, STOP IT! YOU'RE KILLING ME!

Gasping for breath, she shoved a tangle of blankets aside and threw herself out of the bed. She was alone in the room. Alone.

No! Bannon?

It took a moment to find him amidst the terror, hers and his.

Bannon, are you all right?

His voice shook. *You tried to push me out. Why, Vree? Why?*

I didn't mean it. All at once, her legs couldn't hold her and she sank to her knees. *It was a dream. I didn't mean it. I didn't mean it.* Her hand came up to clutch the onyx pendant that hung between her breasts. But there was no strength there. This was not a battle-field Jiir ruled.

The door opened, and she whirled to stare into the soft light of a shielded lamp.

"I heard you cry out . . ." Gyhard's voice trailed off as she turned and laid her head on her knees, exposing the vulnerable curve of her spine.

"Go away." She forced her voice to carry as far as the door. When she heard him leave, when she heard the door close, she started to tremble.

Vree?

I didn't mean it.

"Want to talk about it?"

Vree scowled at nothing. "About what?"

"About last night."

"Why?"

Gyhard shrugged although he knew she couldn't see the gesture. "I just wondered if you often had night-mares like that."

Never like that. Never so obvious. Assassins exam-ined their dreams for messages from the goddess, warnings of weaknesses or fears that could rise up to defeat them as they moved alone in the darkness. But to learn that Bannon was her weakness was merely to relearn something she'd known most of her life.

Slaughter it, Vree, it's perfectly normal for you to want me out of your head. Just don't do it again and stop flogging yourself over it. Bannon, once his terror had calmed, had found his balance with practiced ease. As usual, he'd placed himself at the center of the problem and looked no deeper.

Deeper. Vree had glanced once into the shadowed depths of her heart where dark desire hid and refused to look again.

Gyhard watched the tiny movements of muscles beneath the surprisingly delicate angle of her jaw and found the answer to his question. *So her sleep is not entirely peaceful.* Somehow he doubted that the lives she'd taken over the years haunted her. "Still sane?"

The expression she threw at him held anger but no taint of madness. "Why are you asking?"

"Curiosity."

"Eat it."

They rode in silence for the rest of the morning. He couldn't get the image of the vulnerable curve of her back out of his mind.

At noon, they stopped in a small village that seemed to have grown up merely because it was exactly half a day's leisurely travel from Kiaz. Oblivious to Gyhard's indulgent smile and pig noises made by her brother, Vree devoured a bowl of honeyed figs and felt her mood lift a little. Perhaps there'd be a way out after all.

When the sun had moved a safe distance past its zenith, they remounted and continued toward the Capital. The South Road was deserted, and Vree actually found herself relaxing into the movement of the horse. For a glorious moment, they became one creature, not two, and she began to understand what Gyhard saw in this method of transportation.

And then she saw the rider, hidden by a sharp bend in the road until he was too close to avoid.

"What is it?" Gyhard demanded as she stiffened.

"Army courier," Vree snapped, squinting to bring the sunbursts on the flapping pennant into focus. "I can't tell which army."

"What are the odds you'd be known?"

"Long," she admitted, but shifted to ready a dagger.

The courier was almost on them, close enough to count the sunbursts on his tunic. Six sunbursts. Sixth Army.

Shit!

Probably on the way back from telling the Emperor about Ghoti.

Lousy slaughtering timing!

The eyes under the crested helm flicked toward them as the courier passed, then widened with sudden recognition. "Bannon?"

Avor, said the Bannon in her head, not the one wrongly identified beside her.

Avor put his heels to his horse just a heartbeat too late.

Gyhard had never seen anyone move so quickly. One moment Vree sat stiffly beside him, the next instant she launched herself from the saddle, slammed into the startled courier and rode him to the ground, landing almost impossibly in a crouch straddling the body.

No, not a body. Not yet. He had the breath knocked out of him by the fall but appeared to be unhurt. Before he could move, a dagger pressed against his throat.

"They think you're dead, both of you. You were killed getting out of Ghoti!" By the time Avor's brain caught up with his mouth, the damage had been done. The information he'd just blurted out had been the only thing keeping him alive. "I won't tell!" His heels dug impotent trenches in the dust.

Vree nodded. "I know."

Avor paled, wet his lips, and somehow found the

courage to face the inevitable with dignity. "Don't leave me for the crows," he said softly.

Slitting a throat does not bring instant death. Consciousness can linger as the heart pumps blood out onto the ground and the lungs fill with scarlet froth. The razor edge of Vree's dagger flashed through soft tissue too quickly for pain, found the spine, slipped between two ridges of bone, and ended it. There was, at that moment, no separation between herself and her brother. It made it easier.

Blood shared, sister-mine.

She felt Gyhard's eyes on her as she stood. "Get the horses." Sheathing her dagger, she bent to drag the body farther off the road.

"What are you going to do?" The curve of her back as she'd bent over the messenger had been almost identical to the curve that haunted him—except this time, there had been nothing at all vulnerable about it.

Vree didn't answer. A grove of trees up ahead would provide both shelter from prying eyes along the road and dirt deep enough to bury Avor and the gear they'd stripped from his horse.

"We leave the mare outside the next village we come to. I'll give good odds that whoever finds it will keep their mouth shut."

"Your commanders will still know he's disappeared."

Vree shrugged. "Nothing to connect him to us." With a silent prayer that the goddess would take the courier into her company, even though he hadn't exactly died in battle, she lifted the onyx pendant over her head and dropped it onto the crimson gap at Avor's throat. Her life had been Bannon and the army. Now there was only Bannon. "And they're not my commanders anymore."

At least you were right about Emo.

Thank you. That makes me feel so much better.
Avor began to disappear beneath double handfuls of
earth.

Bannon remained silent for a long time. *So now
what'll we do?*

Save the prince. She threw a rock into the hole.
After that, I don't care.

*We don't need the army, sister-mine. You'll see. It
was like a weight around our necks, holding us down.*

Her hand lifted to where the pendant had hung for so
many years. She clutched at nothing, then spread her
fingers and began to smooth the grave, blurring the
edges into the surrounding dirt.

Working across from her, Gyhard frowned. He
would give a great deal to know what Vree and her
brother were discussing.

"Why, when as far as he knew he was facing a pair
of deserting assassins and had every right—or even ob-
ligation under the law—to kill us, didn't our young
messenger go for his crossbow?" he asked when they
were once again on the road.

"Crossbows take time to load. He didn't have that
time and he knew it. His only hope was escape."

"Not much of a hope."

She snorted softly. "No."

Gyhard couldn't quite identify the new tone in her
voice. It sounded almost melancholy. "Does it bother
you that you killed a comrade?"

Her profile tilted enough to fix him in a scornful
glare. "Having my throat slit in the dark would bother
me a lot more. If Avor told the garrison that he saw us,
they'd send out comrades harder to kill."

"We're not so very different, then, you and I. I also
kill to stay alive."

If he'd hoped to provoke a reaction, he was doomed to disappointment. "Everyone kills to stay alive. Even if it's only meat for the table."

Yeah, but the rest of us live the lives the goddess gave us. Ask the carrion eater how many lives he's lived.

"Bannon wants to know how many lives you've lived."

"Bannon wants to know?"

She shrugged.

Gyhard considered the question. It felt strange to be talking about it. Strange, but not unpleasant. "Counting the life I was born into, and not counting this borrowed one, six."

So five people have died for you to live.

When Vree repeated Bannon's words, Gyhard threw back his head and laughed. "Oh, more than that. Many more than that."

"He meant innocents," Vree snapped.

"I beg your pardon," Gyhard graciously inclined his head. "Can I assume by this condemnation that a pair of military assassins have never taken an innocent life? What of poor old Governor Aralt? He was no threat to you." He lifted a hand to cut short his protest. "Oh, wait, I forget, he had to die for the sake of the Empire. Well, I consider myself to be of at least as much worth as your Empire."

Worth as much as the Empire? You're a worthless piece of shit!

Vree ignored Bannon's protest. "So you died five times . . ."

Gyhard sighed. "You've missed the point, Vree. I *don't* die."

She turned to face him, trusting—or not caring—that the horse would continue to follow the road. "You've left behind five lives, that's the same as dying. How did you do it?"

He got lost for a moment in the intensity of her gaze. Because it looked very much as though she *needed* to know the answer, he heard himself say, "Except for the first one, I left by choice. That made it easier."

"Choice," she repeated, and her tone cut with the same precision her dagger had.

There was no point in misunderstanding or in pointing out that she could have chosen not to save her brother. "You could have chosen to let that courier live. Chosen to die."

"No one chooses to die."

"My point exactly."

She stared at him for a moment longer, then whatever need it was in her eyes vanished and, her expression carefully neutral once again, she turned back to face the road, the moment when something could have been shared between them gone.

In a hundred and twenty-two years, Gyhard mused, trying unsuccessfully to push away a rising memory, *everything reminds you of something else.*

"Why, Kars?" Because he couldn't look at the other man, he stared at his own reflection in the polished goblet, dark eyes wide with betrayal.

Kars smiled sadly. "I love you. If I kill you, you'll never leave me."

"I wasn't going to leave you." But even with the taste of poison on his lips, his protest sounded weak.

"You were. I saw your face when I Sang Ora back to into her body."

"She was dead, Kars, it isn't right."

"You've had three lives. Why shouldn't she have

two? It wasn't right for her to die. It isn't right for you to leave me. I'll kill you, then I'll Sing you back to your body."

Kars, his beautiful tragic Kars, gifted with the ability to Sing all four quarters but born in Cemandia where bards were seen as demon-kin. His life had been one of torture and torment before he'd finally escaped to hide in the mountains, no longer entirely sane. Gyhard could no longer ignore that insanity. He should never have told him how he'd moved his kigh from body to body. Should never have given him the idea of turning his incredible twisted power to Singing a fifth kigh.

"I didn't drink the wine, Kars. I tasted the poison before I swallowed."

Full lips trembled. "I thought you loved me."

"I did. I do."

"Then stay with me, my heart. Please, stay with me."

He remembered how Ora, neck broken in the fall that had killed her, had struggled to her feet, head lolling to one side. Perhaps they might still have a chance. "Free Ora."

"No. The dead won't leave me."

"Then the living will. Choose."

Tears welled up in deep blue eyes. "The dead won't leave me."

Gyhard stared down at the young hands that held the reins, seeing for a moment the hands that had guided his horse down out of the mountains, away from a crazy bard and his dead companion. He'd gotten rid of that body as soon as he could because every moment in it reminded him of the life he'd left behind. Of Kars.

Old choices. He'd lived almost a hundred years since then. Kars was long dead.

Chapter Six

"Gyhard i'Stevana isn't an Imperial name."

"Very true."

As he left it at that, Vree searched desperately for a way to keep him talking.

You stink at this. You sound like you're going to shove hot metal under his fingernails if he doesn't answer.

*Look, I said exactly what you told me to!"

It's not what you're saying, sister-mine, it's your own unique way of saying it. Ask him where he's from and try to sound like you care.

Slaughter it, Bannon, she growled. *Wouldn't it be easier just to rip off my clothes and impale myself on him?*

Not on horseback. Should've tried it last night. *I told you so,* was implicit in his tone.

Vree took a deep breath and forced unwilling lips up into a smile. "So where are you from?"

Gyhard tore his gaze away from a plump young woman spreading manure in a field by the road and glanced over at his companion. "Why do you want to know?"

Well, Bannon? Why?

You're just ... curious. He layered heated meaning onto the final word. Vree had no idea how he did it. Her own response fell sadly flat.

"How odd." Gyhard's smile suggested he knew how Vree's answer should've sounded. "I'm rather curious myself."

He's patronizing me, Bannon.

Shut up and listen to him, or we'll never get on with this.

"I was wondering," he continued, "how someone so beautiful could allow her entire youth to be eaten up by the army."

We didn't have a choice.

A morning spent trying to echo Bannon's words and Bannon's tone in what was essentially Bannon's seduction betrayed her. This time, she got the tone right. The bitterness surprised her.

"You didn't have a choice?" Gyhard repeated.

"We were raised in the garrison." She wasn't sure why she was answering. She wasn't sure who. "Our mother was in the army. We weren't very old when she was killed. The army raised us; fed us, clothed us, housed us, trained us. We owed them everything."

"Did they raise all their orphans as assassins."

Her shoulders straightened and her chin rose. "No, only the best."

"Did they often tell you that, that you were the best?"

She swiveled in the saddle so she could stare full into his face, not understanding either the question or the almost gentle way he asked it. What right did he have, sitting there in her brother's body without a life of his own, to pity her? A flick of the wrist and she could kill him as they rode. He'd be dead before he even saw the blade.

Why are we talking about us? You're supposed to get him to talk about himself.

Bannon . . .

Get him out of my body, Vree.

"You never said where you were from." She turned her attention back to the road, all at once very busy with reins and riding.

Why not? Gyhard, fully aware that this delving for information most likely had ulterior motives involving his removal from Bannon's body, frankly didn't care. Whatever she . . . they were planning wouldn't work anyway. And whatever he told her could hardly be called secret compared to what she'd known right from the beginning. It was, in a way, very freeing. "I was born and raised in Shkoder. Do you know where that is?"

Vree smashed a bug against her thigh and wondered if he thought she was stupid. "Shkoder's on the other side of the mountain range that guards the Empire's north border. They have no standing army, a well-trained militia, and usually base rank on birth rather than ability." His flummoxed expression drew a scornful laugh. "If an army's to keep the Empire, it has to know about the surrounding countries."

"For defense?"

"Or attack." Everything kept coming back to the army. She supposed it was like losing a limb but having the pain go on in parts long rotted and food for worms.

"Or attack," Gyhard agreed. "Although I doubt that Shkoder would even consider something so innately suicidal given the respective sizes of the two countries. Also, Her Imperial Majesty, the Empress Irenka is a younger sister of King Theron of Shkoder."

Lifting her face to the heat of the sun, Vree sighed.

They'd—she and Bannon—once removed an old army commander who'd gathered a group of veterans around her and attempted to set up a private little fief inside the Empire. "Allies change."

"Very true."

Something in his voice pulled her head around again. Something in his eyes drove her heels in hard against her horse's sides.

Vree, what are you doing? He's supposed to get interested in you. How to explain that she wasn't running from his reaction but hers. That she was in danger of responding to the face Gyhard wore and not the enemy who wore it. Slitting her eyes against a heated wind, she thought of nothing at all save staying in the saddle.

Hooves pounded behind her. Challenged, her gelding increased his pace. For a time they raced neck and neck, and then both horses began to slow. *Too much to hope that they'd run on forever . . .*

Are you afraid of him, sister-mine?

Easy to respond to Bannon's arch tone and brush aside the actual question. *Don't be an ass.*

"Well," Gyhard began when they were walking again, "that was interesting. I assume you're unaware that racing on the Imperial roads is against the law and can result in heavy fines."

Vree carefully leaned forward to stroke the damp curve of chestnut neck, her heart beginning to drum less violently. "It doesn't count as racing until a second horse joins in," she pointed out. "*I* wasn't racing. You were."

"You were merely allowing your mount to work off excess energy?"

"If you like."

Clearly, she wasn't going to tell him why she'd so

suddenly needed to get away. All things considered, he wasn't certain he wanted to know. "So, what were we talking about?"

"You. Who you were."

"Why not who I am?"

His question abruptly turned her mood. Her mouth twisted, and her eyes flicked over the length of his borrowed body. "I know what you are."

Gyhard i'Stevana squinted at the rapidly setting sun and tried, unsuccessfully, to convince himself that he could be home before dark.

"You should've stayed in Caraford," he muttered. "Should've diced with that toothless old man, choked down a bowl of disgusting mutton stew, and slept safely with the bedbugs until morning."

But he hadn't. And now it was almost dark.

He hunched his shoulders as a chill Fourth Quarter wind tried to push an icy gust down under his collar and kicked his horse into a trot. He should've stayed in Caraford, but he'd wanted to get home and surprise his family who weren't expecting him back for days.

Shadows in the forest flanking the trail grew deeper.

Fortunately, he'd traveled between the village and home a hundred times or more over his twenty-three years and couldn't possibly get lost. He knew every rock and every tree. Unfortunately, he also knew what might very well lurk behind them.

His horse suddenly shied sideways and he pulled it back to a walk, senses straining. He could hear nothing but the wind in the evergreens. See nothing but branches tossed against a darkening sky.

Moving slowly, so as not to attract undue attention should there be watchers in the dusk, Gyhard slid his light crossbow from its strapping and fumbled for a quarrel. Loading it would have been easier had the young stallion not continued to fight his control.

"Might be nothing," he muttered, hooking the string back under the steel claw and resting the loaded bow on his thigh—but he didn't believe it.

His eldest sister, who'd taken over the forest contract when their mother died, had sent him to ask their lord, the Duc of Sibu for help. An early freeze and a desperately cold Fourth Quarter, had driven a small band of rough men whose lives had always been marginal onto the dark side of the law. Gyhard had insisted they could handle it themselves. His sister had disagreed.

I should've waited for the Duc. Come back with him.

A branch snapped. He twisted toward the sound.

Something hit him between the shoulder blades with enough force to lift him out of the saddle. His finger tightened on the trigger and the crossbow bolt slammed into the frozen ground barely a heartbeat before he did.

A small panicked voice in his head shrieked at him to roll over, to draw his long dagger, to fight. Gasping for breath, right arm folded under him at a torturous angle, he wished the voice would shut up. He swallowed, tasted blood, and struggled to suck air through teeth he couldn't unclench.

The boot caught him under the ribs and kicked him over onto his back. Jagged ends of bone grated together in his arm. He screamed.

The sandy-haired man standing over him smiled, slabs of yellow teeth barely visible in the midst of a bristling red beard.

Time slowed and Gyhard stared in horror at the descending spear.

I don't want to die!

The crude point dimpled his heavy fleece jacket, parted the leather and the fabric beneath it, then finally touched the skin of his chest. To his surprise, it hurt less than the constant agony of his arm. The audible crunch as the heavy steel forced its way through bone was the worst.

Terror opened his bowels.

Then time took up its normal speed again and whatever gods had cushioned him from the initial blow retreated. He felt the spear slam out through his back and into the earth, and he jerked like a worm on a hook. He no longer felt the pain in his arm because pain was all he had left.

Almost all.

Out of the waves of scarlet and black came one coherent thought. *NO. NO. NO. NO!*

Somehow, he focused on the pale-blue eyes staring down at him in rapt fascination. Frantically, he began to claw his way up the spear shaft toward them. He could feel the rough wood ripping new abrasions around the edges of the wound. It didn't matter. Nothing mattered but not dying.

Then his right hand reached out and touched a filthy cheek and the pale eyes widened.

Smoke and fire and strange faces. Women he didn't know writhing under him. Blood lust. Hunger. Rage. Too many images to make sense of. Gyhard pushed at them, shoved them away. When something called Hinrich pushed back, Gyhard clawed his way toward the center of the maelstrom.

Then he swayed, dropped to his knees, and stared in horror at the body impaled beside him. A body that quite unmistakably had not moved since it had been spiked to the ground. A bloody froth stained the golden mustache crimson as the dying man tried to speak. Failed. Died.

He was looking out of Hinrich's eyes.

But was still Gyhard.

Still alive.

Vree wet her lips and swallowed hard. Death happened. To friends, to foes, to everyone in time. She couldn't remember a time when she hadn't known she would die and she clearly remembered a day in her early teens, a dagger in her hand and a crumpled body spilling blood onto the ground at her feet, when she'd accepted it as inevitable.

But to suddenly be in another body, staring down at the lifeless shell she'd worn since birth . . .

"What did you do?"

Gyhard rubbed his cheek, wondering why the telling of something that had occurred so very long ago affected him as it had. He had to clear his throat before he could speak. "I ran. The other bandits didn't even bother trying to catch me. Why should they? As far as they were concerned, they now had one less partner to share the spoils." His laugh held no humor. "I doubt they could have caught me anyway."

"Where did you run to?"

She could barely hear his answer. "Home."

The palisade around the steading had originally been built to keep out the bears and wolves and mountain cats that hunted in the forests of Sibu. Recently, it had served as a barrier against the approach of human predators.

Ice crystals forming in Hinrich's coarse red beard, Gyhard stumbled to the gate, fighting to breathe through the stitch in his side.

"Open," he gasped. "Let me in."

Ten feet and he'd be safe. Ten feet more and the nightmare would be over.

The crossbow bolt caught him in the left shoulder, flung him back, spun him around, and saved his life. The second shot whistled through the air a hand's span from his nose.

"No!" But pain and terror had hold of his throat and the best voice he could manage was a hoarse croak. "No, please. It's me. It's me, Gyhard."

He could hear them gathering behind the wall, could hear shouts of *Bandit!* and *Murderer!* and his sister demanding to know why the first two shots had missed.

"No. It's me." He staggered back a step, then another. "It's Gyhard."

A quarrel smashed into the frozen earth at his feet. Another hissed his name as it drew a line of pain just above his ear.

He didn't want to die.

He turned and ran back into the shelter of the night.

Three days later, carefully hidden in a childhood sanctuary high in an evergreen, he watched his own funeral. Amidst the grieving were many howled vows of revenge and every adult member of the family carried a weapon close at hand. They knew the face he wore and would never allow it close enough for explanations.

Hinrich had killed him twice.

"I was in Hinrich's body seven years until I found the courage to . . . move on. Tomas was a distinct improvement. Young, dark, handsome; he had the most beautiful eyes . . ."

"Was he trying to kill you?" Vree interrupted.

"No."

She closed her eyes for a moment and almost wished she hadn't asked.

"Don't try to make me a tragic victim, Vree." His voice had picked up an edge. "I've turned the life I lost into an eternal life. Not a bad trade, in my mind."

Your mind, my body, Bannon muttered.

From the corner of her eye, Vree could see his hand—all right, Bannon's hand—holding the reins. The white-knuckled grip seemed at odds with the tone of his voice. "Have you told this story before?"

This wasn't what he'd expected her to ask. The edge disappeared and he shrugged, the graceful motion seemingly dictated as much by the body he wore as his mood. "Once."

His face pleated into a thousand wrinkles as he smiled across his small camp at the young woman who sat crooning to her stillborn baby. As was common in the Capital when mother and child died in a birthing, Wheyra's body had been laid to rest with the infant cradled in her arms. Although no kigh lingered to be Sung back into the tiny body, the distraught mother had refused to leave the tomb without the baby. He had finally given in. He was fond of children.

One by one, he checked on the rest of his new family as they waited out the hottest part of the day in the shady hollow. The dry summer heat acted to preserve their tissues but direct sunlight did them no good at all. As the shadows moved and lengthened, he had to remain constantly vigilant lest one of them blacken and burn.

He called them by the names they'd answered to in life; names learned, for the most part, by clinging to the fringes of funeral processions.

Wheyra, Kait, and the cousins Aver and Otanon.

Once, he'd thought the dead would never leave him. He knew better now.

Tenderly, he reached out and lifted Kait's clutching hand off the heavy brace of scavenged leather she wore around her neck.

"I know you don't like it," he told her, "but your head flops so without support."

Kait's brows drew slowly in above eyes narrowed with revulsion. "Noooo," she said.

He patted her hand. "Yes." The teenager had only joined the family the night before when the distance between two of the flat-topped tenements had proved to be just a little farther than she could jump. Her wealthy parents had spent most of the funeral procession loudly complaining about the type of friends she'd been hanging around with.

"Noooo," Kait repeated, and she would have gone on had he not quickly hushed her.

Something was happening over by the tombs.

"Don't move. Any of you." Leaning heavily on his staff, he started toward the road. He had no fear of leaving his family alone. They'd do what he said, they had no choice, and not moving was something the dead did very well. Nor did he fear that they'd be discovered by accident for living kigh would not come near. Three times guards had nearly stumbled on his camp. Each time they'd veered off without realizing they had.

It wasn't another funeral, he saw with disappointment as he shuffled into place behind a pair of merchants—who were not at all pleased at having their journey to the Capital interrupted by an advance wedge of guard wearing the Imperial sunburst.

"Yeah, hide behind that helmet," muttered the first.

"If I knew who you were, I'd take your spear and stuff it where the sunburst don't shine."

"The roads are for the citizens," snarled the second. "Not some polished flunky in a . . ."

"The Emperor!" came the call from the crowd closer to the city. "It's the Emperor!"

Instantly, the irritation disappeared, and both merchants cheered as loudly as everyone else who'd been pushed to the side of the road.

Sunburst pennants snapped in the wind over the heads of those members of the First Army riding escort. Richly dressed in the muted colors thought appropriate for the hunt, a group of nobles preened under the attention. The Emperor, a huge hawk balanced hooded and jessed on his left fist, acknowledged the crowds, and managed to make everyone feel that they, personally, had been noticed.

As the pair of merchants yelled themselves hoarse, he turned to go. He had no interest in a living Emperor, who would, after all, end up as dead and wormeaten as any of his subjects. Then one of the riders directly behind his Imperial Majesty caught his eye.

Laughing, the young man pushed shoulder-length black curls back from his face with a slender hand. His mouth was wide; his teeth very white. Broad shoulders filled out a cream silk shirt and burgundy vest over a narrow-hipped, long-legged body. But his eyes—dark and thickly lashed and almost too large for his face. Intense eyes. Beautiful eyes.

He remembered what it was he'd been looking for. Years ago, he'd lost his heart.

Jabbing the knob of bone on the head of his staff at the closest merchant, he pointed a trembling finger at the young man and whispered, "Who?"

"Prince Otavas," the merchant snapped, rubbing her

side. "And watch where you're poking that thing, old man."

He ignored her and stood staring in the direction the prince had gone long after traffic on the road returned to normal. Memories fought their way through the confusion the years had wrapped around his mind. He remembered a dark-eyed young man. He remembered joy. He remembered pain.

"I know you," he murmured at last, tears streaming down withered cheeks. "I know you."

"It's in the Capital, whatever it is." Karlene tossed her pack to the floor, then gently lowered her instrument case down beside it. "A day's walk out in any direction and the kigh are fine—but none of them would carry a message into the city."

"Did they give you any more information?" Gabris asked without much hope.

"No. Give me a chance to clean up and I'll do a full recall. Not," she added, moving through their workroom toward her own chambers, "that there's much more than what I just told you."

"Karlene . . ."

She froze, took a moment to wonder what had taken him so long, and turned to face the door. "Highness."

Still dressed in his hunting clothes, Prince Otavas bounded into the room. "I came up as soon as I heard you were back. How was your trip? Is there any news? News that I should pass on to His Majesty, my father, that is. You know how he hates to wait for official reports."

Karlene glanced at the senior bard—who nodded—before answering. "Whatever it is that's frightening the kigh, Highness, it's centered in the Capital."

Dark brows sketched a frown. "That's not good." A

pause while he looked from one bard to the other. "Is it? I mean, nothing's happened. Perhaps whatever it is only affects the spirit world?"

"Perhaps." The bards had discussed the possibility, but neither believed it. Anything that so affected three of the four kigh—and quite probably the fourth as well—*had* to involve something at least potentially disastrous. But there was no point, Karlene decided, in mentioning that to the prince. She gestured at his clothing. "I see you've been out hawking."

"An afternoon's amusement." He smiled wistfully at her. "My heart was elsewhere."

"And now it's back," Gabris murmured.

The prince's smile broadened; Karlene pretended she hadn't heard. "You'll want to clean up, Highness. I know I do."

Otavas sighed dramatically. "Such a pity that the palace cisterns are full and we've no need to conserve water."

Karlene, who'd been expecting a less oblique suggestion, burst out laughing. "Yes, Highness," she agreed, "a pity."

Ghoti secured, a temporary tribunal in place until the Emperor could appoint a new governor, the Sixth Army began the march back to their garrison. Marshal Chela, riding up front out of the dust with her commanders—in spite of the roads there was always dust—glanced over at the officer riding to her right and shook her head.

"Slaughter it, Neegan. Are you still brooding?"

Commander Neegan turned a dark gaze on his superior. "They shouldn't have died. They were too good."

Wishing she had a crescent for every time she'd

heard that over the last ten days, the marshal sighed. "Then their luck ran out. It happens."

"Then why," Neegan continued, "did the Ghotians deny it happened?"

"For fear of reprisals," the marshal answered as she'd answered a hundred times before.

"And what happened to the bodies?"

"The bodies could've been anywhere, Neegan."

"Maybe they chopped them up and fed them to the pigs," suggested Commander Leesh archly, from her place on the marshal's left.

Marshal Chela frowned. Her youngest commander hadn't yet learned to tread warily around the assassin— Chela couldn't decide whether that kind of bravado came out of ego or stupidity. As Neegan would endure either for only a limited time, sooner or later there'd be an accident.

"You're only put out," Leesh went on, clearly relishing the opportunity, "because the governor poisoned himself before your precious assassins could get to him. They died for nothing."

"They shouldn't have died at all." Neegan's hoarse whisper had an uncanny way of covering the distance when he wanted it to.

The marshal hid a shiver as it passed her and noted with approval that it had wiped the smile off Leesh's face. "I think," she said, her tone turning the thought to an order, "that we've heard quite enough ..." A slight, black-clad figure following a small herd of goats down a scrub-covered hill to the east of the North Road caught her eye, and the thought she'd been about to voice marched on without her. "Neegan. Your eyes are younger than mine; what is that child wearing?"

Neegan rose in his stirrups, shading his eyes with a

palm. A moment later, he spurred his horse off the road. The goats scattered. The goatherd screamed and tried to run.

"What's going on?" Leesh demanded.

"A very good question." The marshal raised her hand; behind her, officers shouted the orders that would stop the column. "And one Commander Neegan is attempting to find an answer to. Unless I'm very much mistaken, which I am not, that child is wearing the remains of an assassin's uniform."

"Aye, two of them. First a young man and then a young woman." The goatherd's mother stared at Neegan suspiciously. She didn't like soldiers and she didn't like this husky-voiced soldier in particular. "Governor Aralt told us the young man'd be coming and he had the signet like he was s'posed to. Didn't mention the woman, though."

"They came alone?"

"Just said that. First him. Then her. Left together."

"Were they injured in any way?"

She shrugged. "Can't say. Didn't look it the way they rode out."

"Rode?"

"Aye. On horses. Not the best in the stable, mind, but good ones." Her eyes narrowed. "You gonna want them uniforms back? 'Cause I didn't take 'em. Those two left 'em behind. Got all new stuff out of the governor's stores. Hers was ripped up, that's why Ilse is wearing it with the goats, but his is still in good shape. Person could get a lot of wear out of it."

"Who else spoke to them?"

"Can't say. Steward probably."

Hands clenching and unclenching, a muscle jumping in his jaw, Neegan strode toward the villa.

"Hey, Captain! What about them uniforms? You want them back?"

Neegan half turned, somehow managing to keep a fingernail grip on his temper. "Keep them," he growled.

Well, sod you, too, she thought and went back to mucking out the stables.

"I want to go after them myself."

Marshal Chela watched tension twist the muscles under the surface of Commander Neegan's face and kept her own carefully expressionless. "I need you with me."

"No." He shook his head. "With Ghoti settled, the whole sector is quiet. You don't need me."

The marshal ignored the direct contradiction. She allowed Neegan much more leeway than she allowed the rest of her staff. "And what if there's an uprising while you're gone? The sixth Army will be a commander short."

"Then promote Captain Lyhit. She's ready."

"You'd resign your commission?" Chela frowned slightly and locked her gaze on the commander's eyes. "These two mean so much to you?"

"They were mine." Neegan's voice had picked up the sound of a wire brush rasping against flesh. "Mine. When they deserted, they betrayed me."

"They betrayed the *army.*"

For a moment he looked as though he'd argue the correction, then he nodded once, very slightly. "They have to be hunted down. You know the law."

"There are other assassins, less essential to the smooth running of the Sixth Army, that I could send," the marshal pointed out.

Neegan dismissed them with a barely controlled

wave of his hand. "No. Vree and Bannon are too good. I have the best chance. Perhaps the only chance."

Chela remembered the cold touch of a blade against her throat and granted Neegan the point. "Very well." she said after a moment, her tone indicating this was the final word on the matter. "Go. Your commission stands unless we go back into the field. At such time, I'll promote Captain Lyhit to a temporary position and we'll discuss your reinstatement when you return. I want frequent dispatches. Do you know where to start?"

"Aralt's steward said they were traveling to the Capital."

"The Capital," Chela repeated musingly. "I wonder when they learned to ride."

"Does it matter?"

"It may." She waved his dismissal at him, then stopped him with his name as he reached the tent flap. "Out of the thousands under my command, those two should have been low on the list of possible deserters. Before you kill them ..." She stared down into the smooth cut ruby set in the ring that marked her as a priestess of Jiir. No answers rose out of the bloody depths. ". . . ask them why."

"Three days ..."

"Three days for what?" Gyhard asked as the inn's servants carried away the remains of their meal. He wondered how blunt she'd be in front of witnesses. *Three days to kill you. Three days to get my brother's body back.*

Vree leaned uncomfortably back in her chair—they were now too far north to request southern furnishings—and stared at him as if he were an idiot. "Three days to the Capital."

They sat in silence until they were alone again; Gyhard twisting the metal stem of an embossed goblet between thumb and forefinger, but Vree merely sitting, predator patient. Waiting.

"Our association will not end the moment we ride into the Capital," Gyhard said at last. "It will, after all, take time to gain access to the prince."

"Time," Vree repeated. "How much time?"

"That, for the most part, will be up to you. As we will, essentially, be assassinating him, I'll depend upon your expertise to get us into the palace and past his guards."

Do it tonight,Vree!

She watched Gyhard lift a cluster of grapes from an alabaster bowl and cautiously caught the plump, burgundy sphere he tossed at her. A well-known myth told how Kel, the God of Storm, had seduced a nymph by laying a trail of purple grapes from her tree to his bed.

*You are *no* nymph,* Bannon snorted, lifting the thought off the surface of her mind. *But if it's an invitation, take him up on it.*

Vree caught a second grape, and stood.

Gyhard stood with her and smiled. His eyes crinkled at the corners the way Bannon's had.

That's because they are Bannon's eyes, you fool. After a long moment, she took a step away from the table, toward the smaller of the two bedchambers. "If you're depending on my expertise, I'd best begin making plans."

What was all that about?

Head pounding, feeling as though she'd just missed understanding the heart of an unexpected threat, Vree walked over and sat on the edge of the bed. "All what?" she snarled.

All what went on while you ate. The laughing at his slaughteringly stupid jokes, the hanging on his every word like he's the oracle of the goddess, that last, long lingering look.

Vree lay back and closed her eyes. *Don't be an ass. I was just doing what you told me to. I was just trying to get him interested.*

*He's interested. But *you* didn't do anything about it.*

*I want *him* to do something about it.*

Why? You don't know how to make the first move?

Sod off. She rubbed her temples and wished Bannon would shut up so she could think things through. *If it's his idea he'll be less likely to suspect a trap.*

So kick his feet out from under him, beat him to the floor, and keep him too busy to suspect anything. You're not supposed to have a good time, Vree, you're supposed to get me back into my own body.

A good time. She ground her teeth together. *Do you think this is fun for me? Do you think I'm enjoying myself?*

I know when you're enjoying yourself.

You know what I let you know.

He didn't answer for a long moment and when he finally did, he sounded much like he had when he was very young and he needed her to chase the demons away. *Get me out of here, sister-mine. Before it destroys us.*

Before it destroys us. She drew Bannon's face up out of memory but pushed it quickly away. A chill traced icy lines down her back, when she couldn't be certain that she wasn't seeing Gyhard looking out through her brother's eyes.

Gyhard watched until her door closed behind her,

then he dropped his gaze to the remaining grapes nestled in one hand. If he'd made the first move, she'd have allowed it. He'd exploited too much uncertainty over the last hundred odd years not to recognize it.

Dropping the fruit back into the bowl, he went into his own room and pulled his mirror out of the saddlebag. He stared down at the not-yet-familiar reflection. For the first time in too long a time, he had the freedom of his own past. It was a strange but wonderful gift Vree had inadvertently given him by refusing to let her brother die.

So why hadn't he made that first move? He could only be certain that it wasn't from a lack of desire.

"Does the answer lie in my past?" he asked the young man staring back up at him. "Or does it lie in yours?"

He wondered what they were talking about, Vree and her brother. He doubted very much that they were making plans to assassinate the prince.

Chapter Seven

He didn't like going into the city. There were too many of the living, too close together. They frightened him. But the dead couldn't give him the answers he needed.

Flanked by the cousins, their features hidden in the shadows of deep cowls taken from those too dead to rise, he joined the traffic heading toward one of the six gates that breached the wall around the Capital. Although he moved very slowly, no one jostled him or even demanded he get out of the way. The other travelers on the road seemed to be doing their best to deny his very existence. The pattern split as it reached him, swirled around, and, once safely past, closed up again.

Just before the gate, he gestured for his companions to wait where they were and went on alone.

The guard watched the old man approach and wondered how anyone so old could still be alive. She eyed the bone-topped staff, the threadbare robe, and the tangle of dull gray hair and wondered if maybe she couldn't be busy at something when he arrived. In her experience, crazy old hermits, while harmless, tended to stink.

She was surprised to see he still had teeth and more surprised yet to realize he had a very pleasant smile.

"Yesterday, the Emperor rode out." Slowly, carefully, holding her gaze with his, he described the young man he'd seen. When he finished, he took a deep breath and very carefully formed the next words as Command. **"Tell me who he is."**

"You must mean Prince Otavas."

It wasn't the name he remembered, but the past often poured through his memories too fluid to grasp. He nodded, slowly. "Yes . . ." Then he turned on one bare heel and motioned for the cousins to join him.

As they came toward her, the guard suddenly became aware that an approaching wagon would have to be thoroughly inspected and rushed out to wave the startled driver to one side. Those already passing under the arch of the wall began to hurry, all at once anxious to reach their destinations. Those still on the road found a variety of unavoidable reasons to slow their pace. Those about to leave the city found equally important reasons to delay.

The tapping of his staff against the rutted cobblestones echoed within the confines of the gate and with the cousins close behind, he entered the Capital. Jostling mobs gave way before him. Behind him, now that he'd past beyond the enclosed area, the gate filled as folk surged forward from both outside the wall and in.

"I'm looking for a prince," he said to a woman wearing a bloody apron.

She snorted, her gaze sliding by the place where the cousins stood as she backed into her shop. "Try the palace, old man."

"The palace." He peered up into Aver's hood. "Do you know the way to the palace?"

"Yesss."

He tucked his hand in the crook of the dead man's elbow. "Then you can lead me," he said.

A ripple of distress followed them as they shuffled slowly into the center of the city. A crooked-backed man who sat drooling on a doorstep, one wrist secured to a post by a bit of frayed rope, screamed as they went by. The very old and the very young trembled, suddenly cold. Some would never grow warm again.

No one looked closely enough to say, *these men are dead,* for the kigh of the living would not, could not deal with what he had done. Only the cats refused to turn away and watched all three through slitted eyes, ears back, fur lifted in spiked ridges off their spines.

He knew, although he didn't know where the knowledge originated, that it would be safer not to enter the palace. Still leaning on Aver's arm, he made his slow way around the outer wall, ignored by the guards. At last, by a small gate closer to Temple Street than he'd intended to come—long before, pain had taught him to fear those who served the gods—he sent the cousins to stand a safe distance away.

As he approached the guard, he rehearsed his Command. He had neither the training nor the strength to force a compliance that ran against duty, loyalty, or love. When the guard finally turned, he smiled and locked his gaze on the questioning eyes peering out from under the edge of the crested helm.

"Tell me about Prince Otavas. Tell me everything you know."

"Do you feel it?" Eyes wide, arms folded close around her body, Karlene stared down at the city. The stone bulk of the Center, just visible over the turrets and towers of other temples, brought no comfort. "Something . . . Something . . ."

"Is very wrong," Gabris finished. His face above his beard had taken on a grayish cast. "Cold, so cold."

Startled, Karlene turned, took one look at the older bard, and declared, "I'm going for a healer."

"No." He shook his head. "I'm fine. I'm just so cold."

It was almost midday. In spite of thick walls and windows angled to catch the breezes, the room was, if anything, stifling hot.

"Gabris ..."

"No!"

Her own feelings of disquiet pushed aside, she hurried across the room and caught up one of his hands. His fingers were like ice.

"I don't need a healer," he insisted, reading her expression.

"I don't care what you think you need," Karlene pointed out, dropping his hand and heading for the door, wishing her thoughts were not so suddenly dark and terrifying, "but I'm going for one anywa ..."

A small fair-haired page exploded into the room and flung herself at Karlene's legs, her whole body shaking with the violence of her sobs. "Make it go away! Make it go away!"

A darker, older girl followed close on her heels but rocked to a stop when she saw the two bards.

Karlene shot a glance over her shoulder at Gabris, but the older bard looked as astounded as she felt. Gently peeling the thin arms from around her thighs, she dropped to her knees and gathered the girl up against her heart. "Hush, child. Nothing will hurt you here. Tell me what's wrong."

But she only shook her head and continued to sob.

"She just started to cry," the older page explained, shifting from foot to foot, her hands tracing worried circles in the air. "Then she started to run. I don't know why she came here."

"Are you all right?"

"Yes, Lady Bard."

"Then go for a healer." When the girl hesitated, Karlene added, "Hurry." using just enough Voice to ensure she was obeyed. As the footsteps pounded away down the hall, she shifted her grip and Sang comfort, reassurance, safety. Gradually, she felt the tension leave the small body she held and one hand loosed its death grip on her collar. Her eyes still swimming with tears, the girl pulled far enough away to look up at Karlene's face. She was older than the bard had first assumed, at least ten or eleven although small for her age.

Not wanting to frighten her again, Karlene added a quiet question to the comfort of her Song.

To her surprise, the page swallowed, wiped her nose on the back of her wrist, and Sang an answer. Horror spilled out in a rush of discordant melody, the emotions so powerful that the lack of training made little difference.

They Sang together for a moment, the bard directing, counseling, and finally convincing the child to bring the Song to an end. The girl pressed her face into Karlene's shoulder. "Can I stay here until it stops being scary?" she sighed.

Resting her cheek against the soft cap of hair, Karlene nodded. "Of course you can." She felt Gabris touch her shoulder and turned just enough to look up at him.

"I think we've found the Emperor a tenth bard," he said softly. "Or more accurately, the tenth bard has found us."

"Perhaps whatever it is, it's only a bardic problem. First the kigh, now this." Gabris took another swallow of the tonic the healer had left and made a face. "No one else seemed to feel that anything was wrong."

"Everyone else *denied* they felt anything," Karlene corrected. "Not the same thing."

"They felt it and now they're denying it? You're being ridiculous."

"I am not!"

"You are."

"Excuse me." Prince Otavas had obviously been crying—his eyes were puffy, his nose red.

Karlene crossed quickly to his side. Her would-be suitor looked incredibly young and very much in need of comfort. "What is it, Highness? What's wrong?"

He shrugged, shoulders jerking up and down as though he'd forgotten how to manage his body. "I, I just thought you should know that Verika's baby died this afternoon."

"Died?" Verika's baby, born in early spring, hadn't yet lived two full quarters. And now he never would.

"I was there, Karlene, in the garden by the wall. He started to cry. His nurse picked him up and she screamed and I took him." He swallowed and closed his eyes, lower lip trembling.

Without a second thought, Karlene gathered the prince into her arms. He clung to her, the way the page had and under her Song of grieving she heard him say, "He was so cold . . ."

She kept Singing as Gabris hurried from the room, his own health forgotten. The Empress had just lost a grandchild and would need him beside her. Karlene kept Singing as a faint keening could be heard drifting through the halls of the palace. She kept Singing even though she thought she heard the keening echoed in the city outside the palace walls.

Whatever it was, it wasn't just a bardic problem.

* * *

Karlene finished tuning her quitara and tucked it carefully between the layers of padded felt in her instrument case. For the last two days the palace had been mourning the loss of the youngest member of the Imperial Family. She needed to get out, away from the sorrow that filled the halls and chambers like a heavy fog.

"I don't think this is the right time to go to a tavern." Fatigue had flattened Gabris' voice, disapproval flattened it further still.

Her fingers closed around a stiff buckle. She kept her eyes on her hands. "I don't think this is the right time to sit around doing nothing. Someone, somewhere, has to know what's going on."

"And why do you think that someone will come to you?"

Finally, she turned to face him. "I *can't* just sit around and do nothing. And besides, the prince wasn't the only infant to die. It's important that the palace know what the city thinks just now: Are they grieving? Are they too angry to grieve? I can bring that back with me."

Gabris sighed. He didn't have the energy to argue. "Perhaps you're right."

"You know I'm right." Slinging the instrument case on her back, she started for the door. Gabris moved to block her way.

"Too angry to grieve?" he asked gently.

Karlene bit her lip and blinked back a rush of tears. "Too angry to think straight," she admitted and wondered if he'd stop her because of it. He could. Gabris was senior and could order her to remain in the palace. She wondered if she'd listen.

He stepped aside, his expression a clear indication that he'd been following the path of her thoughts. But all he said was, "I hope you find what you're looking for."

No one noticed the teenage girl in the leather neck brace who watched the palace. Hidden by more than mere shadow, Kait stood and stared unblinkingly at a small gate. When it opened, she stepped back into the shelter of a deep alcove, remembering what he had told her.

"The bard may be able to see you. Hide."

Kait had seen the bard once, singing in a market-place, just like any of a hundred street performers who sang or juggled or danced in the Capital every day. Death had taken the memory of how the song had touched her and left only a bitter awareness that it had.

Her fingers scratched at the brace. *"Leave it on,"* he'd said, so she did.

A tall woman with a pale blonde braid drawing a line of moonlight down her back, slipped out through the open gate and strode quickly away from the wall. She carried a padded case, half again as tall as she was.

"The bard isn't important. Let the bard go."

Kait waited. A fly crawled over her face. She ignored it until it danced across the surface of one eye, obscuring her vision, then she brushed it away. He'd told her to watch carefully.

The gate opened again.

"The guard told me that the prince sometimes follows the bard. If she leaves the palace and anyone follows her, you are to follow him. Find out where they are going and then come for me."

She turned and shuffled after the heavily cloaked figure who trailed the bard. While those who passed her in the dusk would not, could not, acknowledge what they saw, she walked without a circle of death surrounding her. Hers was only one young kigh— young enough to adapt.

"You're the only one who can do this. I'm counting on you, Kait." Although she couldn't feel his touch, he'd cupped her face in his hands and gently kissed her brow. She could almost remember wanting someone else to do that. Before she'd died.

She forced the body she wore to move a little faster. She wouldn't let him down.

The Iron Dog was nearly full of quiet, morose drinkers. A dice game in the corner proceeded by rote, the ivory cubes thrown because in that tavern at that time they were always thrown. Singing softly, Karlene made her way unnoticed to a bench by the empty fireplace and settled her quitara on her lap. If asked, she suspected that both tavernkeeper and patrons would insist that they had no desire for music. So she didn't ask.

During her time in the Capital, she'd learned that the Dog, tucked just back of the markets and mews, attracted those whose business depended on knowing the temper of the city. If the information she searched for existed at all, she'd find it here.

Still Singing, Karlene checked to make certain her instrument remained in tune, then she paused, stroked her right thumb gently over the strings, and listened to the multitude of tiny sounds that would tell her the mood of the crowd.

Confusion. Fear. Pain.

The Song she'd intended to Sing, a Song that demanded answers, would have rubbed salt into emotions abraded and raw. Ashamed, she reached beyond her anger for her own grief and formed it into a lament, a sorrowing for all the deaths of all the children. Her voice, wrapped around her listeners and held them while they found comfort in knowing that they no longer grieved alone. She Sang while the crowd drew strength from each other; sang while they shared the loss and began to find peace. The ache in her own heart began to ease.

"I hope you find what you're looking for."

No wonder Gabris hadn't stopped her. *You're very wise, old man,* she acknowledged as she let the Song trail off.

When grief finally gave way to conversation, she moved through the crowd, gratefully accepted a tankard of ale, and sifted information from the babble of voices. Death had followed a path from the east gate to the palace, but it soon became apparent that no one had seen, or heard, or felt anything. Stranger still, although every one spoke of what had happened, no theories or accusations were made. Direct questions were given indirect answers or not answered at all.

Frustrated, and more worried than she wanted to admit, Karlene packed up and headed for the door. With one hand on the scarred wood, she paused, turned, and took a second look at a cloaked figure sitting alone at a table tucked into a shadowy corner. Then she took a third look. Thin gold rings glinted in the flickering lamplight as the figure raised a hand to adjust its hood.

Lips pressed into a thin line, she crossed the room and leaned into the corner. "I assume you're leaving with me?" Her tone made it obvious there could be only one answer.

Outside on the street, Prince Otavas pushed back his hood and lengthened his stride to keep up. "I don't want you to be angry with me, Karlene . . ."

Her sandals slapped against the cobblestones. "Where are your guards, Highness?"

"I didn't bring any. I never bring any when I follow you . . ." She stopped so suddenly he was three paces past her before he realized. When he turned, he flinched back another step at the expression on her face.

"You've done this before? Followed me into the city without your guards?"

"Nothing's ever happened." His smile faltered. "I'm perfectly safe. It's the middle of the Imperial Capital . . ."

"Death is walking through the middle of the Imperial Capital, Highness. Or have you forgotten?"

The night wasn't nearly dark enough to hide the color rising in his cheeks. "*I'm* not a child . . ."

"Then why are you acting like one?" Rage lent an emphasis that bardic training could never match. "Unless you give me your word that you will *never* follow me again, I'm requesting an audience with His Majesty, your father, the moment we get back to the palace where I will tell him about the stupid way his youngest son has been risking his life."

His brows drew in and he stared at her in astonishment. She could almost see the infatuation beginning to fade. "You'd really do that? To me?"

"Your *word,* Highness."

He scuffed one foot against the ground, fiddled with a ring, chewed his lip, and finally sighed. "All right. You have my word."

"Thank you." She swung her instrument case up on her back with bruising force. How dare he make her responsible for his safety. "Come on, Highness, let's get you home."

He hesitated for a moment then fell into step beside her. "Your songs made me feel better," he offered tentatively.

Karlene glanced over at him and found that she wasn't immune to the hopeful look in his dark eyes. Annoyed at her weakness—she'd intended to remain furious with the young fool for a good long time—she muttered, "Thank you, Highness."

As they hurried toward the palace, a dog began to how. And then another.

The hair rose on the back of Karlene's neck. Except for the dogs, the streets were very quiet. Unwilling to even think that they were too quiet, she quickened her pace.

The fastest way back to the palace lay through a tangle of alleys and then into the wider, safer streets of the merchants' quarter. The moon was up and nearly full and the crumbling plaster that coated most of the tenement walls reflected a pale gray light. Alone, she wouldn't have hesitated, but with the prince in tow . . .

Don't be an idiot. There's nothing in there you can't deal with and you've got to get him home as quickly as possible.

She didn't realize they were being driven until they found themselves up against a dead end. Heart racing, differences forgotten, her fingers closed about the prince's wrist. "Do you feel it?"

"I don't feel anything but lost."

The undertone of terror in his voice snapped her gaze up to his face. The dark eyes showed white all around.

He nearly dragged her off her feet as he charged back the way they'd come. "Let's get out of here."

Three figures stood at the mouth of the alley; two young men in hoods much like the prince's and a very old man in a tattered robe.

The night grew darker.

"No."

It wasn't her denial, so it had to be the prince's.

The two young men shuffled forward.

She had to stop this. The safety of the prince was her responsibility. Fighting the black despair that threatened to overwhelm her, Karlene locked her gaze on the nearer of the two. She staggered and would have fallen had she not still been holding the prince's wrist. There wasn't anything to lock onto.

"You're dead." She could barely hear herself form the words over the screaming in her head.

"Yesss."

The worst of it was, it wasn't her screaming, it was him. Or what was left of him.

It was almost a relief when his companion slammed a crude club into the side of her skull. As she tumbled into darkness, she heard the prince cry out and then an ancient voice lovingly Command him to sleep.

Vree stood, shadow silent, and watched as Gyhard lowered himself into the bath.

They'd reach the Capital tomorrow. This was their last night on the road. Tomorrow, she'd be expected to start finding a path past walls and guards so that an Imperial prince could die. If it came to it, would she let him die to save her brother? Would she kill her brother to save him?

You can't put it off any longer, sister-mine.

I know. The night before she'd found a reprieve at the bottom of a green glass bottle of wine—which in itself was frightening for the amount of trust it implied. Had Gyhard suddenly come to his senses and wished to remove what he had to know was a certain threat, she wouldn't have been able to stop him.

*It's just a distraction, Vree, like all the others we've

used to get close to a target. It's a means to an end.
Nothing more.*

Her foot slid forward. She hastily snapped it back.
You're a little too slaughtering eager for this ...

Eager! His response ricocheted about in the confines of her skull. *And don't you think I have every
right to be eager? I want out, Vree! I want my body
back and I want the carrion eater who took it dead! I
want him dead now!*

Stop shouting!

*Then stop acting like a nervous virgin! He's not go-
ing to stay in that bath forever, you know.*

Teeth clenched, Vree strode into the bathing room,
dropped her robe, and stomped down the shallow marble stairs into the steaming water.

*Oh, *very* seductive.*

Sod off, Bannon.

"Head still bothering you?"

She peered at Gyhard through slitted eyes. "You
might say that, yes."

Over the last twelve days, his smile had become
more his own and less a twisted reflection of Bannon's. It had become harder to see her brother in most
of Gyhard's expressions; they were less extreme, less
self-absorbed, more self-involved.

What the slaughter does that mean?

Vree sank lower in the water. *If you don't back off,
I'm not going to do this.*

If you don't do this, Prince Otavas dies.

"Trying to drown yourself?" Gyhard asked, pushing
a wave toward her.

"Don't you start," she snarled, lifting her chin.

He shook his head. "Getting a little crowded in
there, is it? Frankly, I'm amazed you're still sane."

"Frankly," she mimicked, "so am I."

When he laughed, he didn't sound like Bannon at all.

He's not Bannon, I am. He's Gyhard or he's Aralt, but he's not me.

Aralt. Whom they'd been ordered to kill. And hadn't. No need to question desire. Not need to even admit desire. Just follow orders. Once again become a weapon in the Imperial Army's arsenal. A familiar detachment, missing since the moment the campfires of the Sixth Army had been swallowed by the darkness, snapped back into place.

In order to finish the job, she had to get past his guard and his guard was Bannon's body. *Which is not difficult to distract . . .*

That's what I've been trying to tell you.

Reading nuance in the tiny movements of muscles at temple and jaw, Gyhard could tell that they'd come to some kind of an agreement. He wondered if he should be worried. This was, after all, their last night on the road, their last night before they reached the Capital and began moving against the prince. Logic suggested that they would attempt to dislodge him once again.

He lifted himself up onto a shallow ledge where he could see his reflection in a highly polished brass disk and reached for the bowl of soft soap provided by the inn. Working up a lather on cheeks and chin, he considered the options of his unique companion. There were a number of drugs that might be used to loosen his hold on young Bannon's body, but he was certain Vree'd had no chance to acquire them even if she knew what they were.

"Here, let me." Vree crossed the heated pool and reached for the razor.

His fingers closed around hers. "I don't think so."

"If I'd decided to slit your throat, I wouldn't give

you so much of a chance to defend yourself." With a twist of her wrist, the movement both faster and stronger than he'd been able to anticipate, she slid both hand and blade out of his grip. "I'd do it in the night, when you were helpless, and I'd use something just a little more efficient than this." She swept a disdainful glance along the razor's edge then flicked her gaze upward to meet his. "And besides, you're still in my brother's body. While I'd cheerfully slit your throat, I won't cut his." When he hesitated, she added. "I've shaved that face before, you know."

"I wouldn't be at all surprised. But I am curious as to why you're offering to shave it now."

"Bannon says he's tired of looking at the nicks you leave on his chin."

That's good, Vree. Really good.

You just be ready to move the moment I've got him thinking of something else.

"And what is Bannon saying now?" Gyhard asked her, not taking his eyes off the blade.

"He's wondering if you ever thought of growing a mustache."

Smiling a little at her exasperation and her brother's vanity, Gyhard shook his head.

"Good. I keep telling him he'd look like shit in one." As she watched her target settle back into the water, suspicions evidently lulled, she felt her responses begin to quicken, her senses become hyperattuned. The water lapped like warm silk against her belly. She gently pushed Gyhard up against the wall. "Tilt your head back, rest it on the tiles."

"You won't be able to reach me from there," he pointed out as he obeyed.

"I know." In one smooth move, she straddled him,

the outer curve of his thighs pressing against the inner curve of hers.

His eyes snapped open and he lifted his head. "Is this how you shaved your brother?" His voice snagged slightly on the way out.

"We never had access to a bath this large." She bent forward and gently stroked her brother's cheek, Gyhard's cheek, Aralt's cheek, with the razor. "I just thought it would be easiest, but if you're uncomfortable . . ."

"No." He swallowed. "Stay." Eyes closed, he tilted his head back again.

Brilliant, Vree. Brilliant. You've got him.

Just be ready to move, she repeated. The sound of the steel scraping soap and whiskers off wet skin seemed to echo in the bathing room. If she listened hard enough, she thought she could hear even the heartbeat that throbbed beneath the steadying hand she'd rested on her brother's, on Gyhard's, on Aralt's chest.

A weapon.

A weapon didn't have to think, didn't have to reason, only had to do.

Laying a finger on the damp tip of his chin, she turned his head to one side.

She'd lost track of the number of times she'd distracted a guard for Bannon, or he one for her. This was just one more time.

The soft mat of hair in the center of his chest rose and fell more quickly as his breathing became labored. His hands opened and closed in the water—she could feel the currents he created swirl against her hips. Dropping her gaze, she nodded, satisfied, and leaned closer.

His eyes snapped open again and stared directly into hers.

Now, Bannon! She was completely unprepared for the rush of desire. . . .

They'd been naked together a dozen times since Gyhard had taken over her brother's body, but as his hands closed around her waist, they crossed the line where a simple lack of clothing became something more. Breathing raggedly, she moaned low in her throat as her arms snaked around his neck and their mouths pressed together. Desperately trying to hold onto reason, Vree kept her eyes open to give Bannon as much of a chance as possible. Her loss of control, her surrender finally to what she had wanted for so long, her failure to remain a weapon for his use, must not destroy his chance to regain his body.

Bannon . . .

They pulled apart and her hands began to dance over wet flesh as though they'd never touched it before. She marveled at its texture, at its resilience, at its sculpted beauty. She marveled at her own responses, at how the brush of a callused palm across a nipple resonated groin deep.

Which was when she realized that it wasn't her desire she felt, but Bannon's. Bannon. Whose desire to make love to his own body while in hers was so strong it was all she could feel. Bannon, whose desire was blinding him to the one thing he *should* want above all else.

Gyhard murmured her name into the curve of her throat, shifted his body . . .

"No." Her rage burned hotter than Bannon's desire. She twisted away to the other side of the bath, leaving Gyhard reaching for her desperately. "I said no."

He stared at her incredulously. His mouth opened and closed and then he managed a strangled, "Why?"

Struggling to steady her breathing, she turned on him. "Why? I'll tell you why. Bannon was supposed to use this, this seduction, to get back into his own body. You'd be distracted, he said. It doesn't make any slaughtering difference if you are because he's more distracted than you ever could be. Oh, he's having one slaughtering good time being me fucking him."

Vree, I . . .

"Shut up, Bannon." She heaved herself up out of the bath and jerked a drying cloth off the hook.

"What about me?" Grasping the shreds of his composure with both hands, Gyhard waded toward her. "I want you, not him."

Vree stared down at him through narrowed eyes, fingers clutching the warmed cloth tightly so he wouldn't see them tremble. "What about *me?*" she asked. "I know what Bannon wants, I know what you want; what about what *I* want?"

"All right." His voice picked up an edge. "What do you want?"

"I want . . ." The safety of an army around her. Knowing always exactly what was expected. Her place in the Empire secure and unchanging. Her brother; not always kind, not always careful, but hers. "I want what I had before you showed up."

"Even if I left your brother's body, you couldn't have that life again."

She closed her eyes for a moment, trying to block out the terrifying vision of life going on with no parameters she could understand. "I know."

"Learn to want something else."

"Like what? Like you? Like . . ." A quick gesture at the bath sketched in the details of what had almost happened.

His control regained, Gyhard shrugged. "Why not?"

Vree's upper lip curled into a sneer. "You destroyed my life."

"I changed it."

"Same thing."

He looked up at her for a long moment, then he sighed. "If that's what you believe," he said quietly, "then we have nothing further to discuss."

She nodded once and strode out of the room, not angry at him so much as at herself for being taken in by Bannon's plan.

Vree, I'm sorry!

I'm sorry, too, Bannon . . .

It took Gyhard a very long time to sleep that night. It helped only a little that the pair of Imperial assassins in the next room were no doubt having a sleepless night as well.

Over and over, he heard himself say, *I want you.*

Her.

Vree.

The twenty-year-old body he wore would've been willing to couple with any willing partner.

But he wanted her.

She was the first person he'd been honest with, been himself with, in over ninety years. Circumstances may have been responsible for that but it was a strong bond nevertheless. He was amazed that she'd managed not only to provide a refuge for her brother but to stay sane while doing it. He admired her speed and strength and grace, and he thrilled to the danger her presence denoted.

Removing the mirror from its case, he stared into the silvered glass. The expression on young Bannon's face, on the reflection of his face, seemed less cocky than it had.

"I think I may be falling in love with your sister," he told it softly. "If only . . ."

If only he didn't have to kill her.

Chapter Eight

Vree, I . . .

   I don't want to talk about it, Bannon.

   But . . .

   I said no. We'll go on. We'll find another way.

   And if there isn't another way?

Vree checked that both of her wrist daggers would release if needed, then pulled down the long, full sleeves of the silk shirt Aralt's gold had provided to cover the sheaths. Swinging her saddlebags up onto one shoulder, she strode out into the suite's main room, eyes squinted shut against the brilliant morning sun streaming in from the tiny private garden.

   Vree! What if there isn't another way?

Gyhard glanced up as she came in, noted the shadows around her eyes, and handed her a bowl of figs. "Still sane?" he asked neutrally.

   Vree! Answer me!

She chewed, swallowed, and picked another piece of sticky fruit out of the bowl. Turning it over in her fingers, she shrugged. "Sane? Well, nothing's changed."

   And it wasn't all my slaughtering fault either! You added your own hunger to the mix, sister-mine.

"About what almost happened last night." The memory brought a heated buzz that Gyhard ignored. "It was a good idea that could have worked, but I want you to know that you won't get that close again."

"Why?"

He blinked. "Why what?"

"Why do you want me to know?" Dropping into a chair, she poured herself a mug of beer out of the clay carafe on the low table.

"Uh . . ." He rubbed his jaw where the touch of the razor she'd wielded lingered. He'd intended not to even mention their brush with . . . well, with each other. "You're in a strange mood this morning," he observed instead of answering.

No shit.

Lifting her head, she met his gaze.

Her eyes, he noticed, were hard, unreadable; shields in front of her thoughts. The confusion that had lingered in them from the beginning was gone.

He stood. She stood with him. If he reached out his hand, he wouldn't quite be able to touch her. *Will you kill your brother to save a prince who means nothing to you?* He had glimpsed her strength last night and, for the first time, he thought she might.

"Perhaps . . ." His hand came up but he forced it back down again. "Perhaps I should have killed you, killed you both when I had the chance."

Vree nodded. "Perhaps you should have."

Vree!

If there's no other way, we'll all die together. At least we'll die with honor.

Could you kill me, sister-mine?

Her expression softened and, eyes locked on her face, Gyhard wondered why Bannon needed comfort.

Not and live after.

* * *

Vree! Soldiers! Riding up from the road!

I see them. Her heart slammed against her ribs and the large breakfast she'd just finished turned to stone in her stomach. *First Army. Nothing to do with us.* *Couldn't* be anything to do with them.

If Emo talked or they found Arro's body . . .

She dried her palms against her thighs. *Then we can expect a dagger in the night, you said that yourself.*

Sure, but first they have to find us, and all armies must assist an assassin loosed at a target.

First Army guards the Emperor. Even if Marshal Chela sent a courier—and that courier rode by without us noticing—the First Army is not going to leave His Imperial Majesty to search for us.

Yeah? Well, they're heading this way and they look pissed.

Vree stepped back behind a stone lattice and called herself several kinds of fool for leaving Gyhard alone in the inn. While she could easily slip off the small terrace, down the lane to the stables and away, five armed and armored soldiers of the First Army now stood between her and Bannon's body.

Shit. Shit. Shit.

Bannon, shut up.

The captain dismounted. "If any of the honored guests try to leave," she barked, dropping her reins to trail on the ground. "Take them alive." Lips set in a thin line she straight-armed her way through the carved doors and into the inn.

Four left. If it came to it, she could kill two easily. The two remaining would be warned and moving. Not so easy but not impossible either. Trouble was, that left the captain in the inn with . . .

Vree, listen!

Like most expensive inns the Zepher Garden was set well back from the South Road, a row of lindens blocking the sounds and smells of common travelers from the delicate sensibilities of its wealthy clientele. Wafting through the trees came the unmistakable sound of bellowed orders and civilian shouts of outrage.

You're right, sister-mine. There's something bigger going on than us. She allowed Bannon to turn her back around to face the four soldiers waiting by the inn door. *They don't want to be here. They want to be out cracking skulls with their buddies. Whatever's going down, they don't think it has anything to do with this place.*

Every impatient scowl, every unnecessary jerk at the reins clearly said they wanted to be elsewhere. *The one on the right looks like he dressed in the dark, his tunic's on inside out. And all three men need a shave.*

Why would the Emperor send the First Army out of the Capital in the middle of the night?

Looks like we're about to find out.

"Captain, I assure you of my complete cooperation and I am of course shocked and horrified by this attack against the most gracious Imperial Family, but I also assure you that no one involved in such a distressing incident would ever dare to come here." The Zepher Garden's portly owner patted the silver brooch that secured the folds of his mantle on one rounded shoulder with a plump, white hand. "My loyalty to the Emperor is well known. Why, Senator Eraco, who as I'm sure you are aware is very close to the Emperor, keeps a suite of rooms here."

A senator. A member of the Emperor's council. Rumor suggested that the people of the Empire chose the senators they felt would best represent them, but Vree had never chosen one or known anyone who had so it was a rumor she discounted. The presence of the senator did, however, explain the presence of the captain; rank demanded rank.

"I am aware of your loyalty, citizen." A muscle jumped in the captain's jaw as she ushered the innkeeper out onto the terrace. "But I still must speak with those of your people who live in the town and spent the night at their homes."

"None of my people would be involved in such a . . ."

"Of course not. But they might have heard something or seen something and my orders were to speak with them." The captain's tone held a clear opinion of those orders and Vree almost smiled.

"This establishment is, of course, too far from the road for any of my guests to have heard anything."

"I know." Her reply was as blunt and uncompromising as a blow to the head and the innkeeper subsided into a petulant silence.

"Captain . . ."

Vree's pulse began to pound again as her brother walked out of the inn, Gyhard banished by the familiar voice calling out as it had a hundred, a thousand times over the years.

". . . if the stablehands could bring our horses when they come for questioning, my sister and I could be on our way and out of yours."

What is he so furious about? she wondered. Anger radiated off of him in almost visible waves.

Surprisingly, the captain seemed to approve of the emotional excess. "Go ahead." She jerked her head at the innkeeper who rolled his eyes but padded off to find his major domo and send the order to the stable. "You said your sister was out here?" she continued.

Head jerking from side to side, grace lost in his

rage, Gyhard glanced around. Vree froze, trusting the pattern of shadow to keep her hidden.

"Vireyda!"

It was a summons meant to be obeyed.

*What is going *on?** Bannon demanded.

How the slaughter should I know? Hands carefully away from her body, she stepped out onto the terrace and crossed to Gyhard's side. Fully aware that her accent would deny whatever story "her brother" had spun, she merely raised a questioning brow.

Gyhard's eyes blazed as he turned to face her and his fingers kept curling and uncurling as though he were squeezing a captive throat. "Prince Otavas," he growled, "has been kidnapped."

Thumbs shoved behind the thick leather of her sword belt, the captain watched the brother and sister trot their horse down the lane to the South Road. While she had no doubt of their uninvolvement—his anger had been too slaughtering real—there was something about the woman she didn't like. Something familiar in the way she moved touched an icy finger to the captain's spine.

The resemblance chewed at the edges of memory.

Who do I know who moves like that? Whoever it was, she didn't feel good about the similarities. Perhaps it might be best to ask them a few more questions. She opened her mouth to call them back.

"Captain? The servants are gathered."

Jiir take it anyway. She spun on one heel and scowled at the whispering knots of men and women crowded onto the the terrace. *It's not like I don't have enough on my slaughtering plate.* Dragging off her helm, she rubbed her other hand over the sweat-damp bristles of her hair. "All right, which of you lot lives along the road?"

"That's *all* she told you?"

"What was I supposed to do," Gyhard ground out through clenched teeth, "torture her for more information? The prince was kidnapped by three men—two young, one old—late last night. That's all I know." He snorted. "It looks like I'll be wearing this body for a while longer."

I guess we don't die right away, sister-mine.

A trickle of sweat rolling down her side, Vree clutched at Bannon's comment. It could be the perfect explanation for the sudden surge of relief so intense she could barely breathe around it.

"So what do we do?" She hadn't intended to speak aloud.

Assuming the question was meant for him, Gyhard's muscles tightened across his back. "I don't know." He couldn't remember the last time he'd been so angry. His gelding, responding to his mood, began to buck.

He's taking this personally, isn't he? Bannon snickered as Gyhard fought to control his horse. *Like someone kidnapped Prince Otavas just to piss him off.*

All around them, the men and women who lived and worked along the South Road put homes and businesses back together. The unit sent to search the area had done so with a thoroughness that could only be found in those who'd been dragged from their beds in the middle of the night and told they'd been derelict in their duty. Outside the occasional door or window, piles of furniture and clothing lay in tumbled heaps.

Gyhard chopped a wave at the chaos around them. "Capital's half a day's ride away; even if they started at midnight, how could the army get this far so quickly?"

"One unit searches while the others ride ahead, then they leapfrog each other down the road." At his questioning look, Vree shrugged. "Standard search procedure. It doesn't take long when you don't care about civil law."

"Why the blazes are they searching along the Great Roads anyway? Only an idiot would grab an Imperial prince and take such an obvious route away from the Capital."

"It's a big empire. They have to start somewhere. If you're so concerned about His Imperial Highness, why don't you try and find him?"

Vree! What are you doing?

If he goes looking for the prince—if we go looking for the prince—we'll gain more time to get him out of your body.

Yeah, and if he settles for second best, he'll transfer into someone else and I'll get my body back. If he's not going to kill the prince, why should we care? His thoughts tumbled frantically over hers.

If he settles for second best, he won't need our help anymore. The moment that happens he'll try to kill us. Bannon, we're the best. If we think of the prince as a target, we'll find him. But it'll take time, the time we need to come up with a way to get Gyhard out of your body.

And if we don't get him out of my body, we kill him and then ourselves to protect the prince? Vree, honorably dead is still dead.

But if we do get Gyhard out of your body and then we save His Highness we can ask for an Imperial pardon. Everything can be like it was . . .

Why is it always all or nothing with you, sister-mine? She thought she heard him sigh. *Go ahead. Convince him if you can.*

"You're not listening to me, are you?" Gyhard snapped. "I said that finding the prince and rescuing him would still end in my possessing him."

Vree stared at him for a long moment, then she locked her gaze back between her horse's ears. "We'll go over that wall when we come to it."

He'd be on them in three days, four at the most, his mounts supplied by Imperial way stations set along the roads. He rode the horses couriers rode, bred for speed and endurance, their pace slowed only by the needs of his hunt.

He'd learned to ride only when he gained his commission and it became an unavoidable necessity. While an assassin's strength and agility had made the skill an easy one to acquire, he'd never thought much of the beasts. Years later, he still didn't think much of a creature that needed more cosseting than any of the solders under his command, and he'd often been heard to growl that, if it came to it, they make a tasty sausage. Tastier with a little red sauce.

But his targets—however, wherever, whenever they learned—were riding. As forage suitable for horses had long since been stripped from around the Great Roads—especially roads in the southern part of the Empire, that meant they were also stopping every night at inns with stables in order to feed their mounts. That means they could be tracked. Easily.

To Neegan's surprise, they appeared to be heading exactly where Aralt's servants had indicated—straight up the South Road to the Capital. And not very quickly at that. They either thought themselves safe from pursuit or believed that, together, they could handle anyone sent after them. Under normal circumstances either would be an intelligent assumption. Blind luck, nothing more, had put the goatherd in the discarded assassin's blacks so close to the passing army and Neegan himself, in all the Seven Armies, held the only chance of their death.

He had watched them from the beginning. He knew their weaknesses and their strengths. He'd adjusted their training. He'd pulled strings to get them in his company and then in his command. He'd given them everything he could. He'd sent them out after targets that no one else could hope to hit because he believed in them. He'd even talked—if either or both survived long enough—of personally supporting their commissions as Chela had supported his.

They had made him look like a fool.

How could they? How dared they!

"Hey! Watch where yer going', asshole!"

Angry betrayal still dominating his thoughts, Neegan glanced down at the burly young woman pressed up against the stone railing of the bridge. His horse had crowded her but she had sufficient room. He rode on.

A beefy hand grabbed at his ankle. "Hey! I'm talkin' to you! You can't just push me aside, then keep goin' like nuthin' happened."

The grip on his leg got his complete attention. He stared at her fingers, trying to remember the last time he'd been so accosted. The woman was either crazy or crazy drunk. "Let go of my leg." His husky voice held a warning.

"Or you'll what, little man?" Ready for a fight, she tightened her hold and tried to yank him from the saddle.

Then he realized that although he wore a uniform, she had no idea of what he was. He felt a brief pity for her, rapidly overtaken by annoyance, and wondered if Vree and Bannon had met such ignorance. And then he remembered, as his hand snapped down and at least one of the small bones in the woman's wrist shattered, that they had given up their uniforms and all the rights that went with them.

Ignoring the howls of pain, he rode down the arc of the bridge and onto the north shore of Kiaz.

His targets hadn't stopped on the south shore although Kiaz boasted a multitude of inns along the road. If he found no trace of them on the north shore, he'd have to check with the bargekin to determine if they'd taken to the river. He would not allow them to escape. They'd pay for their betrayal.

"Here, at Evion's we respect the privacy of our guests."

"The child who takes the horse," Neegan husked, the scar on his throat tinted pale gray with the dust of three days' hard riding, "has already told me they were here." The commander laid both hands flat on the marble counter and stared up at the tall young man behind it. "But I require additional information."

"The army has no jurisdiction here." Gently patting an oiled curl back into place, he stared disdainfully down his nose at the other man. "We know the value of discretion at Evion's. Now, if there's anything *else* I can do for you?" His tone made the expected answer very clear.

Teeth clenched, Neegan leaned forward, his fingertips pressing grimy ovals into the highly polished counter. "Do you know what a black sunburst means?"

The young man glanced at Neegan's insignia and frowned. "My family paid my deferment, so I'm afraid I know nothing about the army." *Nor do I want to,* his tone added. "Now, as Evion's will not divulge information about its guests, I'm afraid that you . . ."

"There he is! That's the one what did it!"

Wearing nearly identical expressions of distaste, Neegan and the clerk turned together as the burly woman from the bridge—her left wrist bound, the arm in a sling—led a city guard into the inn.

"Him! The short one in the uniform! Bloody army. Think they can walk all over citizens what pay for 'em. Do yer duty, guardsman!"

Her boot soles ringing against the intricate pattern of small tiles, the guard strode across the atrium. "We have a complaint of assault," she declared neutrally to the commander. "This citizen says you broke her wrist."

Neegan nodded almost imperceptibly. "I did."

The guard frowned, recognizing authority, uncertain of how to react. "Imperial law," she began but broke off abruptly as Neegan turned enough for her to get a good look at his uniform. She stared at the black sunburst and slowly moved both hands away from her weapons.

"I am on target and she attempted to detain me," Neegan explained.

"What's he whisperin' about?" the woman demanded, scurrying forward. "Is he tryin' to deny it?"

"Shut up!" The guard spun about on one heel, scowling. "You're lucky he only broke your wrist, you fool. He could have killed you!"

"That little runt?" the protest echoed in the large open room. "Not likely!"

"That little . . ." All at once realizing that repeating the insult, even sarcastically, might not be a good idea, the guard began again. "That *man* is an Imperial Army

Officer *and* an assassin and you attempted to detain him."

Ruddy face suddenly pale, the woman stumbled back a step. "I didn't do no detainin'," she whined, her frantic gaze landing everywhere but on Neegan. He wondered if she thought that by looking at him, she'd release an attack. "I just touched him like. Barely touched him. I didn't know . . ."

"I don't care." The guard jerked her around and shoved her toward the door. "Get out. Go home. And keep your touching to yourself in the future." Not until the woman had scuttled out the door, did she turn back to Neegan.

"If there's any way I can help, Commander," she offered nervously.

"No."

Recognizing a dismissal, she sketched a salute— although the army had no actual authority over the civilian guard—and quickly left the inn.

The tall young man swallowed, hard, but his eyes gleamed. "An Imperial assassin?"

Neegan merely stared up at him.

"And the two you were asking about?"

The silence answered.

"I see. Well, under those circumstances, I, that is, Evion's will be glad to assist you in any way we can."

They had stayed in the most expensive suite in the house.

They had eaten well. Some of the food Neegan had never heard of but Bannon had apparently ordered it by name.

They had both bathed.

They were richly but conservatively dressed.

They had plenty of money and they left a generous gratuity behind them.

"I'm sure you know about their servants . . . ?"

"Tell me anyway." Neegan had known Vree and
Bannon all their lives and none of this made any sense.
Made as little sense as them deserting in the first place.

They were continuing to the Capital, a server had
overheard them discuss it. *"But she don't call him,
Bannon, sir. No, she doesn't. Calls him Gyhard."* At
other, lesser inns, he'd heard they didn't act like
brother and sister. He thought he knew what that
meant, thought it the most likely answer to Marshal
Chela's why.

He didn't care why.

As he turned to go, his target more clearly delineated for the blade, the tall young man repeated almost
coquettishly, "An Imperial assassin. Are you as good
as they say?"

The blade of the dagger went through the hoop of
filigreed gold that hung from his left ear on a slender
chain and embedded itself in the painted plaster wall
behind him, the crosspiece catching and dragging his
head around, pinning it in place.

Neegan reached up and pulled his dagger from the
wall. "Yes," he said softly. "Thank you for your assistance."

Although the morning's traffic flowed around the
high, two-wheeled cart moving east along the West
Road, no one seemed to actually notice it. Heads
turned away and minds fought against chill darkness as
it clattered past.

The cart had been designed to take supplies into the
heart of the Capital where horses were not permitted.
Even fully loaded, the oversized wheels made it easy
to pull and the wrapped pole that joined the shafts offered a solid grip for one or two.

Within the shafts, Aver and Otanon had been running without rest since just after midnight.

He squinted up at the sky and then around at the rest of his family. The sun would soon be directly overhead and the day was growing hot. He should have the cousins pull the cart off the road so they could find shade and sit out the midday heat. He would not neglect his children just because love had returned.

"I'm taking you home," he murmured, stroking a strand of dark hair off the pale face cradled on his lap. "We'll start again, you and I, right where we left off. We'll be happy, you'll see."

Caught in desperate dreams, Prince Otavas stirred but couldn't wake.

The cart jerked over the corner of a paving stone heaved slightly out of place, bounced twice, and crashed to the left as the wheel popped off the end of the axle. Thrown violently against the side of the cart, he did what he could to protect his precious burden, then, as the cousins continued to run, found enough voice to yell, **"Stop!"** Shaken but unhurt, he had Wheyra and Kait unhook the back wall and he lowered himself carefully down to the road.

He sent Otanon to pick up the wheel and called the others to his side. "I know nothing about these things," he told them. "But without the cart, how will we get my heart home?"

While the others stared blankly at nothing, Wheyra, her baby's tiny corpse cradled against her chest, dragged her gaze from the axle to the wheel to the old man. "Los . . . cotter p . . . in," she said. Although death had robbed her voice of most of its expression, the little that remained clearly suggested the solution was so obvious it shouldn't have needed mentioning.

* * *

Traffic became increasingly chaotic the closer to the Capital they rode. The youngest son of the Emperor might have been snatched away in the night, but commerce continued. After thirteen days, Vree had thought herself comfortable in the saddle, able to deal with anything that might come up. She was wrong.

Vree! There's a wagon coming right at you! Watch out for those kids! Who let that slaughtering chicken loose!

Stop flicking my eyes around.

You're not watching!

And you're not helping!

The Capital grew larger, dominating the horizon. At the end of the South Road, one of the city's seven double arched gates gaped wide enough to admit a pair of wagons side by side. Behind the wall, orange-tiled roofs climbed a gentle slope, drawing the eye inward and upward to the domes and spires of a dozen temples and then finally to the jewel at the apex of the city. The cluster of buildings that made up the Imperial Palace shone brilliantly white under the midday sun. Here and there, a flash of gleaming metal marked a polished copper roof and Vree thought she could see the flicker of a hundred flags.

All her life, she'd heard stories about the Capital, but none of them had prepared her for its immensity. It was larger than she'd imagined. Larger, she suspected, than anyone *could* imagine. And for the palace to be so clearly visible at such a distance . . .

The garrison and the town besides could fit into one of the palace courtyards.

Twice, Bannon agreed.

As they rode between the first of the tombs, traffic became even worse. They were part of a solid mass of people heading toward the city, caught up and carried along, their horses held to the pace around them but adding the slight advantage of height. The noise level grew—almost every conversation concerned the missing prince—and so did the smell.

You could close your eyes and know the size of this place by the stench alone, Bannon muttered.

Hovels and shacks of every description leaned against the outer wall. Naked children peered around the edges of elegant tombs while their elder siblings searched for opportunities on the road.

At the gate, years of training took over, and Vree studied the entrance to the Capital the way she'd study any city she might have to one day enter under arms. The wall was about twenty feet high and about ten feet broad at the bottom. Built of concrete rubble strengthened with bonding courses of ironstone, faced with flint and finished with chamfered stone bases, it still looked able to withstand the crash of troops against it but the years had definitely opened the way to more subtle attacks.

Lots of good handholds, Bannon observed. *And I don't think they've got guards stationed in those towers.*

There're two by the gate.

So what?

Maybe they think this place is just too big to attack.

Feeling as though the city were looming over her, Vree could only agree.

To her surprise, the Capital became much less overwhelming once they passed through the gate and turned onto a street that followed the inner arc of the wall. But the people ... In the Sixth Province, in the south of the Empire, there were few variations on dark hair and dark eyes and cinnamon brown to deep olive skin. Even though as an assassin she'd had contact with the world outside the army, Vree was used to people who essentially looked and dressed the same.

Tall, short, pale, dark, fat, thin, long hair, cropped hair, no hair. A group of people—impossible to tell if they were men or women or both—draped head to toe in multicolored flowing scarves, drifted across the road in front of them, their gauzy clothing making it appear they were pushed by an errant breeze. A hugely fat man, a monkey balanced on one shoulder, elbowed his way through the crowd oblivious to the ill will trailing him. A woman, no taller than a child, stomped along, chin thrust out, both hands resting on belt knives as though daring anyone to mention her size.

The language of the Empire predominated although the liquid syllables of the south had been replaced by a harder sound.

Vree recognized a Beltrain mercenary, the gold rings of a dozen successful campaigns glittering in his beard, and watched the stately progress of a pair of Ilagian merchants, their patrician features and ebony skin making the rest of the crowd seem ill-defined in comparison. A yellow-haired couple, spitting guttural syllables at each other, had skin so pale she was certain she could see blood move beneath it. A laughing cluster of young men and women had dyed their left arms green. At least, Vree assumed it was dye.

Bright colors turned the kilts, trousers, robes, shirts, tunics, mantles, cloaks, hats, hoods, and bare skin into an almost painful assault on the eyes.

"He's a holy man," Gyhard grunted, following her line of sight.

Crimson and blue strips circling his body, gray and white feathers stuck into the tangled mass of his hair, he leaped from one foot to the other, painted genitals bouncing about in a separate dance of their own.

Vree tore her gaze away. "He's a lunatic," she muttered.

Gyhard had been looking forward to Vree's reaction to the Capital, had been looking forward to seeing it freshly through her eyes. The loss of the prince changed all that. "We'll be leaving the horses at a stable up ahead. They're not permitted any farther into the city than this." He glanced over at her and noted her expression for the first time. "Are you going to be all right?" His tone dared her not to be.

She snorted. "I can climb into a dark room over the bleeding body of its guardian with no idea of what's waiting for me inside. I can handle this."

"Good." Pulling his gelding's head around, Gyhard deftly maneuvered past a cart of spilled cabbages and its cursing owner.

Glaring an urchin away from her stirrup, Vree followed.

So now what?

I don't know. Vree swallowed the last mouthful of beer in her tankard and covertly watched her glowering companion from over the rim.

So ask.

He doesn't know either.

I thought you were going to convince him to go after the prince.

Yeah, right. He hasn't listened to a word I've said all day.

They'd spent the afternoon collecting a hundred different fragments of rumor ...

"The foreign singer who allowed the prince to be taken'll be beheaded for treason."

"*Lady Death herself run off with the prince and struck the singer woman down as a rival, like.*"

"*The prince is dead, that's why no one saw him taken outa the city.*"

"*If his Majesty's searchin' outside the city, then His Highness ain't in the city.*"

. . . and the evening sitting in the common room of a grimy inn eating food that could have been prepared by army cooks. Rumor had it that the truth eventually ended up at the Iron Dog. Vree broke a splinter of wood off the edge of the scarred table and dug at a piece of gristle caught in her teeth. Rumor, she decided, didn't know what the slaughtering blazes it was talking about.

"If that singer woman says they were dead, I believe her." Across the room, a very drunk woman in the uniform of a city guard slapped her palm against the table. "I seen the dead up and walkin', I tell you."

If not for Gyhard's reaction, Vree would've ignored her; one more rumor that made no sense in a city of rumors that made no sense.

He looks like he's seen a ghost.

Or heard one.

Surrounded by a jeering crowd, the guard lurched up onto her feet, eyes narrowed and jaw thrust out. "I'm tellin' you, there ain't no one robbing them tombs! Them bodies are walkin' out on their own!"

"And then walkin' off with the prince?" someone called.

"Why not? Singer woman says the two young guys was dead!"

"She got hit on the head," someone else yelled.

"I didn't."

"Yeah, but you ain't got enough brains to piss with."

Hands flat on the table, she leaned forward until her

nose nearly touched the nose of the last man to speak. "I don't like you," she growled.

He stood. She straightened with him until she stared up into his face a good six inches above her own. "The dead don't walk," he told her, daring her to argue.

She thought about it for a moment, then self-preservation overruled the beer. Scooping her helm up off the bench, she staggered for the door, muttering, "I know what I seen."

Hot fingers closed around her wrist. Vree stared from Gyhard's hand to his face. His eyes were so completely expressionless that if not for his heated grip she would've thought he'd abandoned Bannon's body and left it empty.

"I have to talk to that guard," he said quietly.

Vree put down her tankard and shook her head. "Look, you don't believe . . ."

But, quite obviously, he did.

They caught up to her before she got very far.

"Why should I tell you anythin'?" she asked, spitting into the gutter. "Yer just like them. Like all of them. Got busted down a rank 'cause I told what I saw. Got laughed at. You heard 'em, laughing. Well, no more. The two of you can just take yerselves outa my way."

"*I* believe you," Gyhard insisted through clenched teeth.

"Sod off." Shoving her helm down on her head, she started to push by.

Gyhard nodded toward the dark crease of an alley. "Vree." A moment later, he picked up the fallen helm and followed.

Her eyes wide shadows in the pale oval of her face, the guard stared at the woman kneeling over her. "I ain't never seen anyone move so fast," she panted, terror chasing the alcohol from her voice. "Yer hurtin' me."

Vree moved the blade a fraction of an inch. "I know. Remember it."

He'd been uncertain of what would happen when he'd given the silent order, uncertain whether she'd even follow it, but years of army training had apparently made some responses instinctive. He stepped over the sprawl of legs and squatted by the guard's right shoulder where he could see her face. Vree shifted her own position slightly to give him room, and it suddenly occurred to him that perhaps it had nothing to do with army training. An argument could be raised that they were working as a team.

A team. He didn't have time for that now, not now, so he pushed it away. "Tell me what you saw," he said softly.

"What I saw . . ."

"You said, you saw the dead up and walking."

Her gaze locked on Vree's face, she swallowed and told him everything.

When she finished, making allowances for darker skin, Gyhard was the paler of the two. "How old was the old man?"

"Real old."

"You're certain that you heard singing?"

"Yeah, but not with words." For the first time she dared to turn her head enough to look at him. "Slaughter it. You *do* believe me."

"I said I did."

"Well, you'll excuse me fer not believin' you."

What a load of crap.

Are you sure?

Dead men don't walk, sister-mine.

Two lives don't live in one body.

It's not the same thing.

Vree stood as Gyhard did, daggers disappearing as she moved. *Are you sure?* she asked again. *Because I'm not.* She could feel Gyhard trembling even though she couldn't see it. "What now?"

"I think we'd best go talk to that foreign singer."

"We don't know where she is."

"If she was knocked unconscious late last night, she's still at the Healers' Hall." He started out of the alley. "You may have to get us past a guard."

Oh no! One whole guard! Can we possibly do it?

Shut up, Bannon. She fell into step at Gyhard's side. "We'll manage."

Lying where she'd been thrown, one finger lightly resting on the bead of blood marking her throat, the guard thanked any gods who might be listening that she'd been forgotten and watched, without moving, until the two strangers disappeared into the night.

Chapter Nine

The two dead men who stood at the foot of her bed implored her with their eyes and pleaded with writhing arms and hands that clutched at nothing she could see. Their need engulfed her and Karlene fought for breath under its desperate weight.

"I don't know what you want," she gasped.

She could hear them screaming although their mouths were closed. The screams became a Song and just for an instant she thought she understood. Then the instant passed.

Flesh began to decay and fall from the ivory bone beneath. Bits of fingers dropped onto the blanket covering her legs. Even while they rotted, both men continued to beg for her aid. Bone followed flesh, crumbling to dust as she watched until only the eyes remained, burning in a pair of shadows.

Terror closing her throat, she struggled to answer them. "I don't know what you want ..."

"We want to talk."

Not the voice of nightmare but the voice of a living man. Sleep fled and the shadows at the foot of the bed gained substance. Head throbbing, Karlene lifted herself up onto her elbows, squinting in the mix of moon and starlight that poured through the small, arched window high above her. "Who ... ?"

The shadow on the left stepped forward into definition, becoming a young woman; sleekly muscled, not
very tall. Her delicate, almost waiflike features were at
odds with both her expression and the deadly, liquid
way she moved. She was beautiful the way poisonous
snakes were beautiful—the certain knowledge that they
could kill without a second thought, without regret,
adding to their glamour. As she came around the corner of the bed, Karlene realized that something was
very, very wrong.

Every instinct told her two people were approaching
where she could only see one.

She'd been told by the healer that under no circumstances should she use her bardic abilities, that the
blow she'd taken could have easily killed her, but
when the young woman lifted her head, moonlight re-
flecting for an instant in her eyes, Karlene caught her
gaze and held it. **"Stop right there!"**

Bannon! I can't move!

Try harder!

*I *am* trying harder!* Vree struggled against the
compulsion, but her feet had rooted to the floor. She
felt Bannon's consciousness race through her body,
then surge to the front of her mind.

Let me take it, sister-mine . . .

They had learned to trust each other in a hundred, in
a thousand situations where to hesitate meant death.
Vree sucked in a deep breath and, as she released it,
gave Bannon control.

She felt herself dive toward the bed, the familiar
weight of a leather-wrapped hilt in one hand. She saw
the blonde woman jerk away and discovered she could
move again. But it was Bannon who held the blade to

an ivory column of throat and Bannon's cry of freedom
that echoed inside her skull.

The kiss of the dagger's point having successfully
banished all other emotions save fear, Karlene pressed
back against the pillow, oblivious to the red heat
pounding at her temples. *I hope I'm still dreaming . . .*

You are a fool, Gyhard i'Stevana. A fool! How could
he not have realized that the foreign singer was a bard?
I've spent too many years in the Empire. Since his first
body had died, he'd been near only one other bard and,
although untrained and emotionally crippled, Kars had
known what he was, had sensed the reforged connection between his life and the physical shell he wore. He
could only assume that this bard would know him as
well and the thought of that recognition paralyzed him.

He'd done nothing to prevent Vree's capture by the
bard's Command and, a heartbeat later when Vree
shook the Command off and dove for the bed, he continued to do nothing.

He'd watched Vree closely for the last thirteen days.
He watched her now and tried to understand the small
changes in her bearing, in the way her fingers wrapped
around the hilt of the dagger, in the curve of her spine.

Vree, please . . .
No.

He held on. She thrust herself past him. He pushed
her back.

I won't. I won't go. I can't go.
*This is *my* body, Bannon! Mine!*

Facial muscles twisted, teeth snapped together, a
shudder ran from neck to ankles but the hand holding
the knife never moved.

* * *

Karlene, sensing the battle, rolled her eyes toward the second shadow. A male copy of the woman who had her pinned to the braided straw mattress; his features fey instead of gamine, the danger he exuded was more subtle than a sudden death. The woman held two lives. The man held his at arm's length. A day ago—or perhaps more accurately a night ago—she would have cried *abomination* and run. But she'd seen the dead up and walking and knowing they were dead, and all reactions had to be measured against that.

"What do you want?" she whispered.

Fighting free of the memories that held him, Gyhard stepped forward. "Exactly what I said we wanted. To talk."

"I'm to talk with a knife at my throat?"

"You'll have to excuse my companion." His tone managed to hold both threat and amusement. "She's an assassin and has only one response to perceived obstacles."

An assassin. Enclosed as they were within the city walls, the First Army had no assassins—they made the citizens of the Capital far too nervous. While Karlene had never met one, she'd certainly heard of them; dark songs called them Jiir's blades and insisted they were safely sheathed by the army. The assassin bending over her looked neither sheathed nor safe.

Following the bard's train of thought with little difficulty, Gyhard smiled slightly. "I wouldn't twitch so much if I were you."

"I'm not twitching." Shallow breathing kept her skin from pressing against the blade. "It's just that I've never heard they were able to overcome Command."

"Usually, they aren't." Gyhard saw no reason to tell the bard what he suspected must have happened and surrender a potentially useful advantage. *She's not one assassin, she's two.* "Give me your word you won't . . . Sing out, and I'll have her release you."

"My word?"

"That's right."

As she had little choice, Karlene gave it, fully aware that even if she called for help she'd be dead before it arrived. It was a strange feeling; in Shkoder bards were honored, in the Empire they were protected by an Imperial decree, but neither honor nor the Emperor would—could—save her now. She was staring death in the face—and she'd never imagined death would be beautiful. *And this is* not *the time to start writing love songs . . .*

"Vree."

Vree straightened. Bannon returned the knife to its sheath.

"Vree? Are you all right?"

Bannon pivoted to face him. Vree spoke. "Don't you mean, am I still sane?"

"Are you?"

Bit by bit, Vree pried up Bannon's will and thrust him to the edges of her consciousness. He was her brother, and if honor demanded she sacrifice him, she would die as well, but she would give him no more of her life than he already had. Her strength surprised them both. Regaining control, she saw Gyhard studying her, a worried frown creasing the bridge of his nose, and realized she hadn't answered his question.

Vree, please, don't . . .

Was she sane? "Yes." But the word came out sounding like she intended to say, *For now.*

Karlene glanced from one side of the bed to the other, wishing that the light was a bit better or that pain hadn't painted quite so many starbursts across her vision. While the physical similarities of her unexpected visitors suggested brother and sister, the tension stretching between them did not. Curiosity aroused in spite of common sense, she shoved the pillow up behind her and slowly, carefully pulled herself into a sitting position. "What did you want to talk about?" she asked, as though having an assassin hold a knife to her throat was a common occurrence.

"I want to know everything you remember about the old man who took the prince last night." His eyes locked on the bard's face, Gyhard sat down on the stone bench built into the wall of the narrow room. Resting his forearms on his thighs, he leaned forward and repeated, "Everything."

On the other side of the room, Vree stepped back from the bed. If anything happened, she wanted space to react. Without looking directly at either of the other two people in the room, she watched them both. The woman in the bed was in pain and no physical threat, but Vree would not be caught by her voice again. Gyhard had lost both his amused detachment and his earlier anger. He didn't *want* to know everything the foreign singer could tell him, he *needed* to know; she could almost see that need rolling off him like smoke.

"There were *three* men," Karlene reminded him.

"I'm only interested in one of them."

"The other two were dead."

"I don't care."

To her astonishment, Karlene heard the truth in his voice. Unlike the others, who didn't believe her—even Gabris had blamed the blow to the head—this mysterious intruder believed but honestly didn't care. Why not? Worrying at it, she slipped into a light trance and triggered a full recall.

Gyhard had forgotten about Bardic Memory. Detail after inarguable detail dragged him toward only one possible conclusion. As the bard's low voice described the way the years had destroyed beauty, he closed his eyes and saw the incredulous smile of a young man who'd always believed that no one could love him and had just discovered he was wrong.

It had been ninety years since he rode down out of those mountains. Kars was dead. Had to be dead.

"Gyhard?"

He had no idea how long ago the bard had stopped talking. Opening his eyes, he stared across the room at Vree.

She took a step toward him, drawn by the misery and confusion on her brother's, on Gyhard's face. Then she stopped as he buried it. Had she not known the features so well, she might have missed seeing the shadow that remained. "You know that man."

"Yes."

Pain forgotten, Karlene jerked forward, crushing a double handful of knitted, cotton blanket. "What does he want with Prince Otavas?"

Gyhard shrugged, the motion too deliberately nonchalant. "I don't know. He's insane."

"Is His Highness in danger?"

"*. . . kill you so that you'll never leave me.*" Gyhard brushed aside the voice of memory. "His Highness is probably already dead."

"Dead." She turned the word over for a moment as though trying to recognize it. Then, like a physical blow, horror replaced the growing sorrow. "Dead like the two . . ."

"Yes."

Karlene swallowed, once, twice, and finally forced her voice past the lump in her throat. "You've got to go to the Emperor with this."

"The Emperor?" Gyhard's brows rose as he leaned

back against the wall. "Shall we go to the Emperor, Vree?" he asked.

Vree struggled to make sense of what she'd just heard. "The prince is dead but not dead?"

"That's right. His body has been killed, and then his kigh has been stuffed back into it."

"Kigh?" The foreign word fell out of her mouth; a click and an exhalation. "Like Bannon?" If the prince was dead, there would be no Imperial pardon. But if the prince was like Bannon . . .

Gyhard nodded approvingly. "Very like. Except that Bannon isn't dead. Isn't aware he's dead. And hasn't been forced to remain in a dead and decaying body." He spread his hands and smiled sardonically. "Bannon can leave any time."

"Kigh?" Karlene repeated, ignoring everything else that had been said, her racing thoughts outdistancing the pain. "The fifth kigh the healers speculate about . . ." She swung around toward Vree. "You have two kigh!"

As it wasn't a question, Vree saw no point in responding.

Then Karlene made another connection although it took her a moment to find her voice. "How does this old man compel the kigh back into the body?"

"He Sings."

"No."

"Afraid so." Gyhard was enjoying her reaction.

"I know all the Songs that name the bards." The air in the room seemed to have gotten thinner. It was hard to catch her breath. "He isn't a bard. He can't be a bard."

"A bard?" Vree had no idea what they were talking about.

"This is a bard." Gyhard gestured at the bed. "She Sings to the spirits and they listen."

Vree's eyes widened until they hurt. "Sings to the spirits of the dead?"

"No, there's only one bard that I know of who can do that." Apparently the skill had kept him alive long after he should have died. Grief flickered across Gyhard's features so quickly Vree thought she might not have seen it. Turning back to the bed, he bowed mockingly. "You wouldn't know him, Lady Bard. He's Cemandian."

The sudden relief made Karlene dizzy. "Cemandian," she murmured. That explained a great deal. Fearing the kigh and those who Sang them, the Cemandians had crippled bardic gifts before. This time, they appeared to have found a gift too strong for them to either use or destroy. No wonder the other kigh were terrified of being trapped. If the old man could Sing the fifth kigh back into the body that death had separated it from, what could he do to the other four? What horrific prisons could he Sing for them?

Gyhard watched conclusions flicker across the bard's face and had to turn away. He raised a brow at Vree's narrow-eyed stare and said, "It seems you're going to get your wish. We're going after the prince."

But he's dead! What good is a corpse?

This has nothing to do with the prince, Bannon. He's going after the old man.

Why?

Old wounds. But for reasons she refused to examine, Vree wasn't able, wasn't willing to expose that much of Gyhard to her brother. *It doesn't matter. If we return the prince's body and the body of the man who kidnapped him, we can still get that Imperial pardon.*

If we get that carrion eater out of my body.

When.

"Do you know where the prince is?" she asked.

Gyhard looked back over ninety years. "I may . . ."

"He's at least a day's walk from the Capital."

They turned together to stare down at Karlene.

"The air kigh have returned," she explained. "They wouldn't come any closer to the Capital when this . . . person was here, so obviously he's gone."

"Gone where?" It wasn't obvious to Vree but Gyhard seemed to think this bard knew what she was talking about.

Karlene shrugged and wished she hadn't. "I don't know." Her fingers hovered over her left temple. "I haven't been able to Sing, to find where the kigh refuse to go . . ."

Tugging down the edge of his vest, Gyhard stood and nodded toward the bed. "Kill her."

Vree wrapped her fingers around the hilt of her dagger. At this distance, she could effortlessly sink it guard-deep into an eye socket. This woman, this bard, knew she was an assassin and could therefore target her.

Probably why he told her, Bannon snorted. *Now he's picked her brain he wants her dead and he hasn't the balls to do it himself.*

Assassins who deserted died. It wasn't enough that Gyhard was responsible for their danger, he was trying to use it to control her. Vree folded her arms and glared at him. "Sod off."

"I beg your pardon?" Gyhard spread his arms in a parody of concern. "Don't tell me you think we *should* go to the Emperor? Or perhaps you believe she won't go herself once we're gone? Life won't be fun with the entire First Army on our trail. In case you're forgetting, Vree . . ."

"I'm not forgetting anything. I think she should come with us."

"What?"

I hate to agree with the carrion eater, Vree, but maybe you're not as sane as you think you are.

Vree raised her left hand and began flicking up the fingers. "First, you're not sure where the old man went. She can find him; the spirits won't go where he is, so we'll go where they won't. Second, a bard brought these dead guys back to life so maybe it needs a bard to kill them again. Daggers aren't much use against someone who's already dead. Third, if the prince is . . . is like that, then I want her along even if you don't. Fourth, what are you going to do when you catch up to the old man?"

All emotion drained from his face. "That's none of your concern."

"Fine." Vree folded the fingers down into a fist and set it on her hip. "But I'm going with you, and she's going with me."

"Perhaps you should consult the bard before you finalize your plans," Gyhard suggested caustically. "Why do you think she'd be willing to help?"

"Because she feels responsible for what happened." Vree turned to face the woman on the bed who was breathing heavily and staring up at her in astonishment. "You don't want to leave His Highness dead-not-dead, but you won't be able to save him without us. No one else believes you and no one else knows what Gyhard does about the old man and these spirits he controls." Her eyes narrowed. "You know the army will never find him. You'd be a fool not to come with us."

"You're the one being a fool, Vree," Gyhard spat through tight lips.

"Then kill her yourself."

The night grew a few heartbeats closer to dawn.

"Can you ride?" Gyhard asked at last. "I know it isn't a bardic skill . . ."

Teeth clenched, Karlene threw back the blankets. "I had a life before the Bardic Hall," she grunted. "I can ride."

Gyhard shook his head at her condition. "You see that she stays in the saddle," he told Vree pointedly.

"Who died and put you in command?" she snarled, but she helped the taller woman up onto her feet. Twisting around, she pulled a pair of full trousers and a long tunic off a hook. "Here. Get dressed."

Fighting nausea, Karlene dragged the tunic down over her head. "We have to free him," she said, her voice muffled in the fabric. "We can't leave him like that. I can't believe a bard would be so . . ."

"Lonely?" Vree asked. From the corner of one eye, she saw Gyhard flinch.

Karlene stared at her, amazed, the trousers dangling forgotten in her hand. "Lonely," she repeated. It was the first thing in two days that made total and complete sense.

"Very profound," Gyhard commented dryly. "I guess you have to know people pretty well in order to kill them."

Gripping the bard's elbow, Vree turned to face him. Head cocked to one side, she stared at him for a long moment. "I guess you do," she agreed at last.

"Karlene, wake up. It's almost sunrise."

"Wha . . ." Struggling with the embrace of the straw, Karlene sat up and tried to focus on the figure silhouetted against the entrance to the livery stable.

Callused hands caught hers up and wrapped them around a warm clay bowl. She heard the younger woman murmur, "I brought you something to help your head."

A cautious sip puckered her mouth and, holding her

breath, the bard drank the rest of the familiar liquid in a half a dozen fast swallows. Although she knew it would take time to work, the bitter taste alone seemed to clear the fog from her eyes.

Hands dangling between her knees, Vree squatted an arm's reach away. Karlene sighed in relief and handed back the bowl. "Where did you find feverfew?"

Vree shrugged. "There's an herbalist just around the corner."

"I can't imagine they'd be open at this hour." Then all at once, Karlene remembered. A locked shop would mean nothing to someone who could commit silent murder in the midst of guards and fortifications. *So if an assassin brews you feverfew tea,* she wondered, swallowing a sudden flood of saliva, *do you worry about poison?*

It seemed that Vree read her mind. "Don't worry about poison. I know herbs. It's safe."

Because it was also too late, Karlene relaxed a little as she heard the truth in Vree's voice. "What about the hot water."

"Oh, that." Another shrug and a dismissive flick of a delicately arched brow. "Over the years, I've learned to improvise."

"Did you get any sleep?"

"Some."

Lip caught between her teeth, Karlene grabbed the edge of the stall where it had been rubbed smooth by the scratching of a hundred equine itches, and carefully stood, her head balanced like an egg on the column of her neck. "You must be exhausted."

"No."

I wonder why she cares. Do you think she's interested?

Vree looked startled, then in one smooth motion rose as well. "I'd better wake Gyhard."

You've gotta admit she's a looker—in a pale, northern kind of way.

It doesn't matter if she's interested or not. Nothing is going to happen, Bannon. Nothing could happen, not when she couldn't tell for certain which needs were hers and which were his.

And if we both need, sister-mine?

She pretended she didn't hear him as she shook Gyhard's shoulder.

After leaving the Healers' Hall, they'd spent the rest of the night in the stable with their horses. From the sounds in other stalls, it was a common enough occurrence.

"We've paid for the space," Gyhard had explained. *"It's ours to use."*

"His Highness needs us now!" Swaying where she stood, Karlene had tried desperately to concentrate through the pain in her head.

"Unless you're willing to run alongside, you need a horse." Gyhard had yawned and settled into a pile of clean straw. *"No one's going to sell us a horse until morning."*

Karlene's head had ached too badly to argue.

The stablemaster, irritated at being woken before dawn, became obsequiously willing to sell them both horse and tack the moment he caught sight of Aralt's remaining gold.

"You could've had the chestnut for less," Karlene pointed out, tying a rolled woolen blanket on behind the worn saddle.

Gyhard continued inspecting his gelding's feet. "I bought the best horse I could afford given our immediate need," he said. "We won't be able to change mounts, and I don't want you slowing us down."

The bard threw her braid behind her shoulder with some force. "Slowing you down? How fast can dead men travel?"

"Dead men don't need to eat or sleep or shit." He straightened and began adjusting the girth. "If K . . . if he left the Capital right after acquiring the prince, he's a lot farther than a day's walk ahead of us—a day and two nights farther."

"The old man isn't dead," Karlene declared.

He should be dead. "And that's our only hope of catching them. They had to have stopped occasionally for him."

Her reins in one hand, a half-eaten piece of flatbread in the other, Vree led her horse over to the corner of the stableyard. "It's a big empire," she said. "After we go through the East Gate, what then?"

Gyhard turned to stare at her. "What makes you think they left through the East Gate?"

"The old man took at least two bodies out of the tombs along the East Road around the time the air spirits first got upset. Makes sense to assume that's the way he approached the city and if he's heading away, it makes sense to assume that's the road he'll take. So," she balanced the flatbread on her saddle and brushed crumbs off her shirtfront, "where do we go after we leave the East Gate? We know he's gone farther than the tombs because when he was in the tombs the air spirits were frightened and now they aren't."

One hand absently stroking his gelding's neck, Gyhard studied her. "You seem very sure of yourself this morning," he mused.

"It isn't you and me this morning," she told him, picking up the flatbread. "It's *find the prince.* I understand how *that* works."

"It'll be you and me again, once the prince is found."

"I know. But it isn't now."

You and him? Bannon demanded. *What about me?*

She couldn't believe that just for a moment, she'd forgotten.

Yeah, I can't believe it either, Bannon snarled.

"We'll go past the tombs." Gyhard swung up into the saddle. "Then the bard will Sing, giving us a better idea of the prince's location and how far they've gone." He glanced down at Karlene. "You will be *able* to Sing, won't you?"

"I'll Sing," she told him through clenched teeth. "You don't need to worry about me."

"Good." He smiled. "I won't."

Struggling to deal with three kigh in two bodies, Karlene could feel the hair rising on the back of her neck—and wasn't at all surprised to discover that it hurt. Thanks to the feverfew, she could function, but the continual throbbing at the point where the blunt object had connected with her skull made curiosity painful in spite of everything the healers had done. She had a hundred questions but they'd have to wait.

Concentrate on getting out of the Capital, she told herself sternly. She stiffened her neck to support her pounding head and mounted awkwardly. *First, the prince.* Nothing could interfere with freeing the prince's kigh.

But once the prince was . . .

Was what? she demanded of herself. *Safe? He's dead, Karlene, you didn't keep him safe.* Teeth clenched, she followed Gyhard out of the stableyard. *All you can do, is get him back.*

* * *

As they approached the East Gate, guiding the horses around a steady parade of farmers heading to market, Karlene realized they had a problem. Gabris would send the kigh to find her—she'd deal with them—but there were also more mundane methods he could use to discover her direction. *If anyone has seen Karlene the bard* ... Bardic recall could add a full description. ... *inform the palace immediately.* Too late to do anything about the people who'd already seen her this morning but at least she could hide her path out of the city. Given the healer's warning, she'd hoped to avoid Singing until they got past the tombs, but she had no choice.

Sitting as straight as she was able, she began.

Frowning, Vree reached over and touched the bard lightly on the arm. "Be quiet. You're too noticeable already."

"I'm Singing so they *won't* notice me," Karlene explained, allowing the Song to trail off while she spoke. In spite of everything, she smiled at Vree's expression. "It's a bardic ability."

When Gyhard nodded in agreement, Vree rolled her eyes and made sure her daggers were ready and her saddlebags secure in case they had to run for it. Making noise so as not to attract attention made less than no sense.

The guard at the East Gate barely glanced at them as they rode by. Obviously, they were none of them the prince in disguise and neither could he be hidden amongst their small amount of baggage.

That might be a good trick to learn, Vree observed as no one noticed the tall, very fair, singing foreigner leave the Capital.

What trick?

Singing so the guards don't see you.

See who?

The bard!

What bard?

Teeth clenched, Vree turned her head. *That bard. The one riding beside us.*

Oh. Bannon remained quiet for a long moment. *I forgot she was there.*

Were you listening to her sing?

I could hardly help it, could I? They're your slaughtering ears and she's right beside you. Now. I mean, I guess she always was, but . . . His thoughts tumbled over each other in confusion. *Vree, I don't like this.*

Don't worry about it. It seems as though she can only affect one of us at a time. Which is weird.

Slaughtering right it is.

No, I mean because, well, like you said, they're my slaughtering ears . . .

They rode until they passed the line of tombs, the pale stone gleaming in the morning sun.

"I think it's time we determine if we're on the right road," Gyhard declared, reining in. He glanced back at the small, square buildings lining both sides of the empty road. "For the moment, there's no one around to overhear."

Karlene lifted her head, eyes squinted nearly shut against the angle of the light. A strand of pale hair lifted off her cheek as she dismounted and handed the reins up to Vree. Trying to ignore the slivers of pain that radiated out from her temple, she walked up a small rise and Sang the four notes that would call the kigh.

Astounded, Vree gaped as the bard's clothing billowed in the sudden breeze.

Do you hear any words? Bannon asked.

No. But she could hear a question. "Is it magic?"

she asked Gyhard as Karlene stroked the air and continued to Sing.

Gyhard started. He'd forgotten how achingly pure bardic tones were. Kars had sounded like that once. Dragged back from contemplating the past, he shook his head. "Not exactly."

"Then what is it?"

"Not magic. She's merely speaking to the spirits of the air."

"Merely?" Vree repeated as Karlene's braid whipped around her head and, flung backward, the bard sat down hard on a small bush.

Handing the reins of both horses to Gyhard, Vree dropped out of the saddle and moved forward cautiously. The air was unnaturally still. Not even her movement stirred a breeze. "Are you all right?" she called softly.

"No worse than I was." Clasping Vree's extended hand, Karlene pulled herself to her feet and nearly pitched forward onto her face. She winced as only a quick transfer of grip from hand to elbow kept her standing. "You're a lot stronger than you look."

She's interested.

Shut up, Bannon. "What happened?" Vree asked as they carefully made their way back to the road, the bard's sandals scuffing a track in the dirt.

"You were right about the East Gate." She raised her voice to carry as far as Gyhard but no farther. "Because the old man is on the East Road heading away from the Capital."

Vree helped the taller woman up over the curbstones and back onto the road. "Did the air spirits tell you that?"

"No." Wrapping both hands around her saddle horn, Karlene rested her forehead against the warm leather.

"But they were quite emphatic in their refusal to follow the East Road. The kigh don't judge distance very well, but if I had to guess, I'd say they went more than a day's walk before they came back to tell me they were afraid."

"And he's at least a day's walk beyond that," Gyhard murmured.

"Yeah." She got her left foot into the stirrup and laboriously lifted herself up onto the big bay. "The chestnut was shorter," she grumbled under her breath. The moment she had the energy, she'd send a kigh back to Gabris and reassure him that she knew what she was doing. They'd have missed her at the Healers' Hall by now and sent a messenger to the palace.

"If he's taking the prince along the road, why hasn't anyone seen them?" Vree asked as she mounted. "They *have* to be pretty noticeable."

"People have seen them," Gyhard explained, "but the next instant, they deny what they saw. The living can't, or won't, acknowledge the living dead and so they look right by."

Karlene stirred in the saddle. "I didn't. I looked right at them." Pain dulled the terror that memory returned.

"You're a bard."

Sucking her breath through her teeth, Karlene pushed her horse forward into a walk. "Is the old man heading where you thought he was?" she asked as Gyhard and Vree fell in beside her.

Gyhard stared down the road—as though, Vree thought glancing over at him, he could see the end of it. "So far," he said, after a long moment.

"But you're still not certain?"

"It's been a long time."

Karlene wondered how long it could *possibly* have

been given his age, but the pounding inside her head
suggested she forgo dealing with a young man's ego.
"So all we can do is follow him along the road? Assume he'll stop sometime and hope we can catch up?"

"For now, yes," Gyhard nodded, "that's all we can
do."

She thought of Otavas trapped screaming within his
murdered body and slammed her heels into the barrel
of her horse. Startled, he leaped forward. She swayed
but kept her seat and hung on grimly as he settled into
a rocking canter, racing in pursuit of the walking dead.

The patterns of light playing against his eyelids woke
him, dragging him up out of darkness. Confused and disoriented by the constant motion and the sound of wheels
against stone, he tried to remember where he was.

He remembered hearing Karlene sing. He remembered the fight they had. He remembered an alley
where the shadows held terror . . .

Gasping for breath, Prince Otavas opened his eyes.

A very, very old man stared down at him, his expression one of rapt adoration. "Good morning, my
heart," he said pleasantly. "Did you sleep well?"

"Morning?" Otavas struggled up into a sitting position. The old man neither helped nor hindered. He'd
been lying on a pallet on the rough plank floor of a
high-sided cart, his cloak folded to make a pillow. Facing him, were two young men, their skin a pale
greenish-gray, their eyes sunk deep above purple crescents. They looked almost familiar. The prince fought
to clear the fog from his head.

. . . where the shadows held terror.

Heart slamming against his ribs, he threw himself
backward, crashing up against the side of the cart. The
old man reached out to grab his arm, but he twisted

away. On hands and knees, he scrambled for the rear of the cart and tried to throw himself over.

Cold fingers clutched at him and pulled him back.

They were touching him.

He shrieked in disbelief, shuddered once, and darkness claimed him again.

Still grieving for her infant grandson, Her Imperial Majesty had taken the abduction of her youngest son very hard. Gabris had spent the night and the early morning at her bedside, playing, singing, giving what comfort he could. When she finally fell into a deep, exhausted sleep, he told her attendants to send for him when she woke and headed for his own quarters and his own bed.

The messenger from the Healers' Hall finally reached him as he left the Imperial Apartments. The message from Karlene reached him a few moments later as he hurried across one of the myriad courtyards honeycombing the palace.

I've gone after the prince. Ask His Majesty to trust me for just a little while.

Although Gabris Sang question after question at the kigh, he got very little information. Karlene was not alone; there were three people with her. She wasn't happy. The kigh wouldn't tell him where she was—had been told not to tell him where she was, and Gabris, even fully rested, no longer had as great a command of the air as the younger bard.

When he reached the bardic suite—having rushed past curious courtiers and servants alike, oblivious to their greetings or stares—he threw open the shutters and stepped out onto the small balcony. He couldn't tell if the kigh he called was the same kigh Karlene had sent to him or a different one as they all shared identical features. Putting everything he had left into the request, he asked it to find Karlene.

It pushed slender fingers through his hair in a mocking caress and disappeared.

Shkodan bards were allowed into the Havakeen Empire by Imperial indulgence. Although the restrictions holding them within the walls of the Capital had been lifted some years before, they were still required to keep the palace informed of their movements. As senior bard, he should be able to tell His Imperial Majesty, at any time, where Karlene could be found.

When the kigh returned a short while later, his relief lasted less than a dozen heartbeats.

Please, Gabris, don't try to find me. This is bardic business and has to do with . . . The translation tattered, but the familiar terror of the kigh came through distressingly clearly. *This is His Highness' only chance to rest.*

Gabris staggered back into the suite, sagged down onto the edge of the scribe's table, and buried his face in his hands. "First, walking dead and now this," he moaned. Obviously, the blow to the head and the shock of seeing the young prince abducted had somehow gotten mixed up with whatever had been upsetting the kigh over the past . . .

But the kigh were back. Gabris slowly straightened, eyes widening. So whatever had been upsetting them was gone from the Capital. Gone with the prince?

He had to admit the slim possibility.

But why had Karlene not come to him? Who were these three others the kigh placed her with? There were still too many unanswered questions.

Ask His Majesty to trust me for just a little while.

Putting himself in the place of a man who barely believed in the kigh at all and who needed a certain healthy amount of paranoia in order to maintain the integrity of far-flung borders—putting himself in the Emperor's place—Gabris could draw only two conclusions.

Either Karlene was involved with Prince Otavas' abduction and had rushed off to join her accomplices or the blow to the head had completely scrambled her brains and a dangerously powerful crazy woman was now wandering the Empire. Either way, it didn't look good.

"No." Swaying in the saddle, Karlene fought to pull the reins from Gyhard's hands, trying desperately to see through the orange and yellow bars of light streaking her vision. "We have to keep going. You said yourself, the dead have no need to rest."

"The horses do." Gyhard told her bluntly. "We've shade here, and water, and I've no intention of wasting either. You can go on without us if you like, but it won't do His Highness any good if your horse founders."

Lips pressed tightly together, the bard acknowledged his point with a reluctant jerk of her head and slid gracelessly to the ground. Leaving her companions to deal with the horses, she staggered to a crude bench under an ancient chestnut tree and collapsed onto it. Directly above the canopy of leaves, the sun blazed white-gold in a sky bleached of color by the heat. Underfoot lay reddish-brown dirt, crushed to the consistency of dust by centuries of travelers leaving the road to rest at this exact spot. If she turned just a little to the left, she could see a one-story building, the same color as the dirt. The world spun, and she closed her eyes.

At the well, Vree pulled the counterweight around and spilled another bucket of water into the stone trough.

"Bards live to ask questions," Gyhard said as he watched the animals suck noisily. "When this one recovers her wits, what have you decided to tell her?"

"What have *I* decided to tell her?"

"It was *your* choice to bring her along."

He was being deliberately provoking. She wondered if Bannon's less endearing mannerisms were beginning to rub off the inside of his body.

Hey!

"You bought her the horse." The sound of the bucket dropping back into the water echoed against the damp sides of the well.

Come on, Vree; what do you mean, less endearing mannerisms?

Gyhard stroked his gelding's damp neck. "After you convinced me she represented a resource we could ill afford to ignore."

What, Vree?

"She reports directly to the Emperor, you know," he continued. "I imagine he'll be fascinated to hear about you and your brother."

Come on, Vree, tell me.

Well, to begin with, you never know when to shut up! She could feel his hurt retreat, as obvious as it had been when they were children and he'd crawl under the barracks and hide if she yelled at him. But things were a lot simpler back then, and right now she didn't have the time to crawl under after him and reassure him that she still loved him best. "We'll trade her silence for our help rescuing the prince."

"You mean for the prince's body," Gyhard corrected with a false smile. "And silence isn't something usually associated with bards; they see all, they sing all."

Vree studied him for a moment and wondered, if she asked, whether he'd tell her why the old man was so important to him. She knew the bard's reasons for wanting to set Prince Otavas' spirit free, she knew her own. She wished she knew his and even more, she wished she knew when it had become so important for her to know him as more than a usurper in her brother's body.

The horses had finished drinking, so she plunged her own face into the trough and raised it, dripping, a moment later. "The bard can ask all the questions she wants, we don't have to answer. Right at the moment, she needs us and we need her and that makes her an ally." Glaring across the well at him, she added, "There've been stranger."

This time the smile was genuine. "I know."

He thought he was on one of the barges that members of the Imperial Family occasionally took out on the water; that the rocking motion came from waves slapping against the polished wooden sides; that he could hear the creaking of the mast as the huge square sail filled with wind; that he could smell the faint stink of rotting fish that always seemed to drift over the river closest to the Capital; that he'd fallen asleep on deck. Without opening his eyes, he dragged his tongue across dry lips and—certain there'd be a servant close enough to hear—murmured how nice a cool glass of wine would taste.

Bony fingers closed on his shoulder.

And he remembered.

"No!" Otavas jerked into a sitting position, tearing himself out of the old man's grip.

Rheumy eyes narrowed in puzzlement. "You don't want a drink?"

Heart pounding, Otavas pressed up against the side of the cart and stared frantically around. Except for the position of sun and shadow, nothing had changed. Afraid to move lest the dead lay hands on him again, he craned his neck and peered out at the road.

They were traveling fairly quickly down one of the

great roads—he recognized a mile marker as the cart rolled past—pulled by . . . by . . . It took him a moment to understand that two more of the dead ran between the shafts of the cart, their gait made horrifying by a unified precision the living could never attain. The younger of the two women had a leather brace around her neck. His stomach twisted as he realized what that had to mean.

Then up ahead, he saw a courier in the uniform of the Imperial Army. Relief hit him so hard he swayed and had to grab the side of the cart to keep from falling.

"Hey!" he yelled, waving an arm over his head. "Help me! Help!"

The courier turned toward the sound, but her gaze slid right over the cart. Reining in her horse, she pulled off her helm and stared back up the road.

"No! Here! Can't you see me!" Voice breaking, Otavas scrambled up onto his knees. "Help me! I order you to help me!"

They'd drawn abreast and for an instant it almost seemed as though she looked right at the prince. Then her eyes widened in terror so that the whites showed all around. An instant later, she shook her head in disbelief and crammed her helm back on.

Then they were past.

Tears cutting through the dust on his cheeks, Otavas turned to stare at the rider, quickly being left behind. "Help me," he cried. "I order you to see me . . ."

"I have watered wine for you."

He jerked around to face the old man who gazed at him with such adoration he felt it as a physical caress. His skin crawled.

"I remembered how you preferred it over beer."

Otavas looked down at the offered wineskin then up at the old man. He swallowed and the sides of his throat scraped together. Slowly, fingers trembling, he reached out. Smiling happily, the old man pushed the yielding skin toward him.

Although he shook so hard he could barely find his mouth, if he concentrated on the wine, and only on the wine, Otavas found that he could drink. The normalcy of the action helped. Clutching the leather sack as if it were the hand of a friend, he found the courage to look around.

The two dead men at the rear of the cart stared, unblinkingly at him. Otavas shrank back but, with nowhere to go, found himself forced to confront the rising darkness. As though it issued out of another mouth, he heard his voice foolishly proclaim, "You're dead."

The taller of the two blinked. "Yesss, Highnesss."

They knew who he was. They were dead and they knew who he was. His leg muscles jumped painfully as his body fought to run while his fear of having them touch him again held him in place.

They were dead, and they knew they were dead.

The world seemed to pause while Otavas realized what that meant. His heart started beating, his lungs pulled in air, terror became laced with pity. They were more dreadfully trapped than he was.

Wordlessly, he offered them the wine.

Equally wordlessly, they shook their heads.

"The dead have no need of drink, my heart." He whirled to face the old man who smiled at him. "You and I alone must share a cup."

"Did you . . ." Otavas wet his lips and tried again. "Did you do this?" A wave of his hand made it obvious what he meant.

"Of course I did, just like you taught me." The old man's smile moved past him to touch the dead. They leaned toward it.

"*I* taught you?"

The ancient eyes filled with moisture. "Did you think I'd forget?"

He's crazy. He's not just old, he's crazy. Wiping his palms on his shirt, the fine cotton already damp with sweat, the prince lifted his chin and made an effort to sound like a son of the Emperor. "Listen to me, please. I'm *not* who you think I am. I am Prince Otavas and my father will send the army out to search for me. They'll tear the Empire apart and when they find me . . ." He stared over the back of the cart, hoping to see some sign of pursuit. "When they find me . . ." But the courier had looked right at him and ridden on by.

The cart turned suddenly and thudded down into wheel ruts cut alongside a field of grain. "We're heading for a small grove of trees," the old man explained, patting the straw basket between them. "We'll eat then, you and I, and have shade to protect us from the heat of the day. When the sun is less dangerous, we'll go on."

The scent of peaches rising up from the basket brought a rush of saliva and his stomach spasmed. He'd never been so hungry. "How long was I asleep?" The old man ignored him. "Where are you taking me?"

"Home," the old man told him with a longing sigh, one gnarled hand holding the necklace of bone, the other reaching out to lightly touch the prince's cheek. "Home, where we'll start again. And this time we'll get it right and you'll never, ever leave me."

Chapter Ten

"We won't catch them before dark."

Karlene turned her head just enough to glare at Gyhard through bloodshot eyes. "How do you know?" she demanded.

"As long as you are able to Sing the kigh," he told her, speaking slowly and just on the edge of sarcasm, "our quarry is at least a day's travel away. You Sang the kigh at the last milestone, and unless I'm greatly mistaken there are still kigh around you now."

"How can you tell?" Her thoughts trailed one another around in pain-filled circles and could come up with no reason for his certainty. For all their strangeness, neither of her new companions were aware of the kigh.

Gyhard exhaled noisily, impatiently. "Your hair keeps blowing into your face and yet the breeze is from the opposite direction."

"Then if we're still a day behind them, we can't stop." Teeth clenched, Karlene straightened out of the slump she'd been riding in for—she didn't know how long, it seemed as though she'd spent her life in the saddle—but before she could drive in her heels, a slender brown hand closed over her wrist like a vise.

"No."

She turned. Her protest died unvoiced at Vree's expression. Short of chopping it off at the wrist, Karlene couldn't move the hand; the hand's owner would not be moved at all. "No," she repeated wearily after a long moment, her tone making it an agreement.

Vree, what difference does it make? Let her gallop off into the sunset if she wants.

Much more galloping and she'll kill herself.

So? He sounded sulky.

Vree recognized the question he was actually asking; *Why are you paying so much attention to things that don't concern me?* He'd asked that question too many times before in too many different ways for Vree to mistake it now. Bannon had always basked in her attention—needed it, she realized suddenly as much as she'd needed him there to give the attention to—and now, when her attention was all he had . . . Guilt gentled an impatient response. *Without the bard, we can't track the prince.*

That's bullshit. The prince is with the old man, the carrion eater's going after the old man, and we're sticking close by my body.

Gyhard isn't certain where we're going, and he has problems of his own right now.

Bannon was silent for a moment, then he sighed. *And you care about his problems, sister-mine?* His voice hardened. *I want that carrion eater in my body to die, Vree. I want him to die, not me, with or without honor. I want my body back and we are doing nothing to take it!*

His rage sizzled through her arms and legs, and Vree snatched the hand around the bard's wrist away before it could spasm closed tighter still.

Honor's easy for you, he sneered, *you're living. I'm existing.* Then abruptly as it rose, his rage subsided and his voice, when she heard it again, sounded close to tears. *I'm sorry, Vree. It's just ... I mean, I want ...*

"Vree?"

Fighting her way up out of Bannon's despair, she discovered the reins were sliding lose through her fingers. Her gelding, taking advantage of her momentary absence, had swerved for the edge of the road and dropped his head to snatch a mouthful of the coarse grass. The bard, physically exhausted by the day's ride and emotionally shredded by the reason for it, appeared not to have noticed, but Gyhard stared at her, his expression looking very much like concern. A heartbeat later Vree decided she had to be mistaken—she'd fallen a little behind so he'd had to turn and face the setting sun. It was a squint. Nothing more. Because it couldn't be anything more.

"You have a suggestion?" Gyhard continued, lifting a hand to shade his eyes.

Vree gathered up the reins and with them her control—of the horse, of herself. "I do. We stop at the next inn. If there's a healer around, we have her head looked at ..." She jerked her chin at the bard. "... either way she eats and goes to bed. We leave at dawn and we ride hard before the day heats up."

Gyhard opened his mouth to speak, but Karlene broke in before he had a chance. "We ride until dark," she said. "It would be stupid to waste the cool of the evening."

"Stupider to die," Vree pointed out. "Much stupider to fall off your horse and break your neck. You look like shit, and you need to rest."

Karlene took a deep breath, the air equally scented with sweaty horse and sweaty bard, and discovered that even her lungs ached. "The prince ..."

"Will be rescued later or not at all. Your choice."

Later or not at all had been Vree's choice from the moment she'd seen another man wearing her brother's body.

The bard stroked at a dark strand of mane with one finger. Finally, she sighed, surrender implicit in the release of air. "Are all assassins so tenacious?"

What does tenacious mean? Bannon asked peevishly, curiosity dragging him up out of depression.

How should I know? Vree lifted her chin. "We're trained to remove anything that gets between us and our target," she said, and because it was important to keep in mind just what she needed to remove, she looked past Karlene to Gyhard.

He raised her brother's eyebrow in what could have been acknowledgment.

Chasing the dead, the three of them had ridden from the Capital much faster than Gyhard and Vree had ridden in, and they'd long passed that section of the East Road where buildings were as frequent as Imperial law allowed and stopping at an inn meant merely making a choice. They rode into the next village as the setting sun dipped below the horizon, their shadows no longer stretching out before them, leading the way, but blending back into the dusk.

Vree lifted sweat-damp hair off the back of her neck and scanned the cluster of buildings grouped as close to the south side of the Great Road as the law allowed. Habit planned routes through shadow, marking doors and windows she could enter unseen.

Then the breeze carried the sound of keening down the road toward them.

The lament came from a tiny cobbler's shop, tucked up against one wall of what appeared to be the village's only inn. As they approached, a burly young man standing outside the shop's closed shutters glared at them suspiciously and shifted his ornately carved cudgel from hand to hand. He watched them pass, the sound of their horses' hooves momentarily drowned out by the cries of grief from within.

When they rode into the inn yard and the bulk of the building cut off the ululating cry, Vree checked her weapons. "I wonder what he's guarding against."

"Death," Karlene replied dully. "It's the custom in this part of the Empire to hire a strong arm to stand guard at the door for a day in case the body calls Death back into the house. The club he was carrying had protections carved into it. He'll lead the procession to the grave."

"We don't do that in the south."

*'Cause we're not stupid enough to think it would make any difference. Death walks where she wants to. Slaughter it, Vree, *we* walk where we want to.*

"In the south, you burn a sprig of parsley and sprinkle the ashes across the threshold to keep restless spirits from returning home." Half her mouth crooked up in a humorless smile. "Bards study these things. I'm so tired of death." She slid out of the saddle. Vree barely managed to catch her as her knees folded and she continued to drop all the way to the hard-packed dirt of the stableyard.

A life spent in the army allowed Vree to recognize and appreciate the stream of profanity pouring out of the bard's mouth even without knowing the language. "Come on," she grunted, heaving the taller, heavier woman back up onto her feet. "Inside. A hot soak . . ." A quick glance through gathering darkness ascertained that the inn did, indeed have a bathhouse. ". . . and then sleep."

"And it'll be better in the morning?" By will alone, Karlene got her legs moving toward the door.

"No." False promises were for children. "But *you* may be."

The common room was empty, hardly surprising as the wailing could be heard clearly through the adjoining wall. Shooting a glance that contained as much irritation as sorrow at the place where the sounds originated, the innkeeper lit one last lamp and hurried toward them. As Vree eased the bard down onto a bench, Gyhard negotiated for care of their horses, three places in the dormitory, and use of the bathhouse.

"Two crescents every time we fill the bath," the woman told him.

He stared at her in astonishment. "What are you filling it with, ass's milk?"

"The water doesn't heat itself," she said shortly, her tone suggesting haggling would raise the price. "Nor raise itself up out of the ground. One at a time or all together?"

"It's large enough for the three of us?"

She pursed her lips, her head rising and falling as she made silent measurements. "It is."

Gyhard looked into his depleted purse and frowned. The bard had better have been in the Empire long enough to absorb a few of the customs she'd studied. "Then all together."

A speculative gaze alighted on the obvious foreigner for a second or two, then the innkeeper took his coin and jerked a thumb back over her shoulder. "Loft's at the top of those stairs, you've your pick of the pallets. I don't provide blankets, so I hope you've got your own." When Gyhard nodded, she continued. "Bath'll be ready by the time you are."

"Who died?" Karlene asked suddenly, her voice surprisingly strong.

The irritation vanished and the innkeeper heaved a

heavy sigh. "Aven—that's the cobbler with the shop next door—it was his son. Only days old."

The bard paled beneath old tan and the crimson blush added that day by the sun. "A baby?"

"Aye. His mother's not recovered from the birthing and now this. Babe just up and died. Aven says one heartbeat he was warm and the next cold . . ."

"Cold," Karlene repeated.

"Aye, cold. And the next thing poor Aven knew, the babe was dead."

"How could I have forgotten about the babies that died in the Capital?" The thick golden mass of her hair spread out over the rim of the bath, her eyes closed, Karlene gnawed on her lower lip.

Vree braced her foot against the broad ledge that ringed the small bath and provided a place to sit while soaking. Lip curled, she dug her fingers into the knotted muscle of the bard's right leg. "You met two dead men up and walking, you were hit on the head, His Highness got snatched, and you spent a day in the saddle when you should've been resting in the Healers' Hall."

"That's not an excuse," the bard began, but Vree interrupted with a snort.

"Maybe not, but it's a slaughtering good reason."

On the far side of the bath, his position dictated by the need to accommodate three pairs of legs, Gyhard swiped at the sweat dribbling down from his hairline. "Why is he doing it," he muttered. "Babies! I don't understand *why.*"

He sounded so confused, Vree found herself wanting to slip a blade across the throat of the person responsible.

What for? Bannon demanded.

Because he's in your body and I keep reacting like it's you that's been hurt. Which made perfect sense, but then, all the best lies did. Mollified, Bannon settled back below the surface of her thoughts. "Maybe he isn't doing it," she suggested, allowing Karlene's right leg to slide under the water and picking up the left. "Maybe it's just happening."

Gyhard glanced up at her. "What do you mean?"

"Well, you said that our spirits . . ."

"The kigh."

"All right, our kigh . . ." The foreign word felt unbalanced in her mouth, like a borrowed dagger. "You said they look away from the dead. Maybe baby spirits, baby kighs, haven't been around long enough to get attached to their body. Instead of looking away, they run."

"And the babies die," Karlene murmured.

Vree nodded. "And the babies die."

"It makes sense." Relaxing, Gyhard shifted position, sending a wave of rapidly cooling water to lap at Vree's chin.

For the first time since they'd peeled off sweat-stained clothing, Vree turned to look full at him. "This is the only death we've run into on the road; I think he stopped here. If it only took the dead passing by, we'd be knee deep in bodies by now."

He played with a bit of loose plaster as he considered it but found himself considering her instead. That she was both dangerous and dangerously loyal, he'd known from the beginning. Adaptable, beautiful, ruthless; he'd discovered that on the road. Since she'd challenged him over the bard in the Healers' Hall, he'd seen that a strong intelligence lurked beneath her single-minded intensity. She was capable of such intense love that she'd agreed to lay her sanity on the line rather than have her brother die. All at once he found himself wondering what Kars would have thought of her.

Kars. He closed his eyes for a moment and wondered if this new love, if it was love, had somehow called back the old. He'd lived too long to believe in blind chance. When he opened his eyes again, Vree was still looking at him. "You want me to find out why he stopped?"

She nodded. "The more you know about a target, the better your odds of success."

"He's not a target, Vree."

"No?" She locked her gaze onto his. "Then what is he?"

Gyhard flushed, but before he could answer, Karlene pulled her leg from Vree's grip. Sucking the moist bathhouse air through her teeth, she pushed herself forward and onto her feet, the water rippling around her hips. Her nostrils were pinched tight and her voice trembled. "We have to catch up to him before he stops again. We have to catch him before more ba . . ." She looked fleetingly surprised, then her eyes rolled up and she collapsed.

The water itself caught the bard and eased her back onto the ledge.

Vree stopped her forward dive so suddenly her muscles locked. Blood roaring in her ears, she glared at Gyhard, silently demanding an answer.

"Water kigh," he said softly, pulling himself up and out of the bath, the quick economy of his movements in direct contrast to the matter-of-fact tones in his voice. "She must be very strong in that quarter for them to manifest without a Song."

"Water spirits?" Vree could feel her skin crawling under the caress of the warm liquid. All the tension the heat had dissipated returned. Between one breath and the next, she stood dripping on an ugly mosaic of cavorting gods that adorned the floor.

Focus on freeing the prince, she told herself, crouching to slip her hands into the bard's armpits and haul her up out of the bath. *The rest of this doesn't matter.*

She's got great ...

Not now, Bannon.

Gyhard reached for a drying cloth and shook his head. "And you thought this would be less complicated than just *you and I,*" he said mockingly.

It was getting dark. Otavas licked the peach juice from his fingers and pressed his spine hard against the rough side of the cart. They'd stopped three times since they started again in the late afternoon; once for him to relieve himself, once to fill the empty skin with fresh water, and once so that the dead could change places between the shafts of the cart. They were not going to stop for the night.

"We have to get home," the old man told him earnestly. "So we can start again."

"I'm not who you think I am!" Over the course of an impossibly long day, the prince had shouted it, whimpered it, wailed it, but every time the old man had merely smiled.

He was losing track of how long he'd spent within the confines of the cart, passing unseen and unheard through the lives of those who lived or moved along the Great Road. Muscles ached from the constant pounding as the high, narrow wheels slammed into every imperfection, every pothole in the stone.

He flinched as the old man lightly stroked a warm, dry finger down the length of his arm.

"It's late, my heart. It's time to sleep. Dawn comes early this quarter."

This quarter? Otavas twisted to stare through the dusk at the wizened face. The countries to the north, Shkoder, Cemandia, and Petrok beyond that divided their year into quarters; the Empire did not. "Who are you?" He wondered why it had never occurred to him to ask before.

Rheumy eyes filled with tears. "You'll remember everything, my heart, as soon as we get home. But now you must sleep."

Sleep. The prince glanced toward the end of the cart where the dead sat. Not the men this time, but the two women. He guessed that the younger, Kait, was thirteen or fourteen and Wheyra his age or a very little older. To his disgust, the old man had introduced them just as though they were people. Kait had stared past him, unblinking eyes locked on the old man's face while Wheyra ignored them both, crooning to a desiccated bundle that crawled with flies. No, he couldn't sleep, not around them. Pity may have tempered the horror, but the horror remained. Bad enough to be trapped in this waking nightmare—worse to be plunged time after time into the terror of darker dreams.

"No." He shook his head, sable hair flinging lines of shadow against the night.

"Yes."

Something in the old man's voice drew him around. Something in the old man's eyes held him.

"Sleep."

"Yesterday, around noon, an old man came into the village and got food and a cotter pin—didn't pay for any of it, just asked and, for some reason no one I spoke to is clear on, they handed it over." Gyhard straddled the bench and leaned an elbow on the tabletop. "No one saw where he went."

Vree glanced toward the group of four travelers at the other end of the common room who were speculating on the prince's kidnapping and making their own loyalties loudly clear. She leaned forward so as not to be overheard should any of the four suddenly stop talking. "No one was willing to look where he went?"

"Very likely."

"What's a cotter pin?"

"Among other things it's used to hold a wagon wheel on the axle."

"He has a wagon?"

"Or a cart."

"Shit on a stick."

He smiled at her expression. "Don't worry about it, nothing's really changed; his horses are going to have to rest as often as ours."

"Oh?" Her brows went up and she drummed her fingers against the table. "What if the dead are pulling it? the dead who never need to rest. The old man can do everything but shit in the wagon and how often are they going to stop for that?"

"Not often," Gyhard admitted. He swung his inside leg out over the bench and leaned back against the table. After a moment's thought, he said, "Perhaps the other wheel will fall off."

"Yeah, maybe." Vree jerked her chin at the stairs leading to the loft. "This is going to really upset her."

"Then maybe we shouldn't tell her."

It could have been Bannon sitting there, offering to share a secret with that exact glint in his eye. *Just between you and me, Vree* . . . But it wasn't Bannon. She shook her head, uncertain of what she was refusing.

"Suit yourself." Gyhard stood and turned toward the door. "I'm going out to get some air." As he passed her, he rested his hand, for a heartbeat, on her shoulder.

He touched you! I don't like it when he touches you! I don't want him to touch you!

It's your body . . .

And just you remember that, sister-mine.

"A skin of watered wine, a dozen cooked sausages, a hunk of cheese, a loaf of bread, and six peaches," Gyhard murmured, pulling a peach from his pocket and rubbing at the fuzz with the ball of his thumb. "Why would Kars have taken peaches?"

Ninety years before, they'd bought a basket from a trader who'd been crossing the mountains on his way to Cemandia. The fruit had made Kars violently ill; closing up his throat, choking off his breath, causing his skin to erupt in painful blisters.

Juice dribbling down his chin, Gyhard leaned back against the well housing. He supposed the passage of time could have changed Kars' reaction; after all, the passage of time should have killed him and hadn't.

Or perhaps it wasn't Kars they followed at all.

Cemandian law produced a steady progression of crippled bards. Perhaps another had torn free and joined Kars in his nest on the Empire's side of the mountains long enough to learn of the fifth kigh, and it was this bard they followed now.

"No." Gyhard chewed and swallowed and tasted dust. Although his head could create reason after reason why the old man who'd raised the dead around the Capital was not the young man he'd abandoned to insanity so long ago, his heart knew otherwise.

Then why the peaches?

His teeth scraped against the pit and he started, pitched into memory.

"That is so incredibly sensual, the way you do that."

"The way I do what?" Gyhard grinned and sucked the juice off the pit, holding it by his fingertips and rolling it between his lips. *"This?"*

"That." Kars lifted himself up on his elbows, eyes gleaming. *"I love to watch you eat those. It almost makes up for not being able to eat them myself."*

Perhaps Kars had taken the peaches in order to watch someone else eat them. But he journeyed with the dead. Or did he?

All at once, it seemed there was a very good chance that his Imperial Highness, Prince Otavas, was alive.

Gyhard tossed the pit into the darkness and stared up at the stars. If Vree thought that the prince was alive, then the simplicity of *find the prince* became lost in the resumption of strike and counterstrike. They'd have to start thinking about killing each other again.

He didn't want to think about killing her.

"And may I inquire what your business is in the Capital, Commander?"

"No." Neegan sealed his message to Marshal Chela and pinched the wick of the sealing wax between thumb and forefinger. "Your marshal can if he wants to, but all you need to know is that I am loosed at a target." He paused then added, "Commander."

The woman on the other side of the desk gave no indication that she heard any insult in her visitor's husky enunciation of her rank. She'd been raised to play the political game that guarding the Emperor required and would not be thrown out of countenance by a grimy provincial who stank of his days on the road. "You're here very early and you've obviously been riding hard;

the facilities of the First Army are, of course, yours to enjoy." Her tone suggested Neegan wouldn't recognize a bath if he fell into one.

Neegan stood and pushed the folded parchment across the desk. "I want a courier sent immediately."

"No trouble at all, Commander. Will you be waiting at the garrison for a return message?"

He leaned forward slightly. "No, I won't. I told you, I am loosed at a target."

The words brushed an edge across her throat. She swallowed and forgot to breathe as she watched him leave the duty room, cross the portico, and disappear behind the bulk of a painted pillar. All at once she understood why the First Army trained no one to wear a black sunburst. The assassins were weapons to be used when a single blade could decide the course of a battle. They had no defensive use and the First Army existed for the sole purpose of defending the Imperial Family. Commander Neegan was a weapon unsheathed. She wondered what battle he was deciding and a not entirely unpleasant frisson lifted the hair on the back of her neck.

It's like having Death herself walking around the city. . . .

He'd been to the Capital once, many years ago, but he'd forgotten how big it was, how many people crammed within the circle of its wall. A pair of assassins—two people trained to disappear—would assume they could lose themselves easily in a city this size. Neegan stood outside the palace wall and swept his gaze over the wedge of the Capital that he could see, wondering why anyone would be willing to live in such conditions. *Stacked up on top of each other six deep . . .*

Under a clean uniform tunic, the flesh between his shoulder blades twitched as the guards on duty at the First Army's gate stared curiously at his back. In a very short time, the rumor of who and what he was would reach them—rumor raced through the ranks faster by far than legitimate information. He was used to being the center of speculation, all assassins were; it worked to their advantage far more often than the opposite case. In this instance it would have no effect at all. His targets, in the short time they had remaining, would stay as far from the army as possible.

Foolishly believing themselves safe from pursuit, they had stayed at the best inns all along the South Road and would very likely continue to do so. He expected to find them by nightfall at the absolute latest. By morning, it would be over.

Although a morning's hard riding had still not brought them within a day's walk of the old man and his dead, when the heat began to rise in shimmering waves off the pale stone, even Karlene reluctantly admitted the need for both water and shade. They guided their lathered horses off the road by a marker indicating a well under Imperial protection and in a short time came upon a copse of trees gathered around a small, contained spring.

The marks of cloven hooves in the dirt indicated that cattle, not travelers, were the usual visitors, but for the moment they had the area to themselves.

"What is it?"

Vree continued untangling the lengths of coarse thread and polished ovals of wood that she'd lifted down out of a slender beech. "A shrine to the wind."

"What's it for?" Karlene knelt beside her, reaching

out to lightly caress the feather carved into one of the pieces of wood.

"Luck." Vree told her shortly.

The bard looked intrigued. "You believe that acknowledging the wind will bring you luck?"

"I don't know what other people believe, but I believe in taking luck where I find it."

You're in a mood.

Sod off, Bannon.

No. She could hear the scowl in his voice and fought to keep his expression off her face. *Why are you being such a slaughtering bitch? You were nice enough to her last night.*

What are you talking about?

The massage in the bath. The helping hand to the pallet.

Helping. Nothing more. I left when the healer arrived.

You're right. Nothing more. His mental voice grew shrill. *It's never anything more, Vree, and I'm tired of it. I can't live like this!*

Look, it's my body ...

So you keep reminding me!

Karlene's eyes widened as Vree's hands began to twitch and writhe in her lap like huge brown spiders. Muscles rolled and strained under the thin silk of the assassin's shirt. It didn't take bardic ability to sense the internal struggle and she wondered what, if anything she should do.

Bannon! Stop it!

I don't want to live like this.

You think I do?

Then get him out of my body!

How? With a desperate grip on her sense of self, Vree forced Bannon back. Chest heaving, she spat out a mouthful of blood from where her teeth had been driven through the soft flesh on the inside of her lip and carefully stretched her hands out on her thighs, gripping her own muscles for stability. "What?" she demanded, suddenly aware of the bard's concerned gaze.

Karlene sat back on her heels and frowned. After a moment she said, "Is it Bannon?"

Startled, Vree looked past her at Gyhard lying under a tree barely a body length away, one arm thrown up over his eyes.

"No." The bard shook her head. "He didn't tell me, you did. In the Healers' Hall. You asked if the kigh were like Bannon, and you carry two kigh, so . . ." Karlene let her voice trail off. Yesterday, she'd only had enough energy for guilt and survival, but sleep and food and the village healer had rekindled curiosity. It had seemed that all through the morning a new question had risen with every fall of hoof on stone. As the oppressive heat pushed her thoughts down dark and self-condemning paths, the answers would be a welcome distraction.

Vree dropped her gaze to her lap, her fingers beginning to unravel the knots again. After a moment, she nodded.

Karlene released a breath she couldn't remember holding. "Who is he?"

"My brother."

"Were you—you and Bannon—born like this?"

Vree snorted. "No."

"Did you choose it?"

"No."

Karlene glanced over her shoulder at Gyhard. Out of the corner of her eye, she saw Vree stiffen. "How did it happen?"

"We fell into a trap." The generous curves of Vree's mouth flattened into a pale line. Did she want this bard to know how easily they'd fallen into Gyhard's trap? Or how Bannon's body had defeated her? Or how Bannon's body had . . .

"I don't want to talk about it."

"Why not?"

Vree stared at Karlene in astonishment. For her entire adult life, no one had ever continued a conversation when she'd said it was over.

"Unless you have some sort of a death wish, I'd drop it," Gyhard contributed, sounding amused.

Karlene twisted around to face him. "A death wish?" she repeated scornfully.

"She's an assassin. As I mentioned before, they're trained to have somewhat limited responses."

Karlene blinked, suddenly remembering the feel of the blade on her throat. Assassin. She kept forgetting. But neither could she believe that Vree would kill her merely for pressing a point and said so.

"I wouldn't be so sure of that." Gyhard sat up and brushed an ant off his arm. "She'll kill anyone who gets in her way."

As much as she would have preferred not to, Karlene could hear the truth in his voice and had to believe him. One hand holding a pale strand of hair off her face, she turned back to Vree. "Am I in your way?"

Vree carefully untangled another bit of the shrine. This foreign singer, this bard, already knew she was an assassin. Had to have noticed that she was no longer a part of any of the seven armies. Although she seemed to have no indication of what that meant, if Gyhard was right and bards couldn't be trusted to keep quiet, Vree would have to decide whether or not to kill her as soon as the prince was safe. She couldn't risk her even accidentally betraying them—betraying her and Bannon, or her, Gyhard, and Bannon, it didn't matter.

"That," Gyhard said, rising lithely to his feet, "remains to be seen."

"I'm asking Vree."

Gyhard bowed mockingly. "Pardon me, Lady Bard."

"Am I in your way, Vree? I'd like us to be friends."

Vree pulled another thread loose. "Why?"

Calm bardic tones cracked slightly. "Because I could use a friend right now, and I think you could, too." Whatever Gyhard was, Karlene would bet the entire contents of the circle that he wasn't a friend.

Iron self-control kept Vree from trembling. There'd always been Bannon . . .

Standing over them, Gyhard braced himself against an unexpected wave of jealousy and tried not to feel the knives twisting. He was suddenly glad he hadn't mentioned that the prince could be alive, that he hadn't offered the bard reason to hope. "Very touching. It's time to go."

Vree shook her head, curls of sweat-damp hair falling over her forehead. "In a minute. I want to finish this."

"You'll never get it untangled. Give up."

"No. Once I find the one thread that releases the rest . . ." Vree hooked a finger through a loop, twisted, and knots seemed to slide apart of their own volition. ". . . everything works out." She rose to her feet and hung the small shrine back in the tree. "Just a matter of finding that one thread."

Gyhard flicked one of the wooden ovals with his fingernail and set the whole shrine spinning. "Very symbolic," he said dryly. "But do you really need the complication of a friend you may have to kill?" He flicked it again, harder this time. The oval began to spin, wrapping about the others, catching up the longer threads, and reentangling the whole.

Vree took a deep breath and came to a visible decision. Her right hand folded into a fist. Muscles moved with purpose under the silk of her shirt.

Gasping for breath, arms wrapped around his stomach, Gyhard dropped to his knees and stared up at her in pained astonishment.

Vree! What have you done?

Something I should have done days ago. The sanctimonious little shitbrain; thinks he can do and say what he wants because he's in your body. Well, he's wrong! She stomped over to the horses, posture leaving no room for compromise.

Karlene smiled for the first time in two days and followed.

Dusk in the Capital muted both the glorious display of colors—statues, mosaics, friezes—and the grime of thousands of people living one on top of the other. Habit placed Commander Neegan in the narrow space between two buildings where he scowled at the deepening shadows. He'd been to every expensive inn in the city, his black sunburst ensuring answers to any question he cared to ask; nothing. For some reason his targets had changed the pattern they'd followed for the last thirteen days.

There were a hundred, a thousand places they could be. Finding them would take a little more time than he'd anticipated.

A rustling behind him dropped a dagger down into his hand. He whirled and threw. The pigeon managed half a wingbeat before it realized it was dead—dagger point driven into the packed earth behind it, narrow hilt pressed tightly against the soft gray feathers of its breast.

There was, however, no doubt that they'd be found.

"Vree told me about the cart."

Gyhard turned from his contemplation of the stars and stared at the bard. "I wonder why."

Karlene crossed the stableyard to stand beside him at the small corral. "Perhaps she doesn't like the intimacy that a shared secret brings."

"And you are her friend, after all." He leaned back against the rails, studying her, weighing her potential threat. "So where *are* the third and fourth members of our intrepid party?"

"She's asleep."

"You should be asleep as well. You still aren't completely recovered. If you want to give your all in the service of the prince, you'll need an all to give."

As her eyes adapted to the dark, Karlene could make out the dim shapes of horses by the far curve of the fence. "I woke up, saw you weren't there, and decided this might be the time for a talk."

"I went to the privy—I never use pots if I can help it—and stopped to admire the night sky." He hooked his thumbs behind the waistband of his full trousers. "Talk about what?"

The bard shrugged. "About what's going on. Why it's going on. Where we're going." Her gaze caught his and held it. **"Who are you?"**

"Gyhard i'Stevana." He jerked free, fully aware that she made no effort to hold him. "That wasn't very nice," he snarled. "I'm quite sure it probably contravenes any number of Bardic Vows."

"So do you; just by existing." Her brows drew down, throwing her eyes into shadow. "You've been assuming that you have all the power here—power over Vree, probably because of her brother; power over me because I need you to help me rescue what's left of a young man who never hurt anyone in his entire life and who deserves better than torture and terror after death. Well, you're wrong. Vree let you know that this afternoon; I'm letting you know it now. You need me as much as I need you, and I strongly suspect you need her more than you need anyone."

"Is it so obvious?"

Taken aback by his almost wistful tone, Karlene stared at him for a long moment, then finally sighed in exasperation. "That *would* be what you'd respond to. And I had such a good mad going, too." She mirrored his position, leaning against the rails. "Even at a full gallop, when both of you have your attention locked on the road, I can feel the attraction humming between you. You're not another brother, no matter what you look like."

"And what do I look like?" Gyhard asked dryly, deeply irritated by his flash of weakness. *It must be love; only love leads to such blatant stupidity.*

"Like a young man, late teens, early twenties. Attractive. Arrogant. You act, however, like a man much older. A man accustomed to command, certain of being obeyed. I hear a man who has spent a lifetime learning to control everything around him." She half smiled, enjoying his discomfort. "Now and then I hear a man who is finding that control slipping through his fingers. Callused fingers, working class fingers. The body doesn't go with the voice or the attitudes the voice expresses."

"You should tell fortunes."

A quick gesture dismissed his facetious statement. "The body does, however, go with Vree. Not only do you share the same features, but your musculature is almost identical; those bodies were meant to do the same thing. Your kigh and your body are not fully meshed. Somehow, Vree's body holds both her kigh and her brother's." She paused and turned to face him. "Your name is Shkodan, not Imperial. I don't know how it happened. The mere fact that it happened at all would terrify me under other circumstances, but you, Gyhard i'Stevana, are wearing Bannon's body."

Across the corral, one of the horses nickered softly.

"You seem to have given this a great deal of thought," Gyhard murmured.

"I can't think about His Highness all the time; it hurts too much."

"And suppose I tell you that you're right. What then?"

All at once, Karlene found it very difficult to breathe. It was one thing to spout incredible speculations in the middle of the night, and another entirely to have them confirmed. "I don't know," she managed at last, amazed at how composed she sounded. "Is this the first time it's happened?"

He rubbed at the fine triangle of hair in the center of his bare chest. Bannon; Aralt; a caravan guard; a chance-met stranger in the foothills of the border mountains; the young man with beautiful eyes who'd loved a crippled bard; the bandit . . . After a moment he said, "No."

"What? Who?"

"What am I? Who am I?" He spread his arms. "Just a man who doesn't intend to die."

Eyes wide, Karlene stepped away from him. Everything died. By refusing to accept that, Gyhard had taken himself out of the Circle and that alone made him as much an abomination as the dead men they followed. When she finally found her tongue, she could only manage a strangled, "How?"

Shaking his head, Gyhard exhaled noisily. "I warned Vree that bards ask a great many intrusive questions. How do I do it? That is none of your business. How do I happen to be in this body? That is Vree's business. If she wants you to know, she'll tell you herself.

"But know this: whatever the situation is, or becomes, between Vree and myself, you can affect it only in small ways." Memory laid his hand over the ridged muscles of his stomach. The point where Vree's fist had connected was still tender. "You can't change anything."

"I Sing the kigh. Maybe I can."

Suddenly exhausted, Gyhard pushed himself up off the fence. "Don't threaten me," he said quietly. "As long as I'm in her brother's body, Vree will do whatever she must in order to keep him alive. I think she's amply proved that."

"Are you warning me . . ."

"No." He stopped, halfway to the inn and looked back at her over his shoulder, the night wrapped around him like a black velvet cloak. "You were warned this afternoon."

"She'll kill anyone who gets in her way."

"What were you staring at?"

The guard swallowed a painful lump in her throat, snapped to attention, and locked her gaze a hand's span to the right of the slender man's left ear. Although the voice had barely risen above a whisper, the question crackled with menace. "You, you look familiar, sir."

Commander Neegan's brows drew in. He'd had too long and infuriating a day to put up with an open-mouthed inspection by a lowly member of the city guard. There were no laws against an Imperial citizen walking the streets of the Capital after dark. "Familiar?" he growled. "In what way?"

Even without the uniform, she'd have known he was an officer the moment he opened his mouth, and not a guard officer either. Only Imperial Army officers could stare in such a way that the person on the receiving end felt like they'd just been scraped out of a public privy. Back ramrod straight, one hand clutching the haft of her pike, the other pressed against the side pleats of her kilt, she breathed a silent prayer to Doyu, the god of fools, that she wouldn't end up on the wrong end of an army lash before morning. "You look like, well, I mean you move like someone I saw night before last. Sir."

The change in his expression almost made the idea of a flogging the lesser of two evils.

"Tell me."

So she did. Everything she could remember of what happened—and she found that under the circumstances she could remember the details with incredible clarity—and everything she'd told the man and woman who'd accosted her.

"And I move like the woman?"

"Yes, sir."

"But not the man."

"No, sir."

"Did they say why they were interested in the foreign singer?"

"No, sir. Just that they were going to the Healers' Hall to see her, and now she's gone."

"Gone or dead?"

"Gone, sir."

"You know that for a fact?"

"My brother's partner's cousin's nephew does laundry at the Hall. Sir."

Neegan nodded slowly, one hand rising to stroke the scar on his throat. He didn't understand how Bannon could so quickly throw off years of training and no longer move like an assassin. He didn't understand why they'd be interested in the foreign singer. But it seemed obvious that if the singer was gone . . . "And I see no reason to doubt your brother's partner's nephew," he muttered aloud.

"Brother's partner's cousin's nephew, sir."

"Of course." He graciously accepted the correction.

The guard's heart began beating again.

If the singer was gone, then Vree and Bannon were gone with her. But rumor implicated the singer in the kidnapping of His Imperial Highness Prince Otavas.

The guard had seen an old man with two dead men in the tombs along the East Road. The singer had said an old man and two dead men took the prince. Neegan didn't for a moment believe that the men were dead. "But I don't expect there are *four* dead men roaming the city."

"No, sir."

"Why didn't you report this to your commanding officer?"

"I reported the dead men in the tombs, sir, and was demoted one rank for being drunk on duty."

"Were you?"

"No, sir!"

"Then your commanding officer is an idiot."

"Yes, sir!" She was beginning to like this dangerous little man.

"Tomorrow morning, I want you to repeat everything you've told me to Marshal Usef."

Her jaw dropped. Up until that moment, she hadn't

believed that sort of thing actually happened. "Of the First Army, sir?"

"Yes. Of the First Army." He pulled a leather square out of his belt pouch and stuffed it into her hand as she seemed incapable of taking it from him. "Tell them that Commander Neegan says they should look for His Highness along the East Road."

"Yes, sir. But why tomorrow morning, sir?"

"Because I want to catch up to them *first*."

In spite of the heat, the guard shivered. She remained at attention until the commander disappeared into the night, then she moved out away from the buildings to give the moonlight a chance to illuminate the piece of leather in her hand. The black sunburst, stamped with the Imperial seal, stared up at her like a single, dark eye in the center of her palm.

Chapter Eleven

"Still sane?"

Vree yanked the shirt over her head, glanced down at Karlene asleep with her mouth open, then back to Gyhard. "Why should you care?"

Gyhard frowned and slowly stood. He tried to get a look at her face, but too little of the dawn light seeped through the slats of the shutters. It was the first time in all the mornings they'd shared that she hadn't simply spat a defiant yes back at him. "I used to ask," he said slowly, almost answering her question, "because I was amazed that against all odds you *were* still sane . . ."

"And now you ask because you think I'm not?" Her whole posture suggested she dared him to challenge her. *"Go on!"* exclaimed the line of her jaw and the set of her shoulders. *"I'm not afraid."*

"And now I ask because . . ." . . . *I'm afraid you're not.* He suddenly realized it himself. Since the night in the Healers' Hall, her movements had lost much of their fluidity, her eyes were shadowed, and she'd begun to do things—little things—he'd never seen her do before. He'd be willing to bet that Bannon, in his own body, had rubbed his palms together while he thought. All at once, he became aware that she was waiting for him to finish, and under her defiance he could sense apprehension. His belief in her sanity might easily be what maintained it. Wasn't it enough that he would be responsible for her madness? Apparently not. He finished the sentence as fatuously as he could. ". . . an insane assassin would not be a comfortable companion."

"If I go crazy, you'll be able to kill me—us—and it'll be over."

Would it? "If you go crazy, you'd be more likely to kill me, forgetting or not caring about whose body I'm in."

She balanced a throwing dagger on the ball of her index finger, flicked it into the air, and caught it. "You're probably right." A burgundy drop of blood marked the place where the point had pierced the skin.

Gyhard couldn't take his eyes off her as she sucked the finger clean. That her action was more fatalistic than sexual didn't seem to matter at all. He shrugged into his clothes, needing their camouflage. "You haven't answered my question."

"Am I still sane?" She moved close enough to bring her features out of shadow. For an instant, Gyhard thought he could see the storm breaking behind the surface calm in her eyes. "I'll trade you. Why are you going after this old man? And don't tell me it's because of the prince; His Highness is no good to you dead."

I don't know.

Because Prince Otavas was mine and I won't have him taken from me. Because Kars shouldn't be an old man, he should be dead and he's lived emotionally crippled far longer than he should have and I'm responsible because I taught him about the fifth kigh. Because chasing a ghost from my past delays the moment when I have to deal with the present. Because I find that loving you makes it impossible to continue to deny that I loved him and abandoned him to madness.

I don't know.

Morning moved a little farther into the room.

Vree nodded as if his silence was all she'd expected. "I'm going down to the stableyard to loosen up. All this riding is twisting me into knots."

"I know the feeling."

"I thought you might."

He closed his eyes as she left the room, but he wasn't able to hear her footsteps on the stairs. *If she does decide to kill me, to sacrifice all three of us just to see me dead, I won't even know she's coming.* Once he'd been sure that Vree would never harm her brother's body. He wondered if it would please her to know how little he was sure of now.

"You know that there's no way you'll find a happy ending in all of this."

Gyhard glared down at Karlene, who raised herself up on one elbow and stared levelly back at him. "I thought you were asleep."

"You were supposed to. I don't want to know what you'd intended to do with His Highness were he alive . . ." Her tone quite clearly said that she thought she did know and had no intention of admitting it. "But why *are* you going after the old man?"

He squatted beside her pallet, forearms balanced on his thighs, careful not to meet her gaze too directly. "I'm going to tell you something that Vree said to me once. It always struck me as succinct and to the point."

The bard lifted a heavy strand of hair back off her face and waited.

"Sod off."

Are you still sane?*

Stop it, Bannon. Don't you start. Saddlebags slung over her shoulder, sandals dangling from one hand, she padded barefoot across the stableyard to a secluded corner between the sandstone wall that separated the inn's property from the road and the small corral. Dropping her sandals onto the packed earth, she hung the bags over the top rail and peered in at the horses.

*Then am *I* still sane?*

He sounded so frightened that she stood where she was, closed her eyes, and took a deep breath. Bannon had never been afraid of anything. Not the things small boys were often afraid of. Not the training that killed one candidate for every two assassins it produced. Not what they were ordered to do, no matter how difficult. He'd never even been afraid of losing her, as she'd been afraid of losing him. She felt her palms rubbing together and as gently as she could, forced her hands apart.

Sister-mine?

You're as sane as you ever were, she told him. *Not that anyone who once carved his name on the wall in Commander Neegan's quarters just to prove he could should be considered sane.*

She felt a smile begin. *I couldn't do it now.*

*That's because you'd never get *this* body into the commander's quarters, especially not when he was asleep in them!*

His mood swung as high as it had been low. *Remember how impressed Neegan was?*

I remember he made you sand it out of the wall.

Slaughter that! He told me I had more balls than the whole Sixth Army!

And that was a compliment?

Instead of answering, he murmured, *You had a dream about me last night.*

Vree's heart skipped a beat, but she managed to keep

near panic from scattering her thoughts. *How do you know?*

I was there. He sounded smug. *I've been dreaming your dreams for a couple of nights now. I just never mentioned it before.*

Heat and the kind of sex that seared its mark on the skin for everyone to see if they only know how to look. Arms and legs entwined, bodies slick with sweat, and a final, ultimate fulfillment.

I was flattered.

Except that it wasn't Bannon. She'd had dreams about Bannon since she was old enough for desire and last night, while she'd dreamed about her brother's body, it was *not* his life controlling it.

She opened her eyes. *It's getting lighter. If we want to work out, we have to do it now.*

He settled, complacent, into the back of her mind, secure of his place in her life if nowhere else. As she stretched flexibility back into muscles and joints, she wished she could feel that same security. *Was* he sane? She didn't know. Even ignoring his attempts to take over her body, his mood swings were extreme and his habits were blurring together with hers. It was becoming harder to determine which was her and which was Bannon but no trouble at all to determine which was Gyhard.

Was *she* sane? It didn't really matter. If one of them went off the edge, the other would follow.

A short time later, skin beaded with sweat, breathing just hard enough to prove she'd put effort into the exercises, she slid her dusty feet into the heavy leather sandals and knelt to buckle them.

Vree . . .

I see them.

Two sets of footprints, pointing away from the fence, the indentation deeper toward the heel.

Those are my prints, Vree.

I know.

Why was the carrion eater out here in the middle of the night, leaning on the rail?

Probably talking.

Bannon sighed. *No slaughtering kidding. Talking to whom? He doesn't know anyone here but you and that bard.*

That bard. Vree slowly straightened and turned toward the inn. The common room stretched the length of the east side of the building and overlooked the stableyard. One of the tall, narrow shutters had been thrown open and Vree thought she could see movement in the depths of the window well. Had Gyhard and Karlene formed some kind of an alliance? They were from the same country after all. Perhaps in Shkoder they thought nothing of stealing another's body.

Don't be an ass, Vree. If they did this all the time in Shkoder, Karlene wouldn't have had to ask how it happened. He paused then continued. *Besides, she wanted to be your friend, not his.*

Secure in the knowledge that he was first in his sister's life, Bannon had never been jealous of Vree's few friends the way she'd been of his multitude.

Karlene had asked for her friendship. So why the companionable chat with Gyhard in the middle of the night?

You know, she's not bad looking for all she's got to be—what, thirty? Maybe they were . . .

Shut up, Bannon.

You could still . . .

No! She didn't know which of the two Bannon was suggesting she sleep with. Nor did she care.

Gyhard remained off limits for an increasingly complicated number of reasons, and she couldn't accept the comfort of a few hours with Karlene as long as Bannon remained in her mind.

*Hey, don't cut *my* tongue out.* He sounded sulky. *I just think it would be slaughtering unfair to go back to my own body without once experiencing sex as a woman.*

Why don't you think about a way to get us out of this alive, instead of worrying about getting laid? Vree snapped and headed back to the inn and food. She could feel the stablehands staring at her as they tossed fodder into the corral and, uncomfortable with her suspicions, only barely resisted giving them something to stare at.

"Marshal? Squad leader Zefra reports a city guard at the gate who says she has something important to tell you."

Marshall Usef sighed and rubbed a little scented oil into his hands. Many of the Imperial Court found sword calluses exciting while at the same time they objected to rough skin. Commanding the First Army had complications he'd never anticipated during his climb to the top. "Commander, I don't *see* city guards. If you think she has something important to say, you see her."

"Sir, according to the squad leader, she said it was about His Highness."

"His Highness?" Usef had spend every moment of the past three days and nights coordinating search patterns and arranging for the questioning of suspects. A few of the more highly placed suspects, he'd questioned himself. Couriers brought back news of failure after failure from the companies he'd sent out along the Great Roads, the prince remained missing, and the Emperor was beginning to lose patience.

"Yes, sir. And she had this."

Usef stared down at the black sunburst. "Neegan's?"

"Yes, sir. She says he gave it to her and told her to speak to you."

"And where is Commander Neegan now?"

"Gone, sir. He requisitioned a new horse late last night. Apparently, he'd ridden his nearly to death getting here."

"Gone?"

"Yes, sir."

"And he's sending me a message by way of this city guard?"

"Yes, sir."

"The bugger." A familiar pressure began to build in Usef's temples. The moment the prince was found, he'd retire to that villa by the sea and spend what was left of his life watching sunsets. "All right," he said at last, rubbing the square between his fingers, the oil on his skin giving the leather a greasy sheen, "I'll see this guard of Neegan's. But she'd better have something intelligent to say or she's going to pay for his insolence."

"First Army."

"What?" Gyhard raised a hand to shield his eyes. Marching toward them, just at the edge of identification, came a troop of soldiers.

"One sunburst on the pennants," Vree snapped. "First Army." The First Army left the Capital only under Imperial orders. An assassin who deserted committed treason, an Imperial offense. Obviously, someone in the Capital had recognized them. *How did they get ahead of us?*

How the slaughter should I know?

The grazing land to both the north and south offered no cover and no excuse to leave the road. Suddenly taking off cross-country would solve nothing. *We can't run . . .*

We sure as shit can't fight!

We haven't any choice. Blood roared in her ears as her body prepared for battle.

"They must've looked right by His Highness when they passed the cart," Karlene muttered. "Just like everyone else."

"Probably went as far as the Third Army garrison at Shaebridge," Gyhard agreed.

His Highness. Of course, the First Army had been ordered along the Great Roads hunting for the missing prince—on the morning after, they'd met a company searching the South Road. Now, four days later, this company would have reached the territory of the Third Army and be returning home. *We should've known they weren't looking for us.*

Guilty conscience, sister-mine.

If they come for us, they'll come as a dagger in the night.

If Emo kept his mouth shut, they've no reason to come for us.

If we're recognized . . .

Like Avor?

We can't kill everyone who knows us, Bannon.

"Vree?" Karlene reached over and touched her lightly on the shoulder. "Are you all right?"

"She's talking to her brother," Gyhard said shortly. "You get used to it." He took another look at the approaching soldiers. The military blur had begun to separate into individuals. *Or as close to individuals as the military allows,* he thought, shooting half a glance at Vree. But the whole mass moved with a jerky vehemence that suggested they were none too pleased about their failure to find Prince Otavas. "I think we'd better expect trouble and take the time we have remaining to decide what our business is along this road."

"They have no reason to stop us," Karlene began indignantly.

"They could come up with any number of reasons if they wanted to, all perfectly legal under Imperial law, but they don't need any of them."

"Why not?"

"Because there're three of us and considerably more of them and they're in a bad mood. Not to mention that an Imperial prince is missing and everyone is suspect until His Highness is found."

"And what if we tell them the truth?"

Vree snickered before she could stop herself. *Bannon!*

Karlene pressed her lips together in a thin line. "And what's wrong with the truth?"

"That we're after a cart pulled by dead men and that cart contains the prince?" Gyhard shook his head. "Even you, Lady Bard, couldn't make them believe that."

"Riders," Vree said abruptly as two of the mounted officers separated from the column and galloped toward them, a squad of infantry following at the jog. "You'd better let Gyhard do the lying while you Sing."

"Sing? Why?"

"First Army's garrison is in the palace. The officers, at least, will recognize you."

"And will anyone recognize you? Us?" Gyhard asked as Karlene swore in Shkodan and began to Sing quietly.

Vree shrugged. "Shouldn't. This is First Army, we were Sixth."

"If they do, you're not to kill them. They'll have no way of knowing you're, we're not out . . ."

"Aimed at a target," Vree supplied when he hesitated. "I'd better do the talking. You don't even know the words."

"You can do the talking, *if* we're recognized."

Don't tell me you trust him?

I trust him to save his own ass and you've got to admit, he's had practice at that. Vree reined in her horse as the pair of Imperial officers stopped in the middle of the road. While sufficient room remained to go around them on either side, their intentions were plain. *Don't do anything to attract attention.*

Me?

I mean it, Bannon. Behave. She rested both hands on the low pommel of the saddle, wondered for a moment where the scar across her knuckles had gone, realized it was Bannon's scar not hers, and pushed the thought away.

"Names?" barked the squad leader, significantly the younger of the two officers. His expression suggested he'd taken the loss of the prince, and his inability to find him, personally.

"Albannon Magaly," Gyhard replied with just the expected amount of challenge in his voice. He wasn't, after all, under this squad leader's command. "This is my sister, Vireyda Magaly."

How does he know Mother's name?

*He's in *your* head, Bannon. Now shut up, I need to hear what's going on.*

Neither officer seemed to think it strange that he didn't mention the third member of their party. "You're southern."

Gyhard looked pointedly down at the dark olive skin

of his arms, then pointedly back up at the peeling tip of the squad leader's nose. "Yes."

"Imperial citizens?"

"The Sixth Province has been part of the Empire for three generations!"

The older officer, a captain, half smiled at the indignant tone but the younger bridled. "Your business on the road?" he snarled at Vree.

"I'm guarding my brother." *Find the lie in that,* she sneered silently. Officers bloated with their own importance were invariably despised by the ranks.

"From what?"

"From danger." Vree locked her gaze over the junior officer's shoulder. Her hearing and sense of smell grew more acute and the edges of her vision expanded. She felt the way she did going through the perimeter into the enemy's camp when death lurked around every corner. Her wits would be her dagger here.

"What danger?"

"Whatever danger there is."

The captain raised her hand as the squad leader prepared to spit out another question. "You served," she said quietly.

"Yes, sir," Vree acknowledged.

Vree, you're sitting at attention.

Bannon, stop it!

Fortunately, no one appeared to notice the twitch.

"Your brother didn't."

Vree glanced over at Gyhard, who was *not* sitting at attention. "No, sir."

"So." The captain swept her gaze across them, her eyes unfocusing slightly as they passed over the bard. "If you are guarding your brother, what is your brother's business?"

"He's a whore, sir."

Hey!

She fought to keep Bannon's protest from showing on her face—not that it would have mattered as both the mounted officers, and the infantry squad that had reached them during the questioning, were studying Gyhard with new interest.

"You're not, by chance, heading for the garrison at Shaebridge?" the captain asked, her eyes measuring the breadth of Gyhard's shoulders.

Gyhard shook his head. Vree thought he might have put more grace into the movement than usual for it caused the sunlight to throw rippled highlights through Bannon's curls. "Not the garrison, no."

"Pity." She nodded to her left. "Carry on." A moment later, she lightly put her heels to her horse and murmured, "An attractive pair, and who would dare take advantage of the brother with the sister around?"

"She was insolent," the squad leader complained, yanking back at the bit.

"And you were an idiot, Orlan. Anyone could see that those three had nothing to do with the prince's disappearance."

"Three?"

For a moment, the captain thought she heard singing. "Did I say three? Jiir take me, I'm more tired than I thought . . . ."

"I thought I was to do the talking," Gyhard complained as they moved out of earshot.

Vree shrugged. "Next time have them ask you the questions."

"Then *why* a whore?"

"They also serve who service."

"What?"

"Just something we say in the army . . ."

Riding a little behind and continuing to Sing, for they had the bulk of the company still to pass, Karlene considered what she'd heard. Had the Imperial officers the benefit of bardic training and the ability to separate the sound of truth from falsehood, they would have realized that they'd been lied to twice; the first time when Albannon Magaly—or more precisely the man in his body—had called Vireyda Magaly his sister, the second when Vree had said that her brother had not served in the army.

When she'd called him a whore, she'd meant it.

Karlene watched the muscles roll across Vree's shoulders and wondered if the younger woman even knew how much barely repressed hostility she felt toward the brother who shared her body.

Half dozing in the lingering heat of the afternoon, Otavas was shaken awake by a sudden jerk of the cart. He grabbed for the side, missed, and found himself sprawled half over the old man's lap, one hand tangled in the necklace of bone he wore. With a grunt of revulsion, the prince pushed himself erect and yanked his foot out from under Kait, who'd also fallen forward and was awkwardly trying to rise. His skin crawled where she'd touched his leg.

He steeled himself for the old man's solicitous inquiries and the feel of the soft, dry hands patting at his arms, but the old man seemed hardly aware of him at all. Instead of performing the expected pawing, he twisted around, pulled himself up to see over the high front edge, and cried out.

"Are you all right?" The prince's question was a conditioned response to the suffering in the old man's voice. Although he reached out, Otavas stopped himself before he touched the ancient shoulder.

"My fault. All my fault. I was too anxious to get you home."

"What's your fault?" The prince stood and, keeping a careful distance, peered out at the dead men running between the shafts—the dead *man* running between the shafts, for the left side of Aver's body twisted under him with every step, causing the cart to lurch as his cousin dragged both him and it forward.

"Stop running!"

With more strength than he'd previously shown, the old man threw himself up at the back and had the tail-gate out before it was completely still. When Otavas tried to follow, Wheyra reached for him. "Okay, I'll watch from here," he said quickly. "I'm staying right here."

Wheyra stared at him for a terrifying moment—in many ways the prince found her the most frightening of them all—then resumed crooning to the corpse of her baby.

He could actually see everything from where he was but, looking down between the shafts where the old man knelt by Aver's fallen body, all at once he wasn't sure he wanted to.

"My fault, my fault." Tears etching tracks through the dust on his face, the old man reached out and patted Aver's cheek. He had forgotten how much movement could be asked of the dead. "Forgive me." His voice quavered with guilt. "I was too anxious to get my heart home." He'd forgotten his responsibility to the rest of his family.

The dead man tracked his movements with wildly rolling eyes.

"So soon, so soon," he murmured as he traced the shattered joints at knee and hip and lightly stroked the black patches of decay that showed through the skin.

Nose, fingers, lips—all had been burned a purple-black by the sun and in other places yellow pus oozed out through baked cracks. He could hold his hand above Aver's torso and feel the heat generated by the rot within. The left foot must have been dragging on the road for most of the day as it was nearly gone.

"You can ride the rest of the way home," he promised. "You'll last so much longer that way, you'll see." Leaning heavily on his staff, he got to his feet and turned to the still standing cousin. "Put him into the cart, Otanon. He'll be fine once he's in the cart."

Although he'd suffered nearly identical sun damage, Otanon's joints appeared to have survived the pounding they'd taken over the last few days. Eyes never leaving his cousin's face, he dropped the supports down from the shafts that kept the cart from tipping forward on its nose, then he bent and heaved Aver up off the ground.

The skin across Aver's stomach split and a rancid mass of organs and tissue spilled out of the body cavity. Up in the cart Otavas gagged, but the old man didn't appear to notice the stench.

Aver twitched in his cousin's grasp. His mouth opened and closed, but he made no sound.

He's still in there, Otavas realized. *Gods protect us, he's still in there.* Fingers locked white-knuckled over the top board of the cart, he began to pray; for himself or for the dead, he had no idea.

"Put him in the cart," the old man said, his face folded into itself with worry. "He'll be fine once you put him in the cart."

Aver, dangling from Otanon's hands, somehow found the strength to jerk his head from side to side in a silent plea. Otanon didn't move.

"You'll be fine once you're in the cart," the old man repeated soothingly. "You'll see."

"Let him go." Otavas almost didn't recognize the voice as his. "Please, let him go."

The old man stared up at him, confusion mixing with the concern on his face. "But I never let them go," he said, reaching out to stroke Aver's shoulder. "They leave me."

It seemed as though the words or touch were a signal, for the dead man stiffened and his eyes opened as wide as destroyed tissue would allow.

"No . . ."

The old man sounded so distraught that Otavas rubbed his vision clear and leaned forward. During the heartbeat the prince looked down into the dead man's eyes, he found himself trapped in a horror too dark to understand with no hope of either escape or rescue. A shriek that could not have been made by a human throat rang in his mind as Otavas threw himself back, escaping into oblivion.

"No!" the old man cried again as Aver's kigh fled the ghastly wreck of his body.

Otanon made a noise very like a sigh, then, keening no less terribly, his kigh followed his cousin's. Both bodies collapsed to the road, wet meat smacking against dressed slabs of stone.

"Oh, my children . . ." The old man rocked back and forth, clutching his staff to his chest. They'd been called with one Song, and so they had to leave him together as they came—but it hurt. For all the times it had happened over the years, it never ceased to hurt.

"Unless you can explain your companion's involvement in the disappearance of my son, I will send a company of the First Army out along the East Road to join the company already searching and together they will beat the information out of her."

Fighting for calm, Gabris bowed deeply as the Emperor paused. "Imperial Majesty, I cannot explain, but I beg you to give Karlene just a little more time."

"She was alone with my son when he was taken." The Emperor gestured toward Marshal Usef standing just to the right of the throne, plumed helmet cradled in the crook of his left arm, his face politically expressionless. "Now I find that two strangers, targeted by an Imperial assassin, removed her from the Healers' Hall. You tell me that she is searching for my son, but if these two had answers, why did she not bring them to me? She has had all the time I am willing to give. I want answers, Gabris. I want my son."

"Imperial Majesty, I . . ."

"No. To whatever you were going to say, no. You will be moved to a secure suite in the center of the palace where you will not be able to warn her. At this moment, I do not hold you responsible . . ." His tone clearly indicated that could change. ". . . but I will not have you interfering."

Gabris closed his eyes for a heartbeat. What he had to say had to be said in such a way that it would not, could not, be interpreted as a threat. "Imperial Majesty, Karlene is a bard, powerful enough to finish the training of the young bards of the Empire soon to be returning from Shkoder."

Marshal Usef snorted. "I think this bard, however *powerful,* will be willing to be reasonable with a hundred swords at her throat."

Karlene Sang a gratitude and hurried back to the road, kicking up little clouds of dust from the dry earth with every step. "They're no longer heading east," she called. "According to the kigh, they're following a river. It would have to be the Shae, unless they've pulled incredibly far ahead, which would mean they've turned off the road at Shaebridge."

"You know this part of the country well," Gyhard remarked as she took her reins from Vree and mounted.

"I'd better." She settled into the saddle and flipped her braid back over her shoulder. "In a very short time I'm supposed to be walking the new Imperial bards over it."

Vree fell in beside Karlene and noted how Gyhard moved to ride on her other flank, as far from the bard as possible. Their meeting in the innyard had obviously not gone well. Karlene had spent the day acting as though Gyhard were something she'd found on the bottom of her sandal.

She's perceptive, I'll give her that.

I want to know what he told her.

Bannon snorted. *Probably lies.*

"I wasn't aware that the Empire had bards," Gyhard said quietly.

"It doesn't yet." Karlene's tone was anything but friendly. "Nine Imperial citizens with the ability to Sing the kigh are nearly finished with their training in Shkoder."

Vree scowled, confused. "It makes no sense for Shkoder to train Imperial bards. You'll lose your advantage in battle."

"What battle?"

"*Any* battle between Shkoder and a country without bards." Vree waved an emphatic hand about. "Sending messages quickly over long distances is an advantage you shouldn't surrender. Not to mention having the air spirits scout for you."

"But what about the people in the Empire who are able to Sing the kigh but are never trained?" Karlene asked.

"What about them?"

"Without training, they'll be condemned to live only half alive."

So what.

Vree repeated Bannon's observation and added, "Untrained, they won't guide an army across the border to slit a few Shkodan throats."

"A bard would never do that. We take vows . . ."

Vree's fingers closed tightly around the reins and her horse danced sideways in reaction to her stiffening. "Vows can be broken; on purpose or by circumstance."

"It's hard to explain, Vree." Wiping sweat out of her eyes, Karlene watched a muscle jump in Vree's jaw and wondered what vows the younger woman had broken. "Once you're trained to Sing the kigh, you're changed. You *know* that you're a part of a greater whole and you *can't* do anything to damage that. It would be like cutting off your own arm."

"*That* she should understand," Gyhard murmured. "Have her tell you about assassin training some time."

Karlene didn't want to know about assassin training; didn't want to know how the Empire created an efficient, conscienceless killer out of a normal, intelligent, honorable, beautiful woman. She wondered what Vree would have been like without the training that had made her so easily accept the unacceptable. *"She'll kill you if you get in her way."*

"So there are no evil bards?" Vree asked, breaking into Karlene's train of thought. "No crazy bards?"

"No. No one knows why, but it doesn't happen that way. I'm not saying that we're all perfect; some of us are lazy, some of us are irritating, some of us are vain and complacent ..." *We should've stayed at that tavern. I should've sent for his guard. I should never have assumed I could get the prince safely back to the palace alone.* She had to swallow the guilt before she could continue. "... but our ability to Sing the kigh makes it impossible for us to not realize the validity of another's viewpoint."

"So the bards of Shkoder send Imperial citizens back into the Empire trained to have more in common with the bards of Shkoder than with their own people," Vree said slowly, trying to make military sense out of it. "So that someday, when Shkoder has trained bards and sent them to every country, bards will run things."

For a long moment the only sound was the hollow clop of hooves on stone and the high-pitched hum of an insect in a distant tree. Then Gyhard chuckled. "Get out of that one," he challenged.

Karlene stiffened at the sound of his laughter. "Well, we're pretty nonpolitical ..."

That was no kind of answer and they all knew it.

"What about the bard we're after?" Vree asked suddenly. "What about the old man? You said there were no crazy bards."

All of a sudden, Gyhard found the conversation less amusing. "He was made crazy because he was a bard. He didn't start out that way."

"Cemandians," Karlene sighed as though that should explain it.

Vree leaned forward, trying to get a look at Gyhard's face around the bard riding between them. "What happened to him?"

Gyhard rode in silence for a while before finally answering. "The Cemandians think that the kigh are outside the Circle ..."

What's he talking about?

I don't know.

"They think the kigh are demons," he amended, obviously realizing he'd lost half his audience. "And anyone who shows an ability to Sing the kigh is—I suppose torture isn't too extreme a word for it—is tortured to drive the demons out."

Karlene shook her head, the protest as much at the Cemandians as at what Gyhard had said. "They're not quite so extreme anymore. Over the last few years . . ."

"The last few years have nothing to do with Kars," he interrupted bitterly. "Torture was their preferred response when Kars was young. He escaped. Hid in the mountains."

So the old man had a name. "You found him hiding in the mountains?"

"Yes." Badly hurt but not insane. Not yet. It took love to push him over the edge that torture had taken him to.

There was such a complete lack of emotion in that single syllable that the pain it masked stood out in sharp relief.

Vree stared down at their shadows, stretching out on the road before them. It seemed her heart had begun to beat just a little faster. *The old man is the other one; the one before us that Gyhard told his past to.*

And it sounds like he drove him crazy, too.

We're not crazy, Bannon.

Not yet, sister-mine. He sounded almost smug.

Karlene chewed her lower lip while she thought, trying to piece together all she'd learned over the last few days. *Considering that neither of them wants to tell me anything, I don't think I've ever been with two people so desperate to talk about what's happening to them.* She'd wanted to help Vree from the beginning, but now she began to wonder if she could possibly feel

pity for Gyhard as well. As things were far too complicated for a horseback analysis, she finally sighed. "I
wish I knew what was going on."

Gyhard shrugged. "I doubt you'd understand it."

The urge to smack that superior tone right out of his
voice was intense, but uncertain of what might cause
Vree to protect her brother's body, she managed to resist. Instead, she recalled the map of the Third Province she carried in memory. "They're—Kars is heading
for the mountains."

"I suppose he feels safe there."

"You're sure of where he's going now, aren't you?"

"I know where he used to feel safe, years ago."

"It's a place to start."

"It's a place to finish," Gyhard corrected. He kicked
his horse forward into a trot and then a canter, his final
word hanging in the air behind him.

The cart had stopped. Otavas pushed himself up on
one elbow and peered sleepily around. He was alone.
He remembered thinking that with both the remaining
dead pulling the cart he could easily overpower the old
man and escape. Then the old man had begun to sing,
a quavering lament for the loss of the cousins. They'd
turned off the East Road at Shaebridge—he'd seen the
city pass in the dusk like a torchlit memory from another life—and eventually, emotionally exhausted, he'd
drifted into a fitful slumber.

But now the cart was stopped and he was alone.

He scrambled to his feet, eyes fighting to become
accustomed to the night, and threw himself up and
over the side. Landing awkwardly, palms flat against
the dusty ground, he took a second to catch his breath
and then leaped forward.

The pale oval of Wheyra's face materialized suddenly out of the darkness, too close for him to avoid crashing into her. His outthrust hands sank into the bundle she carried. He screamed and flung himself back.

When his spine slammed against the cart, it seemed more a refuge than a prison.

"Kait and I are going into the village for supplies, my heart," the old man crooned, stepping forward into the limited vision the night allowed. "Wheyra will stay here to keep you company."

"To keep me from running away!" the prince panted.

"No." The old man sadly shook his head, wisps of long gray hair floating in and out of sight. **"You won't run away.** Not this time."

Thunder grumbled in the distance and heat lightning turned the sky an angry orange as they made their way into the small village tucked between the packed dirt of the road and a bend in the river. The old man hummed as they walked, hoping for an answer.

A dog howled as they passed the first of the buildings, but with that one exception it appeared the village slept.

It soon became apparent that there would be no answer.

The old man studied the collection of houses. Finally, he lifted the latch on a tiny dwelling so close to the river that spring floods had marked the walls. Taking a firm grip on his staff, he motioned Kait in before him.

On a pallet by the empty hearth, a man and a woman lay sleeping in each other's arms. He searched the shadows for signs of children as the sleeping couple began to stir, their dreams prodded by the nightmare standing and staring down at them. When he was certain that there would be no orphans left behind, he took a crude blade from its place on the wall and told Kait what to do with it.

The prince crouched against the high wheel of the cart. Wheyra crouched a few feet away, just close enough so he could neither forget nor ignore her. He had no idea how long the old man had been gone, but his shirt stuck to his back in great clammy patches and the near constant roll of thunder made him want to scream.

Instead, he drew in a long shuddering breath, dried his palms against his thighs, and said, "What's its name?"

Wheyra cocked her head, the movement adding curiosity to a face no longer capable of expression.

Otavas wet his lips. *"The more you know about something, the less terrifying it becomes."* He couldn't remember who'd told him that, but anything was better than just listening to the thunder. "The baby." He couldn't quite gesture at the decomposing bundle in her arms. "What's its name." He hadn't heard her speak, but Aver had been able to and Kait called the old man Father.

Wheyra looked down at the remains of her baby, then back up at the prince and, to his astonishment, smiled. Her face didn't move, couldn't move, but he would have sworn by any of the gods contained in his mother's Circle that she smiled. "Ty . . . am," she said.

The others knew they were dead. If Wheyra knew, she didn't care. Otavas locked his fingers together to keep them from trembling.

"Boot . . . ifoo."

"I don't understand."

The purple-gray tip of her tongue protruded as she tried again. "Boot . . . ifoo ba . . . ba."

He didn't know how he could hurt so much and not bleed. "Beautiful baby."

"Yesss." She smiled again, then her head jerked around to the right.

Otavas looked where she looked and sagged back against the cart, bone and muscles unable to hold him. There were four shadows approaching through the night. He should have realized the old man had gone to replace the cousins.

"I've brought us food," the old man said as he drew near. "Take it up into the cart with you. We still have a long way to go before we're home."

The prince numbly accepted the bulging oilskin bag and did as he was told. He couldn't run, and they'd touch him if he stayed where he was. Once in the cart he turned and peered over the edge.

A flash of lightning lit up the scene.

The man and the woman were neither young nor old nor long dead. The rough cotton tunics they wore glistened, wet, black stains spreading out from the center of their chests. Over the constant and familiar stench of rot, Otavas could smell the sharp, coppery scent of fresh blood.

"Iban and Hestia, my heart." The old man's voice drew his gaze around and he found himself lost in the ancient eyes. "They've come to join our family, to help us get safely home where we can start again."

He started to shake. He wanted to shriek, but the only protest he could force through the horror was a faint and disbelieving, "No . . ."

Chapter Twelve

"Funny," Karlene mused, glancing up at the dawn sky.

"What is?" Vree asked, pulling her girth tight in spite of the gelding's plans to the contrary.

"Gabris hasn't sent any kigh since just past midday yesterday."

"Maybe he's given up."

"Gabris? Not likely. Even if he can't get me to return and he essentially trusts my judgment, he'll want me to know exactly how much he disapproves."

"He's probably trying to trap you. He'll wait until he thinks you've stopped expecting the air spirits to come and have lowered your guard. *Then* he'll send them again."

"Perhaps." The bard swung up into the saddle and yanked the bottom of her long tunic out from under her. "But it seems just a little too military for Gabris."

We did that at Oman; only without the air spirits. Do you remember, Vree? You won ten crescents from One-ball when he didn't think they'd fall for it.

You won ten crescents, Bannon, not me.

I did? Are you sure?

She could hear One-ball cursing as the Fourth Squad breached the gate. Could feel the cold weight of the coins in her hand. But was it a memory of her hand or Bannon's? She'd lost two crescents in a dice game, spent three at Teemo's on a beautiful young man with ebony hair down past his . . .

No, Vree, that was me. I went to Teemo's not you. His name was . . .

Ahlaun. She could remember his name, feel the touch of his body, but Bannon was right; he'd gone to Teemo's, not her. *So *you* won the ten crescents.*

But I watched you collect.

No. But her denial had little force behind it for the edges of the memory blurred too far to distinguish which of them watched and which of them won. Searching for herself, Vree started to get lost in the kaleidoscope of images.

"Vree!" Gyhard watched anxiously as she turned toward the sound of her name and her eyes found a focus on his face.

"What?" Her tone, for all it suggested he was interrupting where he had no business being, had a hint of desperation behind it.

Sifting through a number of responses, he dropped his arm. He'd come very close to shaking her even though he doubted he'd have enjoyed her response. "Do you think you could continue your conversation with your brother some other time?" The near panic in her expression had made it clear it'd been much more than mere conversation, but as she wouldn't accept his concern—not that he really blamed her—he made it easier on them both by not offering it. "We're ready to go."

Without answering, Vree whirled about and flung herself up into the saddle. Then she glared down at him with barely concealed impatience.

Why do I bother? he sighed to himself as he mounted. The bard's expression suggested that he deserved what he got and he supposed he did. *I need to keep reminding myself that when she looks on me with anything but contempt, it's safe to assume it's her brother's body she sees.* Except that once or twice over the course of their journey, he could have almost sworn that she saw him. And at the end of that journey? The bard was right. No happy endings. He slammed his heels into the horse's sides, and the startled animal charged away from the innyard.

Who stuck a spear up his butt?

Bent low over the cropped brush of his horse's mane, Neegan ignored the shouts of those forced to dive away from galloping hooves as he ignored the pain pounded into muscles and joints by his wild ride. He'd traded the courier's horse he'd taken from the First Army's stables at the way station where he'd rested for what little part of the night he felt he could spare. The couriers' horses, bred by the seven armies for extremes of speed and endurance, could half the time it took to travel from the Capital to Shaebridge.

Even if they were riding hard, he'd be on his target by dark.

"We're closer." Karlene whistled the kigh out of the billowing folds of her tunic and remounted. "We're still more than a day's walk away, but the kigh are a lot more agitated than they were."

"It might not be because of Kars," Gyhard pointed out.

"It has to be. He's the only thing that's ever upset the kigh like that."

"The only thing you know of, and you aren't that old."

"This from a man who's barely shaving," Karlene snorted sarcastically, raking him with a disdainful glance. "You want to play elder statesman with me, you should've taken over a different body. In all of *Bardic Recall*, your Kars is the only thing that the kigh have ever been frightened of." She waited for him to deny that it was "his Kars." When he didn't, she turned the information over to examine it. She'd been assuming that when he'd met Kars, the crippled bard was already an old man, but that wasn't necessarily so. Gyhard had admitted that Bannon's body was not the first body he'd taken. Without her quite controlling it, her free hand rose to trace the sign of the Circle over her heart. He could've left a hundred bodies abandoned behind him. There were a thousand questions she should've asked.

Gyhard had made it clear from the beginning he was after the old man, not the prince. Why? Perhaps they'd been young men together, with young men's feelings—which would explain why Gyhard considered the old man to still be "his Kars." But would an old love be enough with a new love, however hopeless by his side? *Get a grip, Karlene,* she chided herself. *Write the tragic ballad when this is over.*

Based on what he'd said to Vree back in the Healers' Hall, Gyhard agreed to go after the prince only when he became certain Kars was involved and raising the dead. Kars raised the dead by Singing the fifth kigh. Gyhard moved his kigh from body to body. If Gyhard met Kars many years and perhaps many bodies ago . . .

Her heart skipped a beat, and she jerked around to face him, nearly unseating herself. "*You* taught him to Sing the fifth kigh!"

Vree started at the sudden exclamation and a dagger appeared in her hand.

Gyhard stretched an arm between their horses and

touched her lightly on the shoulder. "I think she's speaking to me."

"I know that," Vree snarled, sheathing the blade. "Do you think we're stupid?"

"I think you've got highly trained responses," he began, but Vree cut him off.

"Don't patronize me," she said wearily. "It doesn't help. Answer the bard."

Gyhard closed his eyes for a moment and remembered how simple life had been when it hadn't mattered what anyone thought of him—only what they thought of the body and the identity he wore. *How fortunate that I don't care what the other one thinks.* "The bard didn't actually ask me anything. I believe she was making more of an accusation."

"And I'll make another one!" Karlene's horse danced sideways under the prod of his rider's emotions. "You're responsible for . . . for everything!"

"For everything?" His voice, arrogant and cynical, mocked her intensity. "You grant me too great an influence. I may be responsible for bringing the fifth kigh to Kars' attention." *And I may have hastened his descent into madness by doing it.* "But I am not responsible for the rest." And he would not accept responsibility for it either. "*You* lost the prince." The bald accusation, contemptuously delivered, rubbed salt in a wound he knew she kept raw by self-flagellation. "Try to remember that, without me, you're not likely to get His Highness back."

Karlene ground her teeth together, as angry as he'd meant her to be. "If *you* were not an abomination creating other abominations, His Highness would never have been taken!"

"If *you* hadn't encouraged the prince to pant after you—oh, yes, we heard the rumors while we were in the Capital—then he wouldn't have *been* where he could have been taken."

"If you both keep shifting blame so loudly, we're going to attract some unwelcome attention," Vree growled. "Try to remember that we're on a public road, that we'll be stopped if we're identified, and we'll fail if we're stopped."

So close to Shaebridge the road held more traffic than at any time since they'd left the Capital—the back of a brightly enameled carriage could be seen up ahead; two merchants were approaching, loudly arguing about something as they walked alongside the mule who pulled their heavily laden cart; a servant carrying a basket hurried toward the city on a path that ran just off the edge of the dressed stone, safely out of the way of horses and carts. The country villas of the middle class lined both sides of the road and behind them were farms and orchards.

Karlene grabbed hold of her anger and dragged her voice down to an undertone. "Do you think anyone heard?"

"No. If they had, I'd have killed them." When the bard looked aghast, Vree sighed. "It's a joke."

It's not very funny.

Who asked you?

"If you ask me, there's nothing the gods can do for those two now. What I want to know is what kind of sick person leaves a pair of decomposing bodies lying in the middle of a Great Road."

As though they were pulled by a single string, all three heads turned to stare at the approaching merchants.

"Maybe it's a tax protest."

"Yeah? Well, it's our taxes paying for the cleanup."

"Excuse me," Karlene lengthened her horse's stride

and rode forward to meet them. "But did you say there were a pair of decomposing bodies left lying in the road?"

The younger of the two merchants looked annoyed with such a blatant admission of eavesdropping, marked her for a foreigner, and decided to make an exception for barbaric manners. "That's right. Two of them. And no one local's claimed them. There's a whole herd of priests out from Shaebridge trying to decide what to do."

"What to do?"

"Well they can't just leave them there; can they?"

Herd of priests, while somewhat irreligious, was accurate enough. Men and women in every color robes imaginable chanted, prayed, evoked, and argued with each other in a loose circle around a covered mound lying by the north side of the road. Incense burned in censers and braziers and in the beard of a priest of Quindarin, god of metalworkers, the scented smoke filling the immediate area with an oily blue-gray haze. A number of people in the surrounding crowd sneezed continually. While it remained possible to go around— not even the representatives of the Empire's gods dared defy Imperial law and completely block one of the Great Roads—most travelers had stopped to watch, joining the curious who'd journeyed out from the city and in from nearby farms. At each of the compass points stood a knot of soldiers—Third Army from the garrison in Shaebridge—sent to keep the peace.

From horseback it was possible to see over the heads of the crowd and right to the mound at the center of the circle. The worn sole of a leather sandal that stuck out from under one end of the covering canvas defined the objects beneath.

"Why don't they just dig a grave and bury them in it," Gyhard muttered. He disliked funerals; had never, in all his lives, attended one. To make such a fuss over death gave it a validity he wouldn't allow.

Vree stared at him in astonishment. "Just bury them? Without knowing what gods they worshiped? Or what rites to perform? You could deny them the rewards of their life. Condemn them to eternity as a . . . as a . . ."

Carrion eater.

". . . carrion eater."

*He should know about *that*,* Bannon snarled.

"That's a load of superstitious crap and you're too intelligent to believe it," Gyhard told her bluntly. "The only thing you're denying these two, now their kigh have left, is the chance to rot in private."

"You don't know that. *You've* never died." She dropped her voice. "And we don't know that these are two of the dead we're looking for."

"Who else would they be? I don't believe in the kind of coincidence that would put two other unidentified corpses in our path."

"If they are who we think they are, then they have family back in the Capital who want them returned," Karlene said quietly, reins draped loosely over the saddle horn, arms wrapped tightly around her body.

Gyhard rolled his eyes. "They're meat."

"Their families aren't." She drew in a long shuddering breath and exhaled slowly, then dropped to the ground and handed the reins to Vree. "I'm going to go have a look."

Reaching out and grabbing her shoulder, Gyhard leaned down toward her ear. "What about catching up to the prince?" he asked.

She twisted around, just enough to meet his gaze. "Maybe we already have."

"I think someone in this lot would know him."

"Would they? After what he's been through?" Teeth clamped on her lower lip, she fought for composure. "Maybe they would, but I have to be sure. Now let go of me before I have the kigh shove you out of the saddle."

"You're not supposed to do that."

"You're not supposed to exist."

After a moment, Gyhard released her and sat back. Together, he and Vree watched her make her way through the crowd.

"Will she command the priests to let her in?" Vree wondered.

"She probably won't have to; bards usually get their own way."

Vree looped Karlene's reins around her saddle horn and rubbed her palms lightly against each other as Bannon glanced over at Gyhard from the corner of one eye.

I wonder if she had her own way with him?

Vree jerked her gaze back to the crowd. *She thinks he's something that crawled out from under a rock.*

So. She knows he's in my body. He must've told her that night they had their little talk. Maybe she's after my body, not him. You think you'd recognize that, sister-mine? Or maybe you wouldn't.

Her head felt as though it were trapped between a pair of battering rams. *I don't know what you're talking about.*

I'm talking about you and him.

There isn't a me and him. There's me and you. There's me and your body. That's all. Just like it's always been.

A layer of silence spread over the chants and the

prayers and the speculation, separating her from the world. *Bannon? Are you there?*

He snorted. *Where the slaughter else would I be? I was just thinking about what we really have is *us* and my body.*

No, Bannon. She should have expected him to keep pushing. He was used to getting what he wanted.

Again the silence. Then, *What happens if this *is* the prince? Do we go back to the Capital with his body, or do we keep following Gyhard and mine? He doesn't need *us* to find the old man, so I wonder why he hasn't tried to slip a knife under our ribs some dark night. I wonder why he hasn't tried to get rid of two of the three people who know his secret.*

She could feel the slow pulse of his anger.

Do you wonder, sister-mine?

"I've just come from the Capital where tombs have been opened along the East Road and bodies taken from them. If I can see these bodies, I might know who they are." Her words pitched to carry over most of the crowd, Karlene used just enough Voice for them to believe her. Then she waited, shifting from one foot to the other, while the priests of Shaebridge's five dominant temples discussed the implications of allowing a foreigner access.

"What gods do you follow?" an elderly woman demanded abruptly, slapping the strap of her short ceremonial flail against the side of her leg as she separated from the huddle.

Since coming to the Empire, Karlene had been asked that question half a hundred times. "I believe that all life and all gods are enclosed within the Circle."

"Oh, that," the old priest snorted. "The northern all-encompassing heresy. Well, there's little enough damage you can do." She stepped aside. "You might as well take a look. You're lucky, they don't smell as bad as they did. I expect the heat's started to dry them out some."

Karlene could feel the attention of the crowd lock onto her as she crossed the open area around the covered bodies. As she passed one of the priests, he sprinkled her with warm liquid and then began to sprinkle everyone within reach. A young—woman or man, she wasn't sure—knelt to one side, surrounded by acolytes, rocking back and forth and moaning, blood dribbling from three or four places where teeth had closed on the edge of soft tissue.

An expectant hush fell when she dropped to one knee and took hold of the canvas. They were waiting for her to solve the mystery. Put name and faith to these discarded shells that underscored their own mortality. Could she? If one of the bodies was—had been—Prince Otavas, would she recognize him after all he'd been through? What marks would a living death cut into flesh?

Her grip leaving a damp print on the heavy fabric, she quickly flipped it back.

Not the prince. Thank all the gods in the Circle, not the prince.

It was the two men who'd taken the prince, recognizable in spite of advanced decay. She pressed the knuckles of her right hand against her mouth as she started to gag, unable to believe that they could have ever smelled worse. They were as unmistakably dead as they'd been that night in the alley but thankfully, no sign of life remained. Breathing shallowly through her teeth, she gently covered them again.

No sign of life . . . The hair lifted off the nape of her neck as she stood. *But something remains . . .*

The kigh nearly knocked her over, their sudden whirlwind dragging the canvas from the ground and spinning it into the crowd. Someone screamed. The prayers grew louder. Backing away from the bodies, Karlene tried to block out the rising noise and concentrate on what the kigh were trying to say. They acted much as they had back in the palace on the night the terror began but, this time, they were able to tell her why.

"Are you all right?" the ancient priest demanded as one of her burly acolytes stopped the bard from sagging to the ground. "You're white as salt."

"I know these men." While that wasn't the problem, neither was it a lie. The kigh drew back to dive around the edges of her vision, the winds died, and she tried to move away from the stranger's arm holding her upright. Her legs buckled and she stayed where she was. "I saw them in the Capital."

"The Capital?" In varying tones of disbelief the revelation rippled through the collected priests and into the crowd.

"These bodies were two of those I mentioned, the ones that were taken from their tomb," Karlene continued. She began to tremble, in relief as much as anything, as Vree appeared at her side and slipped a supporting shoulder under her left arm. "Their rites have been performed, they only need to be sent back."

"Sent back? How did they get this far down the road?"

She couldn't say she didn't know and be believed, so she asked a question of her own. "How do the dead arrive anywhere?"

The ancient priest looked disgusted. "Well, I don't imagine they walked. I suppose the pertinent question is, who brought them this far and where is that person now?" She turned away from Karlene and began issuing orders. Someone protested that her god had no more right to control the situation than any other, and in another moment, they'd all forgotten the stranger existed.

As Vree took most of her weight, Karlene pressed her cheek against the smaller woman's head. "Get me away from here," she murmured. "Please."

She didn't know how Vree did it—she suspected she didn't want to know—but the crowd melted away before them. It took two attempts to gain the saddle and she was barely in it before she began urging her horse up the road. She heard Gyhard begin a question and heard Vree answer it, *"She has to get away."*

"We have to leave the road," she explained as they caught up and flanked her. "I have to Sing."

"Why?" Gyhard understood the bardic emphasis even if Vree didn't.

Karlene tried to tell them but found she couldn't form the words. To actually say it aloud would make it too real to bear. The kigh continued to skirt the borders of her sight.

"What's going on?" Vree asked, dropping back and then guiding her gelding up against Gyhard's outside leg. The bard looked like soldiers she'd seen sitting in the midst of battle, surrounded by carnage, untouched by sword or spear but wounded just the same.

"How should I know?" Gyhard protested. "I have no more information than you do."

Vree's eyes narrowed. "You have a hundred years more information than I do."

"Not about this."

Then what good are you?

They left the road at the first opportunity; followed a lane that edged a field of cotton, became a path, then disappeared. Karlene reined in at a small hollow and slid to the ground. She dried her palms on her thighs, took a deep breath, and stared at a clump of wild lilies swinging violently in a sudden breeze.

"Well?" Gyhard asked at last.

She sketched confusion in the air. "I don't know *what* to Sing. The air kigh . . ." Her hands traced the area around the lilies. ". . . they say that the kigh from those two bodies are still around."

Vree felt the skin along her spine crawl and only training kept her from checking back over her shoulder—toward the road. "Still in the bodies?"

"No. The air kigh say that the other kigh should go away, but because of what Kars did to them, they're lost. They don't know where away is or how to get there." A trickle of sweat ran from hairline to collar. "I'm supposed to Sing and fix it."

"And while you do . . ." Gyhard glanced up at the position of the sun. ". . . your prince moves farther from us."

"I *can't* leave them like this."

"Neither can you accept responsibility for every life, pardon me, every death that Kars has discarded. He's older than you think and has been doing this for a very long time." Implicit in his tone was the declaration that he, Gyhard, had personally accepted as much responsibility as he was going to.

"Fine. Not all of them." She sent a silent apology to the rest. "But these two are here and I am here."

Gyhard wrapped one leg around the saddle horn, braced his elbow on his knee, and dropped his chin into his cupped palm. "So Sing," he sighed.

"Sing what?" Karlene flung up her arms, frustration chasing the terror chasing the sorrow chasing the Song. "*I* don't know where away is *or* how they get there."

"What about the air spirits?" Vree glared suspiciously from a ripple in the grass to a strand of mane blowing out just a little farther than the rest.

"They're no help. They keep repeating *away* like I should know."

"So sing what you do know. You can talk to spirits, talk to these."

"It isn't that *simple*," Karlene insisted.

Vree shrugged impatiently. "It had better be. Or how were you planning on laying the prince to rest?"

How had she planned on laying the prince to rest? She hadn't. Karlene swallowed. *Here I come, galloping to the rescue with no idea if a rescue is even possible.* Talk to them. Call them. Not the notes that called fire or water or air. She could only Sing three of four quarters, how was she suddenly to Sing a fifth when until a few days ago no one believed a fifth quarter existed?

She wet her lips and Sang, repeating the little she knew about the two lost kigh in every combination of note and tone she could think of. *I can't do this. I don't know enough about them. I don't know enough about the fifth kigh. I . . .*

I have a kigh.

She strongly suspected that pausing to think it through would tie her tongue in knots. But the Song wasn't about thought; it was emotion, it was touching the past and the future, it was sharing pain and joy and truth and self.

Maybe it *was* that simple after all. Maybe the bards had never needed to learn to Sing the fifth quarter because they couldn't not Sing it. Every time they touched an audience, or one listener, or one hundred, they were Singing the fifth quarter.

Karlene took a deep breath, more for courage than for her voice, and put herself into the Song.

Between one note and the next, they were there; frightened, hurt, twisted by the darkness within which they'd been forced to exist. They clutched at her, pleaded for an end. She couldn't heal them, so she Sang them comfort, Sang them their love for each other, Sang them peace.

How had she planned on laying the prince to rest?

Eyes closed, her voice wrapped around them and, just for an instant, she crossed the line and *became* the Song. For that same instant, she knew what the kigh meant by *away* and she knew how to get there. She Sang them how it should have been and then they were gone.

She managed to Sing a gratitude although to who or what she didn't know. The knowledge of *away* faded with the Song, but the loss didn't matter because she knew how to find it again.

"Are you going to fall over?" Vree asked.

Karlene wiped at the tears streaming down her cheeks. She couldn't remember crying. "I'm fine. In fact, I feel terrific."

She looks postorgasmic.

She looks like she just came face-to-face with her god.

That's what I said.

But behind the flippant remarks, Vree could feel the effect the Song had had on Bannon and, somehow, they seemed better defined than they had for a while. She knew where he ended. He knew where she began.

They passed Shaebridge just before dusk, their pace having been drastically slowed by the traffic approaching the city. Walk turned to trot turned to canter turned to full gallop as they tried to make up the time they'd

lost. The sound of their horses' hooves softened as
they moved from dressed stone to the packed clay of
the road that followed the crest of the river valley, but
it remained loud enough to cover the sound of the single horse galloping behind.

"What's the matter?"

Vree turned from the gable window, pulled around
by the bard's whisper, to find the older woman merely
an arm's length behind her. Her muscles tensed, began
to move, but she managed to prevent the response
training and experience dictated.

"Vree?"

Her heart pounded from the effort of holding the attack. "I thought I heard something. On the roof."

"Probably a pigeon."

"At night?"

"A pigeon having a bad dream."

It had been the smallest of possible sounds, snapping
her up out of a fitful sleep. Bannon hadn't heard it. She
was beginning to doubt that she had.

Karlene misunderstood the barely visible tremor.
"Are you cold?"

It would be the easy answer. "I'm not used to this."
A wave of her hand indicated the night outside the loft.
"The nights in the south of the Empire are as heavy
and warm as the days."

Moving a little closer, Karlene smiled. "Very bardic."

"Probably Bannon."

The smile disappeared. "Can't you tell?"

She could feel the ten crescents, cold and heavy in
her hand. "Not always, not anymore."

"Is it getting worse?"

Bannon paced, testing the confines of his cage.
"Yes."

"Is there anything I can do?"

"No."

Can she Sing that carrion eater out of my body?

Unable to stop herself, Vree jerked around to stare at the sleeping Gyhard. *Even if she could, we still need him.*

What for?

To deal with Kars.

The bard can deal with Kars.

She'll be freeing the dead.

Then what will we be doing?

Freeing the prince.

He's dead, Vree. You said the bard will free the dead.

She can't free all of them at once!

You don't know that.

We still need him to deal with Kars.

Why? Kars is alive. We can deal with Kars the way we've dealt with all the others.

Stop it! You're confusing me.

You're confused, sister-mine, but I'm not doing it. Bannon's mental voice picked up the intonation of command. *Ask her.*

Bannon, I . . .

Ask her. Or I will. He began to force his control past hers.

Bannon, I don't want to fight you.

Why, Vree? Are you afraid I'll win? That I'll take over? That I'll keep you imprisoned the way you've kept me? She could feel the accusation stretching back beyond the time they'd shared a single body.

No! I'm afraid I won't stop. That I'll push until you're gone! She slammed herself at him with every phrase. *And then he'll have won! Is that what you want? For me to push you right out of here?*

His consciousness retreated so completely, so quickly, that she had to throw out a hand to steady herself against the age-polished wood of the window frame.

I want my body back. He sounded like he was five; hurt, frightened, betrayed. She wanted to hold him, to tell him everything would be all right, be the anchor and the shield she'd always been for him. But she couldn't.

Who would hear her if she cried that she wanted her body back? Who had heard her when she was five?

Gyhard stirred. Even asleep, her brother's face now bore the patina of the man who wore it. Could the bard Sing him out of Bannon's body? If she did, where would he go?

Vree closed her eyes and collapsed for a heartbeat into the comforting circle of Karlene's arms. She trembled as she felt warm lips touch her hair, then she set her jaw and pushed away. "No . . ."

"Why not? We could both use the comfort."

"I can't, not until Bannon has his body again."

Karlene shook her head in disbelief. "You've made the big sacrifice, Vree. Why continue sacrificing yourself for him?"

Vree spread her hands. "I am him."

There had to be a hundred responses to something so ridiculous but at the moment, Karlene couldn't think of one of them.

He could hear the two women talking, their voices rising and falling in murmured cadences too soft to carry the actual words to his position on the roof. Cloaked in the night, Neegan weighed his options. Until this point, he'd concentrated solely on tracking his targets; now he could begin to plan the kill. When sleep claimed them once again, it would be easy enough to slip through the window, slit their throats, and put their betrayal to rest. The foreign singer would awake beside a pair of bloody corpses and the structure of the Empire would be restored. Assassins who deserted from the seven armies died.

But these targets were a special case, and Marshal Chela wanted to know *why*. Although he considered their reasons of less than no importance held up against the enormity of their faithlessness, it wasn't the first command he'd been given that went against his personal preference. One of the two would have to be taken alive.

No. Both. Threatening Bannon would drag the truth from Vree. He doubted he'd get it any other way. The brother was the sister's only weakness. Bannon was his own weakness as well, but he'd pile lie upon lie to save himself the way she never would to save him. And to save her? Neegan wouldn't want to put it to the test.

Perhaps they *should* have been separated. But so few children became available for training with a sibling so close in age and ability. It had been an opportunity impossible to resist.

And I was right. They both survived, finding strength together where they might not have had it alone. They were two of the best.

Which made it worse when they betrayed his judgment, his decision to keep them together. The army was supposed to be the only family an assassin had . . .

It was the only family he'd ever had.

These two had spat in its face. His face.

Neegan didn't want to kill the foreign singer if he could help it—he could leave her in good conscience for the First Army—but neither would he hesitate if she interfered with his mission.

He wasn't surprised to find they were no longer in a private room. The way they'd spent their stolen coin, he was surprised that it had lasted as long as it had. Right hand working around the leather-wrapped grip of his favorite dagger, he weighed the possibility of success while all three slept grouped together in the loft. On one side of the scale, it would be over. Finished. He could let go of the anger devouring his heart. On the other side, he would have two of the best assassins the seven armies had ever trained to subdue as well as an opponent of unknown skills to deal with.

I will wait the short time necessary in order to face them one at a time. He had survived longer than almost any other Imperial assassin. Long enough to become an officer. Long enough to know that to strike in anger dulled the blade.

"Soon," his dagger whispered as he slid it into the sheath.

Far enough north for snow in the winter, the roof of the small inn sloped gently from ridge to eaves. Over the years, Neegan had slept on worse beds. Though the night was cool, the threat of rain had passed and up above, the stars, the same stars that blazed out over the Sixth Army, divided the sky into a thousand portents.

He saluted the Archer, and, warmed by the heat of his anger, closed his eyes.

He opened them again just before dawn when the sound of the inn door jerked him awake. Rolling up into a crouch, he worked the night out of his muscles and peered over the eaves, waiting to see who the early riser would be.

Bannon.

Neegan frowned, his own action arrested, as he stared at the slight figure crossing the innyard to the privy. It *was* Bannon. And yet . . .

No. The patterns of shadow between the day and night could be deceptive. The angle of observation, looking down from above, elongated some movements while it masked others entirely. And Bannon *had* changed. He had cast aside everything he'd been taught to believe in—surely such corruption would leave a physical sign.

Wrapping his betrayal around him, Neegan waited until the rough plank door to the privy closed, then moved silently off the roof. He would take Bannon as he emerged and it would all be over by the time the sun cleared the horizon.

Vree!

I feel it, too. She lay still on the pallet, senses extended; the sounds, the smells, the feel of the air currents against her skin sifted for threat.

Whatever it is, it's not in here, Bannon declared after a moment.

Outside?

Yes . . . A weapon clasped loosely in each hand, she rolled up onto her feet in a single, fluid motion. *Gyhard's missing.*

What the slaughter is he up to in my body?!

They were at the window, shielded by the side wall of the gable, eyes and experience scanning the innyard.

Privy door's closed.

That this explained where Bannon's body had disappeared to did nothing to lessen the sense of danger they shared.

Do you see anything?

No. But there's enough shadow out there to hide an army.

So they waited, wounds left by the emotional battle the night before buried beneath trained responses.

Tucked into a fetid corner between the stable and the privy, Neegan set his anger aside and narrowed his focus to Bannon's capture. The anger would be easy enough to take up again when it would no longer be in the way. He listened to the sounds from within the small building—the splash of liquid, the rustle of cloth, the creak of wood as a man's weight settled on it—and timed a likely exit.

A blade held across the throat wouldn't be enough, but a sharp pommel blow behind the ear would significantly slow a counterattack. Perhaps even prevent one entirely.

Wood creaked again. Cloth rustled.

Door's opening.
I see it.
Something's down there, sister-mine.
Then so are we.

Gyhard stared in astonishment as Vree flung herself out of the loft's small gable window, hit the ground, rolled, and ended up facing him, crouched with a dagger in each hand.

"If you're trying to make me piss myself, you're too late," he muttered, wondering when she'd cease to amaze him. "*What* are you doing?"

Neegan froze in place, unable to believe what he saw. Bannon's only reaction to his sister's sudden appearance seemed to be surprise. He neither assumed a defensive position of his own nor moved to support hers.

Vree's gaze flicked from one pool of darkness to another. "Something's wrong."

"What? With the stairs?" Gyhard checked to see if his heart had started beating again.

"Something's out here. Something dangerous." *Bannon, cover the corner by the bathhouse.*

How? If he'd had teeth to clench, he would've forced the word through them.

Sorry. Vree slid sideways to shrink the blind spot caused by the angle of the building.

All at once, Gyhard realized she was perfectly serious. The hair rose off the nape of his neck and, slowly, he turned. "I don't see anything."

"That's the worst kind."

Hands out from his sides, wishing he had a sword, or a shield, or even one of Bannon's narrow-bladed daggers, he began backing toward the inn.

Not until he called her name from the doorway, did Vree move to join him.

If Neegan hadn't known better, he would have sworn this man was not, nor had he ever been an assassin. Calling himself several kinds of fool, he shook off the paralysis and tried to understand what he'd just seen. The kind of training Bannon had undergone—the kind of training that made certain responses instinctive—could *not* be discarded.

Except that it had.

Chapter Thirteen

"You jumped out the window?" Karlene stared at Vree in astonishment. "Why?"

With the landlord seeing to bathwater for one of the inn's other guests—and therefore safely out of earshot—and the common room empty except for them, Vree saw no reason for evasion. "There was danger; in the innyard. We had to protect Bannon's body."

"Danger!" The word bounced off the walls and Karlene hastily lowered her voice. "What kind of danger?"

Vree looked confused. "How many kinds are there?"

"No!" The bard waved an impatient hand in the air. "I mean, who or what caused the danger?"

"I don't know." Vree shrugged, tucked the flying tails of her increasingly grimy silk shirt down into her pants, and tightened her belt. "I'd say a who, though, not a what."

The bard pushed past to the door of the common room and scanned the visible wedge of yard. She whistled the four notes that would call the kigh and then Sang a question at them. After a moment she Sang a gratitude and came back inside. "They say there's a man forking shit over by the stable and that's all."

"Now." The sense of danger had faded. Whoever'd

been out there was long gone. Vree didn't need air spirits to tell her that.

Karlene sighed forcefully and turned to Gyhard. "Did you feel it, too?"

He shook his head. "But then no one started teaching me to recognize it when I was only seven."

Six.

I was seven, Bannon. Vree could feel their identities beginning to merge again and desperately hung onto the memory of a small child whirling about barely in time to duck beneath a flailing leather strap, having finally learned to read the air currents and avoid a stinging welt. She only hoped it was her memory and not her brother's that she clung to.

"So you believe there was something out there?"

Gyhard tightened the buckle on his saddlebag and straightened. "Do you know how long an Imperial assassin usually lives after training?"

Karlene glanced from Gyhard to Vree and back again. "No," she said tentatively. "How long?"

"Three years. You see, the sort of people that assassins are used against—traitors, rebel leaders, the officers of opposing armies and such—are usually well aware that they're targets. As a result, they make certain preparations. Now assassins take that into account, but in about three years or so, the odds catch up to them."

"If the assassins know that, know the odds, why do they . . . uh . . ."

"Follow orders? Why are you asking me?" He cocked his head at Vree. "The bard would like to know why you followed orders."

Rubbing her palms together, Vree fought to get around the concept of *refusing* to follow orders.

"You must have known the odds," Gyhard persisted.

"What did you think when you went out after a target?"

"The odds meant nothing." Vree's chin came up and her eyes narrowed. "We were the best."

"There." Gyhard spread his hands and turned back to Karlene. "All assassins are taught to believe that from a very young age. Now, as Vree and Bannon have been working assassins for the past five years, that seems to indicate that they, at least, have reason to believe in what they've been taught. They *are* the best. Or among the best. If Vree tells me she senses danger, I believe her." He slung the saddlebags over his shoulder and picked up a wrapped package of journey food. "I've settled up with the landlord. We should get on the road."

Brow furrowed, Karlene picked up her own bags. "You should have woken me," she muttered to Vree as they followed Gyhard to the stables.

Vree snorted. "If I'd had time to wake you, I'd have had time to take the stairs."

Head bowed, a filthy rag over his hair, Neegan methodically forked horse shit from the stable cart into the manure pile. Clad in a rough tunic and short breeches he'd pulled from a wash line two houses away, he stood hidden in plain sight and watched his targets.

While he had never seen either of them around horses to give him a basis of comparison, Bannon's movements still lacked the deadly grace that marked an assassin and he wore only a single dagger hanging in plain sight from his belt. Vree, for all she retained her training, seemed to periodically lose control of bits of her body—as though she forgot, just for an instant, who she was.

Was she sick, he wondered. Had she picked up some kind of brain disease in Ghoti? Perhaps they left the army rather than risk spreading it. Perhaps they were looking for a cure.

But that theory didn't explain Bannon.

Had Bannon sustained an injury in the assault on Aralt's stronghold? A blow to the head that had caused him to forget who and what he was? Neegan had heard of that kind of an injury although he'd personally never believed such a thing to be possible. Was Vree guarding a brother who could no longer guard himself? Actually, had he not known their relationship, Neegan would not have assumed from what he observed that they were brother and sister.

He studied them for a moment as if they were nothing more than targets. *Not lovers, not yet.* But they no longer flirted with the boundaries blood placed around them. A line had been crossed or the boundaries had been shifted—he wasn't certain which.

They spoke of their horses, or the weather, or the condition of the secondary, packed clay road they now followed but said nothing that would even begin to answer the multitude of questions he suddenly had. Neegan cocked his head as Vree swung into the saddle and turned to Bannon, her exasperation apparent from a distance.

"Can't we beat Kars to his stronghold and ambush him?" she asked. "I hate trailing along at his heels."

"First of all, it isn't a stronghold, it's merely a cabin, or it was. Secondly, it's a long ride to the mountains and I rather think our friend the bard here would prefer to catch up and free His Highness sooner than that. The longer the prince is with him, the more twisted his kigh becomes."

"You never said that before."

"I should have thought it was obvious." He smiled and Neegan fought to keep from staring. Even from across the stableyard, the expression on Bannon's face had nothing of Bannon in it. What's more, it had been Bannon's voice but not Bannon's manner of speaking.

When they rode out of the innyard, galloping off toward the dawn, Neegan dropped the manure fork and raced along the shadowed paths to his horse and gear. Apparently, his targets were helping the bard to rescue the prince. *But that doesn't change anything*, he reminded himself as he buckled on his arm sheaths. It didn't change the fact that they'd deserted, spat on their oaths, turned their backs on everything he believed in, on everything he'd taught them to believe in. Didn't change the penalty. Eventually, Bannon would seek a little privacy by the side of the road and, when he did, Neegan would be waiting. Once he had Bannon, he'd have Vree.

"Before you kill them, ask them why."

He would ask the marshal's question, but now that confusion threatened to overwhelm his personal sense of betrayal, he would also take the time to ask a question of his own. What had happened in Aralt's tower?

When they finally allowed the horses to slow to a walk, Vree dropped out of the saddle to stretch her legs.

We're going to forget how to get anywhere on our own two feet. Gonna end up looking like fat-assed officers.

Vree arched her back, rocked forward, then arched it again, working the stiffness out of her shoulders. *Giving the pounding it's taking, if my ass is getting fat, it's in self-defense.*

She glanced up as the bard fell into step beside her,

then let her gaze drop back to the road. There were always people attracted to danger, who courted a symbolic death by courting Jiir's blades. Vree recognized the bard's fear—*You could kill me at any moment. Would you kill me at any moment?*—so she recognized the other woman's attraction and while she was willing to accept that Karlene honestly wanted to be her friend, she could sense something else as well. Something that confused her.

She pities us, sister-mine.

But she doesn't know that we've broken our oaths . . .

Don't be so slaughtering stupid, Vree. She pities us because of what we are.

You mean with both of us in one body?

Bannon rolled Vree's eyes. *I mean she pities us because we're assassins.*

That's ridiculous.

I don't think so. She felt his resentment, couldn't tell where it was directed. Or at whom. Felt him retreat into a sullen silence.

"So . . ." Karlene cleared her throat and made her voice sound curious, nonthreatening. "What did your parents think about you becoming assassins?"

"Children with parents aren't trained."

"You must've had parents once."

"Mother was a soldier. She died."

"What about your father? Or Bannon's father?"

"Same man. We look like each other but not like I remember her." Brushing a fly off her face, Vree caught it on the wing, crushed it, and dropped the body. "Probably a soldier; but we don't know who he is."

"Didn't he come forward when your mother died?"

"He could easily have been dead, too."

Karlene shook her head slowly in disbelief. "You sound like you don't even care."

"I don't. We don't. The army is our family, the only family an assassin needs."

"But you've left the army . . ."

Vree flicked a glance back over her shoulder, unable to prevent the involuntary motion. The world stopped as she thought she saw a horse and rider moving into the very edge of her vision. A heartbeat later, they disappeared into a dip in the road.

Bannon! Did you see that?

We're not the only people on the road, Vree.

What if the danger from the inn's following us?

What if it is? We can't do anything until it catches up.

He was right. She forced her attention back to what the bard was saying.

". . . and you'd always had Bannon."

"I still *have* Bannon." Vree's right forearm twitched and a throwing dagger appeared in her hand. A twist and it disappeared. She turned and glared at Gyhard, walking on her other side.

Karlene followed her gaze and considered everything she'd learned about assassins since dawn. "Was Gyhard a . . . a target? Was he prepared?" She read the answer in the set of Vree's shoulders and the studied indifference of Gyhard's expression. "He took Bannon's body when Bannon killed *his* body, didn't he?"

"Rough justice, Lady Bard," Gyhard suggested.

All things being enclosed, Karlene had no intention of comparing the immorality of his action to the equally dubious morality of assassination. "How did you do it?"

"That's no concern of yours, but I think you'd do the same if it came to a choice between transferring

and dying." He looked at Vree, his mouth twisted into
a rueful smile and his voice softened, becoming almost
a caress. "I never meant for you to become involved."

Vree jerked back, as though she were shaking off his
touch. "No, you meant for me to die!"

Gyhard's eyes narrowed. "I meant for Bannon to
die."

"I know." Her voice was a hoarse whisper. "That
was Bannon."

"You couldn't stop him?"

She shook her head. "I thought it was me."

The captain raised her hand. The order to halt
echoed down the line. She squinted at the walls and
towers of Shaebridge and could just barely make out
the garrison flag of the Third Army through the reflected glare of the afternoon sun on the yellow sandstone. "Orlan, send a pair of runners into the garrison.
Have them see if Commander Neegan checked in with
the Third Army. If he hasn't, then he didn't enter the
city and neither did they. Send another pair to the
bridge with a full description of the bard and her companions. If it turns out that they're not in the city or
over the bridge, then they must have taken the road
along the river."

"Sir!" The squad leader saluted and wheeled his
horse around, racing back along the road to where his
people stood panting in the sun. They'd had a hard,
fast march since the marshal's courier had met them
two days ago, double-timing back along the road. They
all knew there'd be no rest until His Highness was
found.

Rubbing her eyes, the captain slumped in the saddle.
"Tell the company to stand down where they are," she
growled and reached for her water skin. As she swal-

lowed the tepid liquid, she stared at the city and at the two roads bracketing it as if by will alone she could determine where the fugitives had gone.

I should've held them when I had them.

But she'd had no reason to hold the whore and his sister and no way of knowing—until the marshal's courier told her—that they had a companion who knew where to find His Imperial Highness. She had no reason to feel like a fool, but she did.

The captain swallowed another mouthful of water and wished for something just a little stronger. Her orders were clear; capture and question the bard using any means necessary to discover the location of Prince Otavas. But how the slaughtering bloody blazes was she supposed to capture and question a woman who could sing herself invisible?

The best she could hope for was that the assassin who'd passed them half a day before the marshal's courier arrived—Commander Neegan the courier had named him, although the captain had never heard of an assassin making commander who continued to use his own blade—would hold the bard after he'd slit the other two's throats.

The sudden gust of wind very nearly blew Karlene off her horse. She clutched at the saddle horn as a pair of kigh tried to drag her to the ground. Somehow she managed to whistle them back and then hurriedly dismounted while they swirled around her, just slightly more than an arm's length away.

"Don't tell me he's lost another one," Gyhard muttered, reining in.

Vree glared at him, but Karlene paled at the thought of a third discarded corpse. Unable to banish a vision of Otavas lying rotting on the road, she struggled to make sense of what the kigh were trying to tell her. When she finally understood, anger obliterated the horror.

She Sang a piercing gratitude and, breathing heavily, threw herself up into the saddle. "*Your* Kars has done it again," she snarled.

A muscle jumped in Gyhard's temple. "And what has *my* Kars done?"

"Sang the kigh back into the dead. He did it there . . ." Karlene jerked her head toward a small fishing village, half-screened by giant cottonwoods, squatting between the road and the river. "Night before last."

"We should have expected it." Gyhard shrugged. "He had to replace the two bodies he lost."

The bay shied sideways, reacting to its rider, whites showing all around its eyes. Karlene was so furious, she could hardly speak. "Sure. Should've expected it. Except he didn't rob a grave this time. These two weren't dead. First he killed them. *Then* he Sang the kigh back into the bodies." Her knuckles were white around the reins. "No more stopping. No more sleeping until he's stopped." She slammed her heels into the horse's ribs, and the startled animal leaped forward, the bard bent low over his flying mane, her braid a pale pennant.

"She thinks she's in a ballad," Gyhard snarled, holding his gelding back.

Vree fought to keep her seat as her own horse danced in place, anxious to race after its companion. "She's angry at herself because the prince was killed like these two were and she hasn't rescued him yet."

"Ah, and you can recognize that; you're angry at yourself because I'm still in your brother's body?"

Vree smiled tightly at him. "I wasn't until you

brought it up." She gave the gelding its head and it pounded off down the road.

As the two of them drew away, Gyhard spent a few pensive moments remembering all the years, all the lives, when he'd managed to remain in complete control.

Horse and rider motionless in the dappled shade of a cottonwood, Neegan watched as Vree and the bard galloped off and left Bannon on his own. He moved between one heartbeat and the next, guiding his horse up onto the road, eyes locked on the young man sitting, shaking his head, oblivious to the danger.

In spite of everything he'd seen, Neegan was taking no chances. Bannon had received the same training he had and was younger, stronger, and faster. But Neegan had years of experience Bannon never would, and he could anticipate every defense his target might make.

He put his heels to his horse and, as the animal lunged forward, drew his feet up under his buttocks, then launched himself through the air. Bannon turned, eyes wide, and, to Neegan's complete astonishment, made no defense at all. The force of the older assassin's attack flung both men out of the saddle. Totally unprepared to be holding an unresisting body, Neegan slammed into the ground. Bannon slammed down on top of him. Caught between the double impact, air exploded out of his lungs. Gasping for breath, he tried to twist out from under the frightened gelding's flailing hooves, but the weight across his chest held him in place.

Time slowed as the hoof descended.

Time stopped.

Still clutching the end of one rein, Gyhard swore as a hoof pounded into the meaty part of his shoulder

then, as another parted the world a hairbreadth from
his nose, he managed to scramble clear. On his hands
and knees, desperately sucking in air, he realized his
attacker hadn't been so lucky.

Blood poured from a half circle where the skin had
been ripped from the man's forehead and bone showed
through the red.

"Got your head stomped in," Gyhard panted, stag-
gering to his feet and trying to calm his frightened
horse. "All things being enclosed, better you than me."

And then he noticed the black sunbursts.

"Assassins who desert become targets." Standing
over Avor's corpse, Vree had made the point very
clear.

"Oh, shit."

It was all he could think of to say.

He couldn't see either of his companions although
he thought he could hear hoofbeats growing fainter in
the distance. Ignoring the shakiness in his legs, and the
pain in his shoulder, Gyhard pulled himself up into the
saddle and looked down at the assassin. "All at once,"
he said thoughtfully, "I'm discovering a distinct desire
to get out of this body."

Pushed tight into a front corner, his hands gripping
the top board of the cart, Otavas watched the summer
storm approach, a line in the dust of the road marking
the leading edge of rain. It moved with such delibera-
tion that after he saw it hit the two running between
the shafts, he had time to brace himself before it closed
over him. Lifting his face to the deluge, eyes squinted
nearly shut, he welcomed the force of its cleansing.

He flinched away as the old man pawed at his arm,
the ancient voice lost in the drumming of the rain.

"Don't touch me!" he screamed. It didn't matter if he couldn't be heard because the old man never listened.

The touching and pulling continued, but after that single protest he ignored it. Over the last few days he'd become very good at ignoring things he could do nothing about. Dead things for the most part.

A warm channel of salt water cut a path through the liquid sheeting down both cheeks and ran into the corners of his mouth. Invisible tears. Safe tears. Pain that couldn't be used against him. He wept silently, swallowing the urge to keen and wail lest the old man force him into sleep and nightmare again. He wept until he was exhausted, wrapped in the arms of the storm.

"The dead feel no hunger, no thirst, no pain but can fight and die and joyously rise to fight again in Jiir's army . . ."

Neegan had heard the priests of Jiir proclaim those words over a hundred graves. He clung to the memory, used it to push himself up out of darkness—pain pounded with red hot hammers on his skull, so he *wasn't* dead. A drop of water splashed on his hand, and he used it to anchor himself to the real world.

Only his right eye opened.

His left cheek pressed against the ground, he could see the yellow-gray clay of the road, damp pockmarks multiplying in the surface dust; beyond the road a fringe of grass and weeds thrashed in the wind; above, a wedge of gray-green sky.

He could hear only the wind and the approaching storm—no birds, no insects, no enemies.

He could smell only blood.

Although he sensed no danger, he was lying wounded and exposed and that was danger enough. The single drops of rain merged into a solid sheet of water. In the distance, behind him, he thought he heard someone yell.

A moment later, the roaring pain in his head louder by far than the storm, Neegan lay in the long grass, spewing bile. Finally, stomach empty, he crawled toward a half-remembered tree, pride keeping him moving when he'd rather have just laid down and drowned in the mud. He lost track of time, lost track of everything except breathing and moving forward under the constant punishment of pounding rain.

Then the multitude of tiny blows falling on his head and shoulders eased. He crawled a little farther and flopped over on his back, staring up with his one good eye at the dense canopy above him. Although gusts of wind swept walls of water through his fragile shelter, the leaves were thick enough to halve the power of the storm.

His shoulders against the trunk, Neegan inched his way up into a sitting position, his head balanced with as much care as he'd ever used to balance a dagger. Questing fingers touched bone, then pushed the flap of skin back into place. He lived only because the hoof had stuck the thickest point of the skull a glancing blow. Carefully, he scraped away the dried blood sealing his left eye closed and, more carefully still, opened the eye.

There were a pair of narrow wheel ruts under the tree, signs of four, maybe five people, and blood that wasn't his. No threat, no danger. He could barely see the road—the trees and the village and river on the far side were lost behind a curtain of water. The voice he'd heard, or thought he'd heard, had probably been a protest from the village.

With the sun buried behind the storm, it was impossible to tell how long he'd been lying on the road, how

long it had taken him to crawl to the tree, how long
since Bannon had ridden away and left him for dead.

Bannon had made an assumption an assassin would
never make.

"Yet another ... question." He licked rain from his
lips and swallowed.

Somehow he managed not to slice off a finger as he
cut a strip of wet cloth from the bottom of his tunic.
The moment he had the strength to raise his arms, he'd
bind the flap of skin in place. The moment after that,
he'd aim himself at his targets again.

For now, he sat, the pain in his head beating in time
with his heart, and wondered why, when all logic suggested he should be lying on the road with his throat
slit, he was still alive.

Squinting through the rain, he anxiously watched the
backs of his newest children as they strained to move
the cart and its two living passengers. The narrow
wheels cut deep ruts in the road. The wet clay clung to
the wood, adding to the weight, digging the cart in
deeper.

Slower ... Slower. . . .

He'd sent Kait and Wheyra to push from behind
when the road first began to suck at the wheels, hoping
that it would be enough to keep them moving toward
home.

The cart lurched one final handbreadth forward and
stopped.

Reaching out with his staff, he touched Iban on the
shoulder. The dead man froze in place. Hestia continued to drag her feet up out of the mud, one after the
other, until he touched her as well.

The tailgate had swollen in the rain, so after Kait
and Wheyra had clambered down, he'd had them slide

it inside the cart rather than replace it. With a longing look at the silent figure standing, head bowed, beside him, he walked carefully back to the open end and squatted. His two older children continued to push against the grip of the mud. They'd work themselves to pieces for him, but he wouldn't allow that sacrifice again. Fingers trembling, he lightly caressed the two new bones hanging on the silk cord around his neck, finding them easily by touch alone for a desiccated band of flesh ringed them both.

"Enough," he said at last, shaking loose from grief and pitching his voice to carry over the wind and rain. "We can't go on."

Lost in the storm, Otavas remained unaware the cart had stopped until the old man grabbed his arm and pulled him around. He flinched back, but the clawlike fingers held.

"We must stay here for a while." The old man's voice cut through the noise of wind and rain. "Please, my heart, you must sit."

The prince stared out over the front end. Although it had to be around mid-afternoon, the rain was so heavy he could just barely see the shafts. No one held them. Frowning, he pushed a lock of dripping hair back off his face.

"We pushed the braces into the mud." The old man nodded and leaned closer. "There is no other shelter, we must stay in the cart."

Moving away from the hand shoving down on his shoulder, Otavas found himself seated between the corner and the rolled bulk of the pallet. Spaces between the floor planks had allowed the cart to drain and the close quarters stopped most of the wind—but shelter? The prince swallowed a sob and rubbed at his cheeks with his palm. To his surprise, after the old man lowered himself into the other corner, Kait and Wheyra lifted the tailgate and laid it across the front half of the cart.

The rain stopped pounding on his head and shoulders.

"A roof." The prince watched as the two dead women sat just outside the overhang and the two murdered fisherfolk sat just beyond them. "But you're still getting wet . . ."

"We are . . . dead, High . . . nesss." He thought it was Kait who spoke, but the downpour made it difficult to tell for certain. "It doesssn't . . . matter."

Otavas shivered.

"Are you cold, my heart?"

"Stop calling me that." But his protest had lost its force, and he didn't move away when the old man pulled the mostly dry blanket from the center of the pallet and draped it around him

"Do you remember how we used to sit, wrapped together, by the fire? You always loved to watch the flames . . ."

"We didn't sit together. I didn't love to watch the flames," Otavas broke in wearily. "I'm not who you think I am." He waved a hand at the four silent figures sitting in the rain. "*They* know who I am! Why can't you get it through your thick head that I'm the youngest son of the Emperor, who won't rest until he finds me. He'll order all seven armies out. They'll tear the Empire apart. They're out there now, looking for me. They'll find me. They will." It had become his catechism against the darkness.

The old man smiled and handed him a boiled potato from the nearby empty oilskin bag. "I always said you had the most beautiful eyes."

* * *

It had never been much of a building—ruined it was even less of one—but as far as Vree could tell, the stone walls were solid and enough of a roof remained for them to sleep, if not dry, then no worse than damp. Tying the reins to the overgrown thornbush by the black-on-black rectangle that defined the door, she left the exhausted gelding and made her way back to the road.

Grabbing Gyhard and Karlene each by an arm, she dragged them close and shouted, "I found shelter! We're stopping here!"

"No!" Karlene tried to pull away but Vree tightened her grip. "We have to keep going. We can't waste this chance to catch up. Kars couldn't possibly move a cart through this."

"Look, we only know he's more than a day ahead of us, but we don't know how much more—it might not even be raining where he is!"

"The kigh say it's raining down the whole river valley!"

Vree rolled her eyes and threw up her hands in surrender. "I don't give a shit if it's raining all over the whole slaughtering Empire! If you want to keep going, you're going without me!"

"And me!" Shielding his face with his arm, Gyhard pulled his unwilling gelding forward. "Where is it?"

"There, just a little ways off the road." Vree half turned and pointed into the night.

"I can't see anything . . ."

"Neither can I. Bannon spotted it." She trailed her fingertips over the wet horse as it passed, the mud sucking at its hooves like a living, hungry thing. Wishing she hadn't thought of that, she shifted her weight from foot to foot and watched Karlene take a step up the road, wet reins stretching, the bay staying right where he was. "What are you trying to do, kill yourself?" she yelled, catching hold of the bard's sleeve.

"I'm trying to save the prince!" Karlene yanked the sodden fabric free, dragged her right foot out of the mud, lost her balance, and fell to her knees.

"Well, you're going to do him piss all amount of good if you end up crawling to the rescue!"

The bard put down a hand to push herself back onto her feet. It sank up to her wrist. Breathing heavily, she squinted up at Vree. "You could be right."

It'll never burn.

She seems to think it will. Vree squatted and stared at the pile of wood she and Karlene had gathered while Gyhard hobbled the horses. She could tell by the feel of it that the stuff they'd picked up in the ruin was punky and at least half of what they'd found outside had to be green. Most of it was wet.

Yeah, well, she also thinks that you and I had our lives stolen away by the army.

She's never said that.

She hasn't had to. You can hear it in her voice, see it in her face every time she asks us a question.

Frowning, Vree squeezed streams of water out of her hair and tried to remember every conversation she'd had with the bard. *I never noticed . . .*

She felt Bannon sigh and shake his head slowly from side to side. *You wouldn't, sister-mine.*

Before she could ask what he meant, the shadow that was Karlene bent over the wood and Sang four piercingly high notes.

Vree threw up an arm to protect her eyes from the sudden light. "How did you do that?" she demanded. blinking at the flames.

"Fire kigh," Karlene sighed and sat down in what looked like a barely controlled collapse. "I can't remember ever being so tired."

"And yet you were going to walk all night." A dribble of water made its way through the rotten thatch up above and splashed against the back of Vree's neck. She hurriedly moved to a drier spot.

Vree . . .

I hear it.

Her left hand cautioning the bard to silence, a dagger appeared in her right. Head cocked, eyes closed, she tracked the rustling path of something moving under the debris at the base of the wall.

Just a little . . .

Now!

Steel clanged against stone, and a humpbacked shape scurried to safety through a triangular crack.

"Terrific," Karlene sighed, pulling the package of food closer to the fire. "Rats. First rain, now rats. What else can go wrong."

"The horses have fallen into a sinkhole out back. I don't think we can get them out."

"What!" Karlene had heaved herself halfway to her feet when Gyhard moved into the firelight and she saw the look on his face. "That's not funny!"

"It was for a moment." He turned to Vree, and the grin disappeared. "What's wrong?"

She shook her head and crossed to where her dagger lay almost hidden in the shadows. When she picked it up, it felt as though it no longer belonged in her hand.

"Vree?"

"We missed." The weapon lay cold and unforgiving across her palm. She looked from it to Gyhard; to a familiar face. "We never miss."

Never miss . . . Bannon echoed. Or perhaps he'd

spoken aloud, and she'd been the one who'd merely thought it.

"Everyone misses once in a while," Gyhard said softly. "It doesn't make you less then you were."

"No. More." She tried to hide the fear in a bitter laugh. "We react as one. We throw as two." Dropping her gaze, she sheathed the blade. "What happens if we're attacked?"

Attacked. Gyhard kept his expression carefully neutral. He hadn't told them what had happened back by the village; had ridden behind the two women until the rain had washed away all the visible signs and then the storm had made conversation difficult. And now? Although he remained a target for as long as he remained in Bannon's body, the assassin was dead. He suspected that the moment the army received the corpse the hunt would be up again, but for now he was safe and therefore had no need to set Vree specifically guarding her brother's body. No need to cause her more distress than she already endured.

"Who's going to attack us out here?" he asked, gesturing with his right arm—his left carefully immobilized by a thumb through a belt loop. The shoulder was only bruised, but moving it twisted barbed spikes of pain in the muscle. The storm had helped him hide it all afternoon. "Bandits? They'd have to be pretty stupid ones considering how seldom this road is used."

"And there're no wild animals this close to the center of the Empire," Karlene offered.

"No bandits? No wild animals?" Vree's voice rose. "What the slaughtering difference does that make? We missed a target we should've been able to hit in our sleep!" She stomped back to the fire and dropped down to sit cross-legged beside it.

Gyhard's hand hovered over her hair. When he saw

Karlene watching him, he let it fall back to his side. "I think . . ." He paused with exaggerated politeness while the bard sneezed. "I think we should get out of these wet clothes and let them dry."

Vree had no difficulty identifying the source of a sudden, intense rush of heat. Bannon's thoughts. Her thoughts. All at once, it became very easy to tell them apart.

The four of us, naked by the fire, keeping warm on a cool, damp, summer night . . .

*Slaughter it, Bannon, with everything else that's going on, how can you keeping thinking about fucking *all* the time?*

*Maybe because I can *only* think about it as long as I'm in your body!* He turned her head so she could see Gyhard stepping out of the wide folds of his trousers. *I had no idea you were such a prude.*

As the firelight flickered over the hard curves of her brother's thighs and belly, she felt Bannon's desire. It was easy to hide her desire within it. *And I never knew you were such a pervert,* she snapped, dragging dripping folds of silk over her head. When she emerged, still staring at Gyhard, her eyes narrowed. "What's wrong with your arm?"

"What do you mean?"

"You can't lift it over your head, you've barely managed to get your shirt off and . . ." Vree leaped to her feet and stepped toward him. "There's a huge slaughtering bruise just below your shoulder!"

"I didn't realize you knew your brother's body so well," Gyhard murmured. "The fire is throwing so little light, I can hardly see you at all."

Vree leaned closer, studying his arm. "It's swollen too. What happened?"

"My horse kicked me."

"When?"

"When you two—pardon me, Bannon; you three— rode off without me this morning. I went off the horse, fortunately retained my grip on the reins, and while I was on the ground, he kicked me."

Vree!

Calm down, Bannon, let me find out how bad it is. "Is anything broken?"

"No."

"How much use of it have you lost?"

"About half."

"Are you in much pain."

A dark brow lifted, the upper curve of the arc disappearing under a wet curl. "Why do you care?"

"In case you've forgotten," Vree snarled, "you're in a borrowed body. If you're feeling pain, then you've damaged it."

Asshole, Bannon added.

"Touched as I am by your concern, I assure you that I am not feeling more pain than I can cope with and nothing has been irrevocably damaged." As her fingers danced over the bruise, he became aware of his nakedness and caught her hands in his before he embarrassed himself. "Please don't," he said softly.

Vree looked at him for a long moment, then freed her hands and pulled away. Wetting lips gone inexplicably dry, she said, "Just don't forget that Bannon wants his body back."

On the other side of the fire, Karlene watched and listened and half thought that Vree'd meant that last reminder for herself.

Hours later, Gyhard put another stick on the fire, watched a flame dance onto it, and smiled. He used to love to watch a fire, used to think he could see the world in the flames. The smile faded. All he saw in these flames were complications.

The bard was sound asleep, head pillowed on her arm, one bare and muddy foot sticking out from under her blanket. Her life, for all the unanswered questions, was simple; all she wanted was to Sing the prince's kigh to wherever it was kigh went.

He slid his gaze over to Vree who slept curled around her daggers. Vree wanted to save the prince as well—she had, after all spent her whole life sworn to defend the Imperial Family—but she also wanted him dead. Or out of her brother's body which, without another host, amounted to the same thing. At least now that it appeared the army knew Vree and Bannon had deserted, Vree would not have to kill the bard to protect what was no longer a secret.

But both women knew his secret, so in order to protect himself, they would both have to die.

He didn't think he could kill a bard.

He didn't want to kill Vree.

And what if the prince *were* alive? Did that change anything except the body he'd end up wearing?

And what about me? He looked down at the mirror balanced on his knee. *Ninety years ago, I foolishly fell in love, trusted the man with whom I was in love, and pushed him off the edge of insanity. Why am I racing after him now?*

Because I am responsible for what he has become.

And why am I accepting that responsibility?

Because she's made it impossible for me to hide from myself.

But once I catch up to him, what am I going to do?

He shook his head at the mirror, and Bannon's reflection shook its head back at him. *And why am I sit-*

*ting up, asking myself these questions in the middle of
the night?* Bannon's reflection offered no answer.

Shifting position slightly, he cupped his hand over
the mirror and stared down at Vree.

As though she felt the weight of his regard, she
stirred and opened her eyes, abruptly awake. "Why are
you looking at me like that?

Why not? "Because you're beautiful."

Her brows drew in and her features subtly changed.
"Leave my sister alone," she growled. "She'll only
ever hate you for what you've done to me."

Oh, yes, that was why not. "Are you jealous,
Bannon?"

She half rose, moving fluidly to attack. Then under
the satin sheath of her skin, her muscles spasmed and
she fell to the ground, rigid and trembling.

His hand resting on the dagger by his side, Gyhard
watched, wishing he hadn't spoken, wondering which
of them would win.

Her body lifted off the ground on shoulders and
heels, spine arched painfully, then shuddered and collapsed.

When he moved toward her, she glared up at him
and said, "Don't."

He stopped where he was. "I'm sorry."

Panting, she clutched at the blanket and wrapped it
tightly around herself. "Are you planning to apologize
to Kars, too?" she asked and rolled over, back to him.

Why was it he loved her?

*Because she's made it impossible for me to hide from
myself.*

Vree lay awake for the rest of the night, listening to
him breathe.

Chapter Fourteen

Although the rain had stopped, the road remained deep in mud. More an irritant than an obstacle for those walking or riding who could take to the verges where plants held the soil together, the heavy clay would stick to the wheels of a cart, build up between the spokes, clump around the axle, and stop it cold.

Vree worked her toes in the cool embrace of wet earth and looked up. Between the pink and gold streaks of dawn, the sky was a pale silver-gray brushed lightly with cloud. The air was warm and damp and felt as if it had gone through other lungs.

She heard footsteps behind her and turned slowly.

Gyhard stopped a body's length away.

Birds, insects, even the liquid song of the river seemed to fall suddenly silent.

"You took away everything I had," she said. "Because of you, I broke oaths. Because of you, I killed a friend. The moment I can, I will kill you. That is all there will ever be between us."

"There is, already, more than that."

"No." Bannon narrowed Vree's eyes and drew her lips up off her teeth. "There is not."

"You've never had serious competition before, have you, Bannon? There's never been anyone in her life with enough allure to distract her attention from you.

And now ..." Gyhard spread Bannon's hands.
". . . you're competing, at least partially, with yourself.
How ironic."

"Smile while you can, carrion eater. When you leave
my body, we'll open another smile in your throat."

"Incentive to stay, don't you think?"

"You're a dead man!"

"You're an idiot."

"Sod off, both of you!" Vree snapped, yanking her
body out of Bannon's control. She jabbed a finger at
Gyhard. "I don't give a rebel's tit for what you think is
going on or what Bannon thinks is going on, either.
You are in my brother's body, and I want you out of
him as much as I want *him* out of me. Everything else
is bullshit!" Nostrils flared, she stomped past Gyhard
toward the ruined building, water spraying up from the
saturated sod with every step. "I'm going to wake
Karlene, and we're going to get moving before the
mud bakes dry and we lose this chance."

Slaughter it, Vree . . .

Don't push me, Bannon.

Me push you? You're not the one who's being betrayed! You're supposed to hate him!*

Hatred dulls your blade. It was one of the earliest
lessons an assassin learned. Clutching it tightly, Vree
stepped over the threshold and moved toward the fire
where a small flame still danced along a partially
burned stick. What point in making a stronger denial;
as she felt his betrayal, he felt her guilt.

Broader wheels might not have sunk so deep—
although broader wheels would have picked up more
of the sticky mud with every turning. He thought of
abandoning the cart, but his old bones moved so
slowly that it would add many, many days to the trip

home. Time enough to leave the cart when they had to leave the road.

He patted Kait on her thin shoulder, damp fabric sticking to her graying skin, and answered her slow smile with one of his own. "Keep pushing, child."

"Yesss, Fa ... ther." She threw her weight against the bar that joined shafts, mud churning beneath bare feet. Pushing beside her, Wheyra crooned to what decay had left of her baby.

Slowly and carefully, his robe dragging in the wet, his fingers wrapped tightly around his staff, he walked to the back of the cart where the two most recent members of his family watched over his heart.

It had become necessary that Iban and Hestia push from the back—or the cart would not pull free of the mud's embrace. But that would leave his heart alone and unprotected. . . .

He had lost his heart once before. He would not allow it to happen again. When the beautiful eyes that had haunted his dreams for longer than he could remember lifted to meet his, he said as he had said a hundred times since the turning of the Circle had brought them together again, **"Don't leave me."**

His horse had not gone far. Much as the storm had driven him to seek shelter, it had driven the horse under the roof of a three-sided goat pen in the fishing village. They spent the night together, the assassin, the horse, and the half-dozen goats. Just after dawn, after swallowing a painfully chewed mouthful of journey bread, Neegan led the horse from the shed. The owner of the goats, arriving to check her stock, saw the Imperial uniform and, although she had no idea of what the black sunburst meant, recognized danger when she saw it. Hands out from her sides, she stayed well back as Neegan emerged from the pen, and asked no questions.

"Ya need a hayla," she said after a moment, as he checked the animal's hooves.

Neegan straightened and stared at her in some confusion, one eye swollen nearly shut. "I need a what?"

"A hayla," she repeated. "Fer ya hayd."

"A healer."

"That's what Ah sayd, a hayla."

He glanced over the cluster of weatherworn buildings. "Does this place have a healer?"

"No. Shahbridge's closest."

Teeth clenched, he swung into the saddle. "I'm going the other way."

"Road's gonna be amass."

"A what?"

She sighed and spat. "Amass. Muddy."

"Thank you for your concern. I'll manage."

Her shrug very clearly told him to suit himself.

"We've got to be making better time than he is." Karlene swiped at the sweat rolling down her face with the back of her left hand, leaving a smear of mud behind. "Don't we?"

"Unless he's abandoned the cart," Vree muttered, pulling the sweat-damp silk away from her skin in a futile attempt to find cooler air.

"Do you think that's possible?"

"Anything is possible," Gyhard growled. The offer obviously covered more than the cart.

"Anything is *not* possible." Vree's voice held Bannon's intonation pattern.

The bard stifled a sigh. Between the brooding silences and the beating-with-a-blunt-object repartee, the mood surrounding her companions was very nearly as heavy as the weather. While the latter hung weights of heat and humidity off the body, the former dragged at the spirit. *And it's not like we were lighthearted to start with.*

She would have given anything to know what had happened while she lay asleep and oblivious. *Two years in the Capital have really dulled my senses. I've got to get out on the road more.* She'd asked them both, using the morning's travel preparations to get each of them alone, but neither would talk. Vree had closed her lips with an emphasis that suggested she was preventing Bannon from speaking, and Gyhard had coldly informed her that it was none of her business.

Perhaps not, but she was in the middle of it and couldn't let it go.

Gyhard loved Vree. Vree was, at the very least, physically attracted to Gyhard. Although Vree should hate Gyhard because he was in Bannon's body, it would've been difficult to consider him an enemy and her reactions to him would've been skewed from the beginning. How far skewed? And what would Bannon think about that? Actually, that last question wasn't hard to answer.

Karlene shook her head, trying to shake the mess down into some kind of clarity. It didn't help.

"I'm going to Sing," she announced suddenly. It wouldn't help straighten out the tangle, but it would make her feel as though she was actually doing something instead of merely being carried along by the turning of the Circle.

"You Sang a while ago," Gyhard pointed out as he squelched from one hummock of grass to the next, dragging his reluctant horse along behind. "Don't you think you should save your energy?"

"It was hours ago, and no." Karlene drew in a deep breath of the clammy air, and Sang the four notes that would call the kigh. A few moments later, she frowned and Sang them again. Then again.

Vree turned toward the bard and found herself staring across her at Gyhard, who'd mirrored her turn.

Steadying herself on the bay's shoulder, Karlene spun around and pointed back the way they'd come. "There! Look!"

In the distance, they could see the willows by the river bending and straightening, first one way and then the other, as though they were being brushed by a giant, invisible hand.

"That's as far as they'll come. We're only a day's walk away and that cart's hardly moving!" She Sang a brief, explosive gratitude, then let her head fall against the warm, solid, living flesh of the horse. He shoved at her with his nose as a few hot tears—of relief, of exhaustion, of anger, Karlene wasn't sure—squeezed out onto his shoulder.

Vree and Gyhard stared past her a moment longer then, abruptly, both turned away, a silent question hanging between them.

What happens when we catch up?

He stopped suddenly, cocked his head, and listened to the silence. He could hear . . . He could hear . . . No. Nothing. But just for a moment, he thought . . .

The cart rolled by him, one laborious inch at a time. He turned as it passed until he faced back the way they'd come. In cities and towns and villages, where lives were crammed in close together, he could sense only *life*. Out where lives were spread across the land, he could sense each one. He sensed a small cluster of lives up ahead and to one side. He brushed over the lives of his companions, each one bending toward him like flames in a breeze. And he touched, like a whisper in the distance, four lives following behind.

The mud made a soft wet sound as he poked his staff into it. This was a road. People traveled on roads. Who was to say that these four lives were not just simple travelers, as he was; simple travelers going home.

But there was something about them, something that made him remember old pain . . .

"They are demons, Kars! They are not enclosed by the Circle!" The teacher raised the rod again and again. And again. "Sing to these demons and remove yourself from the Circle! Or surrender your voice to the truth!"

He surrendered his voice to the screaming, the only truth that he could find.

"Fa . . . ther?"

He turned to see Kait staring at him from her new position at the back of the cart, a shadow of concern lying over her face. "I'm all right, child," he told her, managing to find a reassuring smile. He let it drop when she lowered her gaze, and he looked past her at the young man by her side.

He remembered staring deeply into those incredible, luminous eyes and seeing love stare back. He couldn't see it now, but he would as soon as they were safely home. He knew he would.

"They're out there now, looking for me. They'll find me."

He didn't know who *they* were but he wasn't going to lose his heart again.

"Why are we going up here? This is a way station . . ." Otavas swallowed hard. A way station meant soldiers. Young ones or old ones at a station so far from a Great

Road—but soldiers. If he could catch their attention. If he could just make one of them see him.

The cart rolled out of the mud onto the slightly higher ground of the way station's yard, and the old man ordered the dead to stop pushing.

The prince started toward the building and found the old man in his way.

"Wait here, my heart. There are things in this place that we need."

Otavas glanced at Iban and Hestia who were bracing the shafts. "Like what?" he demanded, then he flushed as his stomach growled loudly.

"Like food." The old man smiled indulgently.

An elderly soldier came out of the station house, and peered toward the road. The three sunbursts on her uniform tunic matched the three on the flag hanging limply overhead. "Who's there?" she called, one hand on the hilt of her short sword, the other shading her eyes.

"Help me!" She was so close, Otavas could see the corporal's stripe circling the hem of her kilt. "You've got to help me! Please!" He leaped forward and was dragged back by cold fingers gripping his arms. When he froze, the dead hands lifted away, but he knew they'd be on him again if he moved.

The corporal frowned. "Ash! Get out here!"

"Corporal?" A chestnut-haired boy, old enough to wear a uniform, young enough for this to be his first posting appeared in the doorway.

"Did you hear anything a minute ago?"

"Ah heard you."

The old soldier sighed. "Did you hear anything besides me?"

"No, Corporal."

"You don't see anything over there by the road?"

For a heartbeat, Otavas was sure the boy saw him.
"No, Corporal."

"It's too slaughtering hot. That's the problem." She
scanned the area again, terror touching her gaze for an
instant as it slid over the dead. "I wonder what's gotten
into the horses. Look at them, all grouped over by the
far side of the corral."

"My ma calls this weatha mad dahg weatha."

"Weath-*er*, Ash. Mad *dog* weath-*er*." The corporal
turned and pushed the boy soldier back inside. "I'll
never get used to the way you people talk up here."

"Don't look so sad, my heart." The old man patted
his shoulder; still feeling the grip of dead hands,
Otavas wasn't able to move away. "I won't be gone
long. Come, Kait."

Shaking with frustration and despair, the prince
watched the old man and the dead girl walk across to
the building. To his surprise, just before they reached
the door, the old man started to sing. It was a pretty
song, a comforting song; Otavas stopped shaking and
yawned. His eyes closed and he slowly sank to the
ground.

He heard the dead move closer but, wrapped in the
song, it didn't seem to matter. Pillowing his head on
his arm, he sighed and fell asleep.

The corporal sprawled in the room's only wood and
leather chair, mouth open, snoring softly. Ash lay
stretched out on a narrow bench, tunic off, bare chest
rising and falling to the slow rhythm of the Song. Another soldier, gray-haired but younger than the corporal, was curled up on the hearth, clutching the wooden
handle of a cleaver loosely in one hand.

While he continued to Sing, Kait took the corporal's
short sword and used it as he'd taught her. She found

the fourth soldier, a woman in her thirties with a patch over one eye and a peg where her right leg should have been, asleep on a pile of hay in the attached stable.

As Kait dragged the fourth body into the main room, he stopped Singing and sank down onto the end of Ash's bench to conserve his strength. A pewter tankard by the boy's limp hand held two inches of tepid ale. He drained it, the warm liquid soothing his throat, as the four kigh buzzed about him; confused, unwilling to be dead.

"Kait, please gather up all the food you can find, there's a good girl." His head ached and he hoped he'd be strong enough for what he had to do. His heart needed to be protected.

Otavas woke to see the old man smiling wearily down at him. "Wake up, my heart. It's time to move on."

Rubbing his eyes, the prince pushed himself up into a sitting position, unable to understand how he'd fallen asleep laying in the damp and the mud. He stretched and frowned at the smell of his own unwashed body. The rain had helped, but he hated not being clean; it made him feel less than himself. Hot water, scented soaps, and attendants to shave him seemed part of someone else's life.

Someone else's life . . . Perhaps they were. Perhaps he'd never had anything but this cart and the old man and the dead.

One hand around a spoke, he used the wheel to pull himself to his feet. Shaking off the torpor that threatened to push him back into sleep, Otavas' brows drew in as he focused on the old man's face. The ancient eyes were sunk deep in violet shadows and the skin hung so loosely off his skull that the gray wisps of his beard appeared to drag it from his chin. "Are you . . . sick?"

"I am tired, my heart." Both his hands clutched at his staff, which seemed to be supporting most of his weight. "But, more importantly, you are safe."

"Safe?" Then he looked beyond the old man—at the corporal, at the boy, at the two other soldiers. They all wore full infantry armor; steel helm, breast and back, boiled leather greaves and vambraces, round shield and short sword. Two of them were old, one was very young, and the other had lost a leg and an eye. Blood had turned the blue of each kilt purple-black in places and had drawn scarlet lines down bare arms and legs. The prince's breath caught in his throat as he was forced to acknowledge one final similarity among them. They were all dead.

"Why?" he whimpered, his back pressed against the cart.

"I did it for you, my heart."

"For me?"

"They will protect you." The old man shuffled toward the open end of the cart. "I did it for you."

"No." He wouldn't take that responsibility. They didn't die for him. He shook his head, found himself in the sudden rush of anger and used it to hold his terror tightly in check. "I am Prince Otavas Irenka, son of His Most Imperial Majesty, the Emperor Otavan."

The four soldiers came sluggishly to attention.

Otavas stepped forward—unable to look the corporal in the eye, he glared at the end of her nose. "I order you to escort me safely back to the Capital!"

The corporal slowly shook her head.

"I *order* you!" His voice grew shrill. "You have to obey the order of an Imperial prince! You have to!"

"Nooo, High . . . nesss."

"No?" He hugged himself to try to stop the trembling. "Why no?"

Her gesture was almost an apology. "Weee . . . arrre . . . dead."

"Oh, yes." Hysteria lurked just below the surface. "I forgot."

"Come, my heart." The prince jerked around as the old man leaned out of the cart and touched the top of his head. "We must go."

Otavas flushed as, in spite of the day's new horror, his body made its needs known. "I have to relieve myself."

The old man nodded. "Go with him, Iban."

Ears burning, the prince hurried over to a thornbush growing at the edge of the station yard, the dead man walking by his side, stopping when he stopped. As the prince fumbled with his trousers, an idea fought its way through the fear. Struggling to hold himself free of the returning numbed lethargy, he worked one of the thin gold rings off his right hand. When he turned to go back to the cart and his body hid the movement of his hand, he quickly slipped it over a thorn.

He could see a small cluster of buildings just up the road and a field of grain behind—a farmer taking advantage of the army's proximity to buy land out of the crowded Imperial core. In time, surely they'd check the station. If not, the army would. If the sun was shining that day, perhaps someone would see the ring.

And if someone saw the ring . . .

Back in the cart, the circle of death closed around him and licked at his thoughts like dark flames.

The weather had not improved as the day went on. Neither had tempers. On edge without the kigh, Karlene kept her eyes locked on the distance they still had to cover, her heart beating like a kettle drum every time the road swooped around a blind corner that could hide the prince.

In mid-afternoon, they came on tracks cut into the mud—cut after the rain had stopped.

"A two-wheeled cart, two people pulling, two people pushing, two people walking along beside." Still squatting, Vree pointed back along the tracks. "I'd say they spent the night there, where the mud's all churned up. The rain came down hard enough to pound yesterday's tracks away."

Karlene felt sick. "The kigh said it was a man and a woman killed in the fishing village. If there're six sets of footprints, Kars must have left the Capital with more than just the two young men."

"Must have," Vree agreed, straightening. She rubbed her palms together as she gazed at the road. "They're not going very fast. These prints are almost one on top of the other."

"Do you think we can catch them by dark?"

"No."

"What do you mean 'no', just like that?" Karlene grabbed her elbow. "We still have lots of light left."

Vree twisted her arm free and stepped away from the bard. "I mean no," she said. "We aren't gong to catch them by dark."

"But we *can* close up the gap." Gyhard swung into the saddle as he spoke.

By the time they approached the way station, they were on foot again—the heat and humidity combined with the soft footing had caused the horses to tire quickly. Still some distance away, Vree moved her gelding to the far side of the road and fell back until she was screened by his head. Gyhard, having been made violently aware that the body he wore was as much at risk of being identified as hers, did the same. The way stations along the Great Roads were set back behind palisades, but on the lesser roads, nothing blocked the possibility of discovery.

Directly opposite the station, Vree stopped walking. The horse took another two steps, then stopped as well. Brows drawn in, her blood beginning to sing, Vree stared across the road over the horse's back. "Something's wrong. It's too quiet."

Gyhard snorted. "Isn't that one of your lines," he asked Karlene. "The heroes approach their destination, tension rises, and one of them says, 'It's too quiet.' No one ever says it in the real world."

"Who asked you?" Bannon snapped and Vree repeated, "Something's wrong." The angle of the sun backlit the station, throwing everything between the road and the long, low building into shadow. Nothing stirred in the area of scuffed dirt nor could she see movement through the open doors and shutters that led to the living quarters and the stables. She smelled neither cooking fires nor cooking.

And given the way the army uses onions, Bannon muttered, *that's saying something.*

The only sound came from the two horses who paced round and round the corral—tails whipping at the air. As Vree studied the area, searching for danger, a pair of crows took off from the ridgepole, their calls like cruel laughter. The hair lifted off the back of her neck. "A bad omen . . ."

"They're birds, Vree. Nothing more." Gyhard continued moving slowly up the road. He walked backward, taking small steps, unwilling to stop, unwilling to be a stationary target.

Who asked you? Bannon growled again, but this time Vree caught the words behind her teeth.

She stared at the three sunbursts hanging limp in the sultry air. She stared at the horses. She narrowed her eyes and stared into the shadows. "The cart went off the road here," she said at last and dragged her horse's head around.

"Vree, where are you going?"

"I have to know what happened."

"Vree!"

Karlene's voice stopped her in her tracks, but she didn't turn.

"We're so close. We *have* to keep going."

Vree nodded. "You go on. I'll catch up."

Gyhard threw up his hands and started back toward her. "That's one of the stupidest ideas I've ever heard. We chase Kars, you chase us . . ."

I hate to agree with the carrion eater, sister-mine, but he's right. We have to stay together.

Fine. He can stay with me.

Karlene stood in the center of the road, torn between two directions. They were close to the prince, less than a day's walk away. If they kept moving, kept moving quickly, they might catch him before dark regardless of what Vree thought. But the cart had gone off the road and there were no kigh to tell her if Kars had left behind any of his walking dead. She took one last, longing look in the direction of the prince and turned her horse toward the station.

"Vree, why are you doing this? Don't you realize the risk you're running?" Gyhard knew better than to grab her arm but his hand hovered in the air beside her.

"You don't have to run it with me."

Yes, he does, Vree. He's in my slaughtering body!

"As for why . . ." She paused, searching for the words. "The army is the only family an assassin has. I have to know. I have to . . ."

Vree!

I see it.

Gyhard recognized the source of the interruption. "What does he want?"

In answer, Vree pointed to the cart tracks cutting up into the station yard and the tracks cutting back to the road. "He had at least three more people with him when he left."

The blood inside the building filled in the details.

"Why does he want more?" Karlene demanded, pacing back and forth, savagely twisting a new braid into her hair.

"I told you, he's insane. He doesn't have reasons for what he does." Gyhard stuffed a half-dozen onions into a bag with a canvas sack of rice. The station's food had been disturbed but so inefficiently he suspected that Kars had ordered one of the dead to do it. "Maybe he thought His Highness needed more company."

"No." Vree straightened and let the lid of the trunk she'd been searching fall. "Not company. Defense. Weapons and armor are missing. That cart left with an armed escort. A dead escort," she added through clenched teeth.

Karlene stared at her. "You're angry." Actually, the tone of her voice had been closer to blind fury. "You were never *this* angry about the prince."

"I never knew the prince."

"You never knew these people either," Gyhard pointed out. "You spent your life in the other end of the Empire."

"I knew them." Vree picked up a tin tinderbox stamped with three sunbursts from the plank table and closed her fingers tightly around it. Three sunbursts, not six, but that was the only difference. The sudden sense of loss nearly overwhelmed her and as she struggled under its weight, Bannon usurped control. "I'm going to rip that slaughtering carrion eater limb from limb! I'm going to cut out his living heart and slaughtering feed it to him!"

"Kars is mine." It wasn't a tone that could be argued with for all its quiet. Gyhard set the bag of food on the table and met Vree's eyes. "Stay away from him, Bannon."

"Or you'll what? What can you do to me that's worse than this?" He spread his sister's arms wide. "Go ahead. Take your best shot."

"If I could throw you out of there, I would."

"Throw me out so you can climb in yourself? You'd like that, wouldn't you?" The peal of laughter had a maniacal ring. "Well, you're not going to ever get the chance."

All at once, Gyhard found Vree's hands locked around his throat, Vree's eyes staring into his, Bannon's kigh trying to force his way back into Bannon's body. He staggered, almost fell, and then contemptuously flicked Bannon away.

Vree's hands fell away and she dropped to her knees, head thrown back and mouth open in a silent scream.

"He's in there too tightly to push out," Gyhard murmured, unable to look away from the vulnerable arc of Vree's throat. "He just snapped back."

"She wouldn't have thanked you for killing him," Karlene snarled, moving up behind him. She wanted to help but had no idea of what she could do. "Vree?"

The tendons in Vree's neck stood out like rope. Muscles twisted under her skin. Her throwing daggers slipped out of their wrist sheaths and clattered on the flagstone floor.

"We can't just leave her like that." Karlene pushed

forward and took a deep, calming breath. **"Vireyda Magaly!"**

Gyhard glared at her suspiciously. "What are you doing?"

"There's power in a name." She threw the explanation at him as she stepped closer and used all the Voice she had. **"Vireyda Magaly! I'm calling you!"**

Vree jerked, once, twice, then collapsed as every muscle relaxed at the same time.

Gyhard beat the bard to the floor. Disregarding both the danger and the audience, he scooped her up into his arms and rested his cheek against the top of her head. For a heartbeat, he thought she relaxed into his hold, then there was no mistaking her desire to be released. He let her go before she could reach for a dagger.

Moving slowly, she stood and half smiled at the bard. "Thank you. Bannon, by the way, says you're an interfering, slaughtering sow."

Karlene returned the smile. "You're welcome."

"Are you all right?" Gyhard's voice held only mild interest, but he had less control over his expression.

Vree bent and picked up her daggers. "At least this time I stayed conscious." Her voice matched his for lack of emotion. "Why aren't you asking if I'm sane anymore?"

She was standing so close he could feel the heat of her body. He shrugged. "Because I wouldn't believe the answer."

"Bannon has some names for you, too, but if I repeated them all we'd be here past dark." She returned the daggers to the sheaths and pulled her sleeves down again. "I'm going out to release the horses. There's plenty of grazing and they can drink out of the river. The army can round them up when it arrives."

"Shouldn't we take the horses?" Karlene wondered.

Vree shook her head. "No. There're three of us and only two of them. We'd still be moving at the speed of one of the three we're riding now." She walked slowly to the door without any of her usual grace. "I'll be waiting outside."

When she heard the gate in the corral squeal open, Karlene raked Gyhard with her gaze. "If you drive him insane, you'll lose her, too."

"I know that." He picked up the bag of food.

"Funny way to show you love her."

"What do you suggest I do, die for her." His laugh held no humor. "That sort of thing only happens in bardic tales, not in real life."

"So you'll kill her?"

It took a moment for Gyhard to realize Karlene did not mean a death as simple as a knife slid under the ribs. "As you said, Lady Bard, there's no possibility of a happy ending."

Vree?

Vree stood back from the high gate so that the two station horses could, if they wanted it, have a clear path to the river. Had she still worn a uniform, they might have trusted her. As it was, they rolled their eyes and stayed by the opposite curve of the fence, masking their fear by aggressive posturing. She knew how they felt.

I'm sorry, Vree. I'm really, really sorry. Please talk to me.

She rubbed at her temples and sighed. *I haven't anything to say to you right now.*

You could yell at me.

Why?

*Because I . . . I mean I . . . Slaughter it, Vree, I took

over your body again. You must have something to say about that!*

I wish you wouldn't.

That's it?

She nodded, aware he could feel the motion.

Bannon was silent for a long moment. *You're mad because of what I said to *him,* aren't you? Aren't you? Vree! Talk to me! Don't shut me out! You're all I have!* He paced the perimeter of his prison. *Oh, I get it. You're tired of being all I have. Did you ever think of how I slaughtering well felt during all those years of being all you had?*

Don't give me that crap, Bannon. You loved it. It gave you power over me.

And now you love having me powerless.

Dependent on her as she had made herself dependent on him. *Maybe.*

*I *know* what you're feeling, sister-mine, whether you're willing to admit it or not.*

She picked up a stone worn smooth by the action of the river and carried up from the shore by some third army soldier assigned to the station.

*I know what you think about *him,* Vree.*

He's in your body and I want him out. He destroyed my life and I want him dead.

I know the rest . . .

Good trick, because I don't.

Want me to tell you?

It doesn't matter.

You'd be surprised . . .

*I *said* it doesn't matter!* The stone whispered through the air and into a thornbush on the other side of the yard. Amidst the sounds of breaking twigs came the faint but unmistakable sound of metal on stone.

When Gyhard and Karlene came out of the building,
Vree was squatting by the thornbush carefully probing
the litter on the ground. As Gyhard went to give their
horses a good feed of the station's grain, Karlene
crossed to the assassin's side. "Did you lose something?"

"Not exactly," Vree murmured without looking up.
"I threw a rock and hit metal where I shouldn't have."

Leaning over the other woman's shoulder, Karlene
peered down into the debris under the bush. "Probably
just a piece of junk from the station."

"Possibly." She flicked a somnambulant beetle off a
twig. "But things where they aren't supposed to be are
a good sign that something's wrong."

"Vree, we know what's wrong."

"Do we?" Vree jerked her head to the left. "There's
two sets of prints over there. One of them, a man, took
a piss. The other must've just watched. What does that
say to you?"

Karlene straightened. "One of them just watched . . .
A guard?"

*She's not as dumb as she looks."

Sod off, Bannon.

What are you defending her for?

She's a friend.

And I'm a . . . Vree!

I see it. She took back control of her hand and
picked up the thin gold ring. Still squatting, she studied
it. There were no marks on the band, no way of telling
how long it had hung on a thorn before she hit it with
the rock and knocked it to the ground.

"Well?" Karlene demanded.

Vree shrugged and stood. "It's got me," she said,
lifted the bard's hand and dropped the ring onto her
palm.

Karlene stared at it, eyes widening.

What was she expecting? A scorpion? Bannon snickered.

Looks like. "Karlene? What's wrong?"

"This was under the bush?"

"Actually, it was hung on a thorn until I knocked it off."

With trembling fingers, Karlene lifted the ring off her palm. "This is one of Prince Otavas' rings. He liked to wear about half a dozen on each hand." She swallowed, hard. "Probably because His Majesty preferred heavy rings with colored stones. Anyway, he set a fashion at court."

Vree frowned. "I wonder who the old man has him guarding?"

"No. No." Karlene shook her head and fought to gain control of her voice. "A dead man wouldn't hang a ring on a tree. He's alive. He left this as a sign to tell me he's alive! Someone was guarding *him!*" She spun around, holding the ring over her head so that the gold flashed in the sunlight and Sang out, "HE'S ALIVE!"

Gyhard ran out of the stable, a feedbag dangling from one hand. "Who's alive?" His head jerked back and forth as he scanned the area. "You found another soldier? What?"

"The prince! The prince is alive!"

Eyes narrowed, free hand gripping the top rail of the corral, Gyhard stared at the bard. "How do you know?"

He doesn't seem very surprised, does he? Bannon muttered.

Vree had to agree. *He seems a little defensive.*

Like he's been caught in a lie.

"Vree found one of His Highness' rings under that thorn tree!" Karlene hurried across the yard, waving the ring. "Except he hung it on the tree, earlier, while he was relieving himself. He's alive! Prince Otavas is alive!"

The high-pitched whine of a buzzbug shattered the silence that followed into a thousand pieces. Her brows drawing slowly together, Karlene froze and studied Gyhard's face. Her finger curled protectively around the ring and her other hand made a fist to match it.

"You knew that." She took a step toward the corral. "You knew he was alive." Another step. "You let me think he was dead and you knew he was alive! You low-down ..." Rage merged the words into a single note that got louder and more shrill and became a weapon that flayed the truth away from any further lies.

Gyhard clamped his hands over his ears and dropped to his knees.

He'd barely hit the ground before Vree had the bard by the shoulders. "Karlene!" she shouted, dragging the taller woman around to face her. "It's Bannon's body! You're hurting Bannon's body!"

The note continued to ring for a heartbeat after Karlene released it. When she shook her head, Vree let her go and stepped back. "Why didn't you tell me?" she asked when Gyhard looked up.

Breathing heavily, he sat back on his heels. "I only ... suspected."

"Why didn't you tell me?"

"What good would it have done?"

"I wouldn't have believed he was dead."

His laugh was shaky and scornful both. "You would have rather believed he was alive, surrounded by the walking dead? Every moment aware of what his fate was likely to be?"

Karlene stumbled back, face pale, the fist clutching

the ring raised to her mouth. She trembled on the edge of flight for a long moment, then whirled and ran toward the river.

"You expect me to believe that you didn't tell her for her own good?" Vree growled as Gyhard heaved himself up onto his feet.

He met her eyes and quickly looked away. "No," he sighed. "I don't expect you to believe that."

"Good." She moved to follow the bard then stopped and turned to face him again. "You're a real shit, you know that?"

This time the laugh held only self-mockery. "Yes. I know." He watched her stride off after Karlene and wondered if she realized that he hadn't known it, until her.

"He's alive."

The old man had heard the words as clearly as if they'd been Sung beside him.

"They're out there now, looking for me. They'll find me."

No. They would not.

Chapter Fifteen

Swaying in the saddle, Neegan approached the way station just as the red ball of the sun sank below the horizon. His exhausted horse, ears pricked forward, lengthened its stride as they left the road. There was a stable waiting and grain and rest. It walked into the corral and stopped.

Neegan twisted around just enough to see the open gate. He stared stupidly at it for a moment and turned again to stare at the building. There were no lights lit, no smoke rising, no smell of an evening meal. There were also no enemies, he realized, grimacing in self-disgust, or he'd have been shot where he sat.

He dismounted awkwardly and looped the reins around the upper rail of the fence. The dusk should have been as easy for him to read as the day, but his head pounded too viciously for him to make sense of what he saw. Dagger drawn, he entered the building through the stable, boots kicking through a cluster of bloated flies that had settled around a bloody stain on the packed earth floor. More flies rose as he entered the main room.

A quick search determined that four people had died without a struggle, that the bodies and the armor of the four soldiers who had held the station were missing.

Neegan fingered the onyx medallion around his

neck. He'd never considered himself a religious man, but he knew death in all its many forms and did not understand what had happened here.

When he returned to the corral, the station's two horses had joined his and all three were waiting to be fed. Frowning, he closed the gate. If the soldiers were dead, why had those who killed them taken the armor but not the horses to carry it? And what had happened to the bodies? If the soldiers were alive, why had they left the station and abandoned the horses? And who had died? And what had they done with the bodies?

With the horses tended to, Neegan lit a lantern and searched the immediate area. There were no patches of loose earth large enough for a mass grave. The privy hid no bodies. If the newer parts of the manure pile had been turned recently, he couldn't spot the disturbance. He'd have been furious had he known what to be furious about—massacre or desertion.

"More questions," he growled. His targets had been trailing unanswered questions in their wake since they left the Sixth Army.

Finally, he went inside, found the medical supplies, and built a small fire in the hearth. As little as he wanted to admit it, he needed to numb the pounding in his skull and he needed rest.

Even if his targets had made the distance they'd made every day since the Capital, he'd still be breathing death on the backs of their necks. One more night would make no difference and then he'd find his answers along the edge of a blade.

They'd reached the ford as the night turned to morning. Otavas had moaned once as the cart bounced through the shallow water and headed east in a line

with the mountains, but the old man had Sung quietly
to him and he hadn't woken.

Now, in the tentative light of dawn, the old man
stared down at his heart and decided not to wake him
right away. "Let him rest," he whispered, stroking a
tangle of dark hair back from a grimy cheek. "He
looks so peaceful when he sleeps."

Gripping the top board of the cart with one hand and
his staff with the other, he dragged himself up onto his
feet. The track they followed could no longer be called
a road; soon, he knew, it would disappear altogether.

He looked back the way they'd come. He could no
longer see the river.

Near tears, he lowered himself back down beside the
pallet. He had never left any of his family alone before. He hadn't wanted to do it, had almost changed his
mind when he looked back and saw them standing for-
lornly by the water's edge, staring after him, but he
hadn't had a choice.

"I did it for you, my heart." He drew the dark head
up onto his lap and Sang softly of the life that they'd
share.

"What is it? What's wrong?" Karlene pulled up and
yanked the bay around in a tight circle, sawing at his
mouth with the bit. "What are you doing?"

Vree dropped out of the saddle and threw her reins
up to Gyhard. "When this stuff's dry, it doesn't mark
worth shit," she muttered, kicking at the double ruts
that led down to the river.

"Have we lost them?" The bay bucked, responding
to Karlene's emotions. "Vree! Answer me!" she
snapped. "We've got to rescue the prince today!"

"Sod you!" Vree spun around and glared up at the
bard. "I'm not a scout, I'm an assassin. You want me

to climb over a wall and slit a throat, fine! You want me to track the pattern of guards, fine! But following a bunch of dead guys and a produce cart in the middle of nowhere is not what I'm trained for. I'm doing the best I can!" She stopped, looked confused at her own vehemence, and brushed the hair back off her forehead. *Bannon?*

He sounded amused. *That wasn't me, sister-mine.*

"Vree, I'm sorry." Karlene sucked in a deep breath and made a visible effort to calm down. "It's just that he's ..." Her hand sketched horror in the air. "... alive."

"I know." And there were four soldiers who were neither alive nor dead. She glanced up, met Gyhard's eyes, and hurriedly looked away. "This track probably leads to a ford. I'm going to check to make sure they haven't crossed the river."

"I'll come with you ..."

"No." She slapped the word up like a physical barrier, and it rocked Gyhard back into the saddle.

He watched her move down to the water until the heat of Karlene's gaze pulled him around. The bard had not spoken two words to him since the way station and Vree had stayed close by her side. "If the prince has gone insane," he said mildly, "which is entirely possible given the length of time he's spent surrounded by the walking dead, can you Sing him up out of shadow?"

Karlene jerked back as though he'd struck her and Gyhard found himself not enjoying her reaction as much as he thought he would've. He sighed and shook his head. "Kars has likely kept him asleep for most of the journey—he can't be in any condition to run after the prince should His Highness attempt to escape."

"Do you think that asleep he'd be . . ." She searched
for a word, hope overriding anger. ". . . protected?"

I haven't the faintest idea. But while he cared not at
all for her opinion, he needed *Vree* to stop staring at
him like he'd crawled out from under a rock. "Yes."

Vree squatted at the river's edge and rubbed her
palms together as she stared at the point where the
track disappeared under the water. A shelf of rock
made it impossible to tell for certain, but she thought
she could see the marks made by a recent passage.
She'd have to cross to the other side to be sure.

Lips pressed into a thin line, she unbuckled her sandals and threw them up on the bank. The heavy leather
was still damp from the rain and she had no intention
of getting them any wetter. Two thirds of the way
across, with the river lapping at her knees, she froze,
hair lifting off the back of her neck.

Bannon . . .

I know.

Her gaze slid quickly over the break in the thick tangle of willows, then dropped back to her feet as they
began to search for new footing against the bottom.
Bannon! What are you doing?

We're going back. Something's not right.

Until he attempted to take control, she'd intended to
return as well. But it was her body—hers—and she
would not allow him to move it about like a game
piece. The water roiling around her legs as she all but
danced in place, Vree fought to push her brother back.

"There's something in the trees across the river."

Gyhard rose in his stirrups. They were waiting at the
point where the track joined the road and he had a
clear view. "There's nothing there."

"How would you know?" Karlene snorted. "You didn't even look."

"I did."

"You didn't; I watched you. Your gaze slid right on by."

"The living can't, or won't, acknowledge the living dead, and so they look right by."

"I looked right at them."

"You're a bard."

The conversation from their first day on the road hung in the air between them.

The hair rose on the back of Gyhard's neck as he tried to force himself to look amongst the willows that lined the far bank. It was dark, far darker than it should have been. All at once, he thought of a use for four un-dead soldiers.

"VREE!" He slammed his heels into the gelding's sides and the startled horse charged toward the water's edge.

Vree turned at the sound of her name and kept turn-ing as a crossbow quarrel parted the billowing folds of her sleeve.

We can't go back! We'd be a target the whole way!

We head for the trees. They won't be able to use the bow. She pulled her long dagger as she ducked and raced for the shore, splashing up as much water to screen her progress as she could.

They met her on the bank.

Training—instinct—brought her blade up to break the downward slash of a short sword. The jar against her raised arm, the sound of steel on steel shoved away the self-delusion her kigh had been practicing.

Four soldiers. Two older ones and a boy. The fourth,

with a peg and an eye patch, reloading her bow a short distance away. Walking dead.

If she wanted to live, she could not give in to terror.

Vree marked their positions as she dove to the right, rolled, and came up with a throwing dagger in her hand. The crossbow had to be taken out. She was moving again before the dagger hit, the boy's sword nearly parting her hair at the forehead. The walking dead were slow, but she realized, slashing a bloodless thigh from hip to knee, they had the advantage of not feeling pain.

The horses would go to the water's edge but no farther. Gyhard threw himself out of the saddle and into the river with Karlene close behind.

Watch out! Bannon twisted her body away from the corporal's thrust as the edge of the boy's flailing shield caught her under the chin. She went down hard, spat out a mouthful of blood, and whipped her leg out of the way just before the corporal struck sparks off the rock she was lying on.

This is not the sort of fight we're good at, sister-mine.

The shield blow continued to echo against the inside of her skull.

Vree! Let's get out of here!

She half-stood. Staggered. A sword whistled past her face and she sliced at the fingers holding it, her blade gouging into the hilt. Three fingers fell, but the two remaining continued to hang on.

"Start Singing!"

"Singing what?" Karlene demanded, stumbling on the uneven and unseen bottom. Arms whirling, mo-

mentum carried her forward another three paces, then
she tripped over the weight of the water and fell.

Gyhard dragged her up onto her feet. "Sing their
kigh free! Out of their bodies and away!" He released
her with a shake for emphasis and continued his
charge.

Gasping for breath, water pouring off of her, Karlene stopped moving and started thinking. She could
Sing the kigh away, she'd done that once already, but
how was she to get them out of their bodies? *Don't be
an ass, Karlene,* she told herself as Gyhard reached the
bank, then leaped back into the river to avoid a sweeping length of steel. *They don't want to be in their bodies. Just remind them.*

Vree ducked through a circle of edged steel and
found herself face-to-face with the archer—blind now,
a dagger hilt protruding from the unpatched socket.
She kicked at the peg. An unlucky grab as the soldier
went down buried undead fingers in Vree's hair. Training barely overcame terror as she tried to cut her way
free.

Neegan left his horse a little way downstream and
slid into the river, eyes and nose only above the water.
He could see his targets fighting four soldiers—the
four from the station he'd wager, although he didn't
bother studying them too closely. *They* were not his
concern as long as Vree and Bannon remained alive.

He would watch and wait and move only when his
targets were either victorious or dead.

Gyhard grabbed up a fallen branch about four feet
long. *This is not something I want to go into armed
with only a dagger.* Teeth clenched, he whipped it

around and slammed it into the back of the corporal's head. Her helm rang with the force of the blow. Her head jerked forward, then back. She should have gone down. Instead, she attacked.

"Shit!"

Vree blocked a swing from the dead soldier's other hand, the stock of the crossbow slapping into her palm. Shoving her dagger between her head and the fingers still clutching at her hair, she dragged the razor edge over her scalp and scrambled clear.

What? This isn't enough? You have to be bald, too? Bannon kicked out and slammed her bare heel into the side of a knee. The joint popped and the boy-soldier tilted crazily to the right.

Stepping toward shore, Karlene began to Sing a soldier's song that a First Army captain had taught her back at the Imperial Palace. She kept it simple, for the moment working only at getting the attention of the dead, her voice reminding them of the life they'd been so cruelly cut out of.

The corporal turned first, her face expressionless, then one by one, the other three joined her. Even the blind woman seemed to stare.

"Vree! Are you all right?"

Vree nodded, spat out another mouthful of blood, and grimaced. "It's hard to remember they're dead. We kept anticipating reactions they didn't have." Wrapping her hand around Gyhard's wrist, she allowed him to help her to her feet. His skin seemed hotter than it should beneath her fingers. "I bit my tongue . . ." The Song made it hard to think. Brows drawn in, she turned to face the bard.

* * *

Still in the water, Karlene changed the Song. There were notes played on a horn every night at the First Army garrison. The captain had explained their meaning as a sort of a combination pat on the back and dismissal. *Good soldiers, your duty for the day is done. Rest knowing that because of you, the Empire is safe.* Karlene had never asked if the same notes were played in *every* garrison, but given the efforts made to keep the seven armies unified, she was willing to bet they were.

She Sang the notes over and over, making them both a call to the soldiers' kigh and stressing the dismissal. *Good soldiers, your duty for the day is done* ...

Slowly, Vree turned toward the river, pulled around by the Song.

"Vree!" Gyhard grabbed her by the shoulders and shook her hard. "Vree, she's not Singing to you!"

She knew she should make him pay for touching her, but it didn't seem to matter. Her duty for the day was done ...

Hidden in a tangle of willow roots that extended out into the water, Neegan heard the Song and shook it off. His duty would not be done until his targets were dead.

"Vree! Listen to me! You aren't in the army any more!" Gyhard grabbed her face, pulled it close, stared into her eyes. "Don't you remember! I dragged you away and made it impossible for you to return!"

Vree blinked at him. "I'm a *good* soldier ..."

"No! You were, but you aren't any more."

"I want ... I want to rest."

... rest.

Gyhard pressed his forehead against hers. "You can't," he told her hoarsely. "I won't let you."

Suddenly, the soldiers collapsed, puppets with cut strings. Karlene threw herself into the Song and joyfully Sang away the kigh that whirled about her.

Gyhard felt Vree sag in his grip and at almost the same instant, stiffen. He could feel her breath, warm against his mouth. If he lowered his head just a fraction . . .

He let his hands fall just as hers rose to break his wrists. She frowned, and for the first time, he wasn't sure if it was Bannon or Vree he saw.

"Why didn't you . . ." Her voice trailed off.

He shook his head and stepped back, unable to answer. All he knew was that he had to get away from her, far enough away to be able to think clearly. *I should have killed her when I had the chance . . .*

"Vree! Are you all right?" Karlene splashed up out of the water and squelched across to the assassin's side. "I saw you get hit!"

"It's nothing," Vree muttered, watching Gyhard drift toward the river's edge.

Bannon yanked her head around. *No!*

Bannon, I . . .

You what? You have no defense, Vree. Don't even try.

Neegan watched and waited and, when the moment was ripe, attacked. A heartbeat later, he knelt between Bannon's shoulders, dragging back his head with a handful of hair and pressing the point of a blade into the arc of his throat.

Now, he would get some answers.

Heart slamming up against his ribs, Gyhard froze. The grip in his hair hurt more than the dagger although he could feel a warm trickle of blood run down from the point. If this assassin killed him, thinking he killed Bannon, the circle would have turned to death at last. He couldn't jump bodies without eye contact—all he could see was the riverbank. All thought fled, leaving behind only the terrified question, *Why aren't I already dead?*

Crouched, dagger in her hand, Vree stared, wide-eyed at the commander. Assassins who deserted died. *It's over.*

I'm not going to die, Vree. She could feel him straining against her control. *I'm not going to die!*

"Vree . . ."

"This has nothing to do with you, Karlene."

Neegan turned his head, just enough to meet Vree's gaze. "I need some answers," he husked. "Or Bannon dies."

"No!"

Thrust into the back of her own mind, Vree clawed at Bannon's frenzy. *Bannon! He's giving us a choice!*

"I am not going to die!"

Vree's sudden, irrational charge took Neegan by surprise. In spite of her speed, he could still have opened Bannon's throat before she reached him, but he hesitated. He knew it was Vree charging toward him, shrieking defiance, but it was Bannon he saw.

Bannon, no!

He/she/they dove, hitting the commander under his left arm, using his/her/themselves as a battering ram to throw the older man off Bannon's body. The knife point drew a crimson line toward Gyhard/Bannon's ear.

Bannon, Vree; it became irrelevant whose wrist he held, whose rib he drove his knee into—Neegan had lived this long by adapting to the unexpected. He jabbed three fingers hard under the curve of a muscle, twisted, and nearly got a hand free. An elbow slammed down and pinned his palm to the ground.

"You've been trying to kill me all my life, old man," Bannon hissed through Vree's lips. "But I've always been too good for you." Impervious to pain, impervious to anything but survival, he smashed Vree's forehead against the bloodstained rag tied over Neegan's brow.

The commander grunted, and his grip spasmed around Vree/Bannon's blade hand.

"An assassin who deserts dies," Bannon snarled, shifting Vree's weight to keep Neegan pinned. "And an assassin who stays dies. And this assassin . . ." He laid the blade against the vein pulsing in Neegan's throat. ". . . dies now."

"VIREYDA! STOP HIM!"

Vree grabbed onto her name and used it to cut through the maelstrom of anger, fear, and triumph that was Bannon.

No!

Trembling, gulping in the air, she stopped the knife with the point just below the skin. "Why?" she whispered, her voice no louder than Neegan's would have been. "Why should I stop him, Karlene?"

She almost couldn't hear the bard's answer over the sound of Bannon's shrill challenges. "Look at him, Vree. He's your father."

My what? But the words never made it past the clenched barricade of her teeth. They didn't have to. The commander's face told her everything she needed to know.

Eyes clouded with pain, Neegan stared up at her.

For the first time, she noticed how like Bannon's his eyes were. Recognized the angle of his cheek. Remembered how he'd always been there, forcing them through harder and more deadly training, tangling their responses until the lines between them blurred and they struck as one blade.

Neegan read the thought off her face. "Assassins," he told her, as he had a hundred times before, "have no family but the army."

"I had Bannon."

He closed his eyes. "No. Bannon had you."

Kill him! Kill him! Kill him!

Once, during training, Vree had slipped from a roof. The impact with the ground had knocked the breath out of her and numbed her entire body except for a sharp, focused pain in her chest where she'd cracked a rib. She felt like that now; numb, with a sharp, focused pain in her chest. There should have been a thousand things to say, but she couldn't think of any of them.

She rocked her weight back off her knees and stood. Stepping over the commander, over her father, as though he wasn't there, she walked slowly along the river's edge, brow furrowed. Why did the world suddenly seem to end just beyond her fingertips?

"Vree."

Even before the arrow had destroyed his voice, Neegan had never needed to shout. Vree stood where she was, acknowledging his call, but not turning.

"I have never missed a target."

"VREE!"

The desperation in Gyhard's warning snapped the world back into focus. Whipping around, she found Neegan exactly where he had to be in order to drive a dagger through her spine. She dropped to one knee, pushed the point of her blade through a black sunburst, and up under his ribs. A twist of her wrist moved the double edge from left to right and sliced through his heart.

He was dead when he hit the ground.

"He wanted you to kill him," Karlene said softly. "It was the only way he could stop trying to kill you."

"What? And that was a good thing?" Vree sucked in a deep breath and forced it out through her teeth. "I am so slaughtering tired of being everyone's slaughtering answer."

Gyhard moved toward her, looking very much as if he had no choice in the matter. "Your head's bleeding."

Vree touched her forehead and stared at the blood on her fingertips. "It's not mine."

"Are you all right?"

"Why wouldn't I be?" She was hanging onto a window ledge with fingers and toes. Shadows filled the cobblestone courtyard below, but they were the least of her worries—the fall would kill her. "Why did you warn us? Your life would be so much easier if we were dead."

"If you were dead, my life wouldn't be worth living."

Vree'd never noticed before how much Bannon—Gyhard looked like Commander Neegan. "Slaughter you, too," she snarled and knelt to wash the blood from her face and hands.

When Gyhard stepped toward her, Karlene grabbed his arm and pulled him back. "You're a complication she doesn't need right now." Her voice held a tone that suggested he not argue. "She's falling apart."

"And how long did you have to study to develop that amazing insight into human nature?" Gyhard growled, jerking his arm free. But he remained where he was. As little as he wanted to admit it, the bard had a point if for no other reason than the face he wore was too like the older face pressed into the dirt of the riverbank—a face that in death showed as much emotion as it had in life. "I'm going for the horses. You might start thinking about burying this lot."

"Burying?" Karlene swept a dismayed gaze over the five bodies. "But that'll take so long. We need to rescue the prince!"

Gyhard, wading across the ford, ignored her, but Vree stood and slowly turned. Mud stained the knees of her trousers, water dribbled down from her hair, and her lashes had clumped together into wet, triangular spikes. "We can't leave them for the crows," she said. "They were good soldiers, like you sang." Her cheeks flushed and her eyes shone with an almost feverish heat. "They were *all* good soldiers."

"Vree, we haven't got shovels or anything to dig with, and this whole area is rock and clay."

"We'll have to do the rites," Vree continued as though she hadn't heard.

Unable to step over, Karlene went around Neegan's body, almost frantic with the need to make the younger woman understand. "Vree, these people are dead, truly dead. Prince Otavas is alive, and we have a chance to save him, today. You *can't* want him to spend more time with . . ." Her gesture covered the four soldiers from the station. ". . . this sort of thing. They're dead! He's alive!" She reached out to grab the assassin's arm, but some instinct of self-preservation stopped her hand before it closed on flesh. "Vree, **listen to me**."

"I hear you."

"A soldier expects to die in the service of the Emperor, and these soldiers *are* at rest. I guarantee it." She used as much Voice as she thought was safe. The last thing she wanted to do was overwhelm Vree's conscious control and release Bannon.

"What about *him*?"

"Him, too. His kigh is . . ." Gone would not, perhaps, be the best word. ". . . not here. I'd know if it was."

Vree sighed and nodded, and some of the tension went out of her shoulders. "Then Jiir allowed this as a battlefield death. Good. The army was . . . was . . ." She bit down hard on her lip. When she released it, her chin jerked up as though daring the bard to comment. "Why did you tell us that he was . . . who he was?"

Karlene spread her hands; half in apology, half in helpless discomfort. "I didn't want you to kill your father."

"I guess you should've checked with him first."

"I think he wanted you to know."

"I don't think he gave a shi . . ." Vree's face twisted, her fingers curled into claws, and her toes dug into the wet ground. "You want to know what's funny?" she said a moment later as though Bannon had not spoken. "He was always the closest thing to a father we had." She stepped over Neegan's body without looking down, put her foot on the shoulder of the one-legged soldier, and pulled her throwing dagger from the eye socket.

He felt the Song in blood and bone and in the memory of ancient pain.

"There're out there now, looking for me. They'll find me."

They were the demons of his youth. He knew them now. He should have known they would come for his heart. Long ago, they had taken everything else, flayed his spirit, and left him for dead.

But he had survived.

In many ways, he was stronger than he had been then. His gaze gently touched each of his four remaining companions where they rested in the shade. This time, he was not alone.

"I have run from them for too long," he murmured to the dark head on his lap. "We will make a stand and defeat them, you and I, once and for all."

Otavas stirred, his dreams touched by a dark hand. He would have wakened had he been able.

"We can't just charge in like three of the seven armies to the rescue," Gyhard said, his eyes locked on Vree's profile. "We need a plan, and we haven't much longer to devise one."

Vree touched the crossbow tied on behind her saddle. "We kill the old man. Karlene Sings away the dead. The prince goes home."

"I don't think Kars is going to be that easy to kill." The look she shot him lifted the hair on the back of his neck. Obviously, the pair of assassins sharing Vree's body thought differently. If they were thinking at all. Because he could do nothing to ease her pain, even if she admitted feeling it, he continued his explanation. "Suppose Kars has told the dead to kill the prince if he dies. If Karlene starts to Sing before he's dead, he'll stop her—remember he's had years of practice Singing a fifth quarter she's only just discovered. And it's going to take her a while to find the right Song. These people have been dead longer and they're all different—one Song isn't going to cover them."

"Isn't it?" Vree asked the bard.

Karlene hadn't actually considered it. Worry about His Highness mixed liberally with worry about Vree had kept her thoughts in turmoil since they left the riverbank. But—as much as she hated to admit it—Gyhard was right, they needed a plan. Two of the dead were from the

fishing village, and she had to assume that any others—
two more at least but possibly three—were from the
tombs of the Capital. "Once they're out of their bodies,"
she replied, "I can Sing them all away at once, but to get
them out . . ." She glanced over at Vree and shook her
head. "I'm afraid that may take some time."

"All right." Vree shifted in the saddle, eyes narrowed. "We catch up. We wait until they stop. We go
in and slit Kars' throat. Solves everything."

"We go in?" Gyhard asked.

"Bannon and I."

"No."

Vree turned enough to look him full in the face.
"Slaughter you, too," Bannon snarled.

"It's too dangerous. The dead don't sleep. I'm not
sure Kars does anymore."

"So?"

Gyhard sighed explosively and threw up his hands—an
older man's gesture at odds with the body he wore.
"What happens if you get killed?" he demanded, snatch-
ing up the reins again as his horse headed off the track.

One shoulder lifted and fell. "You get to keep Bannon's body and Karlene Sings one more Song."

I don't want to die!

You think I do?

Yes.

She ignored him.

"Do you see them there, coming up the track?"

Had her eyelids functioned, Kait would have
squinted; as it was she could only lean toward the three
tiny figures down below. "Yesss, Fa . . . ther."

He patted her shoulder proudly. "Of course you do.
When they get to that tree . . ." Kait swayed so she could
look along the line of his outstretched arm to where a

squat and gnarled trunk lifted twisted, nearly leafless branches to the sky. ". . . I want you to pull this branch away and then follow us as quickly as you can."

"Yesss, Fa . . . ther."

He hugged her close, oblivious to the smell. "That's my girl."

Had she been able, she would have smiled.

"Old bones move slowly," he told her as he released her. "We won't have gone far." Leaning heavily on his staff, he began the steep climb back to the top of the bluff where the others waited with his heart.

"Fa . . . ther?"

Balanced carefully on the loose rock, he half-turned.

"Be care . . ." Kait worked her mouth but the "f" was beyond her. ". . . ul."

Rheumy eyes filled. "I will, child."

"Before you decide to die nobly," Gyhard announced caustically, "I want to talk to Kars." And say? He didn't know. *I'm sorry I drove you insane. Don't you think it's time you were dead?* Then what?

Bannon snorted. "You think he wants to talk to you after what you did to him? Do you think he'll just hand you the prince?" Vree finished.

If he gets the prince, then I get my body back!

We're not letting him have the prince, Bannon.

I want my body back!

Two spots of color burned high on Karlene's cheeks. "Rescuing His Highness has to be our first priority."

"*Our* first priority?" Gyhard shook his head. "You presume, Lady Bard, that my priorities are yours. That is not necessarily so."

"But Prince Otavas is alive!"

"So is Kars."

"He's crazy. You said so yourself."

"And therefore deserves to die? I don't think so. Not for that." He reached out and touched Vree lightly, fleetingly on the arm. "If you can go in and slit Kars' throat, can you go in and get the prince out instead?"

She slapped at a biting fly and wiped her palm clean with a handful of mane. "We don't owe you any favors."

"I know. Can you do it?"

"Not if the old man's put him to sleep."

"If he's awake."

"Yeah. We could."

"Will you?"

Vree glanced over at him out of the corner of one eye. Bannon's body ...

I want it back, Vree!

His desperation clawed at her, but she'd been trained to ignore pain she could do nothing about. "I'll think about it," she said at last and kicked her horse into a trot.

"If His Highness dies because of you," Karlene ground out through clenched teeth, "I'll make you sorry you were ever born!"

Gyhard smiled at her, Bannon's features adding a feral savagery to the expression. "It won't be the first time," he said and sent his horse after Vree's.

Hands wrapped around the branch, bone beginning to show through rotting fingertips, Kait watched the three riders come closer and closer to the tree.

They would not all arrive at the tree at the same time.

What would Father want her to do?

By the time the question had been sluggishly considered, the first rider had nearly passed the tree. Long before she found an answer, the second rider was approaching.

Kait surrendered. She leaned back against the splintered end of the branch and levered it free.

Loaded with rock, the cart began to roll. Shafts dragging behind, it quickly began to pick up speed on the steep slope.

The rumble of the cart whipped Vree's head around and up. Less aware of her surroundings than usual, it took her a moment to find the source of the noise. The next moment she drove her heels into the gelding's sides and bent low over its mane as it leaped forward. The cart, heading directly for the one tree of any size, would pass behind her. The chunks of hillside accompanying it, would not.

Still some distance from the tree, Karlene saw the cart crashing down toward the track, half the steep, rocky bluff falling with it. Time seemed to stop as one of the narrow wheels shattered. The cart twisted, splintered, but the fragments continued to lead the swelling wave of destruction.

Yanking back on the reins, she realized that Gyhard was directly in the path of the grinding, wedge-shaped mass. She hesitated while the bay fought the bit and tried to run, then finally screamed a warning.

He couldn't outrun it. His only chance was to get the bulk of the ancient tree between him and the crushing avalanche of rock. Jerking his panicked horse off the track, he dove from the saddle, pressed his back up against the gnarled trunk and grabbed on to the gelding's cheek straps with both hands just as the first impact shook the tree.

Whites showing all around its eyes, the gelding fought

his hold. With a scream of terror, it tore itself free and disappeared into the rising cloud of dust and debris.

The noise was deafening. Gyhard squeezed his eyes shut, swore as a rock glanced off his thigh, and prayed to gods he'd forgotten for four lifetimes. He lost himself in the roar and reverberation, unable to tell where he left off and the cataclysm began.

Then a sudden, dry shriek wrenched his eyes open.

One of the tree's massive limbs, dead from trunk to tip, dropped toward the ground.

Gyhard barely had time to get an arm up over his head.

Vree left her shaken horse at the edge of the rockfall and clambered back toward the tree. Bannon wailed in the depths of her mind, but it was a sound without words and easy to push into the background. Climbing nimbly over and through the treacherous fan of debris, she swung off the track and down to where Gyhard lay, half buried in rock.

If he's dead . . .

Bannon's wail grew louder, but Vree hadn't actually been thinking of her brother at all. *If he's dead* kept repeating over and over, circling the inside of her head, patrolling the perimeter. She couldn't get past it.

There were few rocks directly behind the tree although the area between it and the bluff had been filled to waist level in places. A smashed board from the cart had been flung high into a splintered fork.

Straddling Gyhard's waist, Vree squatted and slid a hand under the branch that pinned him to the ground. Her heart started beating in time to his.

"He's alive," she said as Karlene lowered herself carefully down off the track. A small ripple of dislodged rock bounced away. Both women ignored it.

Karlene had never heard two words spoken with so many layers of emotion. "Is Bannon's body all right?" she asked gently. When Vree turned to face her, the bard wished she'd held her tongue. Vree hadn't forgotten whose body Gyhard wore—couldn't forget—and the last thing she needed was yet another jealous reminder. "I'm sorry, Vree."

The shrug clearly dismissed both question and apology. "We'll have to lift this branch straight off. We'll only do more damage if we drag it."

The branch had done damage enough. Midway between wrist and elbow, Gyhard's left forearm bent where it never had before.

"This is broken."

My body!

Karlene leaned forward. "Anything else?"

That's enough!

"Cuts and bruises. Nothing big." Vree felt the arm move under the gentle pressure of her fingers and looked up to see Gyhard staring at her through bloodshot eyes. Almost without realizing she did it, she blocked Bannon's frantic leap.

VREE! Bannon's shriek flayed her with her name. *I could've had him!*

And a broken arm, Vree told him, desperately searching for an excuse acceptable to them both. *Do you want that kind of pain?*

I want my body. But the shriek had become a sob, and she knew he'd clutched at the chance to believe she still thought of him first. It hadn't taken much effort; she'd spent her life protecting him from pain.

"I'm going to have to set this," she muttered, needing to fill the silence.

Gyhard—who more than anything in the world wanted to know why Vree had stopped her brother from killing him—dragged his tongue over dry lips. "You sure you know how?"

Vree snorted. "No. If we get injured in the middle of an enemy camp, we go looking for a healer. Karlene hold his elbow. Brace yourself," she added as the bard grabbed on where she indicated.

Gyhard swallowed. Hard. "Aren't you supposed to say you won't hurt me?"

"No." And she pulled the bones straight.

"Better him than me," Bannon snarled as Gyhard paled, moaned, and fainted.

Vree lightly brushed the backs of her fingers over the dark bristles that delineated her brother's jaw. *Do you remember when you took that quarrel in the leg and I had to threaten to carry you before you'd stop telling me to go on alone because you'd only slow me down.*

You took the quarrel, Vree.

No, I . . .

A scream from farther down the hill ended the argument.

Gyhard's horse lay panting on its side, unable to rise. A gash deep enough to show bone over one eye explained why it had remained quiet for so long. As Vree and Karlene approached, it began to thrash, as much in terror as pain.

"That front leg's smashed," Karlene said softly, trying not to cry. "We can't leave it like that."

Vree turned to stare at her in horror. "What do you mean?"

"You'll have to kill it."

"No." Vree backed up a step and nearly fell on the uneven slope. "I can't."

"What?"

"I can't."

Karlene couldn't believe what she was hearing. The horse screamed again. "You just killed your own father!" The accusation carried the shrill edge of hysteria.

"He was going to kill me. I had to survive." Her voice held the echo of a hundred lessons then it broke. "But I can't kill a helpless animal. I can't. I can't." She sank down to her knees and covered her face with her hands. "I just can't."

"It's all right." Karlene touched the younger woman gently on the shoulder. If Vree needed to react to this when she'd reacted to almost nothing else, the bard wasn't going to stop her. "Give me your dagger and tell me what to do."

There was a great deal of blood on the ground before the injured animal finally stilled. Karlene kept one hand pressed against its side and Sang comfort in time to its failing heartbeat. She didn't know if it helped— bardic theory was split over animal reaction to Song— but she figured it couldn't hurt. When the last heartbeat faded away, she Sang the horse into the ever-green pastures of the Circle and slowly stood.

Vree still knelt where she'd left her, staring blankly at the crimson puddle and thinking . . . or possibly, not thinking. Karlene wanted to help but didn't have the first idea of what to do or say. She was afraid Vree would have to find her own Song.

From where she stood, she couldn't tell if Gyhard had regained consciousness nor did she much care one way or the other.

They'd be walking now. But with the destruction of the cart, so would the old man and Prince Otavas.

The prince could no longer be kept asleep.

Would he be walking, or walking dead?

* * *

As the sun moved down the sky and the shadows lengthened, the old man gently woke the young man sleeping by his side.

Otavas pushed himself into a sitting position and stared around him in confusion. The brilliant eyes that one besotted courtier had compared to onyx in moonlight were dull and ringed with shadow, the thick fringe of lash broke into crusted clumps. "Where ... where are the cousins?" he asked as he did his best not to see Kait and Wheyra, Hestia and Iban.

"They left us long ago, my heart."

"They did?" Otavas frowned, trying to remember. Why was it so hard?

The old man pushed a rough wooden bowl into his hands. "I have made you mush, my heart."

Fighting to shove aside the hours of Commanded sleep, Otavas scooped the warm mush up on two fingers and wondered when he'd learned to eat like a peasant. Or had he always known? He couldn't seem to reach the memories of his old life—his life before the old man and the dead.

"Eat it quickly, my heart," the old man told him. "For we must flee."

"Flee? Flee what?" When the old man hesitated, Otavas grabbed at a skinny arm. "You have to tell me."

"Demons." The ancient eyes locked onto the young ones. "I never meant to bring you into such danger, my heart, but I will protect you. I swear it."

Demons. Otavas shuddered. Had they brought the darkness that haunted his dreams?

"I will protect you," the old man said again. "You must believe me."

Otavas nodded. The old man was the only thing that stood between him and the darkness.

Chapter Sixteen

"They rested here." Vree straightened, one hand curled around the dagger at her hip, the other curled into a fist—both hands positioned so that her companions couldn't see the fingers tremble. They trembled nearly all the time. She couldn't seem to make them stop. With the side of one foot, she kicked more dirt over the small fire pit. "And not very long ago."

"Then we're close."

"Very close," Vree amended, squinting up the narrow canyon. They'd lost time by following the cart's trail to the top of the bluff for Kars and the dead and the prince had doubled back nearly to the track.

"It goes to an old Imperial mine and smelter," Karlene declared, falling into a light recall trance. *"It played out during the reign of the last Emperor although a few families are still scraping a living out of it."*

"I don't see how," Gyhard muttered. *"The area's been destroyed. There aren't two trees standing next to each other for miles."*

To Vree, it merely looked like the southern parts of the Empire; only without the lizards. There were plenty of trees in other places; she couldn't understand what both Karlene and Gyhard had been so upset about. "Between the dead and Kars, they'll be moving slowly cross-country," she said. "And without the cart, they'll have to stop to sleep."

"Can we watch them?" Unable to remain still, Karlene twisted her hair into an impossibly tight braid.

Vree nodded.

"Tonight?"

"Yes."

"If they sleep," Gyhard reminded them.

Karlene drew herself up to her full height, which was considerably taller than either of the Southerners. "The prince was alive at the way station."

"A lot has happened since then," Gyhard remarked mildly.

"He's alive," the bard ground out through clenched teeth, "or your Kars wouldn't be trying to stop us."

"She's right." Vree forced her gaze up off the rough sling that bound Gyhard's broken arm to his chest. Bannon kept her eyes on it as much as he could, terrified he would have to watch helplessly while his body died. Vree could do nothing about his fear because if it became the only way she could save the prince, that was exactly what would happen. Her own fear, she kept where she always had.

An honorable death.

And maybe Karlene would Sing her to rest.

You. You. Always you! What about me?

If Gyhard stayed away from the prince ... She didn't know what she'd do. Nothing? But Bannon had to have his body back.

"Come on," she said suddenly. "We're wasting time."

He listened for the demons at dusk. Long ago they'd come to him as the sun set, dancing on the evening breeze. They didn't come this night as they hadn't come for thousands and thousands of nights.

He dared to hope they'd died under the rock.

But demons were tricky, and he'd believed them dead before.

When he could no longer see where to place either feet or staff, he led the way to an outcrop of rock and sank to the ground.

Otavas stumbled after him, stomach growling. He didn't want to ask the old man for anything, but the old man was carrying the food. "I'm hungry," he said, sounding much younger than seventeen.

"Of course you are, my heart."

The three plums were not at their best, having spent the better part of two days in a calfskin pouch, but the prince wolfed them down, then licked the juice off his fingers. Two biscuits, hard and dry, and a few mouthfuls of tepid water finished the meal.

"In the morning, I will make mush," the old man told him. "And then we will gather up the bounty of the land."

"Bounty?" Otavas swiveled his head around and waved a hand at the canyon walls he couldn't see. "Of *this* land? There's nothing but a lot of rock and scrub!"

The old man sighed. "Do you remember how you used to set snares for the rabbits far away from the cabin because you knew I hated to hear them scream?"

"That wasn't me."

"Of course it was, my heart."

Otavas flinched back as an ancient hand reached out and unerringly patted him on the thigh in spite of the darkness. He frowned and rubbed at the place the old man had touched. He didn't know how to set a snare for a rabbit. Did he? Still frowning, he barely resisted as he was pulled down to pillow his head on a bony lap. Brushing a dangling finger bone off his cheek, he rolled over and stared up at the stars.

"You must sleep, my heart. We are still far from home and safety."

Otavas traced the Road to Glory with his gaze and twisted just far enough to see the four brilliant white stars that made up the points of the Imperial Diadem. Imperial ... Emperor ... Tears spilled out the corners of his eyes as he remembered. He was Prince Otavas, the Emperor's youngest son. Prince Otavas. He'd never set a rabbit snare in his life.

"Sleep, my heart."

Holding his memories like a shield, the prince fought the compulsion. And lost.

The old man looked to where his family sat, a semicircle of shadows against the shadows of the night. "We must keep watch," he told them softly, "so that the demons do not come on us unprepared." Wheyra, Hestia, and Iban, he turned around where they sat. Kait, he moved up to the top of the rocky outcrop he leaned against.

As she climbed clumsily in the darkness, he stroked the matted hair back off the face in his lap. "Remember how you would hold me when the demons tried to take my dreams? I will hold you now, my heart, and protect you as you so long ago protected me."

"We're staying here until the moon comes up."

"No." Karlene tried to push past her, but brown fingers clamped around her arm like an iron vise.

"You want a busted ankle to go with his arm?" Vree asked, pushing her face within inches of the other woman's. "If we can't see well enough to move safely, you can't."

The bard knew better than to try to pull away. "But we're so close."

"Close enough to trip over them. We don't want

that." When Karlene nodded reluctantly, Vree released her and sank to the ground. Both hands searched for potential disaster—she wasn't certain fire ants even lived this far north, but she had no intention of finding herself sleeping on a nest. She rolled a few loose rocks out of the way and then thankfully shrugged out of the jury-rigged pack.

"We should've kept one horse for the gear," Gyhard muttered as he dropped the little he carried.

"We're trying to sneak up on them, and horses don't sneak worth shit." Vree stretched out, pillowed her head on the pack, then twisted so she could see Gyhard outlined against the stars as he settled down beside her.

He's too close.

You can watch your body more easily.

Vree, he's broken my arm. A broken arm, no matter how cleanly the bone set, would never be as strong as it once was. He would never be able to depend on his body as he had before Gyhard. *He has to pay for that.*

"I know." He was so close, she could see the pain he tried to hide, see the way he held his left arm protectively with his right.

"You know what?" Gyhard asked, wondering why her words had sounded like she pushed them through a blocked throat.

Vree closed her eyes and wrapped her arms around herself. "I was talking to Bannon."

"Out loud?"

As he knew the answer already, she didn't bother responding. She hadn't realized she'd spoken out loud.

"Vree?" Karlene sat on her other side, all the highs and lows rubbed off her voice by emotional exhaustion. They were so close that every rock, every tree, every bend in the trail could hide the prince. "Have you decided what you're going to do?"

Muscles tensed. "About what?"

"His Highness."

His Highness. Vree bit back a nearly hysterical giggle of relief. "We should catch up and follow him for a couple of days, find the patterns, note the weaknesses, and plan a way to use them."

Just like Neegan did, Bannon snorted. *Giving the commander a chance to kill us from beyond the grave?*

Shut up, Bannon.

I can't believe you care that he's dead.

He was our . . .

Father? Yeah, right.

Father. No. *Teacher. Commander. He kept us together.*

His laugh ground salt into open wounds. *Then he'd *love* this, wouldn't he?*

Karlene shook her head, forgetting that night hid the gesture. "We can't go on like this for another couple of days."

Bannon continued to laugh as Vree shoved him back as far as she could. Which wasn't far. "Neither can we," she murmured. "We'll move on when the moon rises."

"But now . . ."

"Now, I'm going to sleep. I suggest you do the same."

Karlene stared down at the Vree-shaped shadow in disbelief. "How can you *sleep?*"

A fingernail cut a half-moon into her palm; teeth clenched, she forced the fist to open. "I can do anything I have to."

* * *

An assassin has no family but the army.

An *assassin* has no family but the army.

An assassin *has* no family but the army.

An assassin has *no* family but the army.

An assassin has no *family* but the army.

An assassin has no family *but* the army.

An assassin has no family but *the army.*

AN ASSASSIN HAS NO FAMILY BUT THE ARMY.

A hundred voices said it. Vree listened for one alone.

She was seven. Her mother had just died. Neegan was absurdly young, with no scar on his throat, and his voice able to roam where it pleased. He had not yet survived long enough to be made an officer.

"An assassin," he said, wiping her cheeks with strong fingers and lifting her face so she could stare into his eyes, "has no family but the army."

The moonlight touched her face and Vree woke trying to hold onto the feeling she'd just been given a gift. *The army was his family, Bannon. He gave it to us.*

Gave us to it. His mental voice held no forgiveness. *If you had no family but the army, Vree, what does that make me? He screwed that up, too, sistermine. But then, he died for *you* at the end. Right after he held a slaughtering knife at what he thought was my throat.*

I . . . *You mean more to me than training,* Neegan had said to her with his death. *I would rather die than kill you.*

He also said he'd rather die than voluntarily miss a target. Look, Vree, you feel what you want about him, but if I feel nothing but slaughtering satisfaction that he's dead and I'm not, well, he has only himself to blame. Isn't that what he taught us? Do anything you must to reach your target. Do anything you have to in order to survive. Fear turned the anger to a sullen crimson pulse. Bannon opened her eyes and turned her head toward Gyhard, repeating, *Anything,* so softly she thought she might have imagined it.

Gyhard was awake and staring at her with a hungry longing that made her want to grab his shoulders and shake him until his ears bled. She'd already killed one man who loved her—in his own dark and twisted way—did this one think she couldn't kill two?

It's all right, sister-mine. I can hate him enough for both of us.

The moon turned Karlene's pale hair into a gleaming silver-white braid that looked too perfect to be real. When Vree stood, the bard's lids snapped up and she whispered, "Is it time?"

Palms rubbing against each other, Vree nodded.

Vree saw the shadow first, flowing down the curve of the outcropping, one dark stream ending in the outline of a hand and moonlight-elongated fingers. Tracing it back to its source, she found the slumped silhouette of a watcher—not a stump or boulder as she had first assumed. She forced her eyes to remain locked on it, fighting the compulsion to look away and then fighting the terrified panic that rose when she refused to give in.

No one sits that slaughtering still. We don't sit that still.

We're alive. She watched a moment longer, then swept the area at the base of the outcrop with a tightly leashed gaze. Two more. No, three—two of them so close together the darkness nearly made them one. Four in all. *That's not so bad. We defeated that many at the ford and these ones don't look armed.*

We were defending ourselves at the ford. If our kigh things won't face them, we can't attack.

We're not going to attack. We'll go around.

She could see a shoulder and some old man hair. Kars. The dark on dark bundle by his side had to be Prince Otavas. Belly to the ground, Vree squirmed closer. It didn't help much. Even allowing for bardic exaggeration, Karlene's description of the prince had little in common with the filthy young man resting his head in Kars' lap.

That looks friendly.

Does everything have to come back to sex with you?

*I said *friendly,* sister-mine.*

The young man moaned and pushed at the air with one long-fingered hand. Four or five thin gold rings winked in the moonlight.

It's him. And he's alive.

Her weight on fingers and toes, Vree started back to Karlene and Gyhard, left safely hidden behind a bend in the canyon with orders to *stay* there. As little as she'd been able to see creeping forward, she could see less now. A rock rolled away from a questing foot and bounced down a rain-cut gully. Vree froze and watched it wide-eyed as it slammed into the knee of one of the silent watchers. A pale oval of face turned toward her.

If she didn't move, it wouldn't see her.

For the first time since she took up a blade for the goddess, Vree was up against greater patience than hers. The dead eyes stared unblinkingly toward her. And stared. And stared.

A tepid rivulet of sweat dribbled down from Vree's temple, across her cheek, along her jaw, to drip off the point of her chin. The night seemed impossibly quiet; her breathing dangerously loud.

The eyes—they're not focused. It doesn't actually see us! Bannon's nerve broke and Vree made no attempt to regain control as they scuttled, lizardlike, back to the bend in the canyon. When strong hands closed around her arm, she came closer to screaming than at any time in her life.

"Is he there, Vree? Is he there? Is he all right?"

The bard's breath touched her ear, no warmer than the night air but so alive Vree found herself leaning toward it.

"Is he there?"

"Yes." As she sat on her heels, she wasn't sure which of them answered, decided it didn't matter. "But he's asleep."

"Kars . . ."

Senses stretched nearly to the breaking point picked the name out of a thousand tiny whispers of air. "I'm not going to kill the old man," she answered, half-turning to Gyhard. "I can't. He has his back against a rock, and there's one of them on it. He's in shadow and the prince is very close, so I don't want to risk a throw." Her fingers laced around each other, the trembling buried in the weave. "I'm going to go back . . ."

Are you out of our mind!

". . . and wait until dawn. When he wakes up, he'll have to take a piss. I'll grab him then. When people think that death hides in the darkness, they're a lot more careless if they make it through the night."

Karlene made a sound very much like a sob. "That could almost be a song."

Vree wiped sweaty palms on her thighs and covered the motion with a shrug. "Sing it later. Gyhard, you'll have your chance to talk to Kars. You've got until dawn to find something to say," Bannon added scornfully.

"But the prince," Karlene protested.

"The old man won't do anything if there's a chance I'll hurt him."

"Are you sure?"

She remembered the gentle, protective line of shoulder, arm, and hand. "Yeah. I'm sure. You just be ready to Sing if you're needed."

It seemed darker over by the rocks, the dead and living equally hidden by the night. She didn't want to go back there . . .

Then don't go!

. . . but the journey that had started in the governor's stronghold in Ghoti was coming to an end and what she wanted couldn't stop it. Vree was as certain of that as she'd ever been about anything.

If the prince is alive . . .

He was.

If we can free him . . .

They were about to find that out.

If Gyhard tries to jump to the prince . . .

Then they'd all be dead and it would be over.

I don't want to be dead, Vree. And what if he doesn't try to jump to the prince?

Then you won't be dead. But you'll still be here. Bannon had become a constant, painful pressure against her—physically and emotionally. She was so tired of failing to sort out which was her and which was him. *Wouldn't death be better?*

Not mine.

"Vree?"

She felt Gyhard's warmth beside her, the way she'd often felt Bannon's warmth pressed close in the past.

"If I had this all to do over again . . ." He paused and in spite of herself, she turned to face him. His expression reminded her of the times Bannon had attempted to apologize for involving her in some recklessness. "If I had this all to do over," he repeated, very softly, "I'd arrange the defenses of Ghoti so that the Sixth Army would only have to send its *second best* assassins."

Vree stared at him for a moment, then pressed the heels of both hands against her mouth to keep from roaring with laughter. When she finally regained control, she rubbed the tears from her eyes and found him watching her, smiling just a little, sharing the joke.

The moment stretched, lengthened.

The silence pulled Karlene around, dragged her attention away from the nearby prince. She'd never heard it speak so loudly.

Then Vree, almost deafened by the pounding of her heart, whispered, "Think about what you're going to say to Kars," and the moment shattered with the old man's name. "Watch and wait," she continued. The training she fought to wrap around her had once fit like a second skin—she couldn't remember taking it off. "Make your move as soon as I have His Highness in my hands."

Gyhard nodded; by the time he raised his head, she was gone.

I didn't think that was so funny.

I did.

My body, Vree.

I know.

When I get it back, I'll make you forget him.

Once, the intensity in his voice would have stoked desire, bringing heat and hopelessness equally mixed. Now, it only stroked a chill down her spine.

Moving as quickly as survival allowed, Vree followed the shadow paths and made a wide arc around the tiny half circle of dead sentinels. Sometimes she

was herself. Sometimes she was Bannon. Sometimes,
she wasn't sure. Unseen, or at least unremarked, she/
they came at last to the ambush site she'd chosen
earlier.

A thorntree, a multibranched and thriving cousin to
the tree at the way station, rose into the night. Vree
tucked herself into the safety of broken shadow, the
separate pieces of darkness together hiding the whole.
This is where the prince would come in the morning.
Men seemed to prefer to piss on bushes and trees, she
didn't know why, and this was the only one of any size
close enough.

"**Wake up**, my heart. The night is nearly gone and
we have so far still to go. **You must wake.**"

Otavas stirred, trying desperately to hang onto the
remnants of a dream. He was listening to a song—a
sad song filled with loss and confusion and pain.
Somehow he knew that if he could just find the singer,
then everything would be all right.

"**Wake up**, my heart."

He had no choice. His eyes opened, and he saw the
dangling bits of bone and the old man's face above
that. Above them both, the sky arced silver-gray. Not
quite day but no longer night. Balancing his head like
an egg on a spoon, Otavas pushed himself up onto his
knees and waited for the world to stop wobbling.

"The demons made no move in the night, my heart."

Demons. The prince whirled around and had to
clutch at the rock face behind him to keep from top-
pling.

"I kept you safe as you once kept me." The old man
smiled tenderly; and Otavas found himself returning it.

He loves me. Black brows drew in as the prince tried
to figure out why that was wrong. *I don't love him.*

Perhaps that was it—but it didn't seem to be enough. Attempting unsuccessfully to push the accumulated residue of induced sleep away, Otavas struggled to his feet.

"Don't leave me," the old man said.

"No, I just have to . . ."

"An Imperial prince does not discuss his bodily functions." The voice rose up out of memory. *"Do you understand me, Highness?"*

"Yes, Nurse." But Nurse Zumi had been dead for years. Hadn't she? "I just have to . . ." He waved a hand at the thorn tree and was relieved when the old man smiled again.

"Go ahead, my heart. I promised you mush this morning."

Ignoring the silent sentinels, Otavas stood by the tree and fumbled with his trousers.

Let him finish, Vree.

No. I thought I'd grab him in mid-stream. Add to the surprise.

It's too early to be so sarcastic.

It's too early to be so cheerful. It was the old banter. As much a part of the loosening up before a job as muscles flexed within their sheath of skin. If she didn't pause to think about it, she could almost believe that everything was all right. *We'll take him just as he turns, hold the blade to his throat, and hold him hostage for Kars.*

Bannon snorted. *I was here when we made the plan, sister-mine. I haven't forgotten.*

Will alone swept Vree's gaze over the dead. The three on the ground had pivoted to face the old man, leaning toward him as though he were a fire and they were searching for warmth. The one on top of the outcropping had stood but looked like it would stay where it was.

The prince tucked himself away and, frowning, lightly touched a six-inch thorn. Then he sighed and turned.

Now!

They moved her body together and a heartbeat later her knees drove into the back of his and dropped him down to a height she could better manage. The bard hadn't mentioned that His Highness was so tall— although to Karlene he probably wasn't. Her arm whipped about the prince's throat, pushing up his head, and the point of her long dagger lightly parted the soft whiskers growing under the curve of his jaw. It seemed very strange not to slash through and sever the spine.

"One move and he dies!" she yelled, adding directly into the prince's ear. "We're here to rescue you, Highness. But Kars must believe you're in danger, or we won't be able to control him."

She caught a fleeting impression of horror on the old man's face, then the prince began to struggle and all her attention went to not slitting his throat. "Highness! You are in no real danger! I swear it!"

Unless he impales himself! Watch his elbow!

Otavas heard the voice, but terror drowned out words and meaning. The kiss of the blade had pushed him over the edge and all he knew was that he could not die. He'd seen what happened to the dead.

Had they wanted to kill him, they could have done so easily. Keeping hold of him and keeping him alive was a lot harder. A trickle of blood ran into his shirt from a thin slice on one collarbone.

"Otavas, stop it! She's a friend! Hold still!"

"Karlene?" The prince twisted toward the voice and nearly lost an ear. "Karlene?"

"I said, **hold still!**" Her pale hair streaming like a banner behind her, the bard raced over the uneven ground toward them.

So much for the plan ... But Vree continued to hang on to the Imperial shoulders. Although he didn't seem to realize it, His Highness was safest here with her.

"**You!**"

The old man's voice stopped Karlene in her tracks. She rocked back on her heels as though she'd been hit.

"Demon!" The staff stretched out, the shepherd boy's shoulder bone pointing toward her. "I know you, demon! You will not torment my heart, as you tormented me. Stop her, my children!"

Wheyra, Iban, and Hestia rose. Hestia held a rock in one hand and she let it fly with a precision little touched by death.

"Oh, shit." There had been a boy in the regiment who'd thrown with that same flat, economy of movement. Vree had never seen him miss.

The rock hit Karlene in the forehead, the impact sounding like a fist slamming into a green melon. She cried out, spun around, and dropped to one knee, both hands clutching her face.

As the walking dead bent to pick up another rock and the other two continued to advance, Vree realized they'd made a mistake. Kars could not be bribed with the prince's safety, he was too far gone in insanity for that. Shoving the unresisting young man under the protecting spikes of the thorn tree, she raced the dead to Karlene. The dead were slower, but they were much, much closer.

"Destroy the demons! Destroy the demons! Destroy the demons!" Tears streaming down his cheeks, the old man swayed back and forth in time to the rhythm of his chanting. "Destroy the demons!"

"Kars!"

Still racing forward, Bannon glanced sideways to see Gyhard standing almost close enough to touch the old man. *My body! . . .*

Is in a lot less danger than Karlene's. Vree yanked her head back around, threw herself past the dead man, and drove the point of her long dagger up into the armpit of the dead woman with the rock. As a killing blow would be a wasted effort, teeth clenched and able to look at her target only obliquely, Vree slashed through the tendons holding the muscles of the arm to the shoulder. The arm dropped.

The walking dead would have to be defeated one piece at a time.

The old man stared at the young man standing before him. His mouth opened and closed, but no sound emerged.

Gyhard held his open hands away from his sides, ignoring the pain the movement caused in his splinted arm. He couldn't see the tormented boy he'd loved through the changes the years had layered on, but he'd heard him, just for an instant, buried in that first accusation thrown at Karlene. He'd known since the Healers' Hall that it was Kars who'd taken the prince—taken the body he'd intended for his own—but knowing and facing it, he discovered, were two entirely different things. *What am I doing here? What did I think this was going to prove?*

The dead Vree faced were not soldiers; they had no idea of how to defend themselves and less of how to attack. But they'd been told to destroy the demons and they'd do their best to carry out that command.

Good thing we don't have to kill them . . .

*My body, Vree. My body is over *there*.*

A clumsy blow from a gray fist nearly connected as she struggled with Bannon's desire to keep his body in sight. *Do you want to die in *this* body? Is that what you want.* She got a figurative fingernail's grip on control. *We only have to keep them from reaching Karlene; buy her enough time to Sing.* A club heavy enough to crush joints would've been more use than all her daggers put together.

Although her skin crawled at the thought of touching them, Vree charged at the younger of the two women and threw her to the ground. From the sudden putrid smell, the impact ruptured decaying tissue, but the dead woman merely adjusted the dried and desiccated thing hanging in a sling around her neck and laboriously started to rise.

Blinking back tears of pain, Karlene tentatively took her hands off her forehead and examined them. No blood. She'd been sure that the only thing holding her brains in had been the pressure of her palms. *I'm all right. I'm okay.*

Squinting against the rising sun, she saw Vree fighting two of the dead and another getting to her feet barely a body length away.

By all the gods in the Circle, she's carrying a baby!

A very small and long dead baby.

Swallowing bile, Karlene got herself as far as her knees and started to Sing.

Given the chance, Wheyra was only too happy to follow her baby away.

* * *

The old man cried out as the first pure tones rose into the morning. The demons were taking Wheyra! He couldn't let that happen. Breathing deeply, he took a step forward.

"Kars, no." Gyhard grabbed hold of one skeletal shoulder. "Let her go. Let them all go."

"No! They're my family. If they go, I'll be alone." He stared into the eyes so close to his and his expression changed from outrage to confusion. "You left me alone," he said softly, the Song forgotten.

Gyhard swallowed and tried to force his voice around the ninety years of guilt stuck in his throat. *I would've killed an animal in this much pain. But I left you to suffer.* "I'm sorry," he managed at last. "But you were going to kill me.

"Only so that you wouldn't leave me." A hand rose and stroked the air by Gyhard's cheeks with gnarled fingers. He knew the shape of this kigh the way he knew the shape of his own. "But you went away. I lost my heart. I had to find it again." The shadowed eyes widened. "I found it. I did." He twisted out of Gyhard's grasp, his strength surprising. "There. There." His staff swung out to point at the prince. "I found my heart." Then he frowned. "But you ... My heart," he cried. **"Come here!"**

Otavas jerked to his feet, unable to deny the voice. Unsure he even wanted to.

As Wheyra's empty body collapsed, Vree kicked the legs out from under the stone thrower.

Karlene took a deep breath that wobbled just a little around the edges and began a new Song.

* * *

As the prince drew closer, Gyhard felt his jaw drop. He'd seen those dark and long-lashed eyes before. Ninety years before. He'd seen them widening in terror the instant before he'd taken over the body that went with them and he'd seen them gazing up at him in wonder a few moments later from a mountain pool. The rest of the features held little resemblance, but the eyes were frighteningly similar. All at once, Kars' reason for kidnapping the prince became obvious.

"I have found my heart," the old man murmured as Otavas drew closer. Then he turned to look at Gyhard and his mouth began to tremble. "I have found my heart?"

Gyhard shook his head. "No, Kars, you haven't. This boy is not the boy who left you so many years ago. Don't look at him, look at his kigh." The parchment skin felt cool and dry as he lightly gripped Kars' jaw and turned him to face the prince. When he heard the old man sigh, he released him. "You *know* who I am," he said.

The old man nodded, tears spilling over and into the wrinkled gullies of his face. "I know who you are." He sighed again and desperately grabbed for Gyhard's vest. "Can you tell me, who am I?"

Gyhard had believed, ninety years before when he rode out of the mountains, that he could never be hurt so badly again. He was wrong. "Your name is Kars. If you had another, you never told it to me." He'd never spoken Cemandian fluently, but it was close enough to Shkodan that he hadn't completely lost it. Although he didn't know why it seemed important that he speak it now, it had been what they'd always used together. "You grew up in a country called Cemandia. Evil people tried to break you, but you were stronger than they thought and you ran away. We met in the mountains."

"Gyhard?"

"Yes." The smile was almost the one he remembered—sweet and tentative and disbelieving.

"I am Kars."

"Yes." His hands—Bannon's hands—fit completely around the old man's neck. It was both awkward and painful to use the broken arm and he knew he'd pay for it later, but he'd just realized he had only one thing to say to Kars, the one thing he should have said years ago, before he rode out of the mountains. The ancient flesh compacted as he tightened his hold.

Kars' smile never wavered.

All things are enclosed in the Circle, Gyhard thought. And the turning of the Circle had seen to it that Kars had done the one thing that would bring him together with the man responsible for his madness at a time when that man would be able to accept the responsibility. In a moment, it would all be over.

"I have found my heart," Kars whispered happily, insanely.

Gyhard nodded, thankful that, even injured, Bannon's hands were strong enough for what they had to do. It was time. It was long past time. "Good-bye," he said and squeezed.

The attack took him completely by surprise. The body smashing into him from above drove him back, away from Kars, and slammed him into the ground. He screamed as a dead knee drove into his stomach and dead fists pounded at his face.

Vree whirled at the sound of the scream, but it was Bannon who charged across the uneven ground toward his body. Shoved savagely into the back of her own mind, Vree hurled herself at barricades built of Bannon's terror and tried to claw her way through.

The recoil almost threw her out into oblivion.

His fear fueled by the blood dribbling down from his/Gyhard's mouth and nose, Bannon heard nothing, saw nothing, knew nothing but the need to protect his body. Without checking his speed, he dove forward, planted his hands, and flipped feet-first through the air.

Kait felt no pain when both heels struck her left temple, but the thin bone shattered and the force of the blow lifted her into the air, smashing her into the face of the rock outcropping.

When she tried to put herself between the old man and this new threat, she found she couldn't see.

"Fa . . . ther!"

One hand on his throat, Kars jerked around. What had he been thinking? He had family to take care of. Dropping to his knees, he gathered the dead girl into his arms. Although the demons had the others, they must not have her.

Breath rasping in through mouth and nose, Bannon grabbed two handfuls of the brown silk vest and yanked his body into a sitting position. "Don't you be dead!" he shrieked. "Don't you dare be dead!"

Scrambling backward, the dead man pursuing her like a nightmare that refused to end, Karlene began her third Song.

"My arm," Gyhard gasped. It felt as though it were on fire from fingertips to shoulder. "Stop . . . shaking me."

"You're alive. I'm alive." Releasing the vest, Bannon patted gently at the blood on his/Gyhard's chin.

"You need water." Whipping Vree's head from side to side, he suddenly caught sight of the prince and froze.

Bannon! No! She screamed and fought and threatened but he ignored her.

Leaping to his/Vree's feet, he grabbed the prince and threw him to his knees by Gyhard's side.

Otavas cried out as stones and stonelike fingers dug into his flesh, but Karlene had said this was his friend and Karlene was the one thing he could be sure of, so he put up no resistance.

"Do it now," Bannon gasped. "Hurry, the bard will be finished soon. We haven't much time."

Do it now. Cradling his/Bannon's arm, Gyhard spat out a mouthful of blood and stared at Prince Otavas. The boy was weak and disoriented. It would be easy enough to claim his body. And after?

Easy enough. He stared at Bannon in turn. "I will allow you back into this body," he said, speaking quickly. "You belong here, you'll need no push, but once you're in, you'll have to push me out."

Bannon smiled ferally. "I've dreamed of pushing you out," he snarled.

Vree, still clawing at Bannon's control, felt something give. Redoubling her efforts, she suddenly found herself alone, her silent cries of protest still echoing in her skull.

Kneeling across from her, she saw Bannon/Gyhard, Gyhard/Bannon then all at once, Gyhard alone. She knew it was Gyhard, for Bannon had never looked at her like that. Bannon had never loved her like that. His lips moved and she heard him say, "Good-bye."

Then it was only Bannon.

"NO!" Reaching out, she grabbed hold and hung on and refused to let go. And frankly, she didn't give a slaughtering shit about what he wanted. Her head snapped back, she screamed defiance and the world went black.

"Vree!" Stumbling over bodies that were no longer prisons for their kigh, Karlene ran toward the outcropping. Her last Song had finished in time to hear Vree scream; in time to see her collapse bonelessly to the ground. She moved as quickly as she could but was by no means the first to reach Vree's side.

"Vree? Vree, don't do this to me. You have to be all right. Talk to me, sister-mine. Please, talk to me."

Karlene's jaw dropped. "Bannon?"

He looked up, Vree's head cradled against his chest. "She screamed," he said. "And fell over." The features were the same but the man who animated them was not. He looked younger than Gyhard had, and frightened. Although Vree breathed so shallowly her chest barely moved, Karlene could see no wounds, no reason for her to remain unconscious.

"Karlene?"

A sudden surge of emotion too complicated to describe, too painful to endure, shoved her concern for Vree aside and, for a moment, Otavas clutched in her arms and sobbing against her chest, everything that wasn't the prince was forgotten. The iron bands around her heart burst, and she cried like a baby, rocking him back and forth, saying over and over again, "You're alive. You're alive."

It was Otavas who pulled away at last. He dragged his nose over his sleeve and locked shadowed eyes on Karlene's face. "The old man," he murmured.

"Kars." Vree's voice was weak, but it cut through the fog of emotion that seemed to have them isolated from the world. "Where is he?"

He wasn't anywhere around.

Otavas stared wide-eyed at the last place he'd been. "Kait's gone, too."

Vree struggled to sit up, both hands clutching her head. "We have to find him. We have to stop him or this will begin again, somewhere else. We have to finish this." The last words had risen to a near hysterical shout.

Confused by the changes sweeping over Bannon's expression as he stared at his sister, Karlene tucked the prince under one arm and reached out a comforting hand. Before she could speak, the situation slid sideways.

"No one moves. No one talks." Rough-edged with exhaustion, the voice clearly expected to be obeyed. "And just maybe, no one dies."

Chapter Seventeen

"Captain, my squad has searched the entire area, there's no sign of this *old man*."

"You're certain about this, Orlan?"

"Yes, sir."

It took more effort than she thought she was capable of, but Karlene managed to keep her voice level. "Captain, Kars has a dead girl with him. Your squads won't be able to find him because their kigh won't acknowledge the existence of the girl."

"Kigh?" The captain spat the unfamiliar word out of her mouth like a bug she'd accidentally sucked in. "But you can find him, Lady Bard?"

Karlene was too angry to take further offense at the tone of the honorific. "Yes, Captain."

"And His Imperial Highness can find him?"

"We think so. We think Prince Otavas spent so much time with the walking dead that his kigh stopped lying to him about them."

The captain stared down into the sweaty depths of her helm, cradled in the crook of one arm, and pursed her lips. "So you're suggesting, Lady Bard, that I allow you and His Highness to go out and search for this Kars?" She looked up; her eyes amid the dirt and exhaustion marking her face were hard and uncompromising. "I think not. We will all be returning to the

Capital and you can thank His Highness that you won't be gagged and under guard."

"Captain." Otavas sighed. He'd said it before, but he'd say it one more time. "Karlene and her friends rescued me. They had nothing to do with my abduction."

"As you say, Highness." The captain bowed. Had the old man been around, she would have cheerfully slaughtered him for the pain that continued to cling to the young prince. But the old man wasn't around, nor was there any sign of him, so ... "But I have seen what this bard is capable of and, begging your pardon, Highness, but she could have made you see things that weren't there."

Karlene threw up her hands, frustration fighting with rage. "Highness?"

"Let him go, Karlene." The prince wrapped his arms around his body, unable to stop the shaking that memories brought. The beautiful dark eyes shone with sudden tears. "I want to go home."

She wanted to hug him, couldn't with the army so close, and settled for a light touch on one cheek. "Then that's what we'll do," she said softly. "Will you be all right if I go and talk to Vree and Bannon?"

He nodded, fighting panic. "But don't stay away too long."

The captain watched the bard walk over to her friends and shook her head. She supposed that any woman who could sing herself invisible could do just about anything she wanted to—but the comfort in her voice when she spoke to the prince had sounded too real to be faked.

"He wanted to kill me, Vree!"

"No, not you, he intended to kill the assassin who came to kill him." Her back up against the rock outcropping, Vree looked everywhere but at her brother. "They *all* would've preferred to kill us over us killing them. You can't blame him for that."

Bannon's eyes narrowed. "I can slaughtering well blame him for anything I slaughtering choose! He broke my arm!"

"Half a hill fell on him!" Vree fought to keep her temper from getting the better of her and lost. "You're the one who broke your slaughtering vows and tried to kill a member of the Imperial Family!"

All the anger seemed to leach away as the color drained from Bannon's cheeks. "I wasn't in my right mind. Vree, you know that; you were there, too. I never meant to. I wanted my body back and I wanted you to have yours back and ..."

"It's all right." She felt as if she'd aged about ten years over the last few weeks. "I won't tell anyone. I promise." That Bannon could, in any state of mind, consider his life of more importance than the oaths he'd taken and the prince he'd sworn to serve didn't actually surprise her much. She supposed she'd come to know him too well. "Do you really think I could have you executed for treason?"

"No." Bannon brightened visibly, most of his cocky grin returning. "Especially since I was in your body when I did it."

Vree sighed; she couldn't remember ever having been so tired.

"You still haven't told me why you did it." He'd been alternately hurt and furious. He'd demanded an answer, begged for an answer, and snarled that he had a right to an answer.

"I know."

"Vree, if you don't kill him, we've missed a target."

"I am not my ... our ..." She took a deep breath

and tried again. "I am not Commander Neegan. I chose
to miss this target."

Thank you.

Shut up. "Nobody makes my choices for me,
Bannon. Not any more. Not you and not him."

"Is he listening?"

"You know he is."

"Then tell him I will never forgive him for this. For
the rest, maybe in time I might have, but *never* for this.
Do you understand?"

Vree nodded. It didn't really matter if that last question had been directed at her or at Gyhard. She understood. Probably better than Bannon did. Nothing would
ever be the same between them again.

Karlene had intended to ask them if they were all
right but decided upon getting close enough to see
their faces that there was little point. Bannon, who
should have been overjoyed at being back in his own
body, looked almost petulant. Vree, who had stuffed
herself into a situation far more complicated than the
one she'd just gotten out of, looked almost at peace.

The captain had wanted to wait until the rider she
sent returned with the comforts necessary to an Imperial Prince but Otavas overruled her. He wanted only to
get home.

"Can you Sing away the darkness?" he asked as the
sun began to set, tears trembling on his lashes.

Karlene held him the way she'd hold a child that
needed comfort. "I can do better than that," she promised. If nothing else, Gyhard had given her the knowledge of the fifth kigh and Singing the fifth kigh would,
in time, heal Otavas. She could Sing him, not back, but
through the memories and safety out the other side. In

spite of what Gyhard had done, what he'd been in the past, she owed him for that.

Just after they crossed the ford and retrieved their horses, the kigh returned. Karlene raised her chin, Sang one pure, joyous note, and was nearly lifted from the saddle.

Watching through Vree's eyes, Gyhard murmured, *Kars is gone. I've lost my chance to make it right.*

You're not dead yet.

Neither is he.

Do you think he's gone back to his place, to your place, in the mountains?

Perhaps.

Then at least we'll know where he is. It was almost an offer. Not quite, for the future was still far too tenuous for that kind of a commitment; but almost.

Although Gyhard was a constant presence in her mind, Vree found him easier to coexist with than Bannon had ever been. Unlike Bannon, his life had not been a part of hers from the beginning and there was no question of where she ended and he began.

He was quieter, too, off guard and confused by what she'd done. Most of the time, he seemed content just to be. Three days passed before he found the courage to ask her why.

Vree thought about lying to him, but under the circumstances there didn't seem to be much point, so she gave him as much of the truth as she'd been able to face herself. *Because I didn't believe—don't believe—you were going to jump to the prince.*

The silence lasted so long, she began to grow afraid he'd left her. When he finally spoke, she could barely hear him. *I with I could be as certain, but I guess now we'll never know.*

* * *

Early in the march, Bannon stayed close beside her, sullen and uncommunicative. Once, she'd reached out to touch him, but he'd snatched his arm away.

You risked your life for that little shit, Gyhard snarled, jerked from his reflective mood not so much by Bannon's reaction as by the way that reaction clawed bleeding chunks from Vree's heart. *You'd think he'd remember what he owes you.*

Vree clenched her teeth and let her hand drop back to her side. *He doesn't owe me anything.*

As they reached Shaebridge, Bannon began to spend time with the prince. The two young men were very close in age and Otavas, frantically clutching at the lives around him, could cling to a friend the way he couldn't cling to Karlene. Flattered by Imperial attention, Bannon soon became charming and indispensable.

The captain didn't like it, but even the captain had to admit that once or twice His Highness had smiled in Bannon's company.

It looks like he's replaced you already.

Maybe it's time. No point in hiding the hurt.

Gyhard buried a strong desire to beat Bannon into a bloody pulp. *If he tells the prince about me . . .*

He won't.

How can you be so sure?

Vree stared at the pale scar on the back of her hand. Gyhard had defeated, humiliated, and brought out the worst in Bannon. For those reasons alone, Bannon would be unlikely to share the experience with anyone but, more importantly, withholding the knowledge of Vree's betrayal meant he held new power over her to replace the old power that had been burned away.

Vree?

She tightened her grip on the reins, but all she said was, *I know my brother.*

* * *

Unable to put it off any longer, Bannon having removed the need for her constant attendance on the prince, Karlene brought her horse up beside Vree's and tried to think of the best way to begin. Bards were supposed to be good with words, but she couldn't think of any that would lessen the impact of what she had to say. Finally, she said, "We have a problem."

Vree looked surprised. "Just one?"

"This is serious, Vree." She pitched her voice to carry to the younger woman's ears but no farther. "What are we going to do about Gyhard?"

This time the surprise was unfeigned. "We? I thought that was *my* problem?"

Our problem.

Karlene shook her head. "Over the last hundred years, Gyhard has killed a number of innocent people. We can't let him get away with that. He must be brought to justice."

"Gyhard has killed to survive. So have I." Vree's eyes narrowed.

"It's not the same. He's removed himself from the Circle . . ."

Vree chopped her hand down and cut the bard off. "I don't know about your *Circle*," she snapped. "But I know about justice."

Vree . . .

SHUT UP! Her horse danced sideways. She reined him in and fought for calm. "How are you going to put him on trial? You have no proof. You have no bodies. You have only his word for it that he's killed anyone. In fact . . ."

Her expression lifted the hair on the back of Karlene's neck.

". . . you don't even have *him*. I do."

They rode in silence for a moment, every fall of hoof against stone, every creak of harness adding to the tension between them.

"So what do you plan to do?" Karlene asked at last. "Go back to the army? Go back to being a blade of Jiir? I don't think you could do that even without Gyhard. I'm sure you can't do it with him."

"Bannon . . ."

"Leave Bannon out of this for now." She reached between the horses and touched Vree's cheek with the back of two fingers. "What are *you* going to do?"

Vree jerked away from the contact and at the same time turned almost desperately toward the older woman's touch. "I don't know."

Karlene found herself suddenly willing to do just about anything to banish the stricken look from Vree's eyes. She tried to fight it, sighed, and surrendered instead. "What do you *want* to do?"

"Start again."

Only bardic training could have picked those two quiet words out of the surrounding noise. With Vree on one side of the scale and justice on the other, Karlene silently cursed Gyhard, Bannon, Neegan, the Imperial Army, and the Emperor himself.

"Gabris, you've got to listen to me!" The prince had claimed Bannon and with all the excitement of the return to the palace, Karlene had somehow managed to keep Vree with her.

"But she's got two kigh!" Gabris repeated.

"I *know* that." Karlene grabbed the older bard's arm and yanked him away from Vree before he did something foolish enough to push her over the edge and get himself kissed by an assassin's blade. They had a lot to discuss before their audience with the Emperor and

very little time to do it in. Eyes locked on Gabris' face,
Karlene began talking.

". . . and although by now His Imperial Majesty will
have heard the prince's story," she finished, "His Highness will have been able to tell him nothing about
Gyhard."

Eyes wide, Gabris waved both arms in the air. "Well,
then he has to be told!"

"Why?"

"What do you mean, *why?*" His face flushed, he was
almost shouting. "This man has removed himself from
the Circle by the taking of innocent lives! Have you
forgotten your vows?"

"This man doesn't even exist anymore except as a
part of Vree."

"Then we Sing him out of her!"

"How? The little I know about Singing the fifth kigh
does not include forcing apart two kigh that don't want
to be separated. How do I get him out of Vree's body
without destroying her?"

At that, Gabris turned and pointed a shaking finger
at Vree. "You push him out!"

"No."

There was such a complete and utter finality in that
quiet syllable that it formed an impenetrable barricade.
Under other circumstances, Karlene would've been
amused to see Gabris stopped cold by it. "Wouldn't it
make more sense to have Gyhard make amends for
what he did in the past?"

His angry gaze still locked on the assassin, Gabris
muttered, "How?"

"The fifth kigh. No one knows more about it than he
does—than they do. We can't throw this opportunity
away."

* * *

Having heard the story of his son's ordeal as Otavas sat cradled in the safety of his mother's arms, forgetting age and dignity in the need for comfort; having seen the shadows that lurked behind each word and would forever scar the prince's heart; having been told by the captain how the bard had placed herself between the boy and the darkness during the return to the Capital, the Emperor chose to believe the tale she told.

"For your part in the rescue of my son, I grant you both Imperial pardon. As you remained in my service, we will consider that your desertion never occurred."

And Commander Neegan never died? No. There were limits to Imperial power after all. Heart pounding, Vree shot a look at the elderly bard out of the corner of one eye. If he was going to say anything, inform the Emperor that Gyhard did not die during that heavily edited final confrontation, this would be the time.

Gabris looked uncomfortable, but Karlene's arguments held.

"Take these also." The Emperor continued, indicating the two fat purses resting on the edge of the dais. There were no servants, no officers of the court at this very private audience—only the two kneeling assassins, the bards, and Marshal Usef—so he waited until Vree and Bannon had each taken up a purse before he continued. "It is little enough for the safe return of my son." His gaze moved to Bannon alone. "His Highness has requested that you remain in his service as a bodyguard-companion." For a heartbeat, his expression softened, the pain of the father replacing the authority of the Emperor. "I have agreed."

"Thank you, Your Majesty."

As Bannon spoke, Vree suddenly found it difficult to breathe. It was happening. It was really happening.

From this point on, her brother would officially no longer be a part of her life. She felt Gyhard stir and fiercely willed him to be quiet.

"And you, Vireyda?"

Startled by his tone, she looked up and found him studying her with a mix of sympathy and curiosity. The sympathy was almost more than she could bear. She swallowed hard and tried to keep her lower lip from trembling. Then she remembered how Gyhard jumped his kigh and hastily dropped her gaze.

"You've been through a great deal these last few weeks with this man who lived so long by leaping his spirit from body to body. Are you certain you don't want to return to the security of what you've always known?"

From the moment she'd left Ghoti carrying her brother's kigh with hers, she'd wanted nothing more. From the moment she'd left Ghoti until the moment she discovered she couldn't allow Gyhard to die. "No, Majesty. The bards, they say they can learn about the fifth kigh by studying me and I'd like to help them."

His Imperial Majesty shifted so that he could include the two bards in his gaze. "You are certain, Lady Bard, that you can stop this ancient Cemandian who brings the dead to life should he return again?"

Karlene bowed. "It is unlikely, Majesty, that he will return again. According to the kigh, he was heading toward the mountains where he feels safe." According to Gyhard's kigh—which made it not exactly an untruth. Someday, it would be necessary to go into the mountains after him, to not only lay a tormented fifth kigh to rest but to protect the other four from his insanity. That, however, was bardic business and none of His Imperial Majesty's.

"I did not ask you if you believed he *would* return, merely if you could stop him *should* he return."

Her second bow was considerably deeper than the first. "Yes, Majesty, I am certain we can stop him."

"Good." There was a certain amount of threat lurking behind the word. Turning Imperial attention back to the assassins, his voice took on formal cadences and drew the full attention of everyone in the small audience chamber. "While we are loath to lose your skills in the service of the Empire, we grant all that you have asked in appreciation of the return of our son. Vireyda Magaly, Albannon Magaly, from this moment on, you are released from your duty to the Imperial Army and released from all oaths pertaining to that duty." He leaned forward, away from the brilliantly enameled sunburst carved into the back of the small throne. "We welcome you as private citizens of the Havakeen Empire."

In his place behind the Emperor's left shoulder, safely out of sight, Marshal Usef turned purple.

"I don't approve of this," Gabris muttered as they left the audience chamber and passed through the first in a series of reception rooms. "Bards should not lie."

"Who better than a bard to judge the damage the truth can do?"

"I think you're on dangerous ground," he growled, "but I reluctantly agree that there's no point in ruining the young woman's life further."

"And you have no real urge to study the fifth kigh?" Karlene grinned at him, feeling almost giddy with relief. Considering what could have happened, she thought the whole thing had gone rather well. Then she sobered as she caught sight of Vree. "What is it?"

Vree gestured at Bannon, vanishing around a corner with a senior member of Prince Otavas' household. "What," she asked, trying to keep her voice from quavering, "do I do now?"

* * *

"Begging Your Most Imperial Majesty's pardon, but I *must* protest."

The Emperor paused half out of the throne, and settled down again. "You do not believe their story, Marshal?"

Shoving his short sword back out of the way, Usef dropped to one knee before the dais. "If Your Majesty believes then I believe. But, Majesty, assassins do not *ever* leave the army. It is far, far too dangerous."

An Imperial brow lifted. "For whom?"

"Majesty, the citizens . . ."

"Will never know. You will not tell them, the bards will not tell them, and I'm quite certain our two young assassins will not tell them. Assassins, Marshal, are like well-trained hawks who, even when released from hood and jesses, fly only as they have been taught." Smiling, the Emperor raised his left forearm parallel to his body, fist clenched, and studied the scars of talons made in spite of heavy gloves. "I have flown all types of hawks, Marshal. It will be interesting to see how these two fly."

"Majesty, these are people, and people are much more complicated than hawks."

"Not in this case. I've studied the training assassins go through, how they're conditioned from childhood to respond. The boy will protect my son. What has just happened will *never* happen again. Perhaps we shall see about adding assassins to the rest of the Imperial households. For now, the girl will remain in the palace . . ." All at once, he jerked his left arm up into the air, as though releasing a bird of prey. "We'll find something for her to do in time."

"Vree!" Karlene rushed into the bardic suite and all but pounced on the woman standing by the window. "I think I have a solution to your problem!"

Vree turned, brows drawn into a tight vee over the bridge of her nose, holding her elbows through the billowing fabric of a pale yellow shirt. "I have a problem?"

"He's making you sarcastic, you know. I don't like it." Looking pleased with herself, Karlene dropped into a chair. "The first five of the Empire's bards have arrived from Shkoder. You knew that, of course . . ."

Over the last week, neither Karlene nor Gabris had had more than a moment to call their own and Vree had found herself wandering the half dozen bardic rooms like a lost spirit, trading trivialities with Gyhard as though he were a stranger, afraid to move off the dagger's edge they balanced on.

". . . but you don't know about the news they brought. There's a new, young healer training in Shkoder who Sings the fifth kigh."

Vree spread her hands. "So?"

"So, if anyone can help Gyhard find a body he can use, it'd be her."

A wild, unlooked for hope began to grow in Vree's chest. "A body he can use," she repeated. "Are you sure?"

Karlene leaned forward and took the other woman's face in her hands. "No," she said soberly. "But, dearling, you can't spend the rest of your life hiding out in here." She traced the curve of Vree's lips with her thumb then reluctantly sat back. "Nor can you share the rest of your life with another person's kigh. Gabris and I still have no idea of how to get Gyhard into a body of his own . . ."

"He says he has an idea," Vree muttered, grimacing.

You weren't intended to repeat that.

"Oh, I bet he does," the bard snarled. "But he'd just better remember where he stands."

"As we can neither remove you nor bring you to jus-

tice for the lives you've so callously ended, as long as you remain in Vree's body, you have, for the moment, found sanctuary. And you'd best not forget what you owe her for that. But this is where we draw the line; if anyone else dies because of you, anyone, the bards will see to it that your kigh goes back into the Circle so fast you won't know what hit you."

"Allow me to set your mind at rest," Gyhard said through Vree, the weariness in his mental voice evident in her translation. *"Unless Vree is willing to push me, I can't jump into anyone while she remains whole and healthy. In order for me to leave without her help, her body must be dying. Before you bother to point out the obvious, I agree that in the past this has not been difficult to arrange. For now, you may be certain of one thing at least—I will* never *harm her."*

Karlene's lips drew back off her teeth as she asked, "You mean more than you already have?"

"He isn't going anywhere," Vree said sharply, unwilling to be caught in the middle of that particular argument. "Not unless there's a way to do it so that no one dies. You have our word on it."

Vree . . .

I mean it, Gyhard. No one else dies because of this.

Then we're going to be together for a very long time.

She hugged herself tightly and repeated, *No one else dies.*

As the heavy door to the small audience chamber swung shut, the Emperor looked down at the scars on his wrist. "You see, Marshal, I told you we'd find something for her to do."

Dropping to one knee, Usef was momentarily at a loss for words. *I should've done what I said I was go-*

ing to do and retired when the prince was returned.
"Majesty," he finally managed to choke out, "to send an assassin into Shkoder ... Begging Your Majesty's pardon, but that could be considered an act of war."

"War, Marshal? Not at all. Remember, I'm not sending an assassin. The young woman is a private citizen who has privately chosen to travel."

"But ..."

An Imperial hand lifted to cut off the protest. "A private citizen, who could, if properly commanded, be very ... useful."

"If I may be permitted to remind Your Majesty, you have released her from her oaths. Who is to command her? She is no longer in the army."

"Very true," the Emperor agreed. "But I think you'll find that it is not so easy to remove the army from her." When Usef frowned, he added, "Rest assured, Marshal, I have no immediate intention of expanding the Empire to the north; however, it would be foolish to ignore the possibilities inherent in having a blade on the other side of the border."

Everything the Emperor said made sense, Usef reflected, which put him in the uncomfortable position of reminding His Majesty of a forgotten point. "What of the bards, Majesty? She has obviously been ..." He thought of saying corrupted—assassins were not supposed to *want* to leave the army—but settled on, "... befriended by them. They know what she is and will be watching her."

"The bards." His Imperial Majesty dismissed them with a wave. "They can't see past this whole fifth kigh thing, this body-jumping spirit, mumbo jumbo, singing nonsense. They have no idea of what she is or they'd have left her safely sheathed. As they have drawn the blade ..." He clenched his left fist and flexed the air as though he were measuring the weight of a bird. "I may not use her, but I appreciate having her there, just in case."

The two women were the only nonsailors on the dock, a cloudburst having cleared away everyone without immediate business in the area. Even the gulls had gone looking for more congenial surroundings.

"I'm going to miss you, Vree." Karlene drew the shorter woman into her arms and gently lifted her chin. **"Gyhard, go away for a minute."** Considerably more than a moment later, she drew back and murmured dreamily, "I wish I'd thought of that weeks ago."

Vree struggled to catch her breath. "I wish I'd you had, too," she managed at last. She had no idea if the bard's command had actually worked or if Gyhard had just decided to fade into the background for the duration. Nor, for this moment at least, did she care. She tightened the circle of her arms. "I'm going to miss you." Rubbing moisture that had nothing to do with either the rain or the salt air off her cheek, she touched the single dagger she wore hanging at her waist. "Bannon's still refusing to see me. When *you* see him, could you tell him . . ."

"Tell him yourself," Karlene interrupted, and turned her around.

He wore damp Imperial livery and an uncertain, defiant expression. As Karlene diplomatically stepped away, Bannon walked the length of the dock as if he moved toward a fight. "I decided I was being too harsh," he said before Vree could speak. "You betrayed me, but . . ." He bit his lip and shook his head. "I couldn't let you go without saying good-bye, Vree. We might never see each other again."

She didn't bother hiding how much it hurt—unsure

if she were being honest or trying to hurt him in turn. She understood why he couldn't forgive her for Gyhard and she supposed that in time the feeling that someone had shoved a dagger into her heart would fade, but for now his ease in settling into a new life without her kept twisting the blade.

"If I had one wish," he went on, his eyes searching her face, "I'd wish we could go back to Ghoti and have *none* of this happen."

"You wanted to get out . . ."

His hand chopped her off. "Not like this."

"No." She wanted to touch him, knew she couldn't, knew he'd feel Gyhard in the touch. "Not like this."

An impatient bellow from the ship dropped them both into a defensive crouch, daggers in hand, searching for an enemy. Straightening, first Vree, then Bannon began to laugh. If the laughter took on a hysterical tone and grew to hold more pain than humor, neither of the two listeners were likely to mention it.

Finally Vree sobered and held out her hand, hoping but not hopeful that he'd take it. "Good-bye, Bannon."

Bannon stared at her for a moment, features mirroring the inner battle he fought, and finally yanked her into a quick embrace. His fingers digging into her upper arms, he pushed her away again almost as quickly. The heat that had burned between them all their adult lives had burned away somewhere between Aralt and Kars.

"Good-bye, sister . . ." He stopped and looked lost. "Not mine anymore."

"No."

"But you were."

Because she'd done it all his life, or maybe just because he needed it now, Vree gave him the reassurance he asked for. "Yes. I was."

* * *

Rubbing the moisture from her eyes, Vree made her way to the bow of the ship. With a terse nod to the bard, Bannon had left the moment she'd boarded, but Karlene had still been on the dock, waving wildly, when a bend in the river hid her from view.

I've never been to sea before, Gyhard murmured as a small flock of gulls wheeled about the masthead screaming defiance.

What? In all those lives?

You needn't sound so superior. You've never been out of the Empire before.

Out of the Empire. Vree leaned over the rail and stared down the river toward the sea, fighting the need to race to the stern and search the horizon for some sign of the life she'd left behind. She had no army, no brother, no structure left in a life turned irrevocably upside down. It was a good thing she'd been trained to overcome fear.

Vree, what happens if this healer finds me a body?

I'm going to beat the living shit out of it.

She felt him smile. It felt nothing at all like Bannon's, which was strange because that was the only smile she'd ever seen him use. *And then?*

I don't know.

*Will you tell me when you *do* know?*

Aren't you supposed to be teaching me to speak Shkodan?

*I could teach you how to say *yes,** he muttered. *Then perhaps I'd get an answer to my question.*

Vree lifted her face into the wind. "Teach me to say, no regrets," she said, willing herself to believe it. "And maybe, we'll work our way to yes from there."